THE PORCELAIN MOON

ALSO BY JANIE CHANG

The Library of Legends
Dragon Springs Road
Three Souls

THE
PORCELAIN
MOON

A Novel of France, the Great War,
and Forbidden Love

JANIE CHANG

wm
WILLIAM MORROW
An Imprint of HarperCollins*Publishers*

THE PORCELAIN MOON. Copyright © 2023 by Janie Chang. All rights reserved. Printed in the United States of America. No part of this book may be used or reproduced in any manner whatsoever without written permission except in the case of brief quotations embodied in critical articles and reviews. For information in the U.S., address HarperCollins Publishers, 195 Broadway, New York, NY 10007, U.S.A. In Canada, address HarperCollins Publishers Ltd, Bay Adelaide Centre, East Tower, 22 Adelaide Street West, 41st Floor, Toronto, Ontario, M5H 4E3, Canada.

HarperCollins books may be purchased for educational, business, or sales promotional use. For information, please email the Special Markets Department in the U.S. at SPsales@harpercollins.com or in Canada at HCOrder@harpercollins.com.

FIRST EDITION

Designed by Bonni Leon-Berman

Library of Congress Cataloging-in-Publication Data has been applied for.

Library and Archives Canada Cataloguing in Publication information is available upon request.

ISBN 978-0-06-307286-2
ISBN 978-1-4434-7013-1 (Canada hc)
ISBN 978-1-4434-6482-6 (Canada pbk)

23 24 25 26 27 LBC 5 4 3 2 1

To T.K. and C.H., who have always looked out for their little sister

Europeans understand the logics of matter
and by using the logics of the human spirit are
able to transform a pitch-dark battlefield to a clear
morning sky. But suppose they tried to reach the
logics of Heaven through the logics of matter,
now that would be real civilization.

—*Sun Gan, student worker, after seeing flares light up the
night sky over No Man's Land*

CONTENTS

THE PORCELAIN MOON

CHAPTER 1

Saturday, November 2, 1918

PAULINE

BUT I DON'T want to get married, she thought.

The letter fell from her hand and fluttered to the floor of the study, the neat precision of her uncle's brushstroked Chinese writing at odds with the chaos that churned her insides. Pauline didn't reach down to retrieve it, just stared at the sheet of paper as though it were some malevolent creature, a serpent or venomous spider lying on the wooden parquet.

Her uncle's first wife was now in control of her fate.

First Wife, who had never wanted her in their household. First Wife, whose expression visibly curdled whenever she looked at Pauline.

Her uncle had murmured occasionally about writing to First Wife in Shanghai about arranging a match for Pauline, but in his absentminded way he'd never followed through. Not until now. Now, because he was back in China for Grandfather Deng's funeral. Now, because while he was there he had remembered to ask First Wife to hire a matchmaker for Pauline, his dead brother's illegitimate daughter.

Pauline's gaze fell on a tall vase in the corner, its glazed surface painted with a folktale she knew well: the Lady Ch'ang O escaping from a cruel husband, her robes streaming in the wind as she ascends the night sky toward a full moon. Her right hand is raised, pointing to her destination. A porcelain woman reaching for a porcelain moon.

The air in Pauline's lungs felt chokingly thick. She threw open the study window, oblivious to the frigid November wind that slashed at her throat and swept papers off the desk. She leaned out as far as the wrought-iron window guards allowed and let the familiar noises of life on the Rue de Lisbonne seep into her consciousness. Impatient delivery trucks sounding their horns, two women laughing as they strolled together, their children trailing behind them, chattering like sparrows. The streetlamps that gave Paris its nickname, the City of Light, glimmered brightly as the sun sank lower. When Pauline finally took a deep breath, she drew in aromas of baking, the bistro on the corner preparing its evening menu.

She retreated to the chair, ran one fingertip over the polished surface of the rosewood desk, and rearranged her uncle's writing brushes on the lacquered stand. She waited for her heartbeat to calm. Then she gathered up the papers the wind had blown about on the floor and stacked them under a marble paperweight.

There had to be a way to avoid the fate outlined for her in that letter.

Her dowry was meager, her prospects equally so. She knew what sort of match to expect. She might end up a shopkeeper's second wife, worked to death and at the mercy of a resentful first wife. Or First Wife might pair her with an elderly widower who wanted an unpaid nursemaid.

But worse than anything, whatever future First Wife was arranging for her right now, it would send Pauline back to China, far away from everything she loved. She didn't want to leave Paris. Not this apartment with its tall French doors and high ceilings, or the neighbors along the Rue de Lisbonne. Not La Pagode, the store her uncle owned and all its beautiful antiques.

She hurried down to the ground floor and along the corridor that led to the back of La Pagode. The store was closed most of the time now; few wanted to buy antiques while a war was going on. Once inside, she looked around as if to assure herself everything was as she'd left it that morning.

There wasn't a single object in this store Pauline hadn't cleaned and polished, no display she hadn't arranged, composing pieces into enticing vignettes. She paused by an elmwood table where she had placed ivory statuettes between bright porcelain vases. On another table, densely patterned cloisonné enamelware contrasted with austere celadon bowls. After all these years at La Pagode, she could tell the difference between an ancient jade disc from the Han dynasty and an imitation one carved only three hundred years ago. She knew what every antique cost her uncle and how to price it.

If only Theo were here. Theo, her cousin who was like a brother to her. His Chinese name, Deng Taoling, made foreign tongues stumble, so it didn't take long for their Parisian neighbors to call him Theo instead. Just as she became Pauline Deng instead of Deng Baoling. Just as her uncle gave himself a French name when he printed up La Pagode's business cards: Louis Deng, Proprietor.

At twenty-three, Pauline was housekeeper and cook, bookkeeper and clerk. It was an agreeable little household: Pauline and Theo, her uncle and his mistress. If Louis was prepared to disrupt this harmonious arrangement it meant other factors were at play, undercurrents of family politics to which she was not privy.

She pulled a square of chamois from the bottom drawer of a display cabinet and sighed upon catching her reflection in the cabinet's glass door. If she weren't so short and didn't look so young, her uncle might treat her like an adult. It was also her own fault, she had to admit, in that she was careless about her appearance. She had worn her hair in plaits since she was small and her blouses with their rounded flat collars made her look like a schoolgirl. There was nothing she could do about her features: her small nose, the full upper lip that gave her mouth a childish pout despite the determined lines of her jaw, the dark curve of her eyebrows. She removed a jade horse from its shelf and began polishing. All the while, possibilities and consequences clicked through her mind like beads on an abacus.

Uncle Louis depended on Pauline's skills, a convenience that spared him the extra cost of hiring an outsider. If he was willing to send her back to Shanghai and marry her off, then who would do her work here?

The abacus beads fell into place. Theo's bride.

There could be no other explanation. Louis—or rather, the family— had set a date for Theo's wedding. And this time Theo wouldn't be wriggling out of it.

FIRST WIFE HAD ARRANGED THEO'S marriage years ago, while they were all still in Shanghai. At the time there had been no hurry to set a wedding date since Theo and his prospective bride were not even fifteen years old. The girl's family mailed them a photograph each year, which Louis put in a silver frame, replacing the previous. Each time his father handed it to him, Theo dutifully studied the sepia-toned image that gazed out from the picture, his future bride and her unsmiling features, eyes solemn beneath long, blunt-cut bangs. Her pose varied, sometimes standing, sometimes sitting. One year she sat with ankles crossed, her feet in their elaborately embroidered slippers prominent, almost thrust forward, to show they were not bound.

"I told your mother to choose someone from a more progressive family," Louis said, taking the frame back from Theo. "I said to her, the girl must be able to wear European-style shoes and boots, walk on European streets. She'll be living in Paris, after all."

After Theo graduated from *lycée*, Louis would take him home to Shanghai for the wedding.

But when Theo turned eighteen and as his wedding date neared, he enrolled at the Sorbonne. He refused to get married until he'd finished university. Louis telegrammed Grandfather Deng for a postponement and Grandfather agreed.

In his final semester of university Theo refused to marry again, this time because of the war, which was in its third year. The Allies needed to free up more workingmen to fight, and to do this, they were bringing thousands of Chinese laborers to England and France. Theo heard that they didn't have anywhere near enough translators.

"China is a neutral country," his father said, "there's no need to put yourself in danger."

"I would be a translator, Father, that's not dangerous."

"Your first duty is to your family," Louis said, "to help me run the store. To live where it's safe. Paris is safe, the Germans haven't bombed us in over a year."

"I doubt they've given up"—Theo's voice betrayed his frustration—"and in the meantime, half my classmates have enlisted. I must do something."

As soon as Theo graduated, he signed up with the British Army's Chinese Labour Corps. "The French contract is for five years, Father," Theo said, "but the British one is only for three. I took the shorter option."

On the day Theo left for the train station, Louis didn't go with him. They hadn't spoken in days, not since Louis sent a telegram to Shanghai apologizing for this latest delay to Theo's wedding.

Pauline was allowed to walk with Theo but only as far as the end of the Rue de Lisbonne. She was more than a little angry with Theo, and their parting had been stilted and rather formal.

"There's no need to scold me further in writing," he said, a smile crinkling up his eyes. "I know you're upset with me but never fear. Just seeing your letters will make me miss Paris."

"I'm angry with both you and Henri," she replied. "I blame him for encouraging you to join the Chinese Labour Corps."

"Don't blame Henri," Theo said, a grin breaking across his face. "Please give me some credit for making bad decisions all on my own."

His smile dared her to stay angry, so of course she couldn't and laughed. They rarely showed affection with hugs or kisses, as the French did, but now she lifted a hand to his cheek and he put his arms around her for a brief embrace. Then he picked up his valise and crossed the street, each hurrying step evidence of his impatience to get to the Gare du Nord and the train bound for Noyelles-sur-Mer. He turned briefly to look over his shoulder and said something she couldn't hear over the rattle of a passing wagon, then flashed his easy, confident smile and continued walking away. Theo, tall and straight in the early summer sunlight, in a suit of blue serge, so handsome with the brim of his straw boater tilted just so.

HE HAD BEEN GONE FOR eighteen months. But now Grandfather Deng was dead, and Uncle Louis's older brother was family patriarch. Unlike Grandfather, he wouldn't indulge Theo's whims.

Pauline sighed and gave the jade horse a final rub with the chamois, picked up a jade rabbit and began buffing its rounded haunches. She didn't doubt that as soon as Theo's contract ended, his father would have him on a steamship back to Shanghai. Then Theo would bring his wife back to Paris to help run the store.

As for her, if all went according to the plans in her uncle's letter, she would be in Shanghai by springtime, shackled to a total stranger. Her future husband wasn't the only concern. If her in-laws were difficult to please, every day would be a misery, especially if she didn't manage to bear sons. She had witnessed this for herself when still in Shanghai.

"I could never live in China again," Pauline once told Denise. "The women in our family aren't allowed to speak to men who aren't relatives, and they only go outside the walls of our home to pray at a temple or visit relatives."

"Surely not all families are like yours," her uncle's French mistress had said, lifting an eyebrow.

Denise was right. The Dengs were exceptionally old-fashioned, which meant that when it came to marriages, they preferred in-laws of similar outlook. Pauline was sure that First Wife would go out of her way to pick her an extremely traditional husband.

She couldn't go back to China. She just couldn't. Not when she was free to stroll anywhere in Paris, shop at the markets, or wander through museums. Free to drink coffee and chat with Theo and his classmates. Compared to Paris, the restricted life of the inner courtyard was as good as live burial.

How could her uncle not understand that? How could he not care?

He didn't have to care, she reminded herself. It was her duty to obey because she owed him her life. After her parents died, Louis had brought Pauline into his household when he could've discarded her at an orphanage. She couldn't refuse her uncle's wishes. But perhaps she could find a way to change his mind, to let her stay in Paris and keep working at the store.

She locked the jade animals back inside the display cabinet, then trudged up the back staircase, past their apartment and up the next flight of steps to Denise's flat.

Louis would be home soon, his ship docking at Marseilles after a monthlong journey from Shanghai. Then another day on the train to Paris. His letter said that First Wife and the matchmaker hoped to send news of a suitable match shortly after he returned to Paris, a telegram confirming that all the negotiations were complete and a marriage contract signed for Pauline.

She stopped and sat down heavily on the stairs.

The Dengs prided themselves on always meeting their obligations. As merchants, their reputation depended on it. To revoke a contract of any sort was unimaginable. Once the marriage contract was in place, there was no going back. Her uncle would lose face with the family, not to mention her prospective in-laws, if she refused to obey. Gossip would get out to the Dengs' friends and business associates. She couldn't do that to him. Her uncle could put a stop to the matchmaking, but only before the arrangements were final. If only she could persuade him to change his mind. But Louis wouldn't listen to her pleas, she knew that. She was only a girl and an illegitimate one at that.

Theo, however, was a different story.

Louis indulged Theo as much as Grandfather Deng had, treating him almost as an equal, the son who would inherit La Pagode. If only Theo were here. If only she knew where to send him a letter. Normally he wrote every month. His last note mentioned his unit would be moving to a new location and not to write back until she heard from him again, which she would as soon as he was at the new camp. But it had been more than a month now. Theo would speak to his father on her behalf, she knew he would.

All she had to do was go to the Western Front and find him.

CAMILLE

CAMILLE PEEPED THROUGH the bedroom curtain, the clenching tightness in her shoulders not easing even after her husband walked out the door. The clank of rusty hinges carried through the still morning air as Jean-Paul yanked open the garden gate. His gait was slightly bowlegged, a legacy of rickets and malnourishment, a poverty-stricken childhood. He turned south, where the road forked toward the village of Noyelles-sur-Mer. A cloud obscured the horizon, dimming the early sunlight, and for a moment all Camille could make out was Jean-Paul's silhouette, the canvas knapsack turning him into a hunchbacked monster.

A slight injury early in the war and his stated occupation of railway worker, essential to the war effort, had allowed him to avoid further military duty. Jean-Paul used to come home between shifts, but as the tolls of war mounted and more men enlisted, the railway put their remaining crew on longer and longer shifts, sometimes for seventy-two hours at a time. But even those absences weren't long enough for Camille.

Moments later a small donkey cart came over the rise, their neighbor the farmer Fournier with a load of winter cabbages. Old Fournier was easy to recognize, his broad figure draped in an indigo-blue smock and driving a red cart, bright slabs of color against the dull yellows and browns of harvested fields. The scene could've been painted by Cézanne.

The cart stopped and Jean-Paul climbed on beside the farmer. It was market day in St. Valery-sur-Somme, across the canal beyond Noyelles, undoubtedly Fournier's destination. Jean-Paul would jump off at the Noyelles train station for another long shift on the Nord, the northern railway line. Camille didn't know what else her husband might be doing and she didn't want to know. What mattered was that he would be away.

She lay on the bed and gave in to a moment of weariness, waited until her churning insides calmed, nausea subsiding as her body understood it was safe for her muscles to loosen and breathing to slow.

She turned over so that she faced the window, not wanting to smell Jean-Paul's hair oil on the pillow, the sour sweat of his body on the sheets. She'd change the bed when she came home from work. If he was away overnight, then she could sleep alone in luxury, her limbs sliding under clean linens scented with lavender, her body longing for . . . no. She wouldn't think about him. Or about what she had to do on her own.

At the mirror, she pressed more powder above her left cheekbone. The bruise beside her hairline had faded since the previous evening and as long as she stayed indoors, away from bright sunlight, it wouldn't be obvious. She tied a kerchief around her head and tugged a stray lock to fall across the yellowing mark.

In the kitchen, she boiled some water and dropped a few dried mint leaves in a mug. Their coffee, carefully meted out each morning, was reserved for Jean-Paul. She didn't mind going without coffee, but of all the rationed foods, she missed sugar the most. After a slice of last night's baguette with some cheese, it was time to go. She rolled up a clean calico smock and stuffed it in her satchel for the ride into town.

AS CAMILLE CYCLED TO THE post office, the sun finally broke free of the cloud bank, casting an amber glow across the horizon beyond Crécy Forest. For a moment she thought she heard cannon fire, then reminded herself that fighting in their region had ceased. The rumbling noises more likely came from the reverberation of trucks carrying soldiers to the front. After years of war, her ears were attuned to real or imagined sounds of artillery. Thankfully, since the fighting near Cambrai ended in October, the front lines had been moving steadily east, away from the Somme Valley.

The tide had turned against Germany and its allies, or so the newspapers declared. There were rumors of peace negotiations and news of civilian unrest in Germany, where the kaiser was being pressured by his own government to abdicate. There was talk of an armistice but until then, the fighting continued. But the end was in sight, everyone said. And then their armies would demobilize, their men return from the front.

And she would give up her job at the post office.

Brightening skies promised a clear day, a rare thing this time of year. The walk to Noyelles didn't take long, less than an hour, but after work she wanted to drop by the château in case there was some sewing work to pick up, so she had taken her bicycle and attached the small, homemade trailer to the back. She pedaled slowly through familiar farmland, the shrubbery along the road brown and soggy, bereft of summer's lush foliage. She passed the château and barely gave it a glance. It held too many memories, not all of them pleasant.

Another ten minutes and she reached the fence surrounding the Chinese Labour Corps camp. The yard was already busy, smoke and steam rising from the kitchens, men queueing up outside the mess hall. The camp had been built more than a year ago but Camille still couldn't get used to the sight of its ugly barbed wire fencing. It resembled a stockade more than a camp.

At the post office, she tied on the calico smock and began her half day of work. She started by sorting through mail that had come in the previous afternoon. Her heart clenched briefly at the sight of French Army stationery. In the days and weeks after Rossignol, after Verdun, after the Somme, it seemed as though tragedy cascaded through her hands with every piece of mail. Families destroyed, lives maimed and forever changed. There were only two such envelopes today, thank goodness, but it was still too many.

She paused to look at a postcard addressed to Marie-France Fournier, Old Fournier's youngest girl, from her cousin Thérèse. Thérèse, bolder than most, had left Noyelles to take a factory job in

Paris. Camille knew Marie-France had wanted to follow her cousin, work at a factory and earn money of her own, but both her brothers had enlisted and now only she and her mother were there to help work the fields.

Camille read the untidy handwriting.

Ma chère cousine, I spend all day filling artillery shells and the evenings strolling past store windows filled with elegant things. What fun we could have, if only you could come to Paris. Your loving Thérèse who misses you.

If only you could come to Paris. Those scribbled words seemed meant for Camille. She longed to see Paris again. If she had taken a factory job there, she could've spent her days off visiting museums and galleries— the ones still open—to stand in front of paintings that changed how she saw the world. But, of course, it was impossible since she was a married woman. And Jean-Paul was scornful of women who worked in factories.

"No respectable female would leave their husbands and homes," he said, "only low-class women. Unmarried and willing to work along-side dirty foreigners. Whores."

But when the postal service began hiring women to replace men who had gone to war, it was all right with Jean-Paul for his wife to work at the post office. It was a respectable job in town with modest but wel-come wages. Camille suspected the real reason Jean-Paul agreed was that it gave him a chance to get friendlier with the Dumonts, the post-master and his wife, who were prominent citizens of Noyelles.

Before the Nord railway line got so busy and Jean-Paul was away all the time, he liked to visit the post office around closing time, when Camille was tidying the back rooms, ostensibly to walk her home, but really because he wanted to socialize with the Dumonts. Jean-Paul and M. Dumont talked about the war, the price of food, and often as not, the disruptions caused by foreigners in their little town. British, Canadian, and Australian soldiers were stationed there. And there were also Chinese workers. On principle, Jean-Paul didn't like foreigners, not even refugees from neighboring Belgium, and the Chinese were decidedly foreign. He grumbled at newspaper photographs of brigades arriving in Marseilles from Indochina, at accounts of British troops and Indian Sikhs marching through France on their way to the front. But at least they were soldiers.

"It's one thing to bring soldiers from our colonies to help us fight, even if they're only short little Orientals," he said, "but these Chinois aren't going into battle for us. Digging and carrying. That's all they're doing."

"Digging trenches, loading fuel for tanks and vehicles, repairing roads and railway tracks after aerial attacks. The machinery of war has many parts, Jean-Paul," M. Dumont said. "Napoleon was a brilliant tactician because he understood the logistics of supplying his armies. He could've run a modern postal system." M. Dumont liked pointing to the postal service as a model of efficiency.

He droned on a little longer, reminding his audience that using Chinese labor for the manual work of the war freed up more French and British to fight. That the Allies wouldn't have brought in workers from so far away, at such expense, unless they desperately needed the manpower. Manpower to unload and load cargo at the docks and supply depots, plow and plant fields so that farms still grew wheat for bread, work in armaments factories so that tanks and guns didn't run out of ammunition

But while Jean-Paul didn't like the Chinese, he didn't mind making money off them. When he heard that the workers liked buying

Western clothing, Jean-Paul ransacked the armoire in Camille's father's bedroom, then went to the camp on a payday with a sack full of her dead father's clothes.

"They paid me what I asked for, the stupid *chintoks*," he boasted. "So many of them all wanting these old clothes so much they barely haggled."

A few days later, Camille saw a tall Chinese strolling along the main street in Noyelles, one hand straightening the lapels of a familiar waistcoat. Her annoyance faded when she saw how gently the man touched the garment's brocade front and brass buttons, pride and pleasure evident in his face. Jean-Paul shrugged when she pointed at the man, wearing the waistcoat he had sold behind her back.

"They're like children," he said contemptuously. "Dressing up in our clothes, putting everything on the wrong way. He's got it buttoned over that ridiculous tunic."

"But you're the one who sold it to him," she said, her voice just above a whisper. She winced as his fingers tightened on her arm. Then he loosened his grip to make a slight bow as an elderly couple walked past. The mayor, M. Etienne Gourlin, and Mme Gourlin.

CAMILLE SHOOK HER HEAD AT the memory.

She finished sorting the mail into four bags and set them down by the back door for Emil to pick up. She put a dried-out carrot from her cellar on top of the bags, a small treat for the donkey that pulled Emil's mail delivery cart.

No, she thought, Jean-Paul didn't have a problem taking money from the Chinese.

And he'd kill her if he ever found out she was in love with one.

CHAPTER 2

Noyelles-sur-Mer 1906

The year Camille turned twelve, summer came early and rolled through the Somme Valley scorching fields and forests under a relentless sun. Nights felt barely cooler than the days, and when Camille stepped outside in the morning, the stone slabs on the terrace of the château were still warm, welcoming to her bare feet. Then in July, seemingly overnight, the fruits and vegetables in the kitchen garden were ready to harvest all at the same time. The château's gardening staff was down to old Bastien, who was no longer strong enough or fast enough to keep weeds and shrubbery in check. But he was all Grand-mère could afford.

Bastien harvested and carried sack after sack of beans and peppers, cucumbers and aubergines, berries and stone fruit, all of which he left by the kitchen door. But he also had to chop wood because there were pots bubbling on the ancient woodstoves, all three of them, while the cook preserved and pickled. Bastien declared he couldn't do it all.

The next day, Camille went to the kitchen garden toting a basket. Her grandmother had invited guests for lunch and their cook was making a summer terrine of fresh peas.

"Go tell Bastien you need enough to fill two cups," the cook instructed. "Madame la Comtesse has invited the mayor's wife so we must have only the most perfect pea pods. And a perfect lettuce."

"So we can have a special summer lunch," Camille said, nodding in understanding.

"Yes, ma petite," the cook said rather sadly, "perhaps one of our last special lunches." At the time, Camille assumed she meant for the summer.

But when Camille arrived in the garden, it wasn't Bastien leaning over the lettuces with a watering can. It was a teenage boy, black haired and sunburnt. His gaunt frame made him look young, almost fragile. His eyes were wary, and a strange pale shade of blue, the same ice blue as the kerchief tied around his neck. He drew back a little, as if uncertain what to do. He had rolled up his pants above his knees, which were caked with dirt, and his feet were bare. His shoes, she saw, were carefully placed on a wooden crate beside the vegetable patch.

"Hello, my name is Camille Barbier," she said, politely. "What's your name?"

But he didn't get a chance to answer. Bastien came hurrying around from behind the beanpoles, alerted by her voice. "Mademoiselle Camille, what can I do for you?"

The boy dropped back to his knees beside the lettuces and Camille followed the old gardener as he picked pea pods. They returned to the lettuce patch and Bastien pulled out a leafy head, cutting off its roots with a short knife.

"Batavia lettuce," he said, putting it in her basket. "Tolerant of hot weather, stays crisp and sweet. Wait one moment if you please, Mademoiselle Camille, I'll pick a head of frisée, too, just in case."

The boy lifted his eyes briefly to look at her and suddenly Camille was aware of how dingy his clothes were, how worn the fabric. Of how she must look to him in her ruffled white dress of dotted Swiss, her blue leather shoes, a gold locket at her neck.

She left the kitchen garden, her basket full of greens. Just before she turned the corner she heard the old gardener scolding the boy.

"You don't approach her or speak to her, understand? That was Madame la Comtesse's granddaughter and you, you are nothing."

There was a mumbled reply, words Camille couldn't make out. She felt badly for the boy. She wanted to turn back and tell him he wasn't nothing. But she had to hurry before their guest arrived. She had to select a few of her drawings because Grand-mère wanted to show the mayor's wife how well she was doing with her art lessons. She put the incident out of her mind.

A month later, Bastien's daughter came to see Camille's grandmother. Her father couldn't garden for them anymore. He had suffered a stroke and his entire left side had gone numb. Camille's grandmother gave her a silver vase, told her to sell it and pay for Bastien's medicines, then had the daughter go around to the kitchen and get some eggs to take home. Hoping to hear more about Bastien, Camille tagged along.

"Will he come back when he's better?" she asked.

"No, mademoiselle, he will not get better," the woman snapped. "Your grandmother will have to find someone else willing to do her gardening for practically nothing."

The cook put a dozen eggs in a cardboard box. "What about that boy who was helping him through the summer?"

"That little bastard Jean-Paul? He ran away after Papa's stroke. Good riddance."

Sometimes when Camille thought of the fates that had conspired to shape her life, she couldn't help but wonder. Had the same memory persisted in Jean-Paul's mind? If he hadn't seen her that day at the château, would he have found her so tempting a prize? Would she have figured so prominently in his plans?

GENERATIONS OF EXTRAVAGANCE COULD ONLY continue for so long.

Before Camille was born, her grandfather, the Comte de Beaumarchais, suffered the humiliation of selling the Beaumarchaises' Paris town house almost as soon as he inherited the title. The hunting lodge and its surrounding forests were already gone, sold to pay the family's never-ending debts. When Camille's grandparents moved to Noyelles-sur-Mer, it was only because the château was her grandfather's last remaining property. Set in the middle of farmland, it was as far from the urban sophistication of Paris as they could imagine.

"The château was where I met your mother, so I've always loved it," Camille's father said. "When your uncle Nicolas returned from Madagascar, your grandfather Beaumarchais gave a big party to welcome him home. Nicolas invited fellow officers, those of us who had come back. Afterward I learned your grandfather was hoping your mother would catch the eye of Nicolas's friend, the nephew of General Briere de l'Isle."

But it had been young Capitaine Auguste Barbier whose warm smile and quiet ways won her heart. After they married, the young captain went off to war again and again, wars of conquest to acquire new colonies for France. He returned from his final campaign after resigning his commission only to find that his wife had died.

Six months after Auguste returned, the old count died. His title did not pass on to Nicolas, who had died while serving in West Africa. Not in valorous action but from cholera.

"Auguste was a lackluster army officer, not like our Nicolas," Camille's grandmother said. She didn't care who heard it or even if Camille's father was in the same room. "But Camille is all the family I have now, so I suppose I must take in her father, too."

Grand-mère was so domineering a presence that Auguste always seemed to be in the background, his presence so unobtrusive it barely touched their lives. After the excitement of his return had worn off, Camille might've forgotten he was there if not for the way her father seemed to aggravate her grandmother's resentment just by being in the same room. Resentment that her son had died, but not this inadequate son-in-law. Resentment that they were sliding into destitution.

"We must let you go," Grand-mère said to Mme Tremblay, the cook. "I know you've been wanting to live with your son in Toulouse and now there's no excuse not to go."

"I would stay, madame," the woman wept, "you know I would, even on reduced wages. I've been working for you since you were a bride. But my grandchildren need me now that their mother is so ill."

"My dearest Tremblay. You've been friend as well as cook. But I can't even afford to keep you on reduced wages. Nor the housekeeper."

Grand-mère resorted to part-time help, hiring a Noyelles woman as an all-purpose housekeeper. One day to clean, one day to bake and cook up a large stew, and one day to deal with laundry. The woman taught Camille how to sew on buttons and let out hems.

Camille's grandmother closed off one wing of the château. Then she closed off more rooms until finally they were using only their own bedrooms and a parlor, where they took their meals at a round pedestal table beside the piano. Grand-mère sold the last of their great treasures, the sixteenth-century millefleur tapestries of the Lady and the Unicorn that graced the entrance hall. The gold and silver candelabra were long gone, so now she sold the silverware and porcelain.

"Who needs thirty-six place settings of Christofle and Sèvres?" she sniffed. "We can barely feed ourselves let alone give a banquet."

ON CAMILLE'S FIFTEENTH BIRTHDAY, IN 1909, her grandmother had the bakery in Noyelles deliver an elaborately iced cake. Auguste shot a pheasant in the fields behind the château, the housekeeper made pheasant stew, and Grand-mère opened a bottle of port to go with the cake. Grand-mère wanted one last celebration at the château.

"You're a young lady now, Camille," she said, "I only wish we still had some champagne in the cellar for this occasion. But this port is better than any champagne."

Her grandmother was vivacious and talkative that evening, sparkling with such desperate gaiety that Camille pretended to enjoy the little party even though she knew they were leaving their home soon.

A week later, the château and its few valuable pieces of furniture were sold to an auction house. A month after that, they moved into the last remaining scrap of the Beaumarchais property—the estate manager's cottage and garden, a half-hour walk from the château, with a small plot of farmland beside it. There hadn't been an estate manager in decades and the home stood empty, its flower beds gone to seed, the garden's perimeter marked by brambles.

They brought furniture from the château's storage rooms with them, boxes of kitchenware, plates and cutlery. Looking at the two-story cottage, Camille wondered how all their belongings would fit. She followed her grandmother through the door of their new home while Auguste directed workers in unloading the wagons.

Camille peered through the gloom. The rooms seemed so small. The entire ground floor was smaller than the château's drawing room. She flinched when she realized the crunching noises under her shoes came from dried rodent droppings. Above her, ceiling beams dripped cobwebs.

"I should've had this place cleaned out before we came." Grand-mère sighed. "I wonder if there's a broom in those wagons."

Are we nothing now? Camille wondered.

TO CAMILLE'S SURPRISE, LIFE AT the cottage was more tranquil than life at the château, her grandmother less exacting and judgmental. She even seemed to have come to an understanding with Auguste, asking his advice on repairs for the cottage and how to bring the gardens back to life. On hot afternoons, the three of them sat under the shade of the apple tree and drank tea with lemon and mint.

With help from their neighbors, the Fournier boys, Auguste cleared away weeds and blackberries, uncovered the old flower beds and kitchen garden and began planting. Camille helped him lay out a curved path from the kitchen garden through the flower beds. He showed Camille how the bay laurel tree and rosemary shrubs were coming back after a hard pruning, and how to spread straw around vegetable beds to prevent weeds from growing.

"I wasn't always a soldier you know," he said. "My father loved his garden and I used to help."

"Grand-mère loved her garden at the château," Camille said. "Maybe this one will make her happy again. She seems happier here."

"She has lessened her burden." Auguste paused from digging. "Money from the château paid off debts to the bank with enough left over to live a little more comfortably than before. Although I'm not sure your grandmother can ever forget she's a countess and that makes her unhappy sometimes."

Her grandmother held their lineage like a knife to Camille's throat. As far as Grand-mère was concerned, the first priority now was to arrange a good marriage for Camille. She made Camille pore over a volume by the vicomte Albert Révérend, *Titles and Confirmation of Titles*, to learn the names of France's great families so she could distinguish between old stock aristocracy and newly minted upstarts.

At fifteen, Camille was wise enough to recognize wishful thinking on her grandmother's part. Camille could not bring an actual title to a marriage, which was what the nouveau riche wanted in exchange for their wealth. Nor did she possess beauty, that other currency. She had not inherited her mother's vivacious smile nor her grandmother's imperious elegance. She was pale and thin with a rather long nose that suffered from a tendency to freckle. Her hair was an indeterminate shade of brown that turned an indeterminate shade of blond in the summer, so fine it refused to hold a curl.

After school and on weekends, Grand-mère trained her in etiquette, anticipating a time when Camille would need to know how to behave when dining with nobility. Grand-mère also pawned a pair of heavy gold bracelets to pay for music and dancing lessons in Abbeville, the nearest town of any size. She took Camille there each weekend on the train and every evening at home stood over the piano while Camille plodded dutifully through scales and simple arrangements. She rolled back the rug in the parlor and partnered Camille through dozens of courtly dance steps, scolding her for being too slow to learn, for being clumsy as a peasant.

"If your mother were still alive, Grand-mère might not be so strict with you," Camille's father said when he found her sitting in her room, despondent after a particularly harsh scolding. "She places all her hopes on you, hopes from the days of her youth."

But perhaps he spoke to Grand-mère, because the next day her grandmother called her down to the parlor.

"Camille, you show no aptitude at all for music or dance," she said. "Perhaps I left it too late and you're too old now to learn."

"I love listening to music and watching people dance," Camille said, quite truthfully. "And Monsieur Bertrand says my drawing shows promise."

"Well, the world has changed," her grandmother said, with an air of resignation, "so perhaps none of this matters anymore. And we don't have as many friends as before."

Camille was aware of her grandmother's dwindling address book, of all the names crossed off the densely written pages, the letters on stationery engraved with the family crest that came back unopened.

Her grandfather, it seemed, had lost much goodwill when he failed to pay back personal loans.

"You'll probably never have to manage servants or a household," Grand-mère continued. "I should've come to terms with this reality a long time ago. You must learn other, more practical skills."

The lessons in etiquette, dance, and music ceased. Camille had loved her art lessons and these also came to an end, to her regret. M. Bertrand's classes had been her favorite. But at least she still had a good stock of art supplies and could practice on her own.

Grand-mère sent for Mme Tremblay, who came by train all the way from Toulouse. She taught Camille cooking and homemaking. Plain, traditional fare, nothing fancy. How to tell when ingredients were fresh, which cuts of meat to use in stews and which ones for roasts. With the pragmatism of a woman who had lived through hard times, Mme Tremblay took Camille into the surrounding countryside.

"And here is sorrel. Don't ever pay for this if you can find it wild," she said. "It adds a nice tang to soup."

Camille learned to find mushrooms, picked leaves of dandelion and dock for salad, gathered rose hips for making tea. From the kitchen garden, she learned how to brine nasturtium seeds to use in place of capers, and she hung bunches of herbs upside down in the cellar to dry.

In the evenings, her grandmother and Mme Tremblay sat by the parlor window to sew and reminisce. Camille often heard them talking and laughing late into the night. The two old women no longer treated each other as mistress and servant; their relationship had subsided from formality into friendship. Mme Tremblay finally departed when her son wrote yet another letter asking her to return.

IT SEEMED TO CAMILLE THAT Grand-mère gave up once she finally accepted that her family would not climb out of genteel poverty, at least not during her lifetime. The old woman slid into a decline after Mme Tremblay left, her mind often wandering back to her days as a young wife. When Camille took her to town in the little pony trap, she no longer broke out in bitter tirades when they drove past the château, fuming at her husband's debts, at the bank's heartlessness, at the new owner's lack of respect for the château's noble origins. She didn't even glance at the gates.

Then one day her grandmother asked Camille to turn into the château's gates so they could go home. When Camille reminded her the château no longer belonged to their family, the old woman's brows furrowed with the effort of remembering. Her face caved in with grief, but only for a moment, and then she straightened and sat up with a practiced dignity that revealed no emotion.

After a few more similar incidents, Camille took another tactic.

"We'll go home to the château later, Grand-mère," she'd say. "Right now we have shopping to do in town." Or a trip to the post office to mail important letters. Or to meet someone at the train station. It didn't matter what sort of excuse she concocted, it would be forgotten in a few minutes anyway.

"Honesty is no kindness," her father agreed. "Each time you remind Grand-mère the château has been sold, or that her husband and children are gone, it's like stabbing fresh wounds into her heart."

AS HER GRANDMOTHER'S MIND RECEDED into the past and the years went by, Auguste emerged from the backdrop of Camille's life and quietly claimed the duty of looking after their household. He negotiated with Old Fournier to plant a crop on the small plot of land beside the cottage in return for a small portion of the proceeds. The old pony died and Auguste bought a second-hand bicycle, which did not need hay and oats.

"I hate to see farmland wasted," he told Fournier. "Plant pumpkins, cabbages, daisies, whatever you like."

Several years after they had moved into the cottage, Auguste was sifting through piles of documents stuffed in Grand-mère's walnut secretaire when he found papers that seemed to indicate Grand-mère might have inherited a legacy from her own family. She had never mentioned it, another sign that her distracted mind no longer kept track of events.

"She never talks about her family anymore," Camille said, "because she's embarrassed that Grand-père borrowed from her brothers and never paid it back."

"But it seems there is a small legacy from her mother," Auguste said. "I'll go see our lawyer about this next week. Come with me. You've never been to Paris, Camille. We'll ask Madame Fournier to look after Grand-mère for a couple of days."

They spent Camille's first morning in Paris strolling along the banks of the Seine and under the chestnut trees of the Avenue des Champs-Élysées that Grand-mère remembered so fondly. They attended mass at Notre-Dame and afterward Auguste took her to see the Sainte-Chapelle and its stained-glass windows. Then in the evening, they dined at the Café Anglais, which he said used to be her mother's favorite.

"But can we afford this, Papa?" she whispered, looking at the chandeliers and starched white napkins, at the crystal flute the waiter put in front of her. A Kir Royale, her father called the drink he'd ordered.

"Don't worry, we won't live like this tomorrow," he said, "but for my daughter's first evening in Paris, we ought to dine in style."

"What do we do tomorrow?" she asked.

"I don't want you to waste your time in Paris waiting at a lawyer's office. I'll take you to the Louvre on my way to the meeting and you can spend the day there. It is so huge you could wander for a week and not see the same thing twice."

Camille had never been to a museum before except the one in Abbeville, where the small collection consisted of finds excavated from the region. Here, there was art from all over the world. She explored room after room of marble statues, figures she now realized were the originals of the Roman gods and goddesses that had decorated the château's gardens. There were walls hung with paintings by artists whose work she had only seen in books about the Renaissance.

Then a revelation. More paintings, but not stiff portraits of generals on horseback or bewigged women in sumptuous gowns. Not saints and martyrs with heavy eyelids and blank expressions, not annunciations or cherubs. Here were landscapes rendered in seemingly rough brushstrokes, of golden fields rolling beneath a dazzling blue horizon. Riotously happy people, ordinary workingmen and -women enjoying themselves at an outdoor dance. A quiet canal paved with wind-stippled water, throwing glints of light up at the buildings alongside. The paintings made her feel sunshine on her face, sway to a cheerful country tune, button her coat against chill breezes that carried the dank scent of wharves and boats. The names of the artists were new to her. Monet. Renoir. Cézanne.

These paintings excited Camille, made her want to rush home and set up her easel to lay down streaks of color, to conjure the look of sunlight wavering through wheat, the swelling of wind against clouds.

Then another room and another revelation. Porcelain glazed with colors at once intense and serene. The delicate, finely crafted pieces couldn't have been more different than the free-flowing, joyous paintings she admired ten minutes before, yet their exquisite workmanship exerted just as much fascination over her.

Snuff bottles of clear glass no larger than a man's thumb, painted with detailed miniatures from the inside. Screens carved with scenes of gods and goddesses whose robes seemed to float outside the panels. Porcelains in vibrant yet subtle colors, decorated with flowers, mythical beasts, and stylized clouds. Some of the pottery was austere, glazed in a single color but no less exquisite, the solid color accentuating the elegant shapes.

She began to recognize versions of the same scene. Eight figures circled an urn; were they gods and goddesses? Robes billowing around her, the porcelain figurine of a woman rose above stylized clouds toward the moon. An ivory carving of a man and a woman walking across a bridge of birds and clouds. She understood the iconography of European art, the meaning of lilies and doves, a sheaf of wheat, and the color blue. But here, the hidden meanings behind the images were tantalizing, their significance a mystery she couldn't solve. Camille knew there were stories in plain sight, wonderful mystical adventures, if only she knew the code.

"I see you're a connoisseur of Chinese art," said a voice beside her. She turned to see a smiling face, a middle-aged woman dressed in dove gray, chestnut curls peeking out from under her hat.

"Oh, I'm not," Camille said. "This is the first time I've been able to look really closely at such objects. My grandmother had some Chinese pieces but now I realize even though they were big and colorful, they weren't really very good."

"They may have been European pieces made in imitation of Chinese porcelain," the woman said.

"You seem very knowledgeable, madame," Camille said.

"I work in a store that sells Chinese antiques." The woman rummaged in her bag and gave Camille a card. "Before, I just enjoyed looking at Chinese art. Now I understand the history and function and craftsmanship in each piece, which makes them even more beautiful."

There was a scuffling sound at the entrance to the exhibit hall. Camille looked up. A young woman and a man stood there, both Chinese, their features so startlingly alike it was obvious they were related. They looked at her briefly, then at the woman.

"There you are, Denise," the young Chinese woman said. "We should go."

The woman gave Camille a farewell nod. The three of them left, the sound of their footsteps on the museum's wooden flooring fading as they walked away. She wondered about their relationship. The woman had said she worked for a Chinese antiques store. Camille looked at the card in her hand.

La Pagode. Louis Deng, Proprietor.

At dinner that night, this time at a simple brasserie, Camille bubbled over telling her father about the impressionist paintings and the room full of Chinese objects, making Auguste smile, one of his rare genuine smiles.

"Then I have something to show you," he said, "once we're home and Grand-mère is asleep." He put his hand over hers, something he seldom did.

IT WAS LATE AFTERNOON THE next day when they stepped off the platform at Noyelles, the sun still bright on the horizon. Auguste was visibly tired and leaned on his walking stick. Camille carried his bag as well as hers, wondered how he would manage the long walk to the cottage, but as they walked out of the station, they saw that Old Fournier was on the street with his donkey cart.

"My wife sent me to get you," he said, "so you wouldn't be late for supper."

The house smelled of fresh-baked bread, and Mme Fournier's smile told them she'd had an easy time looking after the old countess. At dinner Grand-mère gazed amiably into the distance, eyes unfocused, her mood buoyed by Camille's obvious happiness.

"Paris, Paris," the old woman murmured on her way up the staircase. Even now, she refused to grasp the handrail for support and Camille held her gently by the elbow. "I loved to promenade on those grand avenues when the chestnut trees were in bloom. That was when your grandfather Beaumarchais first saw me. I was strolling with my parents under that canopy of flowers. The dress, I remember it still, pink with cream stripes, falls of lace on the bodice."

When Camille came out of her grandmother's room, Auguste beckoned her into his. He had removed the oil lamp and books stacked on the large trunk beside his bed and now he opened the lid. The interior was fitted with deep trays, each divided into compartments of different sizes. He handed her an object. Something hard, swaddled in cloth.

She unwrapped it and gasped. It was beautiful. "Is this . . . Chinese porcelain?"

"From the Forbidden City in Peking," he said. His voice was wry. "The spoils of war."

One tray after the other, he brought out a small hoard of treasures that they unwrapped and laid out carefully on the bed. Camille felt giddy. Figurines carved from jade and coral, a snuff bottle hollowed out from a single large garnet, a set of ivory animals. Porcelain bowls and jars, cloisonné enamel vases so brilliantly colored they could've been inlaid with jewels. A wooden box held a headdress of flowers fashioned from coral and turquoise, with butterflies bobbing on stems of gold wire, their wings cut from bright blue kingfisher feathers. A set of eight small plates, each with an intriguing scene of people and animals.

They sat across from each other, Camille on the Turkish carpet with her back against the bedroom wall, her father in the armchair. Lamplight softened his features and he looked young, as young as in his wedding picture, with his gaze fixed on her mother's face, laughter in his eyes.

"Why have you never shown me these before?" She turned a bowl in her hand and held it up to the lamp. Light shone through its translucent sides, the porcelain only slightly thicker than eggshell.

"I came home and your mother had died. So many of these"—he indicated the treasures on the bed—"were meant for her and there wasn't any point bringing them out."

The memories were too painful, both of his wife and the fighting in China. He had unlocked the trunk for the first time when the bank put up the château and its surrounding estate for auction. He negotiated with the bank manager to buy the cottage, to keep it off the auction block. He raised the money by digging into the trunk for a long string of pearls the size of hazelnuts. Pearls he once hoped would gleam around his wife's throat, and later, around Camille's on her wedding day.

"All this time," Camille said, "I thought the cottage belonged to Grand-mère. She said the bank manager told her the château on its own was enough to pay off the debt. That she didn't need to sell the cottage."

Not once during all these years had Auguste held it over his mother-in-law that he owned their home, not even when she was at her most insulting and imperious.

"There was no need to bring it up," Auguste said. "We're all family and she is your grandmother, she deserves my help and respect. In the end, it all belongs to you, anyway, Camille."

But neither had he pawned or sold any more treasures. The trunk had stayed locked against days of dire need.

"Now, after visiting our lawyer and the bank manager," he said, "I believe those days of dire need are upon us. It turns out the legacy from your grandmother's family is only a few items of sentimental value. I will need to sell some of these Chinese treasures soon."

Camille put the bowl back on the bed and picked up another object, an ivory snuff bottle, no larger than a candle stub. A carving circled the bottle, a woman in a dress with long flowing sleeves reached up for the sky, her feet floating above the ground. In the background, tiny pine trees swayed and swirling clouds moved to meet the full moon.

"I wish we could keep them all," she said. "There was a vase at the Louvre painted with a scene like this. I'd love to know the story."

"Take something for yourself," Auguste said, "and I'll never sell it."

She leaned over the bed and surveyed all the exquisite little pieces, then selected a plain white jar with a lid. They wrapped everything up again, placed the pieces back inside the trunk, then closed the lid and put the oil lamp and books back on top.

Back in her room, Camille placed the jar on her dresser. Of the entire collection, it seemed the plainest and worth the least. Her father would not lose much by her taking it. She held it in both hands, the rounded shape slightly rough to the touch, yet comforting to hold. And she had much need of comfort whenever she thought of Grand-mère's inevitable decline.

IN HER GRANDMOTHER'S FINAL YEAR, the year Camille turned twenty-one, there were times when the old countess woke up lucid and clear-eyed, her speech crisp, fully cognizant of her life past and present. During these rare intervals, she didn't complain about her meaningless title or ruined wealth. She simply spoke of them as fact.

"By the time I married your grandfather, the Beaumarchais family was no longer wealthy," Grand-mère said.

Camille had come to take away her grandmother's dinner tray and when she saw that the old woman was articulate and cogent, she sat down on the bed. Opportunities for meaningful conversation with her grandmother were rare.

"I tried to be careful with money," she continued, "but your grandfather did not. That monstrous painting, for example. I hate having it look down on me."

She pointed to an oil painting in an ornate gilt frame, of Camille's grandfather standing with a riding crop under one arm, the other hand holding the reins of a chestnut horse. The château and its gardens stood in the background.

"It's by an eminent artist, Carolus-Duran," she said. "We couldn't afford it but your grandfather paid him with the last of our cash. He even gave the man a bonus, just to make a grand gesture. Shortly after this, your grandfather began borrowing from the bank against the value of the château."

"Should I take it down, Grand-mère, so that it's not looking at you?" Camille stood up from the chair beside her grandmother's bed.

"Sit, sit. There's no need." She reached over and held Camille's hand. When her grandmother's mind was clear, she was affectionate and intelligent, all bitterness vanished, all scolding done.

"I leave it there to remind me how useless it is holding on to a world that no longer exists. This is the picture I love most"—and she pointed at a small framed watercolor on the table beside her. It was one Camille had painted many years ago of the cottage in springtime, apple blossom petals drifting in the air. "We should've let you continue those art classes. You're very talented."

"It's all right. I've improved a lot just painting on my own." She patted her grandmother's hand. "Whenever I go out to forage I take a sketch pad with me."

"Camille, marry someone who will take good care of you," Grand-mère said, "and if you can, find a way to earn your own money."

"Earn money, Grand-mère?" Camille said, perplexed. Her grandmother had never brought this up before.

"I don't have a good answer for how or what you could do to earn money, I'm sorry." She gripped Camille's hand tightly in her arthritic fingers. "France is changing, my dear, especially for people like us. Especially once this war is over."

"I can cook," Camille said. "You made sure of that when you hired Madame Tremblay to teach me."

"My pride has kept you from making friends, you've been lonely," her grandmother said. "Marry a farmer, a shoemaker. A gendarme. Someone kind and forthright who puts your happiness and well-being above his pride. Someone who will not disappoint you, the way your grandfather disappointed me when it came to supporting our family. Yet I must confess, in other ways he made me happy."

"Because he loved you very much, Grand-mère."

Her grandmother snorted. "Let me tell you a secret. Being loved by your grandfather did me no good at all. He left us penniless. Yet the sight of him every morning made me happy because I loved him. Loving is what makes you happy, not being loved."

Grand-mère's eyes dulled, then closed. Camille laid her head on the pillow and felt her grandmother's hand gently stroke her hair, heard the thin voice hum a lullaby. When all Camille could hear were deep, soft breaths, she tiptoed out of the room.

THE NEXT MORNING, CAMILLE RODE her bicycle to fetch the priest. Grand-mère had died in her sleep. It was as though she had simply forgotten to wake up. The manner in which she passed was a blessing and Camille knew it. Tears prickled just behind her eyes. It seemed to her that spring had never been so beautiful or so transient, the scent and colors of each flower and green budding shoot so short-lived in their glory. She cycled past the château, refusing to turn her head to look at it. There was too much of her grandmother and her own child-hood there. Even though she recalled afternoons in the château's rose garden, the lace tablecloths and lemonade, the games of boules and croquet, she'd never been truly happy there. Between her father and grandmother, the days had rarely been free of tension.

Grief, Camille was learning, wasn't a pure and specific emotion. Her sorrow over Grand-mère mingled with a sense of release. She had loved her grandmother dearly, but still—and she berated herself for such thoughts crossing her mind—her grandmother had been a difficult and deeply unhappy person.

They held a simple funeral at the little Église de l'Assomption-de-la-Sainte-Vierge. There wasn't any need to invite anyone, the whole town knew and came to pay their respects. Mme Dumont, the postmaster's wife, put a white lily on the coffin. Outside the church, rain started falling, a spring shower.

"Monsieur Barbier, Camille," she said. "I've made a cake and we actually have real coffee. If you'd like to come home with us, you can stay until the rain stops."

Camille looked up uncertainly at her father, who nodded.

"Good, good," Mme Dumont said. "Édouard, hold your umbrella over Camille. She's getting soaked."

Mme Dumont's son looked at Camille from under long lashes. Édouard was one of the boys her grandmother wouldn't let her speak to, not at church, not on the street, or even at the post office where he worked with his father. But now Grand-mère was gone.

ÉDOUARD PROPOSED TO CAMILLE SIX months later. She and Auguste celebrated Christmas at the Dumont house, where Mme Dumont spent most of the meal pressing them to set a wedding date so that she could make arrangements with the priest. But early in the new year, Édouard was called up. He enlisted.

He was killed during his first week at Verdun.

At his funeral, Camille stood between M. and Mme Dumont.

"Everyone admired your fortitude," her father said when they re-turned from the church. "How you helped Madame Dumont walk back from the gravesite, holding back your tears so you wouldn't cause her more distress."

Camille said nothing, not wanting her father to know she didn't feel any more sorrow over Édouard than what she felt over the death of any young man in this war. That in the months after her grand-mother's death, Édouard's long-lashed brown eyes and kind attentions had been a distraction from the numbness of grief. That on the eve-ning before he went to war, Édouard had attempted an ardent kiss. Dutifully, because he might not come back, she tried to respond as his tongue pried open her lips and his fingers fumbled at her blouse. He pressed her hand against his groin and after a low moan, he staggered away into the darkness. She saw him the next morning at the train station, where he couldn't seem to meet her eyes.

After a while, whenever she tried to picture him, Édouard's face refused to come into focus. All she could remember were his shoul-ders turning away when he climbed aboard the train and the pressure of Mme Dumont's hand on her arm as the train pulled away

IN JUNE, FOUR MONTHS AFTER Édouard was laid to rest, Camille and Auguste went to Grand-mère's grave for one final duty. Although her funeral service had been held at their beloved little church in Noyelles, Grand-mère was buried beside her husband in the seaside town of Le Crotoy, at the far grander Église Saint-Clement. Endlessly busy since the war, the stonemason had finally added Grand-mère's name to the gravestone, an imposing monument of black granite topped with the family crest. The late count's epitaph, and all his names and titles, took up so much space there was only enough room for one modest line for her grandmother.

ELISABETH-AMANDINE, COMTESSE DE BEAUMARCHAIS (1840–1915)

"Grand-mère used to remark that the one thing which made the cottage bearable was this 'Gloire de Dijon' climbing outside her window," Camille said, stooping to put roses on the grave. "It's too bad we couldn't fit more words on the stone, something to say she was beloved."

"In a way it's there," her father put an arm around her shoulder. "Your grandmother's name 'Amandine' means 'much-loved,' you know."

When they stepped off the train at the Noyelles station, Camille could tell her father was exhausted. Auguste hadn't been well for the past year, always suffering from one ailment or another. She had been so intent on caring for Grand-mère she'd only recognized how frail he'd become after her grandmother died. It was a good forty-five-minute walk from Noyelles to their cottage. If they walked slowly, she hoped Auguste would manage.

"Capitaine Barbier?" a polite voice said in greeting. The setting sun gleamed on smooth black hair when the man lifted his cap.

"I'm Barbier," Auguste said, turning around.

The man saluted. "My name is Jean-Paul Roussel. Madame Fournier suggested I give you a ride home after your long day."

The man gave Camille a slight bow and when he straightened up, Camille recognized him immediately. She had seen him when she was a girl, in the kitchen garden at the château. It was Bastien's assistant, the bastard who had run away, the one Bastien had called a nobody. His eyes were a startlingly pale blue, especially in contrast to his dark brows and the black mustache. She had never seen such eyes on anyone else.

They followed him to a donkey cart across the road from the train station. He limped a little as he walked.

"This cart looks familiar," Auguste remarked, "and so does the donkey." He stroked the animal's long nose.

"Everyone around here knows Fournier's cart and donkey," Jean-Paul replied, with a smile. "I remember when this creature was just a foal."

But it was Camille he smiled at when he said this and Camille whose hand he held a little too tightly when helping her climb into the back of the cart. She settled herself on a pile of sacks and leaned against the cart's wooden side in relief. Now her father didn't have to walk.

"Are you from this area, then?" Auguste said, getting onto the seat beside Jean-Paul.

"I was born here," Jean-Paul said, "but I left Noyelles as soon as I was old enough to join the army."

When the war broke out, he had been wounded during one of the first battles of the Marne. Discharged for a bad leg and loss of hearing in one ear, he decided he would return to Noyelles. Camille listened as the men's conversation ranged from news of the war to this year's harvest.

"I'm good with machinery," Jean-Paul said. "I've applied to the Nord railway to be an apprentice mechanic, and I'm doing farm work while waiting to hear back."

"All the railways are shorthanded," August said. "They will not turn down a brave veteran. Your prospects are good."

When they reached the house, Jean-Paul refused Auguste's offer of a drink. "But if I may, I'd like to call on you sometime to talk about army life and hear about your experiences in the colonies, sir."

And this time, when he smiled at Camille, she smiled back.

THE CHEMIN DE FER DU Nord company hired Jean-Paul. He told Auguste and Camille the good news when he came for a visit, the first of many that summer.

"I've always liked trains," he said, "and I'll be learning how to repair locomotives and other mechanical systems."

Jean-Paul became a regular guest and a helpful one, weeding the vegetable bed, climbing on ladders to pick fruit, even chopping firewood. He was always deferential to Auguste, equally polite to Camille. Without actually discussing the matter, they understood that Jean-Paul was courting Camille.

"Jean-Paul is hardworking," Auguste said one afternoon. He had been in bed all day and hadn't eaten a thing. Camille put a cup of tea on his bedside table. "Do you know anything about his family, Camille? Your Édouard, well, we know the Dumonts. What do you know about Jean-Paul?"

She shook her head. "He doesn't talk about his past or his family. He's an orphan."

"He's fought for his country"—Auguste looked thoughtful—"and a career with the Nord is a reliable one. Not the aristocrat your grandmother wanted for you, but he seems a decent man."

Unspoken between them, the reality that once the war was over, there would be a dearth of marriageable men, able-bodied or otherwise.

"I don't want to rush you into a decision, Camille," her father said, "but it would give me great peace of mind to see you married before I die."

The sound of the kitchen door opening sent her hurrying down the stairs. Jean-Paul had come in with potatoes he'd dug from the garden and was taking them down to the cellar.

"You didn't need to do that," she said.

"I enjoy gardening," he said, waving off her protests. Then more seriously, "Capitaine Barbier is not well right now. Let me help."

When Jean-Paul finished in the garden, Auguste came downstairs. He insisted that Jean-Paul take a rest and sit with him outside the garden room. Camille brought out a tray of drinks, beer for the men and lemonade for herself.

The garden room stood on its own, separated from the house by the kitchen garden and reached through paths that wound between plantings of flowers and herbs. Auguste had built it himself shortly after they moved in. Camille always suspected he had done this to have a place to get away from Grand-mère. It was close enough to the road that he could watch wagons and people go past, and sometimes he invited a neighbor in for a drink.

Auguste often fell asleep in the garden after a glass of beer. It was in repose that Camille could see how quickly her father was slipping away. Hunched and shrunken, he seemed eighty, not fifty. His cheeks were pallid and his hands shook.

"He's often short of breath, Camille," Jean-Paul said, walking back to the kitchen with her. "Won't he go see a doctor?"

"He refuses. Says he saw one already in Paris, and there is nothing to be done."

Ostensibly, Auguste was acting as chaperone, but as his head drooped and breathing slowed, he might as well have not been there.

"Come on," Jean-Paul said, "let's go for a walk. Just as far as the d'Amervals' farm."

"All right," she said. He grinned and took Camille's hand.

"I understand you were engaged," he said, "but your fiancé was killed."

"Édouard Dumont," she said, "though I rather suspect he wasn't quite ready to marry. But between his mother and the war, well, that hurried things along. He died only weeks after enlisting, at Verdun."

"Édouard Dumont," he mused, "I'm trying to remember him."

"I think I remember you from a long time ago," she said.

And immediately regretted it when his features hardened and his eyes narrowed. Something about those eyes made her hastily retract her words.

"But I'm not sure. You would've gone to the boys' school, and we girls only ever saw you from a distance on school days."

"They kept us boys and girls separate to avoid trouble." To her relief he smiled. "But I do remember you walking to school, Camille, in your white ruffled dress with blue ribbons."

She had never worn a white dress to school. Jean-Paul was remembering her from that day in the garden. He didn't realize she also remembered that day, remembered that boy, the scrawny teenager with dirty knees. He didn't want to be reminded. And could she blame him? Camille felt a rush of sympathy for that boy, who she thought was still inside the man. She wanted him to know he wasn't nothing.

THE D'AMERVAL FIELDS NEAR THE Barbiers' cottage grew barley. During the first year of the war, only the eldest d'Amerval son had been called up and the family had been able to harvest their crop. They sowed a new crop in the spring even though an aerial attack left a crater in the middle of the field and damaged their barn. But now only the women of the family remained and they had given up on the crop that had sustained them for so many years.

The barn door creaked open on rusty hinges. The wall opposite the entrance had been badly scorched, and the roof above had collapsed into a heap of charred lumber.

"Luckily it's sheltered under the loft," Jean-Paul said, "and the straw is nice and dry." He sat down and patted the floor beside him.

Camille didn't want to, but she also didn't want to offend him, so she sat down and hugged her knees to her chest with a nervous smile. He twirled a lock of her hair around one finger and gave it a gentle tug.

"Look at you and look at me," he said, musingly, "and your grandmother a countess."

He had kissed her before, but only on the cheeks in greeting or farewell, or lightly on the lips. Now he kissed her hard, forcing his tongue between her lips and pressing her down on the straw. His hands slid along her hips.

"Jean-Paul, please, no," Camille said, turning her face away. "We shouldn't be doing this."

He chuckled, pleased. "Did you do this with young Dumont?"

She shook her head and he laughed. "So I'm your first." He pressed his knee between her legs. "Stop pretending you don't want this, Camille. Every village girl knows how this barn is being used."

"I didn't know that, Jean-Paul. I don't know what the other girls know." She struggled as he pinned her down, his smile triumphant.

"That's what I like about you, little countess," he said. "You act so innocent, so virtuous, but that's not true, is it? Otherwise you wouldn't have agreed to come here with me, would you?"

And as Jean-Paul heaved and grunted on top of her, all Camille could think of through the sharp pain as she resisted and then gave up was whether she had encouraged him. Had she given him the wrong idea? Was this her doing?

"There, you see," he said, cheerfully as he rolled off her. "You stopped struggling. You liked it. Let's go tell your father we're getting married. If he doesn't think I'm good enough, tell him you're ruined for anyone else now."

CHAPTER 3

Shanghai 1907

Louis's first wife didn't object when Grandfather Deng announced plans for a store in Paris. Normally quick to make her feelings known, First Wife was strangely silent that her husband and youngest son were leaving home to live for a decade or more in a foreign country, returning to Shanghai only occasionally. But she came from a merchant family herself and didn't question this decision, since it would expand the Dengs' business. Her thinking was as traditional as her rice-powdered face and painted eyebrows.

"Our family's prosperity comes first," she said, "and if we must open a business in Europe, obviously only a family member can be trusted to run it. Grandfather Deng has honored my husband with his trust."

Had Pauline believed for a moment that her opinion mattered, she would've begged Grandfather Deng to let Theo stay in Shanghai. Theo found her weeping silently in a corner of the garden, hidden from sight between an azalea shrub and a stand of bamboos.

"I won't have anyone to talk to when you're gone," she sobbed, "and one else tells the other servants to stop slapping me. Can't you tell Grandfather you don't want to go to France?"

"Grandfather won't change his mind," Theo said. "This is something he's been planning for years. It's why they sent me to the French mission school. Besides, I really want to see France."

"I'll kill myself," Pauline said and wiped her nose on her sleeve. "I'll jump down the well and my ghost will haunt this house for centuries."

He laughed and tugged gently on her pigtail. "Won't your ghost get bored spending all those years hovering around the same well?"

A few days later, First Wife sent for her. Pauline hurried to First Wife's chambers expecting some sort of punishment. The large room was both bedroom and sitting room, the whitewashed walls bare except for a pair of scrolls, watercolors of irises and orchids. First Wife was resting on her daybed, her cheeks puffed out in smug satisfaction.

"Your uncle is taking you to France," she said. "You're going to keep house for my husband and my son in that barbaric country." First Wife almost purred at the thought of being rid of her.

Had she been a boy, her uncle might've adopted her officially. Had First Wife been a more generous soul, she might've treated Pauline like one of her own children, official or not. But Pauline was merely the result of a dalliance between Louis's youngest brother and his mistress, a very expensive prostitute, both dead after an automobile accident when Pauline was a toddler.

Pauline knew it made First Wife happy to think she must be frightened and miserable at the prospect of living in a foreign country, so she stared down at her tattered cloth shoes to hide how radiantly happy she was to be leaving. She'd be with her uncle and Theo, the only two who actually paid attention to her. She would live far away from First Wife's baleful glares, away from the reach of the head housekeeper's slaps. There was nothing within the walls of the Deng estate she would regret leaving behind.

The moment she left First Wife's chambers she ran to Theo's room.

"I'm coming to France with you!" she cried. "And your mother has told the cook to teach me how to make some of your father's favorite dishes before we leave. And I must write down the recipes."

His face mirrored her delight. "I told Father I'd be lonely in France without anyone my own age. You were the only one the family could spare." He was teasing but she didn't mind. "Or maybe the Goddess of Mercy intervened and made Father feel sorry for me."

But she knew the only reason she was going to France was because Theo had asked.

"Thank you, cousin. I'm very grateful." Pauline knelt and touched her forehead to the floor.

FIRST WIFE COULDN'T HIDE HER pleasure at this turn of events. She never addressed Pauline by name. She'd never wanted any responsibility for raising the child.

"The only reason my husband didn't send that child to an orphanage," First Wife often said, "was because his waste of a brother begged us on his deathbed to keep the girl. And my husband was the one who agreed. I mean, he couldn't risk curses from beyond the grave."

First Wife herself had no intention of going to France. She had no desire to leave the comforts of her courtyard home for the hardships of life in a foreign land. How could she lead a decent and proper life in Europe? Even diplomats left their wives and daughters safe at home in China when assigned overseas.

When the time came for farewells, the household gathered in the forecourt where sedan chairs and a cart filled with luggage stood ready to go to the wharf. Theo and his father kneeled before Grandfather Deng and touched their foreheads to the ground. Then Theo did the same in front of his mother. Standing with the servants who had come to witness this leave-taking, Pauline couldn't help feeling that although First Wife looked regretful, she was also relieved that her youngest son was going away.

ON THE MONTHLONG STEAMER JOURNEY from Shanghai to Marseilles, Pauline and Theo only had each other for company. There was a handful of Chinese aboard the ship, all merchants like her uncle, tasked with opening up businesses in Europe. Her uncle had been looking forward to afternoons of mah-jongg with these new acquaintances, but as soon as their ship reached open waters, Louis fell prey to seasickness and could barely stir from his bunk.

The ship's crew was French, and they were intrigued by Theo, a Chinese boy who spoke perfect, if rather formal, French. A steward introduced them to the ship's cook, who made some plain broth to give her uncle. But some days just the thought of eating was too much for Louis.

"I'll eat when I can," he said, not bothering to turn over. "Go outside and play."

Left on their own, Theo and Pauline ran around on the deck every day. When the ship moved into the fierce sun of the Indian Ocean, they quickly realized it was cooler inside. With more exploring, they discovered a corner no one else seemed to use, furnished with a pair of bentwood chairs and a small table.

Theo took out his deck of playing cards, gilt-edged and almost as good as new. They liked to race each other at building a house of cards. The motion of the ship made the contest more challenging and Theo never got upset if Pauline's stack tumbled and brought down his as well; he just laughed.

"Do you ever play games with those cards instead of building houses?" a voice asked in Chinese. They looked up to see a young man in his early twenties. He bowed in exaggerated courtesy, his manner slightly mocking. "My name is Mah. Assistant manager at the soon-to-be-established Wenzhou Stone Arts Emporium, the Paris branch."

"I'm Deng Taoling," Theo said. "This is my cousin Baoling. My father is going to open an antiques store when we get to Paris."

"I can tell you're related," the young man said, "you look very alike. Same face shape, same cheekbones." His own cheeks were pockmarked, his face thin and pointed.

"We've been told we resemble our grandmother," Theo said politely.

"How about a game of cards?" Mah said. "We can play for pennies. Do you know how to play Twenty-One Points? Whoever gets closest to twenty-one without going over wins."

"No. I don't use these cards for games," Theo said. "Shuffling makes them lose their stiffness."

"Some other time then," the young man said, shrugging as he walked away.

WHEN SHE LIVED IN SHANGHAI, Pauline attended school at home. There was a large hall used as a classroom, and the Dengs employed a tutor for the family's sons. Girls and servants' children could sit at the back of the classroom and listen to Teacher Chen as long as they kept quiet. Her uncle wanted her to learn the rudiments of writing and arithmetic, so she had been excused from afternoon chores and allowed to sit in class after lunchtime.

While on the ship, Theo was her tutor. They were both determined that she would learn as much French as possible before the ship docked in Marseilles. He spoke to her in French, breaking into Chinese only when there were words he couldn't explain by making gestures or pointing at an object. He taught her the alphabet and the strange notion that instead of a single character for a word, a combination of letters spelled out the sounds for the word.

"That's the interesting thing about Western languages," he said, "you can sound them out instead of having to memorize four thousand characters. So if you know how to pronounce a word, you'll recognize it in writing. And vice versa. Well, most of the time."

The ship's crew soon realized Theo was teaching Pauline to speak French and amused themselves teaching the two children's songs. They learned to sing *Alouette, gentille alouette* and *Frère Jacques, Frère Jacques*, in rounds. A month earlier, Pauline would've shied away from strangers such as these, with their strange noses and hair in so many surprising colors. She was accustomed to a world of walled-in court-yard houses, had walked outside those walls only a few times, and that was to the market, following behind an older servant who needed help carrying packages.

Each day the ship sailed farther from China, away from the walls of her old life. But the realization didn't dawn on her until she stood on deck beside Theo watching their passage through the Suez Canal: the world inside those walls no longer held her.

DURING THEIR FIRST WEEKS IN Paris, the three of them lived in a small hotel, a *pension de famille*, while her uncle looked for a building suitable for both store and home. Sometimes Theo and Pauline went with him, trailing behind as he inspected one building after another, accompanied by an estate agent and a translator hired through the Chinese consulate in Paris. More often than not, one or two men from Paris's small community of Chinese merchants also joined them, curious to meet the new arrivals and eager to offer opinions.

It only took her uncle a month to find the right building.

Their excitement barely contained, Pauline and Theo stood at the entrance to Number 55, Rue de Lisbonne while Louis unlocked the door. They crossed the threshold and entered a high-ceilinged space.

Tall plateglass windows faced the street, reaching almost to the ceiling. The wooden floors were old, wide-planked, made from the same oak as the smooth posts and beams above. The space was bare except for a long marble-topped counter. A double-hung door behind the counter led to a small office. At the very back of the store, another door opened to a corridor that ran the width of the building and gave access to the storeroom, protected by a black metal grille.

"We'll use this space for storing the most valuable antiques," her uncle said. "Open only to our best clients."

"Where does that staircase go?" Theo asked.

"Upstairs, to the apartments. You'll see."

Pauline pushed her hands deeper into the pockets of her padded coat. The sight of cobwebs draped over light fixtures and ceiling fans dismayed her. The thick oak-planked floors needed scrubbing and after that, frequent waxing. The large plateglass windows were dusty, dotted with fly specks; she'd have to polish them every day. She knew this was all her responsibility, all the cleaning in the store and in their home. And the cooking. It was why she had been allowed to come.

But in the next moment, delight overtook her dismay when she realized that although she would have a lot of hard work, there was no one here who would scold or beat her for being too slow or careless. There were no older servants to tattle on her, no head housekeeper. No First Wife. She was only twelve years old, but here she was the head housekeeper. The only servant, the only cook. Even if she slept on a cot in the storeroom, she was far better off than before.

"Now come see where we will live," her uncle said. "We'll go outside and use the front door."

He took them back out onto the street, to a door a few steps beside the shop. It was a very plain, nondescript door painted a dull gray. Pauline hadn't even noticed it when they first walked past. Two num-

bers in brass were fixed to its painted surface. Number 53 on the Rue
de Lisbonne.

The small entrance foyer was just big enough for a staircase, the
wooden handrail and banisters glossy and brown with layers of paint.
Theo, eager to see their new home, ran to a door facing the staircase
and pushed it open. He and Pauline looked in dismay at the two small
rooms.

"We won't be using those rooms," Louis said, "except perhaps for
storage. Our home is upstairs."

The first apartment was over the store. There was a large parlor
with balconies that looked onto Rue de Lisbonne, a dining room, and
beyond that, a kitchen. There were four rooms across the hall and a
staircase.

"If you go downstairs, that's the corridor behind the store," her
uncle said. "Now, these two rooms are mine, one will be my study.
There's a bedroom for each of you so take your pick."

"I'm taking this room," Theo shouted and ran up the staircase.
"Look, there's another apartment up here! Who'll live here?"

"We can rent it out once we're all settled," Louis said. "Shall we go
outside and walk through the neighborhood? There's a market around
the corner."

Back outside again, Pauline skipped along behind her uncle, ecstatic at the thought of her own room. It was a small apartment, tiny
when compared to the Deng estate with its mazes of courtyards and
houses, a compound crammed with several families and dozens of servants. There she had shared a room with five other servants, two to
a bed. Her bed partner, an older girl, banished her to the brick floor,
where she lay on a straw mat with a thin blanket pulled over her head,
listening to the rustle of rats in the walls.

But here she had a room of her own. Here they were a household of three, and she never wanted to see Shanghai again, not for as long as she lived.

THE FIRST THING LOUIS DID before they moved any furniture into the apartment was to open all the windows and doors, letting fresh air in and ill-tempered spirits out.

"Are French spirits like Chinese ones?" Pauline asked Theo. "Do they like to leave before new people move in?"

"I don't see why they wouldn't welcome the opportunity," he said, "especially since we've brought our own gods with us."

The first item of furniture carried up to the apartment was a long console table of polished rosewood inset with a marble top. Louis had it placed in the hallway beside the kitchen door. On the wall above he hung a scroll inscribed with the names of the last five generations of Deng patriarchs. On the table he arranged a bronze statuette of the Goddess of Mercy, a brightly colored ceramic one of the God of Wealth, and an oval urn filled with sand to hold sticks of incense.

"Let us ask the gods for success in our new enterprise," Louis said, and they knelt beside him. Only after the sticks of incense in the urn burned down did he allow the workmen to bring up the rest of their belongings.

Her uncle filled the apartment with the furniture brought over in the cargo hold of the ship. Elmwood chairs with curved arms, black lacquered tables inlaid with carved soapstone figures of flowers and birds, tall folding screens that could be pulled across balcony doors to keep out the sun. Landscape paintings and calligraphy mounted on long scrolls of silk decorated paneled walls. The only European items were the sconces and lamps already installed on walls and ceilings.

When they had settled into their new home, Louis hired a tutor for Theo to make sure he'd be ready in the fall to attend school at the lycée nearby. The young tutor was a recent graduate of the Sorbonne, keen to prove his worth.

When Louis told Pauline that she could join Theo's lessons, she thought it would be just the same as in Shanghai, when she had listened from the back of the classroom.

"My father says she can sit with us, but not bother you with questions," Theo explained on their first day of lessons.

But their tutor just chuckled. "I don't mind if she wants to learn as long as you do your homework."

He had Pauline sit at the dining table across from Theo, with pencils and paper of her own. Soon he was also coming a few evenings each week to give French lessons to Louis in the privacy of his study.

Their young tutor was nothing like the elderly Teacher Chen, who didn't believe girls needed an education. He gave her almost as much of his attention as he did Theo. While Theo worked on his assignments, the tutor gave Pauline lessons of her own. She was so enthralled with the lessons and their tutor's friendliness, it didn't occur to her she might want companionship from friends her own age.

Not until the day she stood at the church square and watched girls from her neighborhood skipping rope. Their faces were familiar to her now; every day she saw them enter and leave their homes, heard them call out to each other, saw them walk to church together. She peered from behind a news kiosk, moving her lips to learn their chant.

Dos à dos, face à face,
Donnez-vous la main et changez de place!

Suddenly a girl with auburn hair and pale freckled skin left the group and walked up to her. Smiling, she put out one hand. Pauline took it hesitantly, then returned the smile. Soon, Pauline was taking her turn with the other girls, jumping and turning the rope, chanting along.

Lise Girard's parents owned a photography studio and camera shop a few doors down from La Pagode. Like all the other store owners on the street, they lived above their shop in an apartment nearly identical to the Dengs'. Whenever Pauline went to their home looking for Lise, Mme Girard always examined Pauline's work-roughened hands and shook her head in pity. Pauline tried explaining that her life before this had been far more difficult, that in the Deng household servants' children were expected to help their parents until they were old enough to take a job of their own.

Lise's brother, Armand, was the same age as Theo. When Theo wasn't working at La Pagode or studying, he squeezed into the darkroom beside Armand to watch M. Girard develop photographs. Sometimes M. Girard allowed Theo to help him. The studio also sold and repaired cameras and, with help from M. Girard, Theo rebuilt a camera he'd purchased from a flea market. Camera slung over his shoulder, Theo took Pauline to public gardens and photographed her beside fountains and flowers, standing on a bridge over the Seine, or feeding pigeons fluttering in a square.

One day, Pauline realized that without really noticing how or when, she was speaking French. And reading it too.

THAT FIRST YEAR, THE DENGS experienced a winter much colder than anything they'd known before. Theo complained the cold made his right ear ache. But for some reason only the right ear, he said, tugging his knit cap farther down the right side of his head. Pauline didn't mind the cold and she didn't miss Shanghai at all—except in one respect.

She missed being ordinary. When she walked on the streets of Shanghai no one gave her a second look. There she was unremarkable, just another servant girl. No one laughed or stared at her the way some of the neighborhood children here still did sometimes, even after they became her friends. Even after she exchanged her high-collared tunics and loose trousers for blouses and woolen skirts.

"La petite Chinoise, la petite Chinoise," they'd exclaim, pulling up the corners of their eyes, laughing and pointing as if congratulating themselves for making her realize she was Chinese. They only looked more amused if she scowled in response, angry and helpless.

But still, these irritations were minor compared to the miseries she'd be facing had she remained in Shanghai, alone, without her uncle or Theo.

Pauline often wondered whether Louis missed Shanghai. He never mentioned regrets over coming to France, about being so far away from home. Only when he opened a box of records from China did he reveal hints of homesickness. First Wife had standing instructions to ship him all the latest Peking opera. At the sight of those boxes printed with the golden rooster of Pathé Orient Records he would break into excited smiles. He perused each album cover carefully, reading the names of opera performers out loud, nodding in recognition at some, frowning if he thought a particular artist didn't suit the role.

"Look at this one," he would say, "a performance by Tan Xinpei. Sixty years old and still the best."

Louis sat in his study almost every evening and listened to the gramophone. Surrounded by Chinese furniture and paintings, he listened to his music, head nodding slowly, eyes closed in appreciation. For those hours, Louis was back home, and he might have been content to spend his leisure time doggedly doing the same few things: listening to Peking opera on his gramophone, reading months-old newspapers from China, going out only to play mah-jongg with the other Chinese merchants.

Fortunately, Denise entered their lives.

SHE CAME TO LA PAGODE on a quiet morning, a trim woman dressed in dove gray, a black hat with gray ribbons. She took some snuff bottles out of her handbag and asked Louis if he'd be willing to buy the small items, souvenirs her deceased husband had brought back from his time in China. Louis, still waiting for the first shipment of fine antiques from Shanghai, only had inexpensive stock on display, cloisonné vases of mediocre quality, vintage porcelain, and carved stoneware. With Theo translating, Louis bought all the snuff bottles.

On her way out, the woman paused at the door and smiled at the children, who stood beside the sales counter, Theo straight and graceful, Pauline awkward and pigeon-toed.

"Vos enfants sont très beaux, Monsieur Deng," she said, her smile rather wistful.

As soon as the door closed, Theo translated her words. "Your children are very beautiful." And somehow Pauline knew this woman had meant what she said, and that she meant both of them, not just Theo.

The following month, the woman returned with a pair of blue cloisonné vases, and a month after that, an exquisite hair ornament set with seed pearls, the entire semicircle heightened by a flock of tiny butterflies. Their wings, made from blue kingfisher feathers set in gold wire, trembled as though alive. Louis admired it, then took Denise to the storeroom where he was inventorying a newly arrived shipment to show her other examples of hairpins and headdresses decorated with kingfisher feather ornaments. She exclaimed over a hair band of small blue hydrangeas.

"These are so detailed, the tiny petals, the jade leaves," she said.

"It's so fine, my little hair ornament looks crude and cheap beside it." Her voice was low and a bit hoarse, not at all what one would expect from a woman so delicately built.

"Yet there are many who would love the piece you brought in," Louis said, "I will buy it."

Pleased at her interest, Louis walked her around the storeroom, pointing out his favorite objects, promising that when the next shipment arrived there would be more to see.

The Dengs began expecting her slim figure to come through the door on the last Friday of each month. She always smiled at Pauline and never appeared impatient when Louis spoke his halting, heavily accented French. By now they knew her name, Denise Latour. They speculated on her age, possibly midthirties but with foreigners it was so hard to tell.

On one occasion, Louis and Theo went to her home and came back carrying a rosewood table inlaid with mother-of-pearl.

"What's a French person's home like?" Pauline asked. "Did she have lots of mirrors in gold frames? Marble floors?"

She asked this with a fair amount of envy. Theo was fourteen and a boy. Louis took him along on errands and allowed him to wander out on the streets by himself. Pauline was allowed to venture outside by herself only as far as the small market square in front of the church. Any farther and Theo had to go with her. At least until she was older and knew her way around the streets.

"No, it's not a nice apartment at all," Theo said. "There isn't anything much on her walls, the drapes are faded, and the floor is parquet like ours but missing bits of wood. She told me she sells her antiques to pay the rent. She made tea for us and also some little tarts. Really good ones. Better than the ones from the patisserie down the street."

The next month, Denise didn't come by as usual and Louis assumed she didn't need money. But as the weeks wore on, he fussed and worried, and finally sent Theo to check on her. When Theo came back, he had distressing news.

"Madame Latour doesn't live there anymore, Father," Theo said when he burst through the door. "Her landlord told me she's moved to the Sentier district to work at a garment factory. But she still goes back to her apartment on Sundays in case there is mail for her."

The following Sunday, Louis brought Denise home. He gave her the apartment above theirs. Workmen carried up a new stove and kitchen sink. Denise papered the walls herself and painted all the wood trim. The apartment on the top floor, Louis made clear to the children, was Denise's domain and they could go up only when invited.

To their French neighbors, she was the Dengs' tenant who sometimes cooked and baked for them, who sometimes did their shopping, a part-time housekeeper of sorts. Whatever else they suspected, they accepted with a shrug.

When the Chinese community in Paris first learned that Louis Deng had acquired a mistress, there had been raised eyebrows. Not because he had a mistress, for that was common enough in China, but because she was French. Ever vigilant of their own, it didn't take long for word to spread in the community about Denise, and the word was that Deng's foreign mistress was disappointingly ordinary. She dressed very modestly, always in gray or blue, and looked like any average housewife as she made her way down the street, shopping basket on one arm. The matter soon settled down.

Denise, the children quickly learned, loved to cook, and it was thanks to her that their palates adapted to enjoy French flavors. She delivered soups and bread when neighbors were ill, and she always seemed to have treats at hand for Pauline's and Theo's friends when they came upstairs. This was how the Dengs learned that her cooking was considered exceptional. La Pagode also gained from her love of baking; customers could count on a small plate of pastries while drinking tea with Louis.

Denise was also endlessly curious about China.

"Tell me more about your home in Shanghai," she often asked Theo and Pauline. "Did you have gardens?" Denise pictured a China conjured from the delicate antiques on display at La Pagode, a dreamlike and magical place.

Theo described the chaos of the Mid-Autumn Festival and New Year's celebrations. His mother's very old and very pampered Pekingese. A dining hall large enough to hold banquets for the entire family. He painted a charming picture of the traditional courtyard houses where they had lived.

"Every courtyard home has a garden in the center," he said. "Some are quite small and paved, with just a few tall pots of flowering shrubs or small trees. Osmanthus and daphne are family favorites. My grandfather's courtyard is the biggest, with a rock garden and bamboo grove, and a goldfish pond."

From Theo's replies, Pauline wondered if his memories had softened with distance and time. Or perhaps the Deng estate really was that idyllic if you were one of the privileged, a legitimate member of the family. Or perhaps he was simply telling Denise what she wanted to hear.

With Denise at her side, Pauline didn't need Theo anymore in order to leave their neighborhood. Denise took her to markets in other areas of Paris, and she learned from her uncle's mistress how to shop carefully and frugally, how to bargain without offending, how to preserve fruit for the winter months.

When Pauline grew taller and plumper, Denise took her to a dressmaker. Without Denise insisting on this, Pauline was certain her uncle wouldn't have even thought about new clothes for her. He probably would've just had First Wife send something from China.

"You are very pretty, Pauline," Denise said. "You'll be a petite young woman, and you'll keep that little waist, too."

"I wish my hair was blond," Pauline replied, looking at herself in Denise's mirror. "And my nose is too small."

"Your hair is dark as a raven's wing, your little nose will keep your features looking young, and your eyes shine with intelligence." Denise began brushing out Pauline's hair. "You and Theo are the most beautiful children I have ever seen."

"Well, Theo is very handsome. Whenever we go out, everyone stares at him."

Denise laughed. "They might be staring at you, too, ma petite."

In ways Pauline couldn't articulate, the Rue de Lisbonne felt more like a home after Denise moved in with them.

"You could say that Louis rescued me, yes, I call it a rescue," she told Theo and Pauline. "I was working fourteen hours a day in that factory and living in a tiny room with three other factory women. I can never thank him enough. Or you, for making me feel like a member of your family"

As for her uncle and how he felt about Denise, Pauline couldn't even begin to guess. There were evenings when Louis went to Denise's apartment after supper and music would drift down, sometimes Peking opera and Chinese folk tunes, sometimes classical music, an orchestra or string quartet.

"They're both happy," Theo said. "Or at least content. We like Denise, she likes us, let's leave it at that."

When she peeked in Denise's parlor from time to time, Pauline often saw them sitting quietly, her uncle smoking and reading a Chinese newspaper, Denise absorbed in her needlework. It was a far more companionable scene than Pauline had ever witnessed between her uncle and First Wife.

"YOUR UNCLE HAS BEEN RATHER distracted," Denise said. "Is it because of the Chinese New Year event next week at the store?"

Each year they decorated La Pagode for Chinese New Year and the party Louis hosted for his best customers. Nineteen twelve was the Year of the Rat and Louis was giving away silk fans painted with a gray rat sitting up on its haunches, nibbling on red bayberries that had fallen from the tree above. A pair of red silk lanterns with golden tassels dangled over the store entrance and inside, strings of small red lanterns adorned ceiling beams and light fixtures.

In fact Louis had been uncharacteristically preoccupied with matters other than the store. He spent a great deal of time at the Chinese Merchants Guild Hall and when Chinese consulate staff dropped by the store, he took them aside for long conversations. Pauline thought it had to do with news of what was happening in China. Chinese newspapers took weeks to arrive but French papers with correspondents in Peking reported that the Qing dynasty was crumbling under numerous rebellions.

Louis came home one afternoon and went straight to his study and shut the door. He did not emerge until dinnertime. He said nothing until Pauline had served all the food, then cleared his throat.

"Yesterday, on February 12 in China, our emperor abdicated. We are now the Republic of China. There was no bloodshed. It was a peaceful transition to the new government. It was inevitable and necessary. The Qing dynasty was stagnant and weak. China can enter the twentieth century now as a modern nation."

He repeated this in French for Denise, then stood up and took out a bottle of cognac from the sideboard. He poured them each a small drink and raised his glass.

"Ten thousand years of prosperity to the Republic of China."

"Ten thousand years," echoed Theo and Pauline.

In the months that followed, new staff from the Chinese consulate visited the store and familiar ones came no more. Not all the diplomats were replaced; quite a few stayed on, willing to serve the Republic of China. The incoming diplomats seemed a new breed. Younger, already fluent in French, and they brought their families with them.

The new Chinese minister to France came to visit La Pagode, an event that sent Pauline running to the back room to boil water and make a pot of their best tea. The minister had brought his daughter, and Pauline left the back door slightly ajar while waiting for the tea to steep, peering through the gap at the young woman in her expensive fur-collared coat and a stylish hat. The minister's daughter appeared to be fifteen or sixteen, close to Pauline's age, but seemed so much more poised. Her face was a delicate oval and her full upper lip seemed perpetually on the brink of quivering. It gave her a look of beguiling innocence. Her eyes, glancing up from under thick, stubby lashes, were deep brown, hesitant and shy, the eyes of a doe.

Pauline looked down at her faded apron, at her ink-stained fingers. She scrubbed her hands clean and took off the apron before taking the teapot out.

WHEN THEO GRADUATED FROM LYCÉE, Louis treated them all to dinner at the Café Anglais, a sumptuous meal even Denise could not fault. She sighed happily as they left the restaurant.

"It's been a very long time since I enjoyed such a decadent meal. That duck confit was prepared in true classic style. Thank you, Louis."

The June evening was balmy so they strolled back to the Rue de Lisbonne. The leisurely route took them across the Seine, where Denise made them stop on the Pont Royal to admire the view. The splendid façade of the Gare d'Orsay, the lights of boats moored along the banks of the river.

Theo barely glanced at the water. The celebration dinner had been in his honor, but he had been distracted all evening, fidgeting and looking down at his plate, talking very little. Now he spoke up.

"Father, I've applied to the University of Paris."

"To the Sorbonne?" Louis said, frowning. "Why? You'll be working full-time at the store now. And you're going back to Shanghai in a few months for your wedding."

"I can go to university and still work at the store, Father," Theo said. "I would continue as now, working part-time. Please, put off the wedding till after I've graduated."

Days of disputes followed, but the decision was in Louis's hands because Theo couldn't pay the tuition fees. Their arguments, frequent and loud, echoed through the apartment even when the door to Louis's study was shut.

Standing outside in the corridor, Pauline couldn't help but overhear.

"You're the reason I came to France," Louis shouted, "to set you up in a business of your own. A business where you can earn a living. What can a foreign university teach you? Will it teach you the Four Books and the Five Classics? No, you'll learn the history of European civilizations instead of our own. You'll learn their poetry and forget the Three Hundred Tang Poems."

"China is not a backward, feudal nation anymore." Theo's voice was sullen. "I need a Western education. Anyway, haven't you always told me that education was the most important gift you could give your children?"

Pauline could imagine the look on his handsome face, lower lip slightly protruding like a small boy about to throw a tantrum. Until now, she hadn't realized La Pagode was meant for Theo's future.

"You have enough education. Enough to discuss antiques, enough to make customers feel comfortable dealing with us, enough to do the paperwork." Louis had lowered his voice, but it still carried through the door.

A few minutes later Theo left the apartment, slamming the door on his way out, no doubt heading to the Girards' store. He liked to help M. Girard, whether it was developing prints or repairing a camera. Pauline often thought that if her uncle owned a photo studio and camera shop instead of an antiques store, Theo would've been eager to take over the business.

"This is what I get for bringing my son to a foreign country!" Louis came into the kitchen where Denise and Pauline were shelling peas, pretending they hadn't heard the argument. "If we were home in China, that boy wouldn't dream of disobeying. Pauline, don't you make me regret ever bringing you here."

After a week of Theo's silence and sulking, Louis gave in.

"I'll telegram your grandfather about postponing the wedding," Louis said, helping himself to more chicken. He pointed ivory chopsticks at Theo. "The minute you've graduated, you're going home to China and getting married."

After supper Pauline followed Theo to his room.

"If you get married, can I still keep house for you?" she said. "Even if your wife doesn't like me?"

"Don't worry," Theo said, "I'll think of something else in four years. I'm not working in this store and I'm not marrying a girl I've never met. In four years, things could be quite different. Anyway, this means I get to attend university."

WITH THEO AT LECTURES ALL day and studying all night, Pauline found herself pulled into the daily routine of La Pagode more and more. It was the now largest Chinese-owned store in Paris and their countrymen often dropped by to exchange gossip and drink tea. Working on the shop floor instead of merely in the back rooms, Pauline felt she'd met almost every member of Paris's small Chinese community, from craftsmen and traders to students and consulate staff. They came with the excuse of taking a look at the latest shipments of antiques but conversations soon veered away from snuff bottles and porcelain to politics and local gossip.

"It's time to show you how to do the bookkeeping," Louis said one day.

"I already know how, Uncle," she said. "I've been doing the books with Theo all year. I mean, we've been sharing that work. And you've never found any mistakes, have you?"

Theo despised doing the accounts so Pauline had offered to help. Then she found herself correcting his work so often she ended up doing his share of the bookkeeping.

"Before this," she said to Theo, "you must've done the numbers to get them right before showing them to Uncle. Or did you even bother?"

"Father did some correcting," he admitted.

Until now, she'd never said anything to Louis, who had looked startled, then pensive. "Yes, of course you've been helping him," he said.

"I don't mind one bit, Uncle," she said firmly. "One family, one business."

This was her life now and it was more than Pauline had ever hoped for when she was a little girl, shivering herself to sleep under a thin blanket with only a straw mat between her and the cold brick floor, listening to rats scuttle around the room.

CHAPTER 4

Sunday, November 3, 1918

PAULINE

DENISE PRACTICALLY SLAMMED the plate down in front of Pauline. Lunch was three crepes rolled with thin-sliced ham, smothered in a creamy cheese sauce served with lashings of disapproval. It was astonishing how Denise had managed to find ham and cream even though rationing was stricter than ever.

Pauline obediently ate her meal, eyes meekly focused on her plate. When she was younger, she used to sit in Denise's kitchen and watch her cook. There was something soothing about the Frenchwoman's unhurried competence. But right now, Denise was so agitated she didn't even notice that a few chestnut curls had shaken loose from her tightly rolled chignon.

"I've never wanted to get married, Denise," Pauline said. She had wavered on this only once, and very briefly. She put away the thought. "Once the marriage contract is signed, my fate is sealed. I have to bring Theo home to speak with Uncle as soon as he's back in Paris."

Pauline knew Denise wasn't actually angry with her. She was afraid for her, afraid that Louis would punish Pauline for such disobedience, afraid for Pauline's safety. There were rumors the war would end soon, that the Germans couldn't hold on much longer. But in the meantime, artillery still shelled towns near the front and German planes still flew behind the lines to drop bombs on roads and railway tracks.

"It might not be so bad. Your husband might be a shopkeeper," Denise pointed out, "perhaps with a store in the French Concession where your French would be an asset."

Obviously, Denise had more faith in First Wife's goodwill than Pauline did.

"Besides," Denise continued, "have you considered how your uncle would feel if something happened to you?"

"Uncle Louis has been very kind to me," Pauline said, "but I'm still just his brother's bastard daughter."

"Don't say that about yourself." Tears filled Denise's eyes. "Louis told me about your parents. Your father loved your mother very much and wanted to marry her, but the family wouldn't allow it."

"Uncle never told me that. First Wife said my mother was only after the family's money."

"Your mother came from a good family, but they fell on hard times," Denise said. "She had no way to support herself, except, well . . . Louis met her once, you know. He said she was lovely and well-mannered, that she and your father were obviously devoted to each other. She didn't strike Louis as a fortune hunter."

"Perhaps that's why Uncle agreed to take me in. He'd actually met my mother." But she wished she could've learned about her parents from Louis instead of Denise.

"It's not safe for a young woman to travel on her own to a war zone," Denise said.

"Noyelles isn't a war zone. Ordinary folk still live there. The Chinese hospital and camp wouldn't be there if it wasn't safe."

"You know what I mean," Denise said, "a young Chinese woman

alone attracts attention, and some of it may be unwanted." She paused. "Are you sure you couldn't refuse an arranged marriage?"

"If I did, Uncle would be within his rights to throw me out," she said, "or worse yet, send me back to China. Either way, how would I survive?"

In Paris, she wouldn't be able to find work. No one in the Chinese community would give Pauline a chance to prove her worth, not after disobeying her uncle. Nor would any respectable French employer hire her. It was true that factories had been hiring women since the war, but at lower wages than men for the same work. Even so the unions were loudly against women and foreign workers taking away jobs from honest workingmen. Pauline would be paid even less than a Frenchwoman. If anyone bothered hiring her at all.

"Your uncle left you in my care while he's away," Denise said after a long silence, "and I forbid you to go to Noyelles by yourself. You write to Theo, care of Chinese Labour Corps headquarters. And hopefully a letter from Theo is on its way right now, from wherever he is."

The older woman's expression settled into sadness, all anger spent. Denise loved Pauline and Theo, and she was truly fond of Louis. But Denise also depended on Louis's goodwill.

"Yes, Denise," Pauline said meekly. "You're right."

She wouldn't share her plans with Denise. She couldn't have any blame fall on her uncle's mistress.

PAULINE LOOKED DOWN FROM THE balcony window. Below, Denise paused on the sidewalk and Mme Girard joined her. The two women continued on together to church. Sunday afternoon was their preferred time to attend Mass, when the priest offered special prayers for men from the parish fighting at the front, including Mme Girard's son, Armand. Pauline prayed for her childhood friend, too, but not at church.

She lit incense to the Goddess of Mercy on the little altar in their apartment. She did this even though she wondered whether the goddess held any sway here or even had any interest in matters outside China.

Now that she had decided not to argue or share her plans with Denise, Pauline could admit that her courage failed at the thought of leaving Paris. Her confidence extended as far as buying a train ticket to Noyelles-sur-Mer. She had never been outside the city, never strayed beyond the familiar boulevards and monuments, or the shimmering curve of the Seine. Once she reached Noyelles, she still had to get to the Chinese Labour Corps office and find someone who could tell her where Theo's company was working.

And then she had to go there and find Theo. Wherever "there" might be.

She'd manage this on her own if she had to, but perhaps she could persuade someone to help her. Someone she hadn't wanted to contact.

In her uncle's study Pauline pulled open the stationery drawer, took out a lightweight blue letter-card printed with the words *Tubes Pneumatiques Télégramme*. Even if bombs destroyed Paris aboveground, the pneumatic tubes that ran through the city's underground tunnels would still operate. And while the cost to send letters via pneumatic post had increased to 40 centimes since the war, Parisians could always count on a *petit bleu* being delivered within a few hours any day of the week.

Henri, I heard you were back in Paris. I need your help. Please meet me at the fountain by the Église Saint-Sulpice tomorrow at noon. Please come even if you have other appointments, this is extremely urgent. ——Pauline

She threw on her coat and hat. She wanted to drop off this telegram before the next postal pickup. It was only an eight-minute walk to the post office on Rue la Boétie, where she dropped it in the special mailbox beside the one for regular mail. Then she hurried back, not wanting Denise to know she had been out.

He will come, Pauline thought. *No matter what I've said in the past, he will come. He just has to.*

He has to come, he has to come, he has to come.

Her heels tapped the rhythm of those words along the pavement. Henri would meet her tomorrow. Surely it was no coincidence that the one person who visited La Pagode yesterday was a clerk from the Chinese consulate. Or that he mentioned Henri Liu had dropped by his office. Henri was back. Henri, the one person Pauline could ask for help was in Paris, at just the right time.

Surely the Goddess of Mercy had arranged it so.

THEO FIRST MET HENRI IN September of 1916, at the start of the semester. The Sorbonne had invited a guest speaker, a young journalist from Shanghai who happened to be in Paris at the time.

"The interviewer asked him to clarify conflicting press reports on whether or not China will end its neutrality and join in the war," Theo said at supper. Louis was in Marseilles, so he and Pauline were eating at Denise's apartment.

"What does he think?" Pauline asked. "Will China enter the war?"

The war had been going on for more than two years, the death toll already unfathomable.

"He was cautious and would only say that many influential people in China want us to join the Allies. So perhaps China will join later this year."

The journalist Liu Hongmu had made a strong impression on her cousin. Only two years older than Theo, he had already traveled through China and Europe on his own. One day, he hoped to head *Xinwen Bao* newspaper's international desk.

"His family doesn't dictate his decisions." Theo sounded rather despondent.

"Did he give his talk in French?" Pauline said.

"Yes. He's from Shanghai and went to a school run by French missionaries when he was a boy. He said to call him Henri."

"How long will this Henri be in Paris?" Denise said. "You sound as though you'd like to spend more time with him. Why not show him the sights?"

"Yes, that's a good idea." Theo cheered up. "He mentioned he's only been here once before, and only for a couple of days. I'll send a petit bleu to his hotel."

The journalist accepted Theo's offer of sightseeing, and Theo spent a whole day out with his new friend.

Afterward, as she listened to Theo talk about his day with Henri, Pauline got the impression they'd spent more time in cafés chatting with Theo's classmates than doing any actual sightseeing.

"Do you suppose I could meet him too?" she asked Theo. She wanted to know more about this man who had captivated her cousin.

"Yes, you really should meet him," he said. "Come with me tomorrow. We can all three of us go sightseeing."

Theo had arranged to rendezvous by the fountain in front of the Église Saint-Sulpice. They were within sight of the fountain when a man waved madly at Theo from the steps of the church. Henri Liu greeted Theo and Pauline with genuine pleasure, then insisted they start their day with a coffee, his treat for all of Theo's kindness. The coffee at Café Triton, the little bistro facing the square, was terrible, a casualty of rationing, but Pauline hardly noticed.

Henri was unlike anyone she had met before, although admittedly her circle of acquaintances was limited. Pauline thought she had never seen such unruly hair, and that if not for his heavy brows, his round face would've seemed too boyish. But what she mostly remembered was that Henri Liu was the most *alive* person she'd ever met.

And that he paid attention to her.

Not in a leering way, like some of the men she encountered on the streets. Or in a speculative manner, like some of her uncle's acquaintances, who always seemed to be assessing her age, appearance, and health as if sizing her up for their sons. Or worse, for themselves.

"It's quite unusual for you to be here, Pauline," Henri said. "I've met other young Chinese women in Europe, mostly students. Some are daughters of diplomats. But you live and work here."

"I'm here because our family is frugal," she said, stirring her coffee. "I'm housekeeper, cook, shop clerk, bookkeeper."

Unpaid, she refrained from saying. It was true that Louis gave her an allowance, but it was recognition she craved, not housekeeping money. Pauline wanted to earn wages like Theo did. Acknowledgment that she was valuable to the store and to her uncle.

"Well, believe me you're unique," Henri said, laughing. "You're a Chinese woman living in a foreign country, speaking the language fluently."

"I read and write French," she said, "because Uncle hired a tutor for Theo when we first arrived and the tutor was kind enough to let me sit at the table and follow along. History, geography, French, and a tiny bit of English."

"On the ship crossing over she asked me to speak only French to her, no Chinese at all," Theo said. "She was so determined. Within a year of living here, she was haggling at the market like a native Parisienne."

"It helped having Denise live with us," she said, glowing at Theo's praise. "She took me everywhere with her and I learned French so much faster."

"She's too modest. If Pauline had been a boy, she'd be running the store instead of my father."

The conversation moved on to the Chinese laborers Henri had interviewed in Shandong Province just before coming to France. A firm called the Huimin Company was hiring men on behalf of the French government. The first contingent of laborers was coming to France at the end of the year to work at munitions factories. There were more coming, tens of thousands of men.

"Why is a Chinese company hiring workers for France?" Pauline asked.

Normally she would've kept to the background, an unobtrusive spectator, while her uncle's or Theo's friends dominated the conversation. Theo was the only one who listened anyway and that was when they were by themselves. But Henri paid attention and with genuine interest.

"China is supposed to be a neutral country," Henri said, "so if worker recruitment is being done by a private commercial business, we can deny official Chinese government involvement in the war. The Huimin Company is just a front for the French. The British are going to do the same."

"So the British are also recruiting now?" Theo said.

"Not yet, so far they're mostly talking about it."

Pauline glanced at Henri from time to time, at his unkempt hair and the scrape along the jawline where his razor had missed while shaving. His clothing was clean but rumpled, as though he'd thrown them carelessly over a chair overnight. On anyone else, such negligence might've seemed slovenly but to her it confirmed that Henri was wholly unconcerned with fashion. He had other matters on his mind than his appearance. Unconsciously, she tugged down the sleeves of her summer jacket to hide her worn cuffs.

"Are you joining us today for sightseeing, Pauline?" Henri said.

"Yes? Wonderful. Where do we start? There's so much of Paris to see. A day won't be enough."

"But Pauline can show you around next week while I attend classes," Theo said, jumping up from his chair. "Since the war the store only opens three days a week now."

On those days off, Louis played mah-jongg at the Chinese Merchants Guild Hall near the Gare de Lyon, and Denise spent her time at the church making up packages of food and cigarettes for soldiers.

"I accept such a generous offer," Henri said, "but are you willing to do this, Pauline?"

She glanced up at him and nodded, too happy to be annoyed that Theo had volunteered her time. "If Uncle lets me," she said.

"Of course he will," Theo whispered to her as Henri went to the counter to pay for their coffees. "Because we won't tell him."

"THERE ARE SANDBAGS STACKED AROUND the monuments," Pauline said, when she and Henri met the following week, "and the Louvre has moved the most valuable masterpieces to other towns for safety. But the collection is so huge there's still enough to make a visit worthwhile."

"Paris always enchants, I've been told," Henri said. "Springtime is supposed to be the best season to visit, but it's fall and I walked past a public garden on the way here and flowers are still in bloom. And the shop windows. Wonderful!"

"What do you mean?" she said. "All the windows are papered over, it's the law."

"Exactly!" he exclaimed. "And Paris turned it into an art project."

Stores and homes were supposed to paste strips of brown paper over windows to reduce injuries from shattered glass during an air raid. Many Parisian stores responded by crisscrossing strips in decorative ways. Some cut paper into floral and latticework designs, arches and columns. At La Pagode, Pauline had cut out willow trees, arched bridges, and pagodas of brown paper, turning the windows into displays of Chinese papercut art.

"Well, fortunately we haven't been bombed since the zeppelins in January."

And fortunately also, the bombs had not harmed Notre-Dame Cathedral; its arched interiors and flying buttresses still impressed. Pauline knew a little bit about the history of the cathedral and pointed out the Notre-Dame's rose windows, the huge pipe organ, and outside, the gargoyle rainspouts perched on the roof.

"I wish I could tell you more about all those carved figures," Pauline said. She pointed at the balustrade above the western façade of the cathedral. "I'm sure they mean something if you're Catholic. I suppose those are all saints."

"Well, actually those statues represent the twenty-eight kings of Judah."

"How do you know that?" she said. "You said you've never been to Notre-Dame before."

"I attended a French Jesuit school in Shanghai, remember? One of the priests was a devotee of religious architecture."

"And you let me prattle on when obviously you know so much more than I do," Pauline said indignantly.

"But I was enjoying your guided tour," Henri said, "and didn't want to interrupt." His smile was friendly, not sneering, and so cheery that she began to laugh.

"There's a function at the consulate next Monday evening," he said, "and I'm allowed to bring guests. Would you come with me? Theo, too, of course. Supposedly quite a grand affair, the Mid-Autumn Festival celebration."

"We've never been invited to a party at the consulate, not even Uncle," she said. "How did you get an invitation?"

He looked a bit embarrassed. "I suppose because I work for *Xinwen Bao* and the minister wants to stay on my editor's good side."

THEO WAS PLEASED BY HENRI'S invitation and when he told his father, Louis was delighted. It was an opportunity for Theo to mix socially with the elite of Paris's Chinese community. He was mildly astonished that Pauline was included.

"Well, that is extremely courteous of young Monsieur Liu to also invite her," he said, reading the note from Henri. "Has he met you, Pauline?"

Theo winked at Pauline from behind his father's back. "Pauline came with us one day when I took Henri sightseeing."

"I don't know if I'll go," she said. "It's such a grand occasion. I wouldn't know how to behave."

"But Pauline, *chérie*, you must go," Denise said, almost pouting. "I want you to tell me all about it. When would I ever have the chance to attend a fancy party at an embassy?"

"Theo can tell you."

"Men do not notice the things that matter to us," Denise said, very firmly.

"But what should I wear?"

Denise made over one of her own dresses for Pauline, a pale blue-gray silk embroidered with a scattering of tiny violets. She took apart the voluminous skirt and stitched it into a straight skirt draped with an overskirt. She modified the bodice by adding a mantle, and reworked the sleeves to flare at the wrist. Pauline, having no strong opinions on the matter of fashion, sat submissively through the fittings, grateful for Denise's generosity.

"There, that almost looks like a dress by Doucet," Denise said, standing back, "the one in last month's issue of *La Mode Illustrée*. Do you recall it? And this blue-gray color makes your complexion look so fresh."

She twisted Pauline's hair into a chignon and combed her long girlish fringe so that it was sideswept, off her forehead. She fixed Pauline's hair in place with a hair ornament borrowed from the store, a comb decorated with flowers of amethyst and kingfisher feathers.

"You look like such an elegant young lady!" Denise exclaimed. Then a little wistfully: "That was a dress from a more hopeful time. I wore that for my wedding breakfast."

"You shouldn't have, Denise," Pauline said, shocked. "I feel terrible!"

"There is nothing to feel bad about. I kept it out of sentiment, but really, when would I wear such a dress again? It was out of fashion as it was, anyway."

AS HENRI PROMISED, THERE WERE no problems getting Theo and Pauline into the party even though his was the only invitation. He flashed it at the consulate gates and the attendant waved them in.

"Henri," Pauline whispered, "he didn't even look at the invitation."

"We're Chinese," Henri grinned, "and it's our consulate. We are properly dressed and Pauline looks particularly lovely. Why would anyone turn us away?"

Immediately upon entering the consulate's lobby they ran into some of Theo's classmates. The other Chinese students at the Sorbonne came from wealthy families, the only ones who could afford to send their sons abroad. They greeted Henri and Theo with enthusiasm, looked at Pauline with astonishment. She had met all of them at one time or another and ducked away from the group as soon as it was polite to do so. She wandered down the long hall of the opulent building, a belle epoque mansion set in a formal garden.

Amid the gilded mirror frames and crystal chandeliers, the consulate's furniture and decorative ornaments showed off the best of Chinese craftsmanship. Porcelain urns glazed with designs of dragons and phoenixes held orchids and ferns. A pair of gilded marble lions guarded the foot of the curved double staircase, and to honor the occasion, the huge silk tapestry draped from the mezzanine above the lobby was embroidered with a scene from the legend of the Lady Ch'ang O. In robes of white and gold, the Lady flew up to a moon stitched in silver thread.

There were even more people milling about now, both French and Chinese; in fact, guests of all nationalities. This wasn't just a Chinese celebration, Pauline reminded herself, it was also a diplomatic function. She looked back at the lobby and saw with relief that Theo and Henri had detached from the other young men.

"Let's take a look upstairs," Henri said. "I hate crowds unless they're doing something newsworthy. Like rioting or striking."

"That man, over there, staring at us," she said to Theo as they followed Henri. "Why does he seem familiar?"

"I think he was on the ship coming over with us," he said, after a quick glance, "but I can't be sure. It's been so long."

The curving marble staircase led up to a large mezzanine that overlooked the ground floor of the mansion.

"So many people are staring at us," Pauline whispered as they walked up the stairs. "I hate it. Why must they do that?"

"There are very few Chinese girls here," Theo replied. "That's why they're looking at you."

Henri pushed open one of the French windows and they stepped onto a large balcony that ran nearly the entire width of the mansion. The three of them stood by the stone balusters of the balcony between a pair of tall terra-cotta urns planted with ivy. Below them, the garden was bright with colorful red lanterns hanging from trees, their gold tassels fluttering at every slight breeze. The gates to the curved driveway were wide open and attendants helped guests out of cars and carriages. Pauline recognized several of them, customers of La Pagode.

"There's Madame Chang," Henri said, pointing at a woman getting out of a sleek automobile. "She's Undersecretary Chang's wife, rumored to be having an affair with his clerk. Very French, don't you think?"

There wasn't anything about Mme Chang's deportment that suggested she felt any embarrassment over the scandal. Her elaborate coiffure added inches to her height and she strolled up the path beside her husband with great composure, magnificent furs worn open over a stylish evening gown of Chinese silk brocade.

"Perhaps Undersecretary Chang should've left his wife home in China," Theo remarked. "When we first came to Paris, the consulate staff didn't bring their wives or daughters with them."

"Those were the old Imperial days," Henri said. "Many of the new diplomats' wives speak European languages because they attended foreign schools in China or even went to school abroad."

"What about you, Henri?" Pauline said. "You learned French at a missionary school, but do you speak any other languages?"

"The missionaries also taught us English," he said, "and then I went to St. John's University in Shanghai. More English. My father made sure I took all the language courses they had to offer. And he tutored me in Chinese at home. All of that has proven very handy in my job."

"St. John's is a very elite college," Theo said. "Your father must be very proud of you."

"Actually, he's my adoptive father," Henri said.

"Adopted," Pauline said. "How old were you when he adopted you?"

"Perhaps six," he said. "I don't know my real birth date. I was an orphan."

"I thought perhaps you were his illegitimate child and he adopted you." The words came blurting out. She clapped a hand to her mouth, aghast. "Oh, that was so very rude of me. I'm sorry."

"But a reasonable guess." He smiled. "Sometimes it happens that way."

"How did your father find you, Henri?" Theo said.

"I was selling candy for a man who made street urchins work for him when I first met my father. He bought some candy from me and I asked if he could buy more. I told him that if I didn't sell enough, my master would cripple my legs and make me a beggar instead."

Pauline gasped. "Why cripple you?"

"The more wretched the young beggar, the more successful," he said. "So the man bought me from my master."

"And now you're a journalist for *Xinwen Bao*," Theo said.

"My father wanted me to be a journalist," Henri said, "and I owe him everything so here I am. Although I rather suspect he already knew journalism interested me and that's why he asked me to choose this profession."

He was so open about his appalling childhood and the life of hardship that would've been his lot if a kind man hadn't taken an interest in him. He wasn't ashamed of his past.

"I'm really happy you both came," Henri said. "I'm going to England after this, then back to Shanghai. But I'm back in France next spring. I'm planning to go up to Noyelles-sur-Mer to write a piece about workers in the Chinese Labour Corps."

"You know where to find us," Theo said, "still at La Pagode."

Only someone who knew Theo as well as Pauline did could've detected the bitterness in those words, spoken so lightly. She glanced up at Henri to see whether he'd caught the sour note in Theo's voice. Then she blushed and looked away from the intensity of his gaze.

THE MEMORY OF THAT EVENING at the Chinese consulate flashed in Pauline's mind as she walked home from the post office. The way Henri had looked at her, how it made her feel so giddy that she'd put a hand onto the stone balustrade to steady herself. How suddenly noises from the garden below faded and everything except Henri's face blurred and receded into the background.

Henri did come back to Paris the following spring as promised. And despite what happened then, how she had treated him, she was still certain he would meet her tomorrow by the fountains in front of the Église Saint-Sulpice. He just had to. There was no one else she could count on.

CAMILLE

IN THE MORNING, Camille went to church on her own. Jean-Paul was away in Amiens. He could've caught a free ride on any train to come home but she suspected he was glad of an excuse not to attend Mass. She wheeled her bicycle to the edge of the churchyard and paused while a squad of Chinese workers marched past the church to the train station, on their way to some undisclosed location. They worked seven days a week, ten hours a day, with only a few days off each year on Chinese holidays.

Many carried axes, so she guessed they were on their way to a forest, most likely chopping wood and bundling it up into fascines for the tank corps to drop into trenches. Fascines. A few years ago Camille wouldn't even have known that term, or even paused to consider how tanks could get across trenches. The battlefields were a maze of trenches and the British needed a constant supply of fascines to fill the gaps so their tanks could keep advancing. And they needed a constant supply of laborers to extend the trenchworks, which some said would stretch twelve thousand miles laid end to end.

"Those Chinese boys look much older now than when they first arrived." Mme Dumont had come up behind Camille. "But why not? This war has aged us all."

"Why does it always make me feel so sad to see the Chinese arriving and leaving?" Camille said, turning around to greet her with a fond kiss. The woman who might have been her mother-in-law.

"Because we know it means they're still needed," the postmistress said, "and if they're still needed it's because the war is still demanding more men to fight. But come, let's go inside to Mass and pray that the end is indeed in sight."

WHEN AN AMERICAN MILLIONAIRESS BOUGHT the Château Beaumarchais, the town marveled at the changes she'd brought. First to the dilapidated estate, where at least a dozen townsfolk now found employment, and then to the town itself, with a generous donation to repair the church.

But those changes were minor compared to what happened after the British Expeditionary Force arrived. They came at the end of 1916 and took over several dozen acres of farmland at the edge of town. They built a camp and then a hospital. Senior officers and administrators moved into the little Château Franssu, which Grand-mère used to speak of disparagingly because in her opinion, it wasn't a château, just a large and tasteless mansion. Two soldiers now stood guard at the gate, which displayed a sign: BRITISH EXPEDITIONARY FORCES, HQ CHINESE LABOUR CORPS.

Noyelles-sur-Mer became unrecognizable, no longer a sleepy rural town. The streets were busy, men in uniform everywhere. Townsfolk gave up extra rooms to billet officers. Mme Dumont spoke approvingly of the young doctor staying in her son's old room. Approvingly, because not only was he a doctor, but he wasn't British. He was a polite Canadian who spoke French. The bedroom at the front of the house, however, her husband refused to rent out.

"It was my mother-in-law's room," she said to Camille, sighing. "He keeps it like a shrine, even though we could be charging rent."

The influx of military personnel gave Noyelles's small businesses, more accustomed to dealing with farmers, impetus to make changes of their own. The hotel at the train station expanded its dining room. The bakery and grocery store added more types of food to their shelves, including biscuits and candy in tins. The photography studio purchased a new painted backdrop with a landscape of mountains and forests. Some of the town's more enterprising women converted their front rooms to estaminets where they offered home-cooked dishes, buying their ingredients from farms nearby—vegetables and eggs, chickens and rabbits. Growers and vendors from other towns began coming to Noyelles on market days.

On a fine April afternoon in 1917 the first Chinese laborers arrived on the train from Calais. They formed rows of four on the platform and then marched smartly through town, following a British officer to the new camp. The entire population of Noyelles—women, children, and old men—rushed out to see them. Children ran alongside the impromptu parade.

"Les Chinois, les Chinois!" they called.

Some of the men smiled, acknowledging the cheers. Others remained impassive, but none of them broke stride. They wore padded blue cotton jackets and trousers and carried knapsacks of brick-red canvas. Their brown felt caps had earflaps lined with gray fur, tied at the top, since the day was warm. Their presence brought a sudden burst of color to the town, a surge of hope that these men, come all the way from the other side of the world, would help the Allies end the war.

Camille and Mme Dumont had watched the parade from the door of the post office.

"They're so big," Camille said, thinking how splendid they looked, how healthy and broad-shouldered. Many were over six feet tall. "I thought they would be short, like *les Annamites*."

"Our Canadian doctor told Dumont these men are from the north of China," Mme Dumont said, "hired because they're used to cold weather, like we have here, and because they're bigger than Chinese from the south."

After the first few trainloads, the novelty wore off and Noyelles's citizens stopped turning out for the workers. Every few weeks, a new contingent arrived and marched into the camp where British doctors checked them for disease and officers assigned them to work units. And every few weeks, the men who had been processed at the camp boarded trains and left Noyelles for destinations that could not be divulged for reasons of security, a constant churn of manpower to keep the machinery of war moving.

The town grew accustomed to the presence of Chinese. The camp's permanent staff, the cooks and messroom attendants, hospital orderlies, officers' manservants, and various others came into the town during their time off, insatiably curious and eager to purchase what the stores had to offer. Some shopkeepers made the effort to learn a few words of Chinese from the interpreters, recognizable by quasi-military uniforms that differentiated them from the workers.

There was one interpreter who caught Camille's eye. Not because he was handsome, although he was good-looking enough to have been a matinee idol, but because there was something familiar about him. Something that pulled at a memory from long ago, from a happier time.

AFTER MASS, THE CONGREGATION FLOCKED about the church steps, exchanging gossip and greetings. Camille left as soon as it was polite to do so. She pushed her bicycle away from the churchyard, harder work than usual because of the home-built trailer attached to the back wheels. She'd brought the trailer today because of a large sewing project from the château and needed it to carry some rolls of fabric. The trailer's axle squeaked irritatingly. It needed some grease and for that, she planned to try the maintenance yard beside the train station. A Chinese ganger there spoke passable French, but even if he wasn't around, if she took the bicycle into the machine shop and showed them, it would be obvious what she needed. The laborers were always friendly and helpful.

She paused at the gate to the rail yard, which stood wide open. Inside, a crew of workers shoveled coal into railcars and others loaded railway sleepers onto flatcars. Railway tracks near the front suffered aerial attacks nearly every day and needed constant repair. Three shifts of men worked nonstop to make sure the trains kept running to take ammunition and fuel to the front. If not, artillery guns couldn't continue their barrages, aircraft wouldn't fly, and trucks couldn't take food and supplies to soldiers.

Camille saw the ganger, a short man sporting a wide-brimmed hat. He was shouting at two workers, both at least a foot taller than he was, broad-shouldered, their faces smudged with coal dust. When the ganger finished, they shrugged and returned to join their comrades.

"Good afternoon, Corporal Sun," she called, "can you spare a little grease for my bicycle and little trailer?"

He knelt down and examined the chain, serious and courteous, then nodded. "Please wait, mademoiselle."

Camille waited and watched the activity. A team of laborers unloaded a railcar filled with petrol, tossing the heavy metal cans from one man to another, a human chain from railcar to truck. They chanted in rhythm, never missing a toss. They moved with such assurance Camille could only imagine the trust they must have in one another to throw and catch with such confidence. Despite the chill November air, some of the men had doffed jackets and tunic shirts. Bare chests and muscled shoulders gleamed with sweat, and the motion of bodies ceased only when a ganger pounded against the side of the truck to signal the driver that it was full. When the truck moved on, another truck took its place and the line started up again, arms and torsos swinging.

"The men seem to be busier since the spring," she said to Corporal Sun when he returned with a pail of grease, viscous and black.

"The Americans borrowed ten thousand workers, mademoiselle," he said, "so now we're all spread between British, French, and American units. Same number of laborers but more work. But the war ends soon, we hear."

He gave the bicycle pedal a few turns, dabbed more grease on the chain with an old paintbrush.

"I'm sure you'll be glad to go home," she said, "but perhaps you can return to France someday when we've recovered from the war, when everything is rebuilt and beautiful again."

"Perhaps, mademoiselle," he replied, standing up. The polite smile never left his face.

On her way to the château Camille passed another column of Chinese workers marching in quickstep, going back to the camp. They sang as they marched, and moved neatly to one side of the road to let her pass. Several returned her smiling nod of thanks. She knew the tune of their marching song so well she sometimes caught herself humming it while gardening or washing dishes.

Camille looked for Theo walking behind the column even though she knew he wasn't part of this contingent. She couldn't help it. It was habit. Whenever she passed his group on the way back from Crécy Forest—and she always tried to walk back from town at a time when his group might be on the road—she would ring her bicycle bell three times. And then, when they looked at each other, if she smiled and nodded, Theo would know it was safe to meet that night.

She cycled up the long driveway to the château. Camille waited just inside the servants' entrance for Frances, knowing it could be some time before her friend came downstairs. When the war began, Mrs. Newland had turned the château into a hospital, bringing over nurses and doctors from the United States all at her expense. The wealthy American woman, however, left the running of her hospital to others. She saw her main role as that of hostess, setting a good table each night for dinner with her guests, which included any wounded officers well enough to dine sitting up.

Unlike her mother, Frances Newland wasn't above bathing lice-infested soldiers or pulling soiled bed linens off a mattress.

"Mademoiselle Frances asks you to wait just a little longer," a maid said to Camille. All the servants were rushing around looking more harried than usual.

"Thank you, Lucie," Camille said, "you seem very busy tonight." Camille knew most of the servants at the château. They were all hired from the area and some had been her classmates.

The maid sighed. "Very busy. We only just learned Madame Newland has invited houseguests and some arrive tomorrow. One is a general. We have five guest bedrooms to make ready."

Mrs. Newland had never invited Camille's family to the château. Looking around, Camille thought that even if the woman had meant to snub Grand-mère, it had been a kindness. The hubbub of activity in the château would've made the old countess melancholy. This was the sort of life her grandmother had been raised to expect, been trained to manage. A troop of servants, extravagant social gatherings, moving between country and city homes according to the season. Grand-mère had lost all of that just a few years after her wedding, when the truth of the Beaumarchais finances came to light.

At last Frances came along the hallway, a striped pinafore tied over her dress, hair bundled into a cotton scarf. Her plain face lit up when she saw Camille.

"Mother is planning a huge party for the armistice," she said. "One of her friends has married a French general and Mother gets all the military gossip now. They think the war will be over within a week, ten days at the most. But whether or not there is an armistice, she wants a party."

"I hear your first guests arrive tomorrow."

"Yes, some of Mother's friends from Paris. And from the town she's invited the mayor, the deputy mayor, their wives, all the British officers, including the doctors. So we need party decorations. Ninety red, white, and blue rosettes by Sunday. Thirty of each color."

"But of course. Just show me how you want them."

"Like this one, but bigger. About the size of a large cabbage." Frances pulled out a small rosette from her pinafore pocket.

Camille took the rosette from Frances and examined it. "It won't be a problem. I can start this evening."

FRANCES TOOK HER TO A storeroom lined with wide shelves and deep drawers. Camille dimly remembered this room from her childhood.

It had been filled with a jumble of broken furniture pushed against the walls. Frances pulled out two large burlap sacks from a drawer and filled them with rolls of red, white, and blue cloth, threw in some spools of thread. They each carried a sack to the side entrance where Camille had left her bicycle.

"The infamous trailer-wagon," Frances said, dropping in the bag of fabric.

"Much repaired and much used," Camille said, laughing. "You mentioned that all the doctors from the Chinese hospital are invited to this celebration. Your nice Canadian doctor, will he attend? Perhaps you'll get a dance or two."

"Very likely," Frances said, "since Mother will be too occupied with French generals and British officers to notice who I dance with. Listen, I really need a cup of tea. Will you join me?"

Camille shook her head. "I'd like to get home while it's still light." There were things she needed to do before Jean-Paul came back.

After Camille bid Frances farewell, she continued home, her bicycle and trailer no longer squeaking. If it had been summer, she would've stopped to gather edible plants. It had been a lean year, food rationing even stricter than the year before. In the village, flower beds had long since been dug over and replaced with vegetable patches. She and many others foraged in the forests and fields, something city folk couldn't do. Sorrel, purslane, and dandelion for salad, nettle for soup, wild chicory for its bitter brew. In August, hedgerows of blackberry and wild rose dangled bunches of shining black fruit and red rose hips. The summer of 1918 had been hard for everyone yet Camille had never been happier, barely heeding the daily privations that had been so hard to endure.

And it was all because of Theo.

Even just the memory of his face warmed her. The way afternoon sun glowed on his cheekbones, the sideways glance that suggested the beginnings of a smile, and when he smiled, it made her think of music drifting unexpectedly out an open window. Or the first daffodils of spring.

They never wrote each other when he was away, no matter how long he was absent; it was too risky. Although she worked at the post office, she couldn't always get to the mail before the Dumonts. Even one slip would lead to questions.

Camille shivered slightly in anticipation at the thought of being with him again. Theo had been away in Wimereux for weeks, but before being transferred he'd promised to get some leave this weekend.

At home, she put away her bicycle, brought the fabric indoors, and began heating up some soup. Outside the light was falling. While the soup simmered, Camille walked through the house and closed all the drapes, pinned the blackout curtains in place to make sure no light leaked out through the windows. The dining room window faced west and sunset lit the glass front of the vitrine. She unlatched the cabinet door and picked up the jadeite figurine that was one of her favorites, a rabbit whose rounded body always made her want to stroke it.

When her father was alive, before she married Jean-Paul, all they'd had to live on was Auguste's small army pension. The most valuable pieces from the château had been sold off, some to antique stores in Paris, and since the war, some to Mrs. Newland. The American woman collected many things, including Chinese antiques. She had even come inside the cottage once to look at the contents of the cabinet, sniffing at some pieces and setting aside others that interested her.

Camille put the rabbit back in its place and closed the dining room drapes, pulled down the blackout curtains.

The Chinese Labour Corps would remain a bit longer after the war. Theo said they were needed for the work of clearing the battlefields. It meant Theo had a plausible reason to stay. There was so much going on right now to distract Camille's neighbors and the townspeople. But once the war ended and the soldiers had gone home, the town would shrink back to its usual population of farmers and shopkeepers. Gossip would shift focus back onto the townsfolk. And the longer their affair went on, the more likely their movements would be noticed, and the more dangerous it would be.

And when Jean-Paul found out—there was no "if," only "when" . . . Camille shuddered. She couldn't bring herself to imagine the consequences. She needed to do some things before Jean-Paul got home, if he came home at all today. She needed to look through train schedules, study maps, and calculate costs. She needed to make her plans.

And she needed to hide those plans from Theo. She couldn't let him know anything was amiss. She couldn't let him know it would be their last time together. She had to vanish from Noyelles and from Theo's life.

For his sake. For all their sakes.

CHAPTER 5

Monday, November 4, 1918

PAULINE

IN THE SQUARE by the Église Saint-Sulpice, Pauline picked a bench facing the church, a spot where it would be easy for Henri to see her. Not that he could miss seeing her in that empty space. The four stone bishops at the center of the fountain sat silently inside their carved niches, each facing a cardinal point of the compass. The fountain was turned off, so not even the sound of splashing water added liveliness to the setting. The only movement in the square came from dry leaves swirling around its perimeter.

This was the spot where they'd first met two years ago, on a much warmer day in September. Henri had entered her life like a pebble thrown into a pond. That was how Pauline thought of it, the ripples of his presence inciting new thoughts, feelings, and events into motion.

She saw him approach from across the square. A stiff gust of wind sent more leaves tumbling and he hunched his shoulders against the cold. Then he saw Pauline and gave a little wave, hurrying his pace. Henri's winter coat was almost military in style, making the bright blue scarf knotted around the collar seem incongruously childish. A small surge of joy shot through her. It was a scarf she'd knit for him.

"Pauline," he said. He sat on the bench beside her, his gaze searching. His voice was hesitant, his manner subdued, not his usual confident demeanor. "I was glad to get your petit bleu. I thought you wouldn't want to see me again."

She looked straight ahead, fixed her eyes on the fountain, on the limestone figure of Bishop François Fénelon. "I didn't want to bother you but this is really important."

"You can ask me for anything. You know that, Pauline," he said.

"I'm going to Noyelles-sur-Mer and I want you to come with me," she said.

He sat up. "But why?"

"Because I need a guide. You've been there, you know people there."

Because she feared no one would pay attention to her once she got there. And because Denise was right, it wasn't safe for her to travel alone.

"No, I mean, why are you going to Noyelles, Pauline?"

"I need to find Theo, get him to come back for a few days," she said. "He needs to speak with Uncle Louis about something important. Uncle won't listen to me, but he will listen to Theo."

"Can you tell me what this is about?"

"I'd rather not. It's a family matter." Pauline saw his hesitation. "Henri. You said I could ask you anything."

"If you want to find Theo, stay here. Let me go on your behalf," he said. "The war isn't something you want to see close up."

"Paris has seen its share of bombs this year," she said. "I've seen war. Anyway, the Chinese camp and hospital are in Noyelles, how dangerous can it be?"

"Perhaps things aren't as dangerous as before, Pauline," he said, "but you'll see things just traveling there. Horrible, brutal things. Scenes that will invade your nightmares."

The bleak look in his eyes gave her pause. But she wasn't going to change her mind.

"I've already suffered nightmares, Henri, every day since Theo went to the front." She couldn't keep the anguish out of her voice. "I've wondered if he's wounded or ill, if he's met with an accident. I must see him face-to-face. It's a family matter and I must be the one to tell him."

Henri was silent for a few moments, then nodded. "All right. When do you want to go?"

"Tomorrow morning. There's a train to Noyelles-sur-Mer at five thirty."

"Then we need to queue up today to get train tickets," he said. "They're not so easy to get right now. Let me do that."

"We'll need a place to stay in Noyelles. There's always hotels near the train station, aren't there?"

"In Noyelles, there's just the one," he said. "Let's hope they have room. The Gare du Nord tomorrow morning then. Five o'clock?"

"Gare du Nord," she said. "You promise?"

"You have my word." A pause. "The Café Triton is open. Would you like a coffee?"

"No. No, thank you." She stood up. "I have other errands to run."

Pauline wanted to get home before Denise. And she didn't want the conversation with Henri to veer into uncomfortable waters, not just yet. She wouldn't be able to avoid it on the long train ride to Noyelles, but she'd put it off as long as she could. She'd been avoiding Henri since last year, in the spring. He thought she was angry with him for encouraging Theo to join up with the Chinese Labour Corps. What he didn't know was that it was also because of what Mah told her.

AFTER THE 1916 MID-AUTUMN FESTIVAL at the consulate, Pauline saw Henri one more time before he left France. He came into La Pagode on a weekend, when Theo was there. Louis was at the store, too, and glad to finally meet the journalist his son talked about so often. The three men quickly fell into a conversation about the latest conflict between two of the strongest warlord cliques, each fighting to be acknowledged as the dominant faction in China. The Nationalist government was ineffectual, its military weak.

The discussion stopped when two customers entered the store. Louis and Theo hurried to greet the men, knowledgeable and long-time clients.

Pauline had been plying a feather duster over perfectly clean displays of porcelain, not wanting to look as though she was hanging about. Henri sauntered over.

"If I write to you, will you write back?" he said. "I know you'll be more conscientious than Theo when it comes to answering letters."

For the rest of the day, she caught herself smiling.

PAULINE WAITED FOR HENRI'S FIRST letter to arrive, knowing it would be weeks before he reached Shanghai and perhaps more weeks before he wrote to her. She remembered how often he had made her laugh, how often he teased her, but most of all, how he listened to her as though her opinions held value. Would the letter be addressed to her, but meant for both her and Theo to read? Would he hint at his feelings for her? It was far too soon for a letter from Henri, but she made sure she was the one to greet the postman each day.

She looked up one day when the bell on La Pagode's door tinkled, announcing a visitor to the store.

She recognized the man from the party at the consulate, the one who had stared at her. He looked to be in his early thirties, neatly dressed in the dark-gray suit worn by Chinese embassy staff. He was short, with pockmarked cheeks and somewhat vulpine features. Suddenly she wished Theo was in the store beside her.

"I'm here to see Master Deng," he said. His smile, when Louis came out of the office, became even more ingratiating.

"My name is Mah," he said. "I don't know if you remember, Master Deng, but we came over on the same ship many years ago. At the time, I was with the Wenzhou Stone Arts Emporium. When the Imperial consulate staff left, I found a job with the new consulate."

It had been five years, Mah said, and he felt the work didn't suit him. He preferred working in a store. His family owned one in Wenzhou and he knew something about antiques.

"I'd make a good sales clerk," he said, "but I'll start in any position to prove myself. I want to learn from you, Master Deng. Everyone knows what an expert you are."

Louis stood a little straighter but shook his head. "First of all, I can't have the consulate blame me for hiring you away. Second, I don't need help. War is bad for business."

Mah left and Pauline thought no more of the incident. For the rest of the day, she was busy, but not with customers. The store shut its doors for the afternoon and some of her uncle's friends arrived for a game of mah-jongg. It was something the shop owners took turns hosting. Louis set up a folding table and chairs at the back of the store, amid inlaid screens and cabinets of porcelain. Pauline ran between the store and their apartment, bringing tea and snacks for the men. She forgot about the visitor.

But the next day, when she opened the store, Mah was outside the door.

"I've resigned my position with the undersecretary," he said to Louis. "Hire me on a trial basis, you'll see what I can do. I've kept a list of all the names and addresses of diplomats from all the foreign embassies. I'm not afraid to knock on doors. I can give them invitations to visit La Pagode. If you don't hire me, I'll be penniless and without prospects in a foreign land."

"I rather doubt it," Louis said dryly. "You've got initiative and will always land on your feet."

"Sir, La Pagode has an excellent reputation. There isn't another antiques store I want to work for in all of Paris. I will work on commission only until you deem otherwise."

Louis leaned back in his chair and tilted his head to one side, considering.

"All I ask is food and a roof over my head," Mah said. "I can sleep at the back of the store if need be."

Under such an onslaught, Louis agreed but warned that any position was a temporary one. "My son graduates from the Sorbonne next summer and then he will run the business with me."

"I understand, Master Deng," Mah said, "but by then I hope I've helped you make the store so successful that you'll need both of us."

"That will be difficult. During a war, antiques don't matter."

"For wealthy collectors, war only gives them more opportunity," Mah said. "I know this. I've seen it."

Louis let Mah live on the ground floor of Number 53, in the two-room suite meant for a concierge. Mah arrived to work at La Pagode each morning impeccably turned out in a tunic vest of dark silk brocade worn over a traditional long gown. In his round cap with a red agate button on top, he was the picture of a Chinese gentleman-scholar. He took his cue from Louis, who always dressed like this at work. Louis believed foreign customers came seeking atmosphere as well as antiques; they wanted to feel as if they'd been to Peking or Shanghai. With Chinese staff dressed in Chinese garb, La Pagode offered more atmosphere than rival antique stores owned by Laurent Héliot, Siegfried Bing, or the Sichel brothers.

Mah was very organized and proved good with numbers. He had

been in France for nine years and easily added the language of antiques to his vocabulary. True to his word, Mah brought in new customers. He paid his respects at the homes of diplomats and wealthy business-men he had met while working at the consulate. He presented them with an invitation from La Pagode and a small gift, some pretty but inexpensive item from the bric-a-brac box. One good sale of a quality piece, Mah pointed out, would more than recover the cost of all the gifts. This proved the case and La Pagode acquired some new custom-ers, the sort who could afford antiques whether or not there was a war going on.

Louis was pleased, but Mah made Pauline uncomfortable. He was attentive and polite to her, his employer's niece. Always a morning greeting, and always standing back to make way if she passed him in the narrow hall. But the prospect of his presence day in and day out for the next few months disturbed her.

"I don't like him," she said to Denise as they set the table for sup-per. "I always get the feeling his smile turns into a sneer the moment he looks away." And she didn't know how to explain it to Denise but every now and then, Mah stood too close to her when there was no need.

"Theo finishes at the Sorbonne soon," Denise said, "and once he joins the store full-time, Mah will be gone."

Pauline found more reasons to dislike Mah's presence. Her favorite work was helping Louis unpack and inventory new shipments from China. This was when her uncle took the time to show her the differ-ence between Tang and Ming ceramics, how to identify Qing dynasty reproductions of older pieces. He explained why he preferred blue-and-white porcelain to five-color *wucai* glazes.

But now Mah joined them, ruining it for her. He was surprised that Pauline was literate, writing in the inventory ledger as her uncle dictated.

"Perhaps I should look for another job, Master Deng," Mah said jokingly. "Mademoiselle Deng seems quite capable of taking over the business."

"You don't need to leave right away," Louis said, absorbed in examining a snuff bottle. "Not this week anyway. Why did they send so many of these? It'll take days to inventory and price them all. Pauline, write this down: snuff bottle, amber, shaped like a pear, carved with a design of bats, dark green jadeite stopper shaped like a leaf. Matching dish of amber, Qing dynasty."

Mah then handed him a green bottle with a stopper of ebony.

Louis looked at it, then set it aside with a grunt. "Opaque glass, not real jade." It went into the box for bric-a-brac, to be priced later. These were the inexpensive items they placed around the store as decorations beside more valuable pieces.

Mah gave Louis another. "Snuff bottle, clear quartz crystal, double-gourd shape," Louis said, "decorated with a white crane and pine boughs, image painted on the inside of the bottle. Early Qing dynasty. What's next, Mah?"

Mah had unwrapped the newspaper around a red bottle and was peering at it. He shrugged. "Red glass. Old, but not valuable. Am I right?" Louis squinted at the object and nodded, pointing at the bric-a-brac box.

"Pauline," Louis said, "the shop opens in five minutes. Go make sure all is ready. Yesterday you left a mop by the back door."

She sprang up and hurried out of the storeroom, making a quick survey of the shop. Denise carried in a vase newly arranged with silk flowers and set it on the counter of the cash desk. Pauline flipped the sign on the window to Open and unlocked the door. They were ready.

Pauline returned to the storeroom. She had left the door open and could hear her uncle and Mah talking. Or rather, Mah trying to make conversation with Louis.

"You're a lucky man, Master Deng," Mah said. "A well-educated son. A devoted niece. When does Pauline go home to be married?"

Pauline froze.

"I leave marriage arrangements to my first wife," Louis said. She could tell her uncle was absorbed inspecting another item and not really paying attention to Mah. "Pauline is illegitimate so my wife doesn't consider her matchmaking a priority. Anyway, it's my fault for leaving it too late; she's already past twenty."

"Ah. Your niece is . . . illegitimate," Mah said. "Yet you treat her so kindly."

There was no following comment. Pauline turned away from the door. She walked up the stairs to their apartment.

Marriage. If she had still been in China, if she had been a true daughter of the Deng family, she'd be married already, her future sealed. *Just as well I'm too old and illegitimate*, she thought.

IT WAS MAH WHO SUGGESTED putting Pauline to work at the store dressed in Chinese costume. After all, if he and Louis wore traditional garb to add an Oriental atmosphere to the store, how much more effective would it be to have a beautiful Chinese girl greet customers at the door? She could wear the silk clothing leftover from the costume party.

He was referring to the embroidered tunics and pleated skirts Louis had brought in the previous summer, a special request from one of his best customers. The man wanted to show off his collection of Chinese antiques and was planning a party with a Chinese theme. He wanted his wife and daughters to wear Chinese gowns for the occasion. Louis sent a telegram to Shanghai, and six weeks later a crate arrived containing a selection of women's clothing and embroidered shoes. The society columns declared it the soirée of the year, with articles that

featured pictures of the charming hostess and her daughters delight-
fully dressed up as Chinese maidens.

The client's wife sent back what they didn't wear and Louis hadn't
yet decided what to do about the clothes.

Pauline didn't much like the idea of being a walking mannequin but
Mah had brought new business to the store, which made Louis more
open to his ideas.

"You were so thin when I first met you, a waif of a child," Denise
said.

Pauline stood on a stool while Denise pinned and measured to take
in the pleated silk skirt. "Now you're a lovely young lady. I can't think
why you don't have a suitor among the Chinese here. It's too bad that
Henri lives in China and not France."

Pauline turned her head to look at the mirror. She no longer knew
what to think of her looks. She knew that to the French her features
were odd, her nose too small and flat, eyebrows too sparse, chin too
small. Her chin made her look childish, Armand Girard often teased.
Would she be considered pretty in China? On the night of the Mid-
Autumn Festival, Henri had said she looked lovely. Everyone said she
and Theo resembled each other, and if Theo was handsome, perhaps
she was attractive too.

"Don't tease, Denise, I'm not getting married," Pauline said, stepping out of the skirt and putting on her own clothes. "I'm going to be
an old maid who looks after Theo. Even after he marries."

Henri was just a friend, she told herself firmly. He said he would
write to her, but he hadn't yet. What if he became something more?
Did she dare hope?

PAULINE DREADED BEING ON DISPLAY. Denise fixed a silk orchid in
her hair, with petals that matched her lilac blouse, a high-collared

tunic with ornate knot buttons. She dusted powder on Pauline's face, smoothed the line of her eyebrows with a dark pencil, and dabbed the tiniest amount of lipstick on her mouth.

Then Pauline stood by the plateglass window near the door with a reluctant smile. Casual passersby paused and stared, some pointed and made faces at her. Their smiles were friendly and amused, but Pauline's cheeks still burned with resentment. Out of curiosity, simply because she had made them stop and look closely at the shop window, more people entered the store that day. Especially men.

"Why did you ever suggest it, Mah?" Pauline said, when they closed the store. "We could just as easily have put up a poster outside or dressed up a mannequin."

"Ah, but you're prettier than any model on a poster and definitely more alluring than a mannequin," he said with a chuckle. "I saw you at the Mid-Autumn Festival party, you know. I could hardly believe you were the same girl I met on the ship, all pigtails and bony knees."

Pauline hurried to the back of the store and up the staircase to the apartment. It wasn't only Mah's attentions that made her long for the privacy of her room. A letter from Henri waited there, tucked under the mattress. When the postman handed her the bundle of mail in the morning, she had sorted quickly through the pile, put Henri's letter in her room before putting the rest on Louis's desk. Now she could savor the letter.

It had been sent first class, by rail, postmarked Shanghai, a date from more than two weeks ago. It was addressed to her at the store. Sent to her, not Theo. The return address was his father's, she assumed. The envelope, a creamy eggshell white, was unexpectedly heavy and expensive. She drew out the letter, written on matching stationery, and saw there were other things in there. Newspaper clippings. She put them on the pillow and began reading.

Dear Pauline and Theo. She sighed. He was writing to both of them. As a friend.

He thanked them for their hospitality, for taking him to see the sights in Paris. He had written some articles during his time in France and the newspaper had published them, clippings enclosed. Henri's words seemed stilted; nothing of his buoyant personality came through.

But still, she thought, he had written to her as promised. She would take some time composing a reply. Something cheerful and chatty. Something to make him yearn to come back. More museums and monuments they could visit together, the city's public gardens in bloom. The banks of the Seine on weekends, lined with artists and secondhand book stalls.

Henri's words were meant for both her and Theo, and whenever she wrote back, Theo always added a short message below hers.

In January, Henri sent a greeting card for the Lunar New Year. *My most sincere wishes to your family for a prosperous and happy 1917.* It was his fourth letter, proper and impersonal as always. But for Pauline his words mattered less than the fact that he was writing to her, a steady and reliable correspondence that proved he meant to stay in touch.

Perhaps, to stay in her thoughts.

"HAS HENRI MADE PLANS YET for coming to Paris?" Theo asked, taking the cream-colored envelope from her desk. The desk in the storeroom was where she kept La Pagode's ledgers, now her responsibility.

"Not that he says in this letter," she said, pulling a heavy notebook out of the drawer, "but I'm sure he'll let us know. Once you've read the letter, can you help me?"

"The year-end accounting?" Theo put the envelope on the counter. "That's a lot of work. Let's start now. I can read the letter afterward."

"Perhaps I can help instead," Mah entered from the door of the shop. Pauline turned to Theo with a warning look as Mah approached the desk.

"There's no need, Mah," Theo said, grinning at the scowl on Pauline's face. "This is something my cousin and I always do at year-end, it's our job."

"Of course, I understand. Family business." Mah glanced down at the envelope on the desk. "Come get me in my rooms if you change your mind."

FOR THE NEXT SEVERAL WEEKS, Mah seemed underfoot all the time. He hovered around inside the store just before it opened, while Pauline was finishing up the dusting and cleaning. When she and Denise came back from the market, he'd somehow manage to be at the apartment's front door, holding it open and carrying their shopping upstairs. Whenever she was in the storage room, Mah would come in to look for something. He kept her company while she stood by the door of La Pagode, always too close, his eyes upon her, calculating and appraising.

"I saw you with that journalist, that Liu fellow, at the Mid-Autumn Festival," he said. "I notice you've been writing to each other."

Ignoring him, Pauline smiled at the couple coming in the door. "Monsieur Janvier, Madame Janvier. Welcome back to La Pagode. Let me tell my uncle you're here."

She served tea to the Janviers, then brought out the little vases her uncle wanted to show them. She returned to her post by the door and Mah joined her.

"What do you know about Henri Liu's family?" he continued as though the conversation had never been interrupted. "He belongs to the Liu clan of Shanghai. It's why he was invited to the Mid-Autumn Festival. They own banks and shipping companies, real estate all over

Shanghai. They own newspapers. Henri Liu's uncle is Liu Sanmu, editor-in-chief and owner of *Xinwen Bao*. How do you think he got his job?"

Henri had spoken fondly of his adoptive father, but he never mentioned his family's wealth or status.

"Families like that, they only marry others of their class," Mah said, "so if he made you any promises, he was just leading you on. His family would never allow it."

Pauline's heart plummeted and in the next moment she berated herself for having dared hope that she might mean more to Henri someday. But she'd rather die than let Mah know the impact of his words, that her daydreams had turned to strips of torn newsprint.

"He's Theo's friend," she said, as calmly as she could. "Why would he make any promises to me?"

IT WAS ONLY WHEN LOUIS called her into his study the next evening that she realized what Mah was up to. Her uncle was all smiles, looking pleased. She wondered what good news he was about to share with her.

"Mah has offered to marry you," he said. "I know it's not usual that the bride and groom should know each other, or even see each other before the wedding day, but we're in France and not China. We can't do everything according to tradition."

All breath left her body. She sank into the chair facing Louis. "No, Uncle. Please, no."

"But why not?" He leaned across the desk. "I've been remiss in planning your future. You need to marry and have a household of your own, and now it's settled. Mah is a good addition to our business."

"I'm happy to obey you in all else, Uncle," she said, trying to keep her voice from rising. "But I thought we agreed years ago that I'm to remain single and keep house for you and Theo."

"That was when you were a child." He shook a finger at her. "Now you're a young woman and must take things seriously. Your prospects are limited, both here and at home. Mah doesn't mind that you're illegitimate. As his wife you would continue living here, working here. You want to stay in France, don't you?"

"Uncle, please."

Louis stood up behind his desk. "I've given him my word."

"IT'S FATHER'S RIGHT TO DECIDE who you marry," Theo said.

Pauline had fled into his room and gasped out the news. This explained so much. Mah's boldness, the proprietary tone he took when speaking to her, the way he trailed her like a wraith. She hadn't been imagining things.

"I know. But Uncle promised," she said, thumping her fist on a pillow. "He agreed, we all agreed, that I wouldn't marry."

"I think Father thought that rather amusing when you were a girl," Theo said. "He probably didn't think he was making a serious promise. I'll speak to him, but he seems quite taken with Mah."

"That's because Mah flatters him," she said. Then sighed. "And Mah has been good for La Pagode."

Pauline knelt at the little altar to the Goddess of Mercy and pressed three sticks of incense into the sand-filled urn. Then pressed in a dozen more. She owed Louis her very existence, her education, this life in France. She would not go against his wishes. But she would pray to the Goddess every day for a way to be rid of Mah.

HER WEDDING DATE WAS SET for the first of May, enough time for wedding clothes to be sent from China. Now that they were engaged,

Mah sidled up to her more boldly than before, to whisper how much he looked forward to married life. Whenever she handed him something, he'd contrive to touch her hand even when it wasn't necessary. Sometimes he kissed her hand, in what she supposed he imagined was a gallant French gesture, his fleshy lips damp against her skin.

She knew he was angling for Louis to give them Denise's apartment once they were married. Sometimes Mah invited friends to his two little rooms, but he remarked to Pauline that a married man needed a more welcoming home to entertain properly.

"DO YOU KNOW WHAT I don't understand?" Denise said, spooning up the last of her soup.

Pauline and Theo were having dinner at Denise's apartment, but Pauline had made the meal, a stir-fry of shredded ham and winter vegetables, not really Chinese but it stretched out the ham and they had to make do in these times of rationing.

Louis was in Marseilles, seeing to a shipment headed for Shanghai. Grandfather Deng had decided recently their business would not only sell Chinese antiques in France, they would also import European goods. Louis now sourced the expensive soaps, perfumes, and other luxury items for Deng Family Enterprises to sell in China.

"Mah told me what he earned at the consulate." Denise picked up her chopsticks. "He had a good job, a reliable income. Why did he come to work here for next to nothing?"

"Maybe he got tired of filing papers," Theo said as he shrugged and put more rice in his bowl.

"When he first came here he was willing to work for commission alone," Denise said, "something only a desperate person would do, believe me."

Theo looked thoughtful. "Desperate. Do you think he'd lost his job at the consulate? Why didn't we hear about it?"

ON THE DAY LOUIS CAME back from Marseilles, it was Theo who went to the Gare de Lyon to meet him. A few days later, almost at closing time, a clerk from the Chinese consulate came to La Pagode, accompanied by two gendarmes.

"The minister asks for your cooperation, Monsieur Deng," the clerk said quietly. "We understand a man by the name of Mah works for you."

"Yes, I know why you're here. I sent him on an errand so he would be out of the way."

"Then would you please take us to his quarters?" one of the gendarmes said.

"Pauline, I may be gone for a little while," Louis said. "Stay here."

He led the men outside and opened the door to Number 53. Pauline was dying to know what was happening, but she couldn't leave the store untended. Not more than fifteen minutes later, Louis returned carrying a small box. The other men did not come with him.

"Uncle, what was that all about?" she said, the moment he set foot over the threshold. "What's going on with Mah?"

"Go home but take the back staircase," Louis said, setting the box down on the counter. "Do not go in or out the front door of the apartment."

She rushed up to Denise's rooms. "Something's going on, Denise. Two gendarmes came looking for Mah."

They went to her dining room balcony, the one that gave them a good view of the street. They craned their necks to look up and down the Rue de Lisbonne. Finally, Mah came strolling around the corner. They heard his cheerful whistling and the jingle of keys as he reached the door of Number 53. He paused, shook his head, pushed open the already unlocked door.

Not ten minutes later, the consulate clerk came out, followed by the two gendarmes, one carrying a small sack. They walked Mah to the police vehicle that had pulled up to the curb.

Pauline ran down the staircase to the ground floor and opened the door to the foyer. Mah's door was wide open. Inside, every drawer had been pulled out, every cupboard opened, even the mattress on the bed turned over.

"Mah won't be coming back," Theo said. He stood at the door.

Theo had a classmate whose father worked at the Chinese consulate.

"He took me to see his father," Theo said, "so I could ask about Mah. They suspected him of stealing, but they had no proof and couldn't accuse him of anything."

Theo had searched the two rooms while Mah was busy at La Pagode. He found a sack pushed to the very back corner of the cupboard beneath the sink. Most of the items were unfamiliar to him, but there was a box with three pieces Theo knew came from La Pagode. Small items: a red glass snuff bottle, a small ivory statuette, a lacquerware dish. When he met his father at the Gare de Lyon, he told Louis what he had discovered.

And now of course there would be no marriage.

"A thief." Louis was both glum and relieved. "Think how this would've harmed our reputation."

"Without proof, they couldn't really do anything," Theo said, "and then Mah quit. But now the consulate has identified those other valuables as theirs. I wonder what they'll do to Mah."

For the next few days, gossip trickled through. The consulate decided against having Mah arrested. The stolen items had been returned, all except the few Mah had already sold off. The matter was hushed up. To have one of their own in jail would only tarnish the

Chinese community's reputation. The consulate put Mah on the next steamship back to China.

CAMILLE

CAMILLE USED TO find comfort in her cellar, in the tidy wooden bins of potatoes and cabbages, the crates filled with rutabagas, carrots, and turnips. In the fragrance of apples, lined up on ledges, carefully placed not to touch one another so they'd keep longer. She used to glory in her jars of preserved fruit and pickles, the round cheeses protected by a thick layer of wax. Now the bins were only a third full and there were still many months of winter to get through. The last of the ham was gone and only dried herbs and garlic braids hung from the beams, along with a mesh bag of onions. Out of habit she flicked a rag across the bare shelves, just to keep the dust off.

But she wasn't there to regret the paucity of her pantry. Camille knelt in the darkest corner and set down the lamp, reached past a box of rags for the canister hidden behind some empty jars. She twisted open the lid, remembering when the blue tin had been new and not scratched up, the garland of painted roses on the metal still bright. What it contained now gave her more comfort than the biscuits it used to hold. A thin roll of banknotes and some coins. A few rings and earrings, a heavy gold bracelet Jean-Paul didn't know she had. Most important of all, the money she had found at the back of a drawer after her grandmother died, ten gold Napoleons in 50-franc denominations, wrapped in an old sock.

Camille knew her grandmother had meant for her to find this money. Her father's sense of propriety would've made him hesitate to look through a drawer of his mother-in-law's undergarments. Camille had found it while clearing out Grand-mère's clothing, getting the room ready before her wedding. Some niggling doubt, some early seeds of insecurity stopped her from telling Jean-Paul or even her father about this find. The fact that her grandmother had never spent any of this money, even as their finances grew more precarious, meant she'd wanted Camille to use it in a time of dire need.

Like now.

She'd been saving what she could for her escape fund. Camille did as much sewing as she could get from the château, but she could only keep what she earned if Jean-Paul didn't know. If he saw her working, she had to hand over the payment. She added a few coins to the tin and returned it to its hiding place. Did she have enough? It would have to do.

She took two carrots from the bin, a bit shriveled, but once scrubbed and sliced perfectly adequate for going into the soup. She also put some apples in a small pot to poach. As it heated, she leaned over to sniff. It never failed to amaze her how spices could transform humble ingredients. One clove, crushed and sprinkled into the cooking liquid, and dry apples became meltingly fragrant.

"Camille!" The kitchen door opened and Jean-Paul hung his coat on the rack of wooden pegs. He turned to her, his smile carefree, the same smile that had disarmed her when they'd first met.

"Marcel is coming for dinner tonight," he said. "Bake that mushroom thing he likes. A celebration. We've just made a lot of money." His smile turned into a sly grin. He didn't need to say more.

We've just made a lot of money. Camille knew what that meant. They'd made that money on the black market. She didn't like it, but at the same time she was grateful for Marcel's illicit connections. And for his love of baking, which meant he brought them butter, sugar, and flour.

Jean-Paul ate his lunch of bread and soup without comment, studying a hand-drawn map as though memorizing it. Silently Camille took away the empty soup bowl and put a dish of stewed apples in front of him.

"Are we out of flour?" he said, looking at the chunks of glossy fruit.

"Yes. We'll need some for the mushroom galette that Marcel likes. Also butter."

He responded immediately. "I'll go out and get that now, and some sugar so you can make a fruit tart for dessert." Anything for Marcel.

It was a perfectly ordinary domestic conversation, a couple discussing what to serve a guest for dinner. Except that if Camille spoke one wrong word, Jean-Paul would turn on her. She never knew what that wrong word might be. It depended on his mood, on what had happened that day, what he'd been brooding on. She managed not to startle when Jean-Paul reached over and touched the edge of her sleeve, stroked the frayed cuff.

"When this war is over, we won't be one of the poor," he said. "I know it feels like we're scraping by right now, but I've been putting money aside. I'll always provide for our family, Camille. We'll be comfortable after the war. Comfortable and respectable."

She let out her breath as he turned his attention back to the map. He spooned up the last piece of apple and wiped his mouth on his sleeve. He put on his coat and pulled his knapsack from beneath the bench by the kitchen door and slung it over his shoulder, whistling on his way out. To get flour, sugar, butter from sources unknown.

It occurred to Camille, and not for the first time, that if Grand-mère had been alive, she'd never have allowed her to marry Jean-Paul. Even though he'd spoiled her for anyone else, as he put it. Grand-mère would've seen through him, seen that streak of viciousness. But her father had been desperate to see good in Jean-Paul, a man who could take care of his daughter once he was gone. Auguste believed what Jean-Paul wanted him to see.

FOR HER WEDDING GOWN, CAMILLE altered one of her grandmother's dresses and used some of the leftover brocade to sew a matching cravat for Jean-Paul. Jean-Paul borrowed a morning suit from her father, who wore his captain's uniform to the wedding.

Jean-Paul moved into the cottage with them after the wedding but left soon after for training at the Chemin du Nord's main repair center in Paris. He was anxious for a promotion from apprentice to fully qualified mechanic.

"We can put off our honeymoon for a while, can't we?" he said, "When I get my promotion, we'll celebrate our marriage and the promotion."

Camille nodded, not upset at the prospect of her new husband being away for weeks. She hadn't enjoyed her wedding night or any of the nights that followed. Jean-Paul's weight on her, his breath hot and grunting by her ear, his hand forcing hers down to touch between his legs. She wasn't eager for a honeymoon.

Besides, Auguste was dying.

As her father's health faded, the stories he kept from her when she was younger now poured out, a river of confessions and guilt. On his deathbed, Auguste told her how the armies of the Eight-Nation Alliance plundered the Forbidden City after the Siege of the International Legations.

Until then, none of the foreigners had any idea of what lay inside those walls. The empress dowager and her ministers had always received diplomats in sparsely decorated rooms with ordinary furniture. It was only when the siege was over and they entered the heart of the Forbidden City that foreign missionaries and diplomats realized the true wealth of the Imperial court. Pillars gilded with dragons and phoenixes. Screens inlaid with ivory and mother-of-pearl, lions carved from blocks of jade. Beaded bed-curtains with pearls as beads. So much wealth it was unbelievable.

Officers managed to prevent their soldiers from pillaging the inner palaces but they couldn't stop the looting outside. Auguste and his comrades ransacked rooms full of treasures; they went mad from wanting it all, everything was so beautiful and valuable. They took what they could carry, plundering shops and breaking into mansions and small palaces. They watched a great library burn.

Recounting all this to Camille, Auguste stared out with clouded eyes, his vision deteriorated to the point where his world was no more than a dark blur of shapes, but in his memories he gazed at chambers filled with wonders, streets filled with wreckage.

The headdress of coral and kingfisher feathers had come from a small palace.

"There were three coffins in the courtyard, surrounded by eunuch attendants," he said, his voice hoarse. "Chinese women were terrified of foreign soldiers. The three coffins held the bodies of three princesses who had committed suicide because they were so afraid of what we might do. And they were right to fear. We had become monsters."

Eight small plates, each showing a scene from Chinese mythology, had been the only plunder he'd taken from a fine mansion. The owner had pleaded with them while his wife and children hid behind the piano. But Auguste and his comrades didn't speak Chinese.

"The poor man sat at the piano and began to play," Auguste said. "He played Schubert's 'Ave Maria.' We listened until he finished, and we left. We were brought to our senses, reminded that we were from a civilized, Christian nation. I was ashamed to find I was holding the box with the little plates, but I was too ashamed to go back and return them."

When Auguste's troop was dispatched to rescue European civilians and soldiers inside the International Legations, under attack by Chinese Boxers and the Imperial Chinese Army, he had been told they would be fighting barbarians. But everything he saw, the architecture and gardens, the exquisite craftsmanship, the private libraries, told him otherwise. They were plundering a civilized society. One whose emperors had refused to allow in new ideas and new inventions for hundreds of years. A country unable to stand against Western fire-power and Western alliances.

"I went to confession at the first opportunity," he said. By now Auguste's voice was weak, a mere whisper. "The priest told me to be at ease because I was doing my duty as a soldier. And as for all that we had stolen, they were merely the spoils of war. 'Spoils of war.' Why does no one understand the ugliness, the brutality of those words?"

AFTER AUGUSTE DIED, JEAN-PAUL CHANGED. Camille wondered why he ever married her in the first place. When he courted her, he'd been modest about his service with General Maunoury's Sixth Army, listened intently when Auguste told stories about his long-ago military career. He teased that she was shy and quiet and he liked quiet women. That the way her hazel eyes gazed into his made him feel strong and capable.

She'd been flattered by his attentions, but she didn't know how to pull away, hadn't wanted to offend him when he first put his arm around her. Didn't know how to refuse when he took her into the barn. And now she couldn't seem to do anything right, and nothing pleased him.

Camille never asked Jean-Paul about his childhood; something warned her not to. When she began working at the post office, however, Mme Dumont didn't hesitate to fill her in.

Jean-Paul's mother died when he was fifteen, but they had been estranged already for many years. He had distanced himself from her as soon as he could and as far away as he could. Away from the tawdry café bar where she worked. Away from the little room she called home, a shack behind the café in a dirty yard lined with garbage cans and cases of empty wine bottles. The shack admitted patrons who wanted something more than a beer and cheese sandwich after the bar closed. That was Jean-Paul's childhood.

"As far as I'm concerned," Mme Dumont said, "what matters is that your husband worked hard to rise above his circumstances. There's no shame in humble beginnings."

And then the war changed everything.

Jean-Paul was one of the lucky ones. He'd fought in one of the first major battles at the Marne and lived. His wounds left him limping and nearly deaf in one ear, just enough so that he was given a medical discharge. At the rate men were dying, not many of the classmates who used to taunt him would survive the war. In another twenty years there wouldn't be anyone left to remind people that Jean-Paul's mother had been the town whore.

The war and its ordeals were trampling over people's memories, plowing under whatever they remembered of the past. The past was another world. Even if they restored shattered landscapes and rebuilt devastated towns, the survivors' lives could never be repaired. Not when your loved ones had been mowed down like wheat. Had anyone really noticed Jean-Paul much in the first place, a skinny boy skulking at the edges of their lives? In time, the citizens of Noyelles would remember only that he had fought for his country and worked for the Nord railway company.

Camille finally understood why he'd married her when Jean-Paul boasted about his plans for the future. After the war, he would become a person of importance in Noyelles. And Camille with her fine name, a name that meant something in this town, would help in this effort.

"You and your long straight nose and that small chin," he said, "which shouldn't look so arrogant in such a plain face but it does. That's breeding, I suppose."

He had married her because he wanted respectability and Camille's grandmother had been a countess. Never mind that the Château Beau-marchais now belonged to an American. Camille was the closest he'd ever get to aristocracy, impoverished or otherwise.

And someday, Jean-Paul told her, he would be mayor of Noyelles-sur-Mer.

NOTHING WAS TOO GOOD FOR Marcel, as far as Jean-Paul was concerned, and Camille knew what this meant. She laid the dining table with her good china and table linens, with real silverware. Grand-mère had sold all but four place settings so they could dine in style on occasion, even if the meal was only bread and cabbage stew. With all the rationing Camille had only been able to get a pork hock from the butcher, but with vegetables from the cellar, it had been enough to make a stew, with a garnish of chopped herbs that brightened up the flavors.

"Camille, your mushroom tarts are the most delicious things I've ever tasted," Marcel said, wiping his mouth with a large linen napkin. He left a smear of gravy on the fabric. "I used to think my grand-mother made the best tarts in the world but yours are even better."

"Marcel knows his food," Jean-Paul said, leaning over to kiss her hand. "Consider it a big compliment. Well, *mon ami*, have we put your flour and butter to good use?" He beamed, his cheeks ruddy from wine and pride.

"Jean-Paul, if your wife ran a café, her cooking would put all others out of business."

After her father died, when they learned how little money was in Auguste's will, Camille had mentioned the same idea, that she could run a little café, an estaminet. Jean-Paul had been furious because he didn't want his wife doing work beneath her station. He didn't want people remembering she had cooked and served others during the war, like a servant. He had slammed her against the kitchen door for even making the suggestion.

But when Marcel suggested this, he just hooted and slapped his thigh.

"Camille? Her delicate bones would snap if she had to cook more than two meals a day."

She couldn't understand what bonded her husband to this man apart from their underhanded business partnership. From a distance, Marcel's slight build and curly blond hair made him look like a teenager. A lean face and full lips reinforced that impression, but closer, lines on his forehead betrayed age, and the hard glitter in his dark eyes made her nervous.

"My grandmother made sure I could cook," she said, standing up to clear the plates. "She hired a woman who used to work for us at Château Beaumarchais. She lived with us for three months and taught me."

So that she would know how to keep house on her own. So that she'd be more marriageable. So that she could earn a living someday if she had to.

"The perfect ending to this meal would be some coffee and cognac," Marcel said, leaning back in his chair.

"I'm sorry," she said. "We don't have any more real coffee. Just a bit of chicory if that's all right."

He grinned and reached into the shoulder bag he'd hung on his chair. "A kilogram of real coffee. And some very fine cognac. As thanks for your hospitality." He handed her a parcel and gave Jean-Paul a bottle wrapped in burlap.

Camille couldn't help holding the brown paper package to her nose and breathing in the warm rich aroma. The two men laughed and in spite of herself she smiled, glad of the coffee and the chance to busy herself in the kitchen again. When she carried the carafe and cups into the dining room, Marcel and Jean-Paul were hunched close together, speaking quietly over a sheet of paper. Another hand-drawn map.

"I'll be in the kitchen washing up if you need anything," Camille said, putting down the tray. Jean-Paul nodded, a quick dismissive gesture. Neither of them looked up. She had a half hour of peace in the kitchen before the sound of chairs scraping across the floor told her Marcel was leaving.

"Camille!" Jean-Paul's voice called out. "Come say adieu to Marcel."

She hurried to the front door, drying her hands on her apron.

"Tomorrow then, in Abbeville," Jean-Paul was saying. He turned when he heard her. "We'll have Marcel over again soon, won't we, Camille?"

"Yes, yes, of course. Whenever you like," she said, "you're always welcome."

They waved as Marcel cycled away, a typical couple bidding their guest good night. From the darkness of the road, they heard his bicycle bell ring twice in farewell. If anyone had been watching them that evening, it would've seemed a very ordinary scene, some friends sharing supper, talking and laughing, taking their leave of each other.

But a closer look and they would've noticed that only the men were talking and laughing. That the woman kept to the edges, hoping to be inconspicuous. And that she flinched when her husband led her upstairs to bed.

CHAPTER 6

Paris 1917

Henri was returning to Paris in May. Pauline wrote back, a brief reply with a few tidbits about the latest rationing restrictions and worker strikes, the sort of news she knew interested him. When she gave her letter to Theo so that he could add a message of his own at the bottom, she asked him not to mention the episode with Mah.

"It would only embarrass Uncle," she said, "that he almost brought someone so unsuitable into our family and the business."

Louis had agreed so quickly to Mah's offer of marriage. She still cringed at the memory of how helpless she had felt all those weeks, trapped into an unwanted marriage, still felt bewildered that her uncle could've been so oblivious to her distress, all the while believing he was doing what was best for her.

"It's a private matter," Theo said gently. "There's no need for anyone else to know."

Pauline went down to the storeroom to finish cleaning some lacquer boxes Louis had bought from a collector for whom food and fuel now mattered more than fine antiques. She only half paid attention to the lacquer box she was cleaning as her fingers worked the soft brush bristles gently into the swirls and grooves of the round box, its surface covered with a carved pattern of intertwined peonies and leaves.

Henri's family, the Liu clan, was one of the most powerful in China. Even the most ambitious member of the Dengs wouldn't dream that a daughter of theirs, legitimate and with a sizable dowry, could ever marry into such a family. Henri had been kind to her because he was kind to everyone. He was charming to her because people brought up with wealth could afford to be kind and charming. He listened to her because he was a journalist, it was his job. She was nobody.

How had she ever allowed herself to hope? Pauline wondered how she would feel on the day Henri strolled through the door of La Pagode. She imagined it daily and schooled her features to feign indifference.

THE FIRST WEEK OF MAY came and went. Tulips and irises bloomed on doorsteps and in public gardens. The city approved bringing a carousel into the Jardin des Tuileries and children stood in line while the sprightly notes of the "Radetzky March" swirled through the park. Denise hung rugs over balcony railings to air, and when she came home from the market her basket was filled with fresh greens.

"Look who's here!" Theo called. He entered, opening the door of La Pagode with a flourish. Henri followed behind, his unruly hair and broad grin just as she remembered. For a moment, Pauline's throat constricted.

"Hello, Pauline," he said. "Thank you for the letters. They made me feel as though I was still in Paris."

"Welcome back," she said, and turned away. "Let me get some tea. And I'm sure my uncle will want to see you." Anything to bring more people into the room so that she wouldn't be alone with him.

Since there were no customers, they gathered at the counter and listened to Henri gossip about Shanghai—a scandal involving a pair of famous opera singers, the price of property, the most popular new restaurants.

"As soon as this war is over," Henri said, "foreigners will be spending money again to buy property and prices will shoot up. My uncles are buying up houses and land. Shanghai will look completely different in a few years' time."

"I would love to see the old hometown," Louis said with a sigh. "It's been years. But I don't relish the ocean voyage."

"Some things about Shanghai never change, sir," Henri said. "The Huangpu River, for example, is as muddy and malodorous as ever."

"How long are you in Paris this time?" Denise asked when Louis stopped chuckling.

"I just came back from Noyelles-sur-Mer," he said, "so I'll spend another couple of weeks here writing up the stories, and then I'm going to England. There are companies of Chinese workers there, too, many in Liverpool."

"Well, you must have dinner with us tonight," Louis said, "and tell us more about Shanghai."

This offer sent Denise rushing to her kitchen and Pauline to the market, from where after standing in line for an hour, she returned with sugar and eggs. Dinner was not as lavish as Denise would've liked and she apologized.

"But given the cost and scarcity of food," Louis said, "this is the nicest supper we've had in a long time."

"We could've made a Chinese meal for you," Pauline said, "if we hadn't run out of ingredients."

Their relatives in Shanghai always tucked some food into the shipping crates along with antiques, since Chinese delicacies were hard to come by in France. They were even more welcome these days and Pauline loved opening a box and finding packages of dried scallops and mushrooms or brown earthenware jars of pickled vegetables and duck eggs preserved in brine. The last shipment contained sacks of rice and strings of dried Chinese sausages, which Louis especially liked. The dried mushrooms ran out months ago, and they had finished the sausages last week, along with dried bamboo shoots and pickled vegetables.

"I wrote your uncles," Louis said, "and told them to start sending us a package of food every month."

"Then I must time my next visit very carefully," Henri said. He looked at Pauline and smiled. Pauline almost had to sit on her hands to keep from reaching out to touch his face. "I need to get here when the dried mushrooms arrive."

After dinner, Louis retired to his study while Theo and Henri went onto the balcony to smoke. Denise started washing the dishes, but Pauline stopped her.

"Not after you worked so hard making dinner," she said. "Let me clean up. You go join Theo and Henri."

Denise shook her head. "I'll go upstairs for some needlework."

While she washed up, Pauline listened to the conversation drifting in through the window.

"Why aren't you writing about the war?" Theo said. "You must be the only Chinese journalist here."

"The British and French barely allow their own correspondents near the front lines, let alone a Chinese reporter. They censor heavily and don't allow anything that might damage morale."

"Well, I suppose *Xinwen Bao* is more interested in how the workers are doing here," Theo said.

"The British have made many mistakes," Henri said, "but at least the hospital is well-run. The doctors are mostly missionaries who have spent time in China, and there are Chinese medical aides and pharmacists."

"So you'll write about the hospital?" Theo said.

"Yes, that will be one of my articles in a series about the Chinese Labour Corps. And there's a worker whose words I can't get out of my mind."

Henri had interviewed a man named Sun who had been in Calais for six months, unloading and loading supplies on the wharves. Then a Franco-British offensive stalled from lack of manpower, more workers were needed to transfer trainloads of ammunition and fuel to the trenches. Sun found himself temporarily assigned to a town closer to the fighting. There, at the Western Front, Sun saw flares for the first time.

"The flares flew straight up, high into the air," Henri said, "and he was amazed because they lit up the night skies as bright as day."

Sun had never seen anything like it. He and his teammates cheered at the sight until they realized the flares were for lighting up the battlefield so that the artillery could see where to aim their guns.

"All the way back to Calais, he wanted to weep," Henri said. "He said it was because Europeans possessed the knowledge to turn night into day, but used it for the purpose of killing. He said to me, what might the world gain if they turned that knowledge to seek heaven instead?"

There was a long silence. Pauline put away the dishes and went to stand by the balcony doors.

"I have another idea for an article," Henri said. "Many of the workers who joined the CLC came because the British used missionaries to help them recruit. The churches have spent decades gaining the trust of Chinese, and for most of the workers missionaries are the only foreigners they've ever met. But now that the men are here, they've realized that not all British are like the missionaries. They'll never trust foreigners again."

There was another long silence.

"I'm thinking you should sign on as an interpreter, Theo," Henri said. "The CLC is desperately short on translators."

"Uncle will never allow that," said Pauline. "Theo, don't you dare.

Henri, if you encourage him in this, I'll never speak to you again. I'm going to bed. Good night."

THE NEXT DAY, HENRI GAVE a talk at the Sorbonne. Theo told Pauline it had been extremely inspiring for the handful of Chinese students attending. China's government hoped that the workers' contributions would give China some leverage during the peace negotiations follow- ing the war. The government would ask the Allies to take the Shan- dong Peninsula away from Germany and give it back to China.

"And then he told us how badly our men need interpreters," Theo said, "and urged us all to sign up with the Chinese Labour Corps as interpreter-clerks. That's what I was planning anyway, Pauline."

She whirled around to face him, almost dropping the platter she was holding. A fourteenth-century porcelain platter. She put it back carefully in the cabinet and shut the glass front.

"Theo, you can't!" she said, in as quiet a voice as she could manage. "Workers have been killed. Those camps are too close to the front."

"There are so few people fluent in both Chinese and English. And French. I'm going to bring it up with Father," Theo said. "I think he'll give in if I keep trying."

Pauline exhaled, a silent sigh. University for Theo had been a major concession from Louis, with the understanding that he'd work at the store full-time once he graduated. And get married. How much more could Theo push his father?

"Theo," she began, but he held up his hand.

"Pauline, little cousin, I know this is right for me," he said. "For once, I'd like to do something that makes a difference to the world, and selling antiques is not that something. I'd like you on my side for this one."

"In this family, my opinion counts the least," she snapped, "so having me on your side won't do anything at all."

She ran up the back staircase to her room and slammed the door shut, threw herself on her bed and pounded at the pillows. She didn't know who made her more furious, Theo or Henri. Mostly Henri, she decided. All the more reason to keep him out of their lives. Her life.

When she had finished punishing her pillows, Pauline went to find Theo. He wasn't in his room. She ran upstairs to Denise's apartment.

"Denise, have you seen Theo?" she asked, over the piano concerto playing on the gramophone. "Do you know if he's gone out? Will he be home for supper?"

In reply, Denise pointed to the French doors in the dining room and returned to her knitting and music. Pauline stepped out to twilight, the sun falling quickly toward the horizon. Theo was smoking on the balcony, looking down at the street. It was colder than she'd expected and she wished she had put on a shawl. Theo was wearing his favorite cap, a navy-blue one Denise had knit for him.

He moved aside to make room, offered her his cigarette. She took a cautious puff.

"I hope you don't do this at night," she said. "What if a German pilot sees the glow and drops a bomb on this building?"

"When we hear air-raid sirens I promise to put it out. Are you cold?" He took off his jacket and draped it over her shoulders. Then he tugged the knit cap lower over his right ear.

"Theo, how will we run the store if you're gone?" she said. "How can I do the bookkeeping without you?"

He laughed. "Pauline, we both know you do all the bookkeeping. You have been since you were fourteen. And since the war, it hasn't been that difficult."

"You have to stay. Your father set up La Pagode for you," she said, "and one day it will be yours. Can't you be grateful?"

"I never asked for it," Theo said, "and the real reason Father and Grandfather opened a store in France, well, one of the reasons, anyway, is that they didn't want people in Shanghai to notice that I'm mentally defective."

"Mentally defective?" She stared at him, then punched his arm. "That's nonsense, Theo. You passed your baccalaureate. You breezed through your university courses."

"Well, literature and philosophy don't need mathematics," he said, taking another drag on the cigarette. "I have a very specific defect, Pauline. I can't add or subtract or perform any other sort of arithmetic. Something's wrong in my head when it comes to that."

She frowned. "You're joking!"

"What do you remember about Shanghai?" Theo said. "Do you remember when I was taken out of Teacher Chen's classes?"

"I remember you were eight years old," she said slowly, "and they sent you to school in the city, the school run by Jesuit priests. I thought it was because you were special. Grandfather Deng told everyone you'd been chosen to learn foreign languages."

But that excuse obscured the problem their tutor had identified. The old scholar informed Louis and Grandfather Deng that Theo was mentally deficient. That he was quite normal until it came to arithmetic. Theo could write down numbers and mathematical symbols, but he couldn't work with them even though he appeared to understand the concepts of addition and subtraction.

"I was terrified when they called me into Grandfather's study," Theo said. "Father and Grandfather sat me down with Teacher Chen and they tested me. They had to see for themselves. Teacher Chen suggested a foreign school, to try a different approach, he said. He was being kind, but I think he wanted me out of his classroom, so that my failure wouldn't reflect on him."

The Jesuit priests were equally puzzled by Theo's issues. In every

other way he was normal, quick to learn French and English, literature and geography, any subject—until the lesson involved manipu-
lating numbers. Comparing the size of one country to another. The
number of years between historical events.

One of the priests wrote to a colleague in France, who replied
that he had encountered this type of mental handicap once before.
It was as though the child lacked any ability to work with numbers;
furthermore, the condition couldn't be cured or surmounted through
intensive instruction. There was no point in making Theo unhappy.
It would be more useful teaching him ways to get around his defect.

Something in Pauline's memories clicked into place and suddenly
she saw a different explanation for what she'd witnessed all these
years, incidents she had always accepted without attaching any significance to them.

Theo's notebooks in his desk drawer, filled with arithmetic problems and tally marks, because Theo had been attempting to work out
simple exercises.

Theo not bothering to count the coins handed back by vendors, not
because he was lazy or didn't care but because he didn't know how
much change was due.

Theo murmuring to customers that all matters of price had to be
discussed with his father, not because Louis had to be consulted on
everything but because Theo couldn't calculate discounts.

Theo shirking his bookkeeping chores, writing down only a description of items sold and their prices, leaving Pauline to add up the
amounts. In the end she had quietly taken over his share of the work
just so everything would be finished in time for Louis's inspection.

"Do you think Grandfather was already making plans back then for
a store in Paris?" Pauline said.

He shrugged. "I think so. Maybe they accelerated those plans because of me."

"Theo, listen. Listen to what you're saying. Your father has done so much for you. So has Grandfather. Take the business they've taken such pains to create for you. You owe them."

"Whether it's here or in Shanghai," Theo said, with a tight smile, "whatever job the family gives me, it's a charitable gesture. Sometimes I think Father hoped I might grow out of this defect if he kept me here, away from our family's relentless scrutiny. But no, not one bit."

"What if Uncle Louis opened another business, a different kind of shop? A photo studio, like the Girards. Work you would enjoy."

"As long as our family supports us, we must do as they wish, in the manner they wish," Theo said. "If we were still in Shanghai, I never would've known it was possible to question our elders. But here I've seen friends chart their own course. If I join the Chinese Labour Corps, it will be the first time I earn money that doesn't come from our family. I'd think that you, of all people, would understand."

But he was wrong. She, of all people, owed her uncle everything. Unlike Theo, Pauline never had the privilege of believing otherwise. If Mah had not been caught stealing, she would've married him out of duty.

Theo stubbed out his cigarette and for a while they just sat watching the stars wink to life.

"Theo, please think again," she said. "What if those British officers treat interpreters as badly as they treat the workers? Remember all those stories Henri told us. Some behave as though they were dealing with beasts of burden instead of men."

"All the more reason why I must go," Theo said. "There's not much I can do to rid ignorant people of racist attitudes, but at least with more translators there would be fewer misunderstandings."

"Are those Henri's words?" she said.

"My words. And strangely enough, when we went for a coffee

together after his talk, we didn't talk about the war or the workers," he said, "he wanted to talk about you." He reached into his shirt pocket and pulled out a note. "This is for you. From Henri."

Frowning, she took it.

Pauline, I'd like to take you for lunch tomorrow. If you're willing, meet me at noon in the Café Triton, by the Église Saint-Sulpice. ——Henri

"I told him most people find you too direct in your speech," Theo said, with his widest grin, "a most unattractive quality. He said that was what he liked about you."

Pauline read the note one more time.

"I think that of all the people I know," Theo said, lighting another cigarette, "Henri Liu is the one whose advice I trust the most. Do you want me to go with you when you meet Henri tomorrow?"

"There's no need. I'll go on my own."

"PAULINE, OVER HERE!" SHE HEARD Henri's voice before she saw him.

The term was over and the Café Triton was crowded with students. She'd just been to the market where the queue for vegetables had been longer than usual, the crowd more fractious. It had been a tiring day and it was only noon.

Henri pushed his way through the crowd to her and took her basket. She followed him to a table in the back corner.

"Good luck shopping today?" he said.

"Two pig trotters," she said, crossing her arms as she sat down. "Turnips and carrots. Some peas."

"Pauline, what's the matter? Have I offended you?"

She glared at him. "Theo is badgering Uncle about letting him go to the front as an interpreter. I hope you're pleased with yourself for convincing him to put himself in danger."

"His translation skills are valuable," Henri said. "He'll make a difference to men's lives, for their safety, for the way they are treated. So much depends on understanding, on clear communication."

"It will make a difference to us if he's killed," she snapped. He caught her by the hand, but she snatched it away.

"Pauline, think of your own experiences with your neighbors," he said. "They've known your family for years. Most are good to you, but there are some who still look down on you, who always will, no matter how well you or Theo speak French. Imagine what it's like for those laborers, with no language skills, no knowledge of European customs, trying to make their way in a world where no one even wants to understand them."

"I understand what you're saying, Henri. But Theo would be working near war zones."

"That's what makes the job even more important," he said. "Our men work under dangerous conditions, under the so-called care of commanding officers who don't know our language or traditions."

Pauline understood, because Henri had told them how a misunderstanding could lead to undeserved punishment, usually flogging. Or how simple requests were denied, small things that could make a huge difference to the men's health, comfort, or simply peace of mind.

"Sometimes it isn't just language," he said. "They also need to negotiate differences in culture and attitude, both ways. They need more people like Theo."

"Henri, I understand," she said. "And I sympathize. But you need to understand that if anything happens to Theo I will never, ever, forgive you."

"I don't want that, Pauline, but Theo is an adult. He will make up his own mind."

"Do something for me, Henri."

"Anything. You can ask me anything."

She took a deep breath. "Theo trusts you. He respects you. Please convince him to stay here in Paris. If not for Theo's sake, then for mine. He's all I have, the only member of the family who cares about me."

"That can't be true. I'm sure your uncle cares. He brought you here to Paris."

"It was Theo's idea to bring me," she said. "I owe my uncle a lot, but Theo is the only one who looks out for me."

Henri was silent. She interpreted this as doubt.

"You've never been an illegitimate and unwanted daughter, have you?" she said. "That's what I am, Henri. My father was Louis's youngest brother, my mother a prostitute, his mistress. If anything happens to Theo, Louis will close La Pagode and take me back to Shanghai. Where I'll be at his wife's mercy because she hates me."

She had never put her parentage so bluntly before to anyone. She wanted to shock, to be harsh. To lay bare the difference between his position and hers.

"I do understand, Pauline," he said, finally. "All right, I'll speak to Theo. I'll try and convince him not to go."

"Do it soon," she urged. "Promise, Henri. This is the most important thing I'll ever ask you."

"I give you my word that I'll speak to him," he said. "But I can only promise to do my best."

THREE DAYS LATER, PAULINE SAT on her bed sobbing, a blue envelope crumpled in her hand, a petit bleu from Henri.

I'm sending this from the train station, on my way to England on an urgent assignment. I've been so busy preparing for the trip

I haven't had a chance to speak with Theo but I'll do it as soon as I'm back. My warmest regards, Henri.

She cried out of frustration, out of anger at this betrayal. Henri knew—she had told him—how important this was. That she was trusting him with Theo's fate and her own. But he hadn't made time to fulfill his promise, had gone running off to England, hadn't understood the urgency of her request.

And now it was too late.

Too late because Theo was gone. After a final blowup with his father, he had enlisted with the Chinese Labour Corps. And this morning, she had walked with him to the end of the block on his way to the train station.

The news that Theo had left for the Western Front quickly spread through Paris's Chinese community. Louis was furious. "All his classmates talked about signing up with the Chinese Labour Corps. He was the only one stupid enough to actually do it."

Henri returned from England a week later and came to La Pagode. Pauline greeted him with cold courtesy.

"Pauline, I had no idea he would join up so quickly," he said. "I am so sorry. Let me take you for lunch tomorrow. There's so much to talk about."

"There's nothing more to discuss. Unless you're buying something, I suggest you leave the store."

She moved behind the marble counter with great deliberation, pressed her hands on the surface to hide their shaking. She couldn't bear to see him standing there, crumpling his hat in his hands, sorrow in his eyes. But she couldn't look at him without also seeing Theo, the nonchalant way he had crossed the street.

CHAPTER 7

Letters from Theo

JULY 1, 1917

My little cousin,

Where to begin? It turns out that Noyelles-sur-Mer is where
I'll be stationed most of the time. The British Expeditionary
Force's administrative headquarters for the Chinese Labour Corps
is here. Noyelles itself is a town of around nine hundred, now
grown to thousands thanks to the military and workers. One of
the châteaux near the town houses a large contingent of British
officers who run all this, plus there are soldiers, military police,
and doctors billeted with local families, so who knows what the
local townspeople think of all this disruption.

The Noyelles camp processes thousands of workers each week,
new arrivals and companies of workers being moved to different
postings. "Processing" takes five days—checking for fitness and
infectious diseases at the rather impressive camp hospital here.
I received a thorough examination from an English doctor who
spoke excellent Mandarin; he spent fifteen years as a missionary
in Tientsin. In fact, the doctors are mostly British or Canadian
missionaries previously stationed in China. It's comforting to

know that when our men need medical attention, they're able to speak to a doctor in our own language.

There are more than thirty CLC camps in France. Once processed, the men are sent from Noyelles to those camps. However, I've been assigned to Noyelles. The British Royal Engineers have a logging camp nearby in Crécy Forest. There is a train from Noyelles to Crécy Forest, but there isn't always room for the workers, so some days it's a brisk march of ninety minutes there or back. My company consists of: 24 British officers and noncommissioned officers reporting to a British major, 443 laborers, and 32 gangers (who are like foremen or supervisors). And now, one humble interpreter-clerk.

While we were chatting during my physical examination, the doctor commented that a worker's well-being depended greatly on the quality of officers in charge. He said I'd be treated well enough because I'm fairly fluent in English, and also because interpreters rank higher and get more privileges.

I may be breaking regulations already, cousin. Letters are supposed to go through censors at the Noyelles camp, but since I'm only writing to you in Paris, I'm using the regular postal system instead of the military's.

T.

SEPTEMBER 18, 1917

Dear Pauline,

Yes, it's a good thing that China has officially joined the war. Some government factions have been wanting to do this since the very beginning. What isn't so good is that it means some higher-ups here are more willing to put CLC companies closer to the front. Since China is no longer neutral, they think we should risk more.

You asked about the people in my company. I've met a real character, a peasant from Shandong province named Zhao who is approximately the size of an ox. He's one of those with a belly full of stories and a gift for telling them. He's rather vague on details and I suspect he exaggerates, but it's all in the service of a good tale.

Zhao was one of the early recruits. He walked for two days from his village to get to the British recruitment camp at Weihaiwei. His family was penniless after two years of drought and then a flood. With so many mouths to feed, when he heard the British were hiring Chinese to work overseas and for very good money, he hurried to Weihaiwei before all the jobs were gone.

He boarded a ship at Weihaiwei (the *Empress of Russia*, a Canadian ship—a detail I learned later from a Canadian officer who came over on the same sailing). Zhao said some of the others (but not him, of course!) at first thought the ship was a building attached to the wharf, not believing a boat could be so big. The men traveled steerage class, packed into bunks. Some men didn't have bunks, just mattresses on the floor. Their officers had to convince the ship's crew to provide hot water every day for washing and drinking.

Something that made me angry—the men had never seen Western-style latrines or washbasins before and no one explained the workings to them. So they used the toilets for garbage disposal and plugged up the drains. The latrines flooded and the floors were a filthy mess. Only then did their officers and doctors, the ones who could speak Chinese, explain proper use of the facilities.

It's this sort of misunderstanding that makes Westerners look

down on us Chinese, when all it takes is a simple explanation in
advance. Yet a French peasant accustomed to chamber pots and
outhouses would've made the same mistake.

You ask how I'm being treated by the British. Well enough, I
suppose. At least language isn't a problem for me, and I've never
had a problem getting passes to go into town.

T.

NOVEMBER 30, 1917

Dear Pauline,

Thank Denise for the jumpers she sent. I've never been so cold
and damp, the little kerosene and charcoal stoves for our huts
don't make much of a difference against these temperatures, but
still, a hut is better than living in the trenches. They say that 1916
and 1917 have been the coldest winters in living memory up here
in northern France.

Some of our squads have been helping at another camp (I can't
say where), and it means getting on a train every day. In addition
to the French rail lines, the British operate their own railway
system to transport troops and supplies. I must confess that until
I came here, the enormity of operations required behind the front
lines wasn't something I understood or appreciated. Every sort of
necessity, from guns to fuel, food, and blankets—all these must
be unloaded from ships, loaded onto trucks, and loaded again onto
trains and so on, until finally they reach the front.

I've been visiting the hospital every week. Some of our men
were wounded during an aerial attack in mid-November (I can't
tell you where), including Zhao. He is most indignant because
he considers his time at the hospital a forced convalescence. He

insists his wounds don't bother him anymore. The real reason is that if he doesn't work, he doesn't get paid. He told his surgeon to write the doctor who examined him in Canada, because that doctor said he is as strong and healthy as a man of twenty. He meant the doctor at the quarantine camp in Canada.

This led to reminiscences about his Pacific crossing and his time at the quarantine camp, which was on a spit of land on the west coast of Canada. To keep themselves busy, the men spent their time improving the grounds, digging better drainage, building paths between the buildings, even planting flower and vegetable gardens.

I'd never seen Zhao dejected before and offered to write a letter for him. He dictated a long list of instructions to his wife, all about using his wages to add a room onto their house for his parents, admonishments to his children, and he asked why they hadn't written to him in such a long time. While I was there, three other patients beseeched me to do the same for them. It made me feel very useful. The chaplain at the hospital asked if I'd like to volunteer to write letters for the men.

Of course I miss Paris. I miss the comforts of home, who wouldn't? But I'm still glad to be here. It makes a difference to men like Zhao, who are sacrificing so much—sometimes their lives.

Again, thank Denise for me.

T.

CHAPTER 8

Noyelles 1917

Eight months into her marriage, Camille believed herself happy. Her early months of pregnancy had been free of trouble and Jean-Paul was thrilled. She felt strong and vigorous, cycled to her post office job each morning as usual, enjoying the warm spring air. This early in the day, she could almost forget the war or that she had buried her father only six months ago.

Madame Dumont dabbed at her eyes when Camille shared her news. "Don't mind me, chérie," she said, "I can't help wishing this baby was my grandchild, the one you would've had if our Édouard had come back from the war."

"Well, you can be godparents," Camille said. "That is, if you don't mind."

The older woman had her husband bring in a tall chair from their home so that Camille could sit at the counter if she ever felt tired.

When Camille and Jean-Paul attended church, he fussed over her, holding her arm at all times, visibly proud of the slight swell under her dress.

He was in an especially good mood because he'd completed training as a railway mechanic. There was such a shortage of mechanics the Nord was sending him up and down the line to work at different train yards and repair shops. Jean-Paul took multiple shifts, sometimes he was away for three days at a time. It was exhausting, but whatever else Jean-Paul might've been, he wasn't lazy. With a baby on the way, he was intent on earning extra money.

"Perhaps you should give up the post office," he said. "You need to be careful of your health. And the baby's."

"But I haven't been there very long and the Dumonts need me," Camille said, smiling at the way he pressed his hands gently over her belly. "It's very light work standing around the post office. And the extra money is nice. I will stop after the baby is born."

"But promise you'll quit if you find yourself getting tired," he said, kissing her, "or if cycling to town gets too strenuous. We must lighten your workload."

Later, when she thought back to those weeks of contentment, Camille couldn't remember what Jean-Paul actually did to lighten her workload. She still fed the chickens and gathered eggs each morning, still walked or cycled to the post office, still carried buckets of water from the rain barrel to water the kitchen garden. And without much notice, she still had to cook dinner for his guests, doing her best with what was on hand, and what was on hand dwindled away as the war went on.

THAT DAY—SHE HAD COME TO call it That Day—Camille walked home from church by herself. Jean-Paul was out of town but would be home by evening. She anticipated an easy supper, a little leftover ham from the day before and a tart filled with preserved plums. Summer wasn't far away and soon she'd be picking fresh fruit again. She stopped at the cottage long enough to change out of her Sunday dress, picked up her basket and a drawing pad, then continued on to the woods to see what she could forage.

Sunlight broke through the canopy, leaves on trees were changing color from the pale green found only during the first weeks of spring to a deeper, more permanent green. Camille brushed bits of dry leaf from her skirt and picked a burr off her stocking. She had time, so she sat with her back against a tree and pulled out the drawing pad and began to sketch.

Camille felt pleased with the results. A stand of birches, a tangle of ferns growing at the base of their white trunks. Two large dog rose shrubs, their arching stems budding with green. A cluster of pale mushrooms nestled in a bed of moss and lichen. As she made her way out of the thicket, birds sounded their alarm calls, and she smiled that they were warning each other about her, the intruder in their midst. Foraging had only been an excuse. She loved these woods. It had been a good day.

Then Jean-Paul came home.

He brought his friend Marcel and a man she had never met before, who Jean-Paul introduced as Julien, no last name. They had brought bottles of wine and sat on the grass under the apple tree.

"They're staying for dinner," Jean-Paul announced, when he came into the kitchen.

"We don't have very much food," she whispered, not wanting his guests to overhear and think they weren't welcome.

"Don't worry, just cook what we have. They're not particular." She could tell he'd already had a lot to drink.

The best Camille could do was check for eggs from the henhouse and chop up what remained of the cheese and ham to make a quiche. She hoped that with bread, salad, and a fruit tart, there would be enough.

It was a warm evening, warm enough that she left the kitchen door and window open. She hardly paid attention to the snatches of conversation and laughter drifting in from the garden. It was only when she slid the tart out of the oven that she paused for a moment to listen.

"Our little Chinaman says he can get drugs." Marcel's voice. "Morphine and laudanum fetch the most money and are easy to hide, easy to carry."

"We found someone at the docks in Boulogne," the man called Julien said, "who supervises a team that unloads the supply ships from England. I've told him nonperishable food is what we're after. Tinned meats and fruit, canned butter, powdered milk. Flour and sugar. Big crates, big sacks. Not as easy to carry but easy to sell. Everyone wants food."

"We have more places to hide goods now. As long as Marcel can find a way to transport the supplies once he's off the train, there's no problem," Jean-Paul said.

"You were always interested in locomotives," Marcel said. "Who would've thought when we were boys sneaking rides on boxcars that you'd end up working on the Chemin du Nord."

Julien hooted. "Just proves they'll take anyone these days."

Camille tensed, worried Jean-Paul would take offense and start a fight. But instead there was laughter all around, Jean-Paul's loudest of all.

The men praised her cooking, but Jean-Paul grew quieter and quieter as he drank, and a familiar anxiety thrummed through her. Their guests left when the last bottle was empty, calling out good-natured insults in farewell as they staggered up the road toward Noyelles. She sank into a kitchen chair and sighed with relief at being able to rest her aching back. Just a few minutes sitting down and she'd wash the dishes.

Jean-Paul came in and she smiled. "It was kind of them to leave when they saw I was tired."

He slammed his fist on the table. "They left because they were still hungry. They've gone into town to get more food. What kind of a meal was that? Eggs? Salad? When we have guests you serve good, solid food."

"But Jean-Paul, that was all we had," Camille said, "and it's Sunday, the shops are closed."

"Why didn't you kill a chicken? You shamed me!"

She shrank back. "But the hens are for eggs. All we had in the cellar was . . ."

"The cellar. The cellar you're supposed to keep filled with food. Hams. Sausages. Terrines."

It had been a long time since anyone's cellar contained such treasures, she wanted to retort, but she said nothing because it would only make things worse.

Camille didn't cry out, not even when he dragged her by one arm toward the cellar door and shoved her through. She stumbled and lost her balance, crying out as she fell, the edge of each wooden step striking her ribs and shins, the side of her head, like blows from a cudgel. She twisted to protect her stomach and one shoulder took the brunt of the fall. She landed facedown, winded. She lay in the dark, legs splayed, unable to do anything but gasp for breath. Through her pain, she heard the cellar door slam and the latch clatter as Jean-Paul pulled it across. She was in total darkness, locked in. Her shoulder throbbed.

Only then did she begin sobbing. She felt her limbs and body for damage and used her apron to dab at the blood she felt running down her face. *Let my baby be safe*, she prayed.

She crawled to the wall and felt her way to the potato bin, where she had folded empty sacks over one side. She layered a few down on the ground so she wouldn't have to sit on cold brick and pulled another one across her chest for warmth. She sat in the corner with her back against the wooden slats and faced the steps.

Jean-Paul was leaving for work in the morning. He'd be gone for three days. If he forgot about her, if he forgot to unlatch the door before he went away, was three days long enough for her to die here, all alone in the dark? She placed a hand over her belly.

What sort of life would her child have with a father like Jean-Paul?

Camille had no illusions that he'd treat his own children any better than he treated her. Her last thought as her head drooped into exhausted sleep was that she didn't care anymore whether she lived or died.

She had been stirring salt into a bowl of water, telling herself she had the ocean.

CAMILLE WOKE, BLINKING AT THE shaft of light cutting down into the cellar's darkness. Jean-Paul had left the door ajar. She realized the sounds she'd heard in her dream had been him stomping around in the kitchen. Had he come down the stairs at all to check whether she was still alive? The kitchen door slammed. Had he really left the house, gone to his job? She listened until she was certain the house was quiet, then made her way cautiously and painfully up the cellar stairs.

She inspected her scrapes and bruises, wiped dried blood from her face, and set her bloodstained clothing to soak in a basin of cold water. The bump on the side of her head had swollen overnight, but her hair covered it. Her ribs ached and she felt weak, but she washed up and got dressed. She had to get to work. And she had to get away from the cottage.

Jean-Paul had done much that was unforgivable, and one of the worst was that his cruelty had driven away any pleasure she took from this cottage. The rooms no longer held comforting memories. Her grandmother had been here, in the parlor's hand-painted wallpaper, a roll brought over from the château. Now there was an ugly blot of blue ink on one wall where Jean-Paul had flung a fountain pen in anger.

Her father used to be here, in the faint scent of pipe tobacco that still lingered on his armchair. His presence was gone now, chased away by shouts and the reek of fear. Her fear. There was no comfort to be found in her home anymore.

Camille ended up walking her bicycle much of the way to work, unable to pedal on the uphill sections of road. Every slight incline felt like a steep climb.

"I'm sorry to be late this morning, Madame Dumont," she said when she entered the post office.

"Don't worry, ma chère, we're still a few minutes away from opening," Mme Dumont said. "And you should take things slowly. For today's cleaning, just sweep the floors."

"Yes, madame," she said.

The heavy broom with its stiff bristles was perfect for scraping clods of dirt from the wooden floor planks, but today every push took all Camille's strength. She leaned against the doorframe for a moment just to catch her breath.

Then she screamed as pain slashed through her. A warm, wet trickle ran down her legs, trails of red seeping through her stockings. She stared in horror and dropped the broom. Mme Dumont came bustling out from the back room, just in time to catch Camille as she fainted.

She drifted in and out of pain and consciousness, aware of kind and capable hands lifting her onto a bed, of conversations taking place around her. There were several voices. Mme Dumont, hovering. A man's voice, speaking French with a slight accent. Another female voice, saying yes all the time to Mme Dumont's orders. Their maid. M. Dumont's voice, not in the room, from out in the hallway.

"I fell down the cellar stairs," she repeated, over and over. But she couldn't be sure the word actually left her lips.

The tinkling of metal, the sound of utensils being dropped into a basin. A prick on her arm. Then blessed, blessed numbness and the serenity of total sleep.

Camille spent the next two days at the Dumont home. When they took her there, the local doctor could not be found, he'd been called out to one of the farms and Mme Dumont didn't want to wait. She had M. Dumont close the post office and sent him to the Chinese hospital to fetch Dr. Adams, the Canadian doctor. He had come immediately and dealt with the most urgent care, making sure her miscarriage would not lead to infection.

When Camille opened her eyes, she sat up, then fell back again.

"Not so fast, not so fast," Mme Dumont said. "Your ribs aren't broken but the doctor thinks they are cracked."

"What day is it? I must get home. Jean-Paul comes back on Wednesday." She pushed herself up and Mme Dumont put an extra pillow behind her.

"It's only Tuesday and don't worry. Monsieur Dumont left a message at the station for your husband that you're here with us. And you can stay for as long as you like, until you feel well enough to go home. Now that you're sitting up, I'll bring you some consommé."

The room was on the ground floor. Judging from the large crucifix on the wall, the old-fashioned furniture, and framed daguerreotype of a solemn wedding couple, Camille guessed she was in old Mme Dumont's former bedroom. The room the postmaster kept like a shrine. She wondered who owned the nightgown, which had long sleeves and a ruffle around the neck, the pin-striped flannel soft from years of washing. Then she realized that the postmistress, and perhaps the maid, had undressed and washed her. And therefore had seen the scrapes and bruises from her fall down the stairs, which she could explain away. And also the scars across her back and thighs, which she couldn't.

Jean-Paul returned and thanked the Dumonts profusely for looking after Camille. They commiserated with him on Camille losing the baby, urged him to put a handrail on the cellar stairs. Mme Dumont repeatedly told Camille she should only come in to work when she felt strong enough. M. Dumont drove Camille and Jean-Paul home in the post office's little mail delivery cart.

Jean-Paul tucked her into bed and kissed her tenderly on the forehead. "You get some rest. I'll stay in your father's room tonight so you can sleep undisturbed."

For the next three days Jean-Paul came home every evening. He brought flour and butter, sugar, and a leg of ham. Then he brought two ducks, which she plucked and cooked, removing the legs to preserve as a confit. It was laborious work, but it pleased Jean-Paul to see her in the kitchen. Content enough that he just sat on a kitchen chair smoking and studying train schedules and maps. Then he signed on for multiple shifts. He'd be away for days.

Camille went back to work as soon as she felt strong enough to get on her bicycle. Her route to Noyelles took her past the d'Amerval farm. Camille usually looked away when she passed the ruined barn, not wanting to remember how Jean-Paul had taken her there, forced himself on her, sealed her fate. Now she stared at the shattered roof beams jutting toward the clouds, the scorched edges of the bomb crater like the edges of an abyss. And found herself wishing she'd been standing there when the bomb fell.

Sometimes mercy is merely the absence of pain.

THE FIRST TIME AFTER HER miscarriage, Camille lay submissively in the dark with her eyes shut, trying not to show revulsion while Jean-Paul strained on top of her. She waited for the relief that came when he rolled off with a grunt. When he did, he pulled the covers over himself and soon, thankfully soon because of the wine, his breathing slowed and he emitted a snore. When his snoring grew regular and he turned onto his side, she slipped out of bed and down the stairs. She took a bottle of white vinegar from the kitchen cupboard. She didn't have a douche—that might've aroused Jean-Paul's suspicions if he'd found it—so she had been using a funnel, one she kept at the back of a kitchen drawer.

She lay on the floor of the small bathroom, the tiled surface icy cold on her back, but it didn't matter. Because she would not give Jean-Paul what he wanted—children. Sons and daughters, but mostly sons. A small troop to follow him into church on Sundays, the girls in frilly white dresses, the boys in sailor suits, his wife by his side, holding a lace parasol. And Camille wasn't having that.

MME DUMONT SAID NOTHING TO Camille, but it was clear she didn't believe her story about falling down the cellar steps. Each morning at work, Camille could feel the older woman's eyes on her, knew Mme Dumont was scrutinizing her for new bruises or cuts. Whenever Jean-Paul came to the post office, Mme Dumont was cordial, but if Jean-Paul could feel a chill in the air he never showed it.

Camille brought in a watercolor sketch of the post office as a gift to the Dumonts. Mme Dumont hung it in a frame on the wall behind the counter.

"Those British soldiers are eager for souvenirs," she said. "I hear they're buying up pictures of Noyelles as quickly as Monsieur Antoine's photo studio prints them up. You could sell little watercolors here at the post office."

"Are you sure it's all right to do that?" Camille said. "Wouldn't Monsieur Dumont mind?"

"He will not mind," Mme Dumont said. "You should make some money of your own." She said this rather pointedly.

Camille was curious to see whether people would actually pay for her sketches. Painting scenes of the countryside would be easy, a pleasant diversion to keep her mind off the miscarriage. She would work on some pictures whenever Jean-Paul was away with the Nord. They wouldn't be large pictures, perhaps twice the size of a postcard.

IF NOT FOR THE WATERCOLORS, she never would've had reason or the courage to speak to him.

Mme Dumont had rushed into the post office that day to tell Camille to manage on her own. M. Dumont had put his back out again and had to lie still in bed with hot water bottles and plenty of poultices.

"If he'd just follow the doctor's orders," Mme Dumont said, shaking her head, "but Dumont refuses to stay in bed and delays his recovery. I must watch him with great vigilance."

Camille dealt with customers all day and found no time to sort the mail. A large pile of it waited for her in the back room and not just because so many families had sons or husbands in the military. As part of the government's morale-boosting campaign the women of France had been asked to write to soldiers so that every man in the trenches would get letters. According to M. Dumont, a fountain of statistics when it came to the postal service, French citizens sent four million pieces of mail each day to men in uniform and received just as many. With only three of them sorting the mail—actually two, since M. Dumont preferred chatting with customers—the small post office could barely keep up. And now with Christmas coming there was even more to handle, greeting cards and packages. Camille couldn't afford to fall behind.

At four o'clock, the post office finally emptied and she felt quite justified in turning over the placard in the window to Closed. But when she saw him walking toward the post office, she flipped the sign back and moved behind the counter.

Some of the Chinese interpreters seemed to have only a basic understanding of French and spoke with a heavy accent. But then, they'd been hired for their English skills, not French; they were there to translate for the British. This man, she noticed, spoke flawless French. What's more, he tipped his hat to all the women with a polite smile, as though such courtesies were second nature. He strolled down the main street of Noyelles as though he were promenading along the Seine.

Camille tried not to stare whenever he walked past, not because he was Chinese, but because she wished she could draw him. It wasn't just because of his features, although he was very handsome. It was the way he held himself, the way he walked with a slight swing to his shoulders, the way he strode along so confidently. She wondered how she could capture that carefree movement in a pencil sketch or on canvas. And he looked familiar somehow.

He handed her money and an envelope. A Paris mailing address. *Pauline Deng, No. 53 Rue de Lisbonne, Paris. A sister or wife?* she wondered, as she pasted on a stamp.

"Are these for sale?" He pointed at the watercolors she had slipped beneath the glass top of the counter, beside the samples of stamps and the price list for parcel post.

"Yes. Would you like one?"

"This one." He pointed at the one of her cottage, a summer scene, climbing roses in a tangle over the garden gate. "We walk past this little stone house on our way to the forest."

"It's where I live," she said, taking the coins he pushed across the countertop. Then flushed at offering this information.

"And are you the artist?" he said, turning from the pictures to look at her. "These are good. An impressionist influence?"

She nodded. "Since I saw my first impressionist paintings at the Louvre."

"Do you manage to get to Paris often?"

"Just once, but I spent a whole day at the Louvre," she said, "and I'll never forget a single moment of it."

She closed the post office as soon as he left, all the while thinking back to her day at the Louvre. Remembered the woman who had chatted with her in the porcelain room. And the young man and woman who came to find her, both Chinese. And realized why the interpreter looked familiar.

WHEN CAMILLE REACHED THE COTTAGE, the windows were dark, the drapes still open, and for a fleeting moment her heart lightened. Perhaps Jean-Paul wasn't home. If he wasn't home by now, he wouldn't be home until the next afternoon. But then a light came on.

"Camille, ma petite," Jean-Paul said, as soon as she entered the kitchen door. Lamplight shone on the wine bottle and the tumbler in his hand. He was drunk, but smiling. In a good mood. "How was your day at work? Happy that the weekend is here?"

The thing about Jean-Paul was that no matter how drunk he was, he never slurred his words. In fact, he enunciated more precisely. It was how she could tell.

"Monsieur Dumont wasn't well," she said, "and the doctor says he must rest in bed for a few days, so Madame Dumont went home. I had to do everything. It was very busy."

"Why don't you make some soup for the Dumonts? Take it over to their home tomorrow."

Anyone else would've thought Jean-Paul was being considerate. Except that she knew Jean-Paul made a point of cultivating the good opinion of all the town officials. In their little world, the postmaster was an important man, a member of the church board.

"Yes, Jean-Paul. That's a good idea. I'll make the soup tonight after we eat."

"One more thing. Marcel is coming for supper tomorrow. Make that thing with mushrooms he likes so much."

No wonder he was in a good mood. Marcel was coming to discuss their illegal business. She knew now, from casual inquiries, that sometimes when Jean-Paul was absent for a day or two he was more likely to be working the black market with Marcel, not working extra shifts as he claimed.

They ate dinner in silence. When Jean-Paul was lost in his own thoughts it was best to leave him there. After the washing up, she put vegetables in a large pot to simmer for soup, then snatched up a linen tea towel and went into the parlor. If she could keep herself looking busy until he fell into bed, everything would be all right.

"What are you doing now, Camille?" He leaned against the parlor door. Quite drunk, but his face and movements, like his speech, never betrayed any inebriation. Not unless you knew what to look for, the way he tilted his head slightly to give you a sideways look.

"I'm doing a bit of cleaning. Marcel is coming tomorrow and I want our home to look nice for him." He was drunk but she couldn't discern his mood. She had to be careful. She gave him a bright smile.

"House must look nice. Yes." He turned away from the door and to her relief, she heard his heavy tread on the staircase, then the creak of the bedroom door and the headboard banging against the wall as he fell into the bed.

She dusted off the glass-front cabinet and stood back to look. She used to think of the decorative objects on the shelves inside as merely souvenirs, objects her father had brought back from his time in China. Now that she knew how her father acquired them, the painted goldfish on the lacquered platter seemed less content in their shining black pond and the ivory Goddess of Mercy looked at her with a reproachful gaze.

Back in the kitchen Camille boiled water and took the white porcelain jar from the mantel. It was the one her father had given her out of his trunk that day. It was simple, a muted off-white glaze. It wasn't decorated in blue and white like some of the ones in the bow-front vitrine, or painted with flowers and butterflies like the large vase on the mantel. But she liked its contours, rounded and elegant, the little finial on the lid shaped like a lotus bud. She used it to store dried chamomile. At least she'd never run out of chamomile, not with so much of it planted around the garden.

As softly as she could, Camille climbed the stairs and went into the small bedroom that had been hers. She pulled out a leather suitcase from under the narrow bed, opened it to look through the drawing supplies inside, pencils and watercolors. She wouldn't do any painting tonight, not while Jean-Paul was home. But she could do some sketching.

She took a few sheets of drawing paper and a pencil down to the kitchen. She had been wanting to paint a portrait of Mme Dumont as a Christmas gift. Her pencil roughed in the older woman's head and shoulders, her broad face and surprisingly delicate eyebrows. She held it up, satisfied. Tomorrow, she would begin using watercolors, adding some soft background colors before underpainting the face.

Unbidden, the face of the Chinese interpreter came to her mind, his dark eyes looking up as he lifted his gaze from the watercolors on the post office counter, his lips quirked in an amused smile. When she looked down, she had drawn him. She studied the paper for a few minutes wishing she'd made more effort to commit his features to memory. She would paint him one day when it was safe.

She fed the sketch into the stove.

CHAPTER 9

Letters from Theo

JANUARY 23, 1918

Dear Pauline,

Tell Denise I don't know how she managed to scrape together the sugar and butter to make such a wonderful cake. Thank her also for the socks—keeping my feet warm and dry is a constant challenge.

It's as though I've been here for years, but it's been just eight months. It's because of the cold. Temperatures have dropped even lower and the winds don't just bite, they slash. The YMCA has set up a recreation hut for the workers. It's well-heated, so we go there to read magazines and newspapers, enjoy a hot drink, play cards, and chat with the secretaries, as YMCA staff are called. There are five secretaries here, three British and two Chinese students, both from missionary schools.

I haven't mentioned the YMCA before. The British YMCA has recruited missionaries to run recreational and educational programs at various CLC camps. At first the military was reluctant but given that the men are bored when not working, the state of their morale, and the need to offset gambling with other activities, well one day, huts and canteens just appeared!

Last week, I played chess with a laborer named Guo. He's a schoolteacher in China who signed on because he wanted to see Europe. What impresses him most about the West is that everyone can read. Even old women read newspapers. He wants to open a school for girls when he returns to China.

He says he realizes now what a weak country China is compared to Western nations. Every little French boy points a finger at us and says, "Chinois, pas bon" because we're weak, poor, and ignorant. Because of this, the French and British mistreat our workers. He made this observation thoughtfully and when I remarked that he did not sound bitter, he replied it was because this would not always be so, that he had faith China would one day regain her place as a great nation, as great as it had been during the Han, the Tang, or the Ming dynasties. It might take a hundred years, but what was a hundred years compared to four thousand years of civilization?

It's too bad his squad has since moved to another camp; he was an interesting man, and I enjoyed our talks. It gets lonely sometimes. I have little in common with these men. They like to reminisce about their villages and families, festivals and famines. I'm sure some of the British have spent time in Paris, but we do not socialize. The townsfolk are friendly enough, especially the shopkeepers, but it stops there. I don't have Henri's talent for drawing conversation from strangers.

Some of our commanding officers are veterans, wounded and unable to serve in the field and so they were assigned to the CLC. Some have served in China (which doesn't necessarily mean they like the Chinese), others know nothing about us or our customs.

Some are friendly and curious to learn, others lack any shred of humanity when dealing with the workers. You can guess which officers get the best from their men.

A young lieutenant, an Irishman, was transferred to another posting. He was well-liked by the workers in his company and on the morning of his departure they all got up early and lined up in parade formation out in the yard, dressed in their cleanest uniforms. The company captain ordered them all to get back in their huts because reveille hadn't sounded. He threatened them with court-martial. He didn't understand this send-off was the men showing respect, that it's our way to walk distinguished guests to the door to bid them farewell. But even after the company interpreter explained this, the captain didn't care. The men were forced to go back inside.

Imagine the punishment such officers mete out for less benign misunderstandings.

T.

FEBRUARY 20, 1918

Dear Pauline,

Happy Lunar New Year. The eight-treasures sticky rice pudding was wonderful, and I was a very popular man when I shared it among all the gangers. Again, dry sausages are the best food you can send.

There was a Lunar New Year celebration at the Noyelles camp. All the workers at other camps within walking distance came, as this was one of the few days off they had, according to their contracts. Some actually walked all night to get to Noyelles, then back again as soon as the festivities were done. The men held their celebrations in a field beside the camp and put together an entire day of entertainment. They made costumes and scenery with fabric they purchased from pooling their own funds. Some were fairly elaborate, and I'm guessing the performers got those sent from China with help from the YMCA. There was music, some of it on homemade instruments, others on instruments imported from China, again the YMCA. There were martial arts competitions, an opera performance, and stilt walkers in costume wandered around the field.

The townsfolk didn't understand a thing about the music or the story of the opera, but our men had a wonderful time. Afterward there was a huge meal, of course. The men must've saved for weeks to buy the chickens and geese for the banquet.

There is a pagoda—yes, a pagoda—at the entrance to the Chinese hospital, a touch of home for the men. But it's also rather sad, Pauline, because the pagoda was built and decorated by patients from the mental ward. It's separated from the main hospital, and the patients are men whose minds and spirit have been broken by the war. Some are younger than we are and before this had never left the placid lives of their farms and villages.

Both the YMCA's comforts and the mental ward are much needed. I heard that a young worker at another camp killed himself before the new year. His squad came to Noyelles after spending two weeks under continuous shelling. They took cover in a vermin-infested trench for days and came out physically unharmed but shaken. The young man was heard muttering over and over to himself "Two more years is too much, two more years is too much," and the next morning, he was found hanging from the beams of the bathing hut.

I'm sorry to finish what should've been a cheerful New Year's letter on such a sad note.

T.

CHAPTER 10

Noyelles, April 1918

The day was glorious, the sky a bold azure from horizon to horizon. Camille took a moment's delight in the perfection of the weather before entering the woods. To the east, the dark bulk of Crécy Forest loomed, but fruit trees frothing with blossoms dotted the landscape, and the fields that stretched across the horizon were neatly plowed, rows of rich brown soil promising abundance come the harvest. The fresh green scents of a new season lifted her spirits. A pair of magpies soared overhead, black and white wings flashing through the sky. Poplar trees swayed in a light breeze, their green leaves with silvery undersides fluttering a semaphore only Nature could decipher.

Jean-Paul wouldn't be home for at least two days so she could take her time. She pulled her drawing pad from the basket. She worked in pencil, a view of the fields looking toward Crécy Forest. There would be time in the evening to add color. It wasn't how she'd been taught but painting over a rough pencil sketch let her work faster. Her watercolors sold well, and so far Jean-Paul hadn't found out about her little enterprise. Landscapes and street scenes were popular and so were paintings of the mansion where the British had set up their headquarters. Camille was even getting commissions from junior officers who wanted watercolors of the houses where they were billeted.

It was quiet in the grove except for the sounds of birdsong. She tucked the finished sketches in a cardboard portfolio and stood up to stretch. It was already afternoon and there was time to forage while the light was still good. An hour later, her basket was full. Springtime meant morels and there were plenty to be found in this grove. She hunted for them under elms and sycamores but it was the ground beneath an old apple tree that yielded the largest find of the hour.

A few more and she'd have enough if Marcel came for dinner when Jean-Paul returned.

MARCEL HAD BEEN COMING TO the cottage a lot, at least twice a week. This put Jean-Paul in a good mood because Marcel loved Camille's cooking and when Marcel was happy, so was Jean-Paul. She didn't drink coffee with them afterward, not wanting to know what they discussed. Supplies stolen and hidden, drugs sold and traded. These conversations meant Jean-Paul would be gone for one or two overnights, taking advantage of his job with the railway to transfer goods and get Marcel onto trains for free.

Usually in a good mood after Marcel left, Jean-Paul would beckon her into bed, pull up her nightgown. She succumbed wordlessly, turning her face until it was almost buried against the pillows. Jean-Paul didn't like her looking at him when he was satisfying his needs. He preferred a frenzied coupling, quickly finished. A small mercy.

Another small mercy was that he often turned his back to her and grunted "You can go." Then she would leave the bedroom and return to her own room, the one where she'd slept since she was a girl. Jean-Paul complained he couldn't get a decent night's rest with her tossing and turning in the same bed.

But last night had not been one of those evenings. She rubbed her elbow and winced.

Marcel hadn't come for dinner as promised. Jean-Paul had her keep the stew warm. She fed wood into the stove while he loitered by the garden gate, listening for Marcel's bicycle, the broken tinkling of its bell. After two hours he gave up and she served dinner in the kitchen, a silent torment of a meal.

"Something's happened," he muttered, "he wouldn't miss dinner tonight."

"I'm sure he's all right," she said. "Marcel can take care of himself, there's no need to worry."

Jean-Paul pushed his chair away from the table. His glare could've scorched wood.

"What do you know about worry, Camille? Food on the table every night, a roof over your head every night. All your life, looked after by your father, your grandmother. And now, your husband."

He grabbed her by the hair. She screamed as he yanked her out of the chair. "You have no idea of the risks I face to support you! The things I do so that we can have a decent future after the war."

Camille gasped as he threw her against the wall. "I know you work hard, Jean-Paul. Please. Please stop this." She struggled to stay standing.

"Marcel could be in danger. Or sick." He paced up and down the kitchen.

"Maybe he just forgot about tonight." Then she flinched as he raised his fist.

"Forget? Marcel doesn't forget!"

IN THE MORNING, CAMILLE HEARD the creak of the garden gate, four loud rings of a bicycle bell. Heard Jean-Paul answer the door. She peered through the curtains and looked down. Jean-Paul's greetings were loud and jocular.

"No, no, I wasn't concerned," she heard Jean-Paul say. "Camille was the one who worried you might be sick."

"Eh bien, there was a small problem I had to sort out," Marcel said, "and then it was too late for dinner. I thought I'd come early today and we could leave together. Are you ready?"

Jean-Paul disappeared from view and from below, there were rustling noises, then the sound of the kitchen door opening and shutting. But no footsteps coming up the staircase or a shouted farewell. He came out, a cap on his head, knapsack on his shoulders, and hopped onto the back of the bicycle. When Marcel had pedaled over the crest of the road, she felt a moment of elation before plunging into despair.

The course of her life extended before her, its path in perpetual shadow. She had money Jean-Paul didn't know about and jewelry she could sell. She would find a way to escape this marriage.

BUT NOW, A DAY LATER, Camille's resolve faltered. She had to acknowledge reality. If she ran away, how long could she survive on her small hoard of funds? If she ran away and Jean-Paul caught up with her—she shuddered at the thought. She rolled up one sleeve and examined the new bruises on her forearm, felt the bump on the back of her head.

Jean-Paul was careful now, even when drunk. Very rarely did he harm her where it showed. His violence was casual. She'd come to understand he thought it normal to strike out when angry or unhappy. It was how others had used him all his life.

Not wanting to leave the serenity of the grove, she paused a bit longer at its edge and gazed at the familiar landscape, the road cutting between pastures and fields. The woods weren't large enough to be called a forest, not really; it was just one of a number of coppices in the area, a stand of trees left to grow wild, then harvested for firewood every few decades or so.

It was her only sanctuary. Even when Jean-Paul was away from home, it was where she came to think. She couldn't think in the house, not anymore. What had been the everyday noises of an old stone cottage now made her nervous. Every sigh of roof rafters each time the house settled a little, every creak of the floor or rattle of a window tightened her nerves, startling her for a moment, making her wonder if Jean-Paul had somehow returned without her knowing.

But there was no sanctuary anymore, not even in these woods. The freshness of spring, the countryside at its peak of beauty, all of it broke her heart because she knew it could all vanish in an instant. The world was uncertain and dangerous. Just one aerial attack and her little forest would go up in flames, the fertile fields surrounding her home turn into cratered wasteland.

A convoy of trucks had been attacked a few days ago, on a road northeast of Noyelles. Chinese workers had cleared up the wreckage and repaired all damage within a few hours. Repairs to roads and railway tracks required never-ending labor because the Germans kept blowing up transportation lines to prevent supplies from reaching Allied troops.

Noyelles had been fortunate. But even without serious damage to the town, life here would not recover quickly. Not when so many of the young men she'd known since childhood were dead. There were too many bereaved. Widows and fatherless children, elderly couples trying to keep a farm going on their own.

As for her life, it was her own fault. Her fault for letting herself get driven like cattle into a marriage she hadn't been sure she wanted. Her fault for being so naïve that she'd entered that barn with Jean-Paul. Her fault for wanting her father to have peace of mind before he died.

Peace. Camille began to laugh. She leaned her forehead against a tree trunk, slid down until she was crouched at the foot of the elm and her laughter turned into sobs.

She didn't hear the warning calls of birds breaking the silence. Didn't hear the rustle of footsteps across dry grass, didn't know anyone was there until the gentle touch on her shoulder. She gasped and whirled around.

The Chinese interpreter.

"Are you all right, madame?" His dark eyes were anxious, and a slight frown creased the skin between his eyebrows. "I saw you from the road. Are you hurt?"

"No, no. I'm fine." Camille wiped her eyes with a sleeve and managed a smile

He pulled a canteen from his belt. "Would you like some water?"

"No, I'm fine," she repeated. "I should get back home." She sat up, pulled her skirt over her knees.

"You're the postmistress," he said, kneeling beside her. His smile was still anxious.

"No, that's Madame Dumont. My name is Camille Roussel. I'm just a clerk there."

"Not just a clerk, also an artist," he said, "My name is Theo Deng. Your watercolor is pinned to my wall, Madame Roussel. I get great pleasure looking at it every day. Will you allow me?" He pointed to her portfolio.

She hesitated only a moment and untied the string fastener around her portfolio. He sat down beside her. "I've been sketching the countryside," she said, "typical views of the area around Noyelles, the plants and flowers, animals. Then if I like the composition, it becomes a watercolor."

"I've been taking photographs," he said. "They depict the landscape accurately, but a good painting somehow conveys more feeling." He studied each sketch slowly, head nodding.

Then Theo laughed. "This isn't Noyelles!" Behind her latest pencil sketches were older ones. He held up a still life of Chinese porcelains, her white jar and behind it, tilted up on a stand, a painted plate.

"The scene on that porcelain plate, I wonder if you know it," Camille said, stumbling over her words. "Is there a story of the woman flying toward the moon?"

His smile warmed, a flame she wanted to catch in her hands. "Yes. The story is called 'Lady Ch'ang O Ascends to the Moon.' It's a famous folktale."

In ancient times one of the gods decided to place ten suns into the sky. They circled constantly; there was no night, and every day was scorching hot. So the greatest archer in the world, a man named Hou Yi, went to the highest peak in China and from there shot down nine of the suns. He became a hero for this feat and the people made him emperor. But corrupted by power, Hou Yi proved a cruel monarch. His wife, the beautiful Lady Ch'ang O, feared him and wanted to escape her marriage.

Hou Yi made a long journey to see the goddess Queen Mother of the West. He persuaded the Queen Mother to give him the elixir of immortality. When he came home he hid away the elixir, but Ch'ang O found it. She couldn't bear the thought of her husband being emperor for all eternity; just then Hou Yi entered the room so she drank the elixir herself then leaped out the window to escape him. But instead of falling, she floated up, flew out of reach, and continued on to the moon where she lives to this day.

"There are many versions of this legend," Theo said, "but our Mid-Autumn Festival celebrations are always the same. We eat sweet round pastries called moon cakes and sit outside at night to admire the full moon and recite poetry celebrating the moon."

"What about the rabbit?" she said. "There's also a rabbit in the picture."

"There are many schools of thought about that rabbit," Theo said, his voice so solemn she felt sure he was teasing her. "He lived on the moon before Lady Ch'ang O arrived. Some say he pounds herbs on a mortar and pestle to make the elixir of life. Other tales say he pounds rice into flour for rice cakes."

Camille didn't need to go as far as the moon, only far enough that Jean-Paul couldn't find her. Maybe Paris. It would be easier to lose yourself in a big city.

After their talk, Theo walked Camille to the cottage. Their conversation never lagged. She didn't want to stop talking, stop listening, or asking questions.

"Thank you for your kindness," she said, when they reached the house. "When you first saw me, I was feeling sad. Sometimes the world seems a difficult place."

"There's nothing easy about living in a time of war," he said. "We all have our dark days. Thanks to you, today wasn't one of mine."

"Monsieur Deng," she said, then paused. "May I ask a favor?"

"Of course. And please call me Theo."

She asked if he would pose for a portrait. She only needed a few hours of his time but . . . and here she hesitated over the right choice of words.

"When my husband is home, I need to be with him," she said. "Is there a way I could let you know when it's convenient for me? And of course, only if it's also convenient for you."

"I could drop by the post office once a week and we could compare schedules," he said.

She couldn't have anyone know. "Is there a more . . . private way to communicate?"

"I see." His tone was thoughtful rather than offended.

"Please feel free to refuse," she began, but he dismissed her concern with a wave of the hand.

"For the next few weeks, my company will be walking to and from Crécy Forest," he said. "Can you put something out in the garden as a signal?"

"Yes, yes." Camille breathed a sigh of relief. "This time of year, I hang blankets and rugs out to air. If you see one in the garden, close to the road, it means we can meet that afternoon in the woods."

He tipped his hat and nodded. "I will look for it."

She couldn't believe she'd been so bold, but she wanted so badly to continue the conversation, learn more about China, talk about art. Talk about something else besides the war. She paused at the cottage door and watched Theo continue along the road to Noyelles, his silhouette against the shell-pink and coral sunset, kept watching until his figure vanished down the other side of the rise.

SEVERAL DAYS LATER, CAMILLE TIED a rope from an apple tree to a hook on the garden room wall and pegged a red quilt to the line. All day at the post office she wondered if Theo had seen the quilt, whether he'd changed his mind about walking from the camp all the way back to the woods. She cycled home as fast as she could after work, gathered the drawing supplies she would need, then hurried along the road.

She waited at the edge of the forest, far enough under the shade that she couldn't be seen from the road. The shiver of delight that coursed through her when she saw him approach surprised her. His pleasure at seeing her again was evident, and it was a relief that he truly wanted to be here, that he wasn't just being polite. Their conversation picked up where it had left off, as though no time at all had interrupted their talk.

Cézanne was Theo's favorite artist, for the way each of his brushstrokes seemed to paint tree bark and sunlight at the same time, and for how trees looked leafy even though there wasn't a single distinguishable leaf. He told her about an astonishing work by an Englishman named Turner, a landscape of a valley that you could tell was a valley even though the painting appeared to be nothing but mist.

"The greatest masterpieces in Paris have been sent away to safety," he said, "but the Renaissance rooms at the Louvre are open and also the medieval sculpture gallery. The contemporary paintings and the porcelain room still contain most of their collections."

"Even without its greatest works, the Louvre must still be wonderful," she said with a sigh of longing.

"After a day there, I feel so satiated it's almost physical," he said, "as if I'd eaten a good meal. It's not very poetic is it, comparing something as sublime as a Monet to dinner?"

But Camille understood completely. During her visit to the museum, she realized some part of her had been hungry for years, and that she hadn't known it until she gazed upon those paintings. The beauty of her world under a different light, through a different lens, ordinary scenes and ordinary people rendered bold and joyous.

At the end of two hours Camille showed him the results of her work. She had sketched Theo in various poses, different angles. She would settle on a pose next time and work in earnest.

"My grandmother didn't approve of the impressionists," she said, opening up her portfolio to put away the sketches. "She liked pictures to look like painted versions of photographs."

"But I don't think the artists want to paint exactly how something looks," Theo said. "I can't explain what it is they're trying to do, but it's more emotional."

"That's because they don't paint what they're seeing," she said, "they paint what they feel about what they're seeing."

He stared at her as though she had said something wondrous and profound.

They left the woods separately, Theo going first. It was as though they were hiding an affair, she thought, when what she was doing was perfectly innocent. Yet she couldn't take her eyes off Theo as he strode away, shoulders swinging. Bold and joyous.

WHERE DID IT COME FROM, this audacity of hers? One day Camille brought a small vase to show Theo, hyacinth blue with yellow chrysanthemums blooming across its rounded body. The entire vase was covered with tiny curls of metal in a filigree pattern.

"I know this is called cloisonné ware, but how is it made?" she said. "The filigree is so intricate."

Theo took the vase from her. "The metalwork is functional, not just decorative. It's made by bending wire-thin strips of bronze or copper and soldering them onto the surface to form tiny compartments to contain the colored enamel glazes."

He explained how it might take two or three firings before the enamel inside their enclosures smoothed out. Then the surface was sanded down until the patterned wires were exposed, and finally the entire surface was polished.

"The technique reached its artistic peak during the eighteenth century," he said. "The fifteenth-century Jingtai emperor was very interested in the craft and had his artisans perfect an enamel in his favorite shade of blue."

"Imagine," Camille said, entranced, "that an emperor would take so much interest in advancing the creation of such beauty."

"If only our emperors had been less interested in advancing the art of decoration," he said, "and paid more attention to how other nations were advancing the science of war."

When Theo was younger, his father used to take him to the Louvre every week to study the museum's collection of Chinese artifacts, part of his training so he could take over La Pagode one day. Louis passed on what he'd learned from Grandfather Deng. The Dengs traded many types of goods but Theo's grandfather loved antiques and took a personal interest in this part of the business. When he was still in Shanghai, Louis would sit in the room while brokers brought antiques to show Grandfather Deng and debate their authenticity and value.

"How did you come by this vase?" Theo asked, handing it back. "And those porcelains in your drawing?"

"They were souvenirs my father brought back from his time in Peking," she said.

He smiled. "Was your father a missionary?"

She shook her head. "No, he was an army officer. A captain."

"I see," he said, and his smile became merely polite. "Was he there in 1900?"

"Yes, that's when he was serving in China," she said.

The smile left his eyes. "Have we done enough for today?" he asked, standing up.

"Yes, yes," she said hastily, "in fact I won't need you to pose again. I'll let you know when it's finished and you can take a look."

Camille put away her drawing materials and walked with Theo to the edge of the grove, a hollow pit forming in her stomach. Her father once told her that some of the best pieces of Chinese art in private collections came from looting the Old Summer Palace and the Forbidden City. What must such episodes in China's history mean to Theo, the humiliation and loss? How did he feel about men like her father? And by association, her?

CAMILLE DIDN'T GET MUCH OPPORTUNITY to work on Theo's portrait. Jean-Paul had been home for the past ten days. She rose early to watch workers march along the road to Crécy Forest, her eyes straining through the dim light to see whether Theo was among them. Usually he was walking with the British officers at the rear of the long line of men. Even though she couldn't make out his face, Theo's easy stride was unmistakable. On days when she didn't see him, she would cycle past the Chinese camp on her way to the post office, slowing down to look for a tall, elegant figure moving between the rows of bunkhouses and Nissen huts.

At work, she paid more attention when others mentioned the Chinese workers.

"Marie-France got a letter from her cousin Thérèse, the one who went to Paris." The woman who said this was waiting for Camille to weigh her package. "She met a chintok at the factory and wants to marry him. He's nice to her and doesn't spend his wages on drink or gambling. Her parents want to drag her home but what can they do? They need the money she earns at the factory."

"Well, remember my cousin Charlotte who lives near Boismont?" her friend said. "She's quite taken with one of the Chinamen at their farm. Strong, works hard, knows how to handle livestock. He was a farmer back in China, she says."

Mme Dumont shut the door after them, shaking her head. "Those girls," the postmistress said. "But you can't blame them for getting interested in foreigners. Not a lot of marriageable men in this town anymore, so many killed or too crippled to work the land."

Camille bit her tongue. "There's been a lot of people in and out today; I must sweep the floor again."

"Do so, my dear, then take the rest of the afternoon off. It's too beautiful a spring day for you to be working indoors. I'd like to see more color on your cheeks."

Camille was glad of the extra hour. Jean-Paul had been called to work at the Amiens rail yard. The days were longer now and she'd have many hours of natural light left in the day to work on Theo's portrait.

SHE WAS TOO FAR AWAY to see the features of the man walking on the road, but Theo was wearing a Chinese uniform and there was no mistaking that distinctive carefree stride. He was strolling toward Noyelles. Toward her. Camille walked a little faster and, when she knew there was no way he couldn't have seen her, she waved.

She decided to pretend there was nothing amiss, that there hadn't been any awkwardness from their last meeting.

"Good afternoon," she called, "where are your men?"

"Cutting timber and milling duckboards," he said, "something routine. And I have some clerical work to do at the camp. And you? Has the post office closed for the summer?"

"Madame Dumont let me out early," she said, pleased at the teasing tone in his voice. He wasn't upset with her. "I plan to finish your portrait very soon. Would you be able to meet the day after tomorrow and see it? The usual time?"

"I would be delighted. I've missed our chats."

And though she tried hard not to read too much into Theo's words, they made her heart race.

CAMILLE HAD A LOT TO carry to her rendezvous with Theo: her portfolio with the finished portrait, a large basket that held the picnic. Theo was already there in the small clearing, sitting by a clump of ferns. When he saw her, he leapt up to take the heavy basket, but she just set it down and began taking out the food. An old tablecloth to sit on, napkins, an apple tart wrapped in a dishcloth. And a pair of blue-and-white plates.

"There are eight of these," she said, holding them up to Theo. "I brought two for us to use. I wondered if you could tell me about them. Is there a story behind the illustration?"

He chuckled when he looked at it. "Fox Fools the Tiger."

A tiger caught a fox but the fox said to him, "You can't eat me. The gods have made me king of all animals and you'll be cursed if you harm me." The tiger looked doubtful so the fox said, "Let me walk in front and you follow. See what happens." So the tiger walked right behind the fox and every animal who saw them fled in terror. The tiger had to concede that the fox was indeed the king of animals and went on his way, never bothering the fox again.

Camille burst out laughing.

"It's my cousin Pauline's favorite story," Theo said, grinning.

She gave him the second plate. A man dressed in loose robes rested in the shade of a pine tree, eyes closed in sleep. A large butterfly hovered beside his head.

"This is not a story," Theo said. "It's more a topic for philosophical discussion but it's so famous it's become folklore.

"One day the sage Chuang-tzu dreamt he was a butterfly. He fluttered from flower to flower, spread his wings to ride upon soft breezes, and was conscious only of the happiness of being a butterfly. Then he awakened and said to himself, 'But was I Chuang-tzu dreaming I was a butterfly or am I a butterfly dreaming that I'm Chuang-tzu?'"

"I like that," she said, slicing the tart. "How often do you wake from a dream so vivid that for the first few minutes the dream is more real than your waking?"

"And too often, I wish the dream were real."

Theo ate the tart with relish, accepted a second slice. "Now may I see this picture we've been collaborating on?"

She opened her portfolio and took out the portrait. She'd executed it in pen and ink rather than watercolor. It was a three-quarters portrait, Theo's face turned away slightly and looking up. He had lifted his eyes to watch a blackbird, she recalled, and she had caught him quickly in the sketch. Dark eyes raised, the angled sweep of his cheekbones, regulation close-cut hair. There was a hint of a frown on his brow, giving him a quizzical expression, as if he was about to turn back and ask a question.

Theo examined the drawing. "I like it," he said. "You handle shading very well. What will you do with this?"

"I'm not sure." She let out a sigh, a breath she hadn't realized she'd been holding. "I wanted to draw your portrait but I didn't have any plans beyond that." She was stupid. So stupid. She couldn't keep the drawing. What if Jean-Paul found it?

"Could I buy it then? I'd like my father to have it."

"No, I mean, you don't need to pay for it. I'd like you to have it. Really." She put the drawing back in the portfolio and gave it to him.

"Thank you." He said this simply, accepting her gift without false protest. "I've enjoyed talking with you very much. Talking to someone who understands art. "

He turned over one of the blue-and-white plates and examined the marks on the back. He tapped the porcelain with a fingertip. "Late Ming dynasty, seventeenth century. 'Made for the Jade Hall' it says. That's another name for the Hanlin Academy, so the design is very apt if this plate was made for the academy."

"What's the Hanlin Academy?" she said. "A school?"

"Yes, like an elite university. It was for Imperial scholars, opened in Peking during the eighth century. The library there was the most important one in China, possibly the largest in the world. It burned down in 1900."

The spoils of war. Not just treasures stolen but also a library lost.

So much destruction then, so much now. Unbidden, tears came to Camille's eyes and she wiped them with her sleeve. Then she realized Theo was looking at her with concern.

"Please, what's wrong?" he said. He offered her his handkerchief. His voice was so gentle, so genuinely kind. "What have I said to upset you?"

"You've done nothing, it's just . . . a library burned down, it's so senseless," she said, sniffling. "This senseless war, which began for reasons I'll never understand, nothing that threatened France. I can't remember what it was like before. Before every day brought a death notice, someone you know. Before you kept track of places along your route for shelter in case of enemy aircraft.

"Usually I can cope," she continued, giving him back the handkerchief. "But sometimes I feel so helpless. I know others who have suffered worse, so much worse. My problems are silly and self-centered."

"I understand," Theo said. "There are catastrophes beyond our control, natural disasters, plagues and floods. Disasters made by governments, such as wars. But when it comes to our own small lives, surely we should be able to have our say. And when we don't, it makes us feel helpless. Tell me some of your silly problems."

What did it matter if she told him everything? Who could he tell that mattered? She had already broken down in front of him. "My problems? Not being able to continue my art lessons. Making a bad decision because I wanted to please my father. I should've made different decisions when I still could've had my say, as you put it. And now it's too late."

"It's not too late," he said. "You're young with many years ahead of you."

Camille shook her head. "You have no idea how being married can mean the end of so many dreams."

"I hadn't thought of it that way. The end of dreams." Something shifted in his gaze for a moment, as if his thoughts had turned inward.

"I haven't anyone to confide in," she said. Despite her best efforts, tears welled up again. "This is such a small town and everything is fodder for gossip. And now I've blurted out my troubles to you. I've gone and spoiled our picnic."

"Far from it," Theo said. "Don't you know you're my haven from the war, Camille? Please, don't cry. What can I do?"

"Put your arms around me," she whispered, not knowing what might come next. Perhaps he would give her an awkward pat on the back. Perhaps he would pull away.

But he didn't. They sat together for a long time in silence, his cheek resting on her hair, their fingers entwined. She pressed her face against his neck and breathed in the scent of his skin, that faint hint of citrus and cedar. He lifted her hand to his lips and held it there. When she raised her face to look at him, there was a question in his eyes.

She answered by pressing her lips to his.

CHAPTER 11

Tuesday, November 5, 1918

PAULINE

PAULINE SLIPPED OUT the door, almost catching her skirt as it swung shut.

It was early and there was plenty of time to get to the Gare du Nord, but she wanted to hurry away in case Denise woke up and decided to look out the window. She had left a note for Denise begging her to explain everything to her uncle. She promised to telegram as soon as she had found Theo. She could only hope Denise got over this betrayal and that her uncle didn't blame his mistress.

She wished her carpetbag wasn't so heavy, but she had taken an extra skirt, one in heavier wool in case of colder weather, then stuffed more stockings in the bag. The winter sun had not yet come up, and she had bundled up for a cold walk to the station. Her hat with the short veil felt itchy already. Thankfully the sturdy leather boots from the flea market were comfortable.

When she reached the corner, a dark-haired man wearing a knit cap and a long navy-blue coat crossed the street on the other side, walking away from Pauline. His height and haircut, the way he held himself quickened Pauline's heart and she almost called out before realizing it couldn't possibly be Theo. The last time she saw him had been at this very street corner, the two of them parting ways. She remembered it with painful clarity, how Theo had glanced back over his shoulder and smiled, his words drowned out by the noise of traffic, then turned and kept walking.

He used to tease her for being impulsive. Was she being impulsive now?

I can't just stay home and do nothing, Theo, she said to the memory of that beloved face. *I just can't, or my life will fall into an abyss.*

FORTY-FIVE MINUTES LATER SHE HELD Denise's carpetbag in front of her like a shield, pushing her way through the chaos of the Gare du Nord toward the ticket kiosks. From what Pauline could see, there wasn't a line, at least not an organized one. She wasn't aggressive enough to jostle her way closer, unlike the buxom woman who had started out beside her a few minutes ago and was now at the ticket window.

"You need to smile as you shove your way through," a familiar voice beside her remarked. French spoken with an accent. A slight Chinese accent, the way Theo used to speak it. Before they came to France, before he acquired a Parisian accent. "Push and elbow, but always smile. Anyway, you don't need to line up; I did manage to get tickets."

Pauline turned around to see Henri looking down at her, a rather anxious smile on his clean-shaven face. Whatever the state of his hair, it was hidden under a porkpie hat. His cheeks were pink from the cold, rosy as a child's. He carried a valise in one hand and a leather satchel was slung across his chest.

"Oh, it's you, Henri." Pauline tried to sound nonchalant but inwardly she gave a silent sigh of relief. He had come.

"Follow me," he said, beckoning. He reached inside the breast pocket of his coat and pulled out a pair of tickets. "Here, take one. The platform for our train is on the other side of the concourse. We can board now." Then tipping his hat, he pushed his way past an elderly couple.

"What about a place to stay?" Pauline said, hurrying behind.

"We'll have to wait until we get there," Henri said, "but once we're on the train there should be others heading for Noyelles, hopefully people who live there and know it better than I do. I'll ask around."

"You're so resourceful," she said. "I'm grateful for your help, really."

"I'm a journalist," he said, his smile pleased, less anxious. "We use ingenuity and charm to get information. Let's try this carriage." He took her carpetbag and they moved along the corridor until they found an empty compartment. "Do you want your bag overhead or under the seat?"

It would be well past four o'clock by the time their train reached Noyelles. They might be late, since civilian railway schedules were erratic with many delays; troops and supplies took precedence. Even with Henri beside her, Pauline didn't relish the thought of walking through Noyelles in the dark to search for lodgings. But she had set her plan in motion and there was no turning back.

They settled by the window facing each other. Their carriage hadn't yet filled up but the platform was getting busier, impatient travelers nudging and jostling to get to their trains, elderly men wrapped up in scarves and gloves, women dragging children by the hand, and everywhere, men in uniform. French, British, American, the occasional Italian and Portuguese uniforms. Canadian and Australian.

"I'm glad you're here," she said and turned back to the window.

Henri cleared his throat. "If you'd done this on your own and something happened to you, Pauline, I'd never forgive myself."

There was a long silence, and then Henri jumped up. "I see someone who might know about accommodations. Why is he riding on this train for civilians? I'll be right back."

He hopped off the carriage and hurried along the platform to greet a tall man in British uniform. The two shook hands. When the whistle blew, Henri helped the British officer hoist his duffel bag into a carriage and they both climbed on. The train pulled away from the platform and the sound of chatter inside melded with the rumble of the rails, which grew louder as they traveled faster.

IT WAS STILL EARLY, THE sun barely breaking over the horizon, and gray morning light revealed ugly neighborhoods near the station. Broken-windowed houses, blackened brick walls, backyards where laundry on clotheslines flapped above overgrown flower beds. It wasn't the Paris Pauline knew, the city that still glittered with elegance and allure even after being bombed, even with sandbags stacked against its monuments and strips of paper pasted over shop windows.

The view soon changed. Backyards became larger and tidier, fences behind shrubs of red rose hips that bobbed on leafless stems as the train rushed past. Kitchen gardens appeared, and apple and pear orchards bordered by poplars whose few remaining leaves flew off as a gust of wind stripped their branches. Beanpoles played host to the nasturtiums that had clambered over, draping them in cascades of wilting leaves, the orange blooms now spent. Between shrubby hedges and stands of birch trees, Pauline caught glimpses of neat cottages, bright window boxes.

Then the train rolled out past the city and into the countryside as the sun rose higher and Pauline saw real farmland for the first time, rolling fields of stubby harvested wheat, the golden colors even brighter where the horizon touched the sky. When Theo had taken her to see paintings at the Academy of Fine Arts, she'd been convinced some of the impressionist artists had exaggerated the contrast between sky and wheat. But seeing this, she doubted no longer.

A snatch of conversation caught her ear. "It took me a while to pick up the Shandong dialect but I managed to learn more from the workers while on the ship crossing over to Canada."

"Here I am, sorry to take so long." It was Henri. "Mystery solved, Pauline. My friend is riding with civilians because he wanted to escort some American ladies."

"Henri, introductions please," the sandy-haired man said. It was his voice she had heard talking about the crossing from Shandong to Canada. His insignia indicated he was a medical officer.

"Once again I fail at etiquette," Henri said. "Pauline Deng, this is my Canadian friend, Robert Adams. He speaks passable Mandarin, bad French, and terrible English. Bob, you may speak Mandarin or French to Mademoiselle Pauline Deng."

"I'm pleased to meet you, Monsieur Adams," she said. "Please, do you work at the camp hospital in Noyelles?"

"Since May of last year," he replied, also in Mandarin. Dr. Adams had a narrow face with a long nose, slightly bulbous at the end. He was rather homely but his eyes, hazel or green, she couldn't tell which, looked at her with friendly curiosity.

"Your Chinese is very good." She could detect only the slightest accent.

"You're very kind, mademoiselle. I was a missionary in China for some years."

"We met in England," Henri said, "when Robert took some leave in London before coming over to France."

"Henri explained the purpose of your trip to Noyelles, Mademoiselle Deng," he said. "Tell me more and perhaps I can help."

"I need to find where my cousin is right now," she said. "He was in

Noyelles until the end of August, when he was transferred to a different company because their interpreter fell ill. I don't even know the name of his new commanding officer."

The doctor nodded. "I can find out for you from the administration office. They should have your cousin's information on file."

A small knot Pauline hadn't been aware was in her neck dislodged. Surely this was a sign the gods were pleased with her, that they approved of her decision. How else to explain the gift that had just dropped in her lap? She leaned back on the wooden slats of the seat. Her coat felt more comfortable, her stockings less itchy.

"Would you know him?" she asked. "Theo Deng. Deng Taoling. He was in the hospital for a short time with influenza."

"I don't recall," the doctor said, "but those patients were kept in their own ward away from other patients and staff. I wasn't one of the doctors treating quarantined patients. I'm a surgeon."

"Robert has a cot in his office where I can sleep," Henri said, "but we haven't quite figured out where you could stay, Pauline."

"Isn't there a hotel near the railway station in Noyelles?"

"There is, but it's rather a rough one," Dr. Adams said.

"I don't need anything luxurious," she said, "just a bed and a wash-basin, really."

"Mademoiselle Deng, when I said rough I didn't mean the rooms were plain although they undoubtedly are," he said. "I meant the clientele and the area."

"It will be all right," she said. "It's just for a few nights."

The doctor looked doubtful.

SHE WAS REALLY ON HER way. With every mile of railway track that went by, more anxiety sloughed off Pauline's shoulders. She had worried about Henri agreeing to come, about getting to the Gare du Nord on time, about getting tickets for the train. As for Denise, whatever she chose to do, to telegram Louis now or wait until he came home, it was out of Pauline's hands.

The doctor had gone back to his carriage, to speak with the Americans. They were nurses, he said. Pauline hoped he came back soon to sit with them; his presence prevented her and Henri from conversation that ventured into the personal. Fortunately, Henri was preoccupied, pencil scribbling busily across a notepad, his expression serious, a slight squint as he worked.

Living in Paris, all Pauline knew of trees and plants was what she saw in parks and city streets. Box hedges and roses, pots of herbs and geraniums on windowsills. Outside, more fields and a forest, the distant gleam of water, the sheen of sunlight on a pond as the landscape alternated between harvested fields of grain and sprawling untended land. With so many able-bodied men called to fight, too much farmland lay fallow, too much work for the women and elderly left behind.

The door from the vestibule opened and Dr. Adams came in. He sat down beside Henri, looking pleased.

"Mademoiselle Deng, I've taken the liberty of finding you accommodations in Noyelles," he said. "The young women in the other carriage are nurses reporting for duty at a small private hospital run by an American, Mrs. Newland. Her daughter accompanies the nurses. I spoke with her and she feels certain they can find a bed for you."

"How can I ever thank you, Doctor?" Pauline said. "You didn't have to do this for me."

"Nonsense. I'd feel terrible if you ended up at the train station hotel."

PAULINE HADN'T COUNTED ON SO many stops along the line. Amiens, Picquigny, Hangest, Longpré, Pont-Remy, Abbeville. At every station, signs of the war. Uniforms and wounded men. Railcars shunted off to the side waiting to be loaded with supplies.

Amiens had been evacuated in April when the Germans began shelling the town. The train station was damaged, but once the Allies secured Amiens, it was the first building restored to working order. The approach to the town was lined with burnt-out barns and farm equipment abandoned in fields. Closer in to the city, the remains of homes and shops were everywhere. Ruined buildings, houses with charred walls and fallen roofs. Staircases climbed up to empty door-ways, and a church crouched like a stone skeleton, vaulted arches for ribs, its bell tower a long, headless neck. There had been cleanup ef-forts, though; there were slate roof tiles stacked against walls and cra-ters filled with gravel.

Paris had endured bombing raids, but nothing like this. Until she saw Amiens, Pauline had not imagined so much destruction.

At Amiens the conductor announced a one-hour delay and Dr. Ad-ams offered to get off the train and bring back something to eat, an early evening meal. He walked briskly, obviously familiar with the streets. He returned with a paper bag and passed around bread and cheese, opened a packet of sliced ham. The bread was good, slathered with real butter, not the strange-tasting margarine that was all they could get sometimes in Paris.

Henri finished his sandwich and was about to say something when he stood up and ran to the other side of the carriage to look out the window. In the rail yard, a locomotive was slowing down. It pulled a dozen open flatcars with tanks chained down to their decks. Six Chinese men were perched on the flatcars, some riding on top of the tanks. When the train stopped, the men jumped off to walk around. Henri opened the vestibule door at the end of the carriage and got out, climbed over the coupling between carriages and hurried over the tracks to the flatcars.

The workers were tall and brawny, dressed in long winter coats and close-fitting caps with earflaps. Pauline saw that all the tanks were damaged; some had no turrets and others were missing sides, their machinery showing. Henri spoke to a Chinese man who, unlike the others, wore a military-style uniform decorated with two stripes. A young British officer joined them, nodding his head and gesturing at the tanks. Then the train began moving again and the Chinese man shouted for the workers to get back on. The officer slapped each worker on the shoulder in a friendly way as they climbed on.

Pauline could hear them singing as the train gathered speed.

"Those fellows are working with the British Tank Corps," Henri said when he returned to their compartment. "I've heard that CLC men are working there, but couldn't get permission to visit the central workshops where they do all the repairs. Its location is a secret. That officer didn't tell me where, either, but he did confirm that CLC mechanics do practically all the maintenance and repairs on tanks."

"Some of those tanks looked like salvage," Dr. Adams said.

"The ganger said they go with the salvage team so they can look around for spare parts and assess which tanks are worth bringing back. He said they've rebuilt tanks that are in worse shape than what's on those flatcars."

"Do you know that song they're singing?" she said. "Weren't they singing in English?"

Henri turned deep red and Dr. Adams laughed. "Mademoiselle Deng, it's a very crude song. They probably learned it from Australian soldiers."

DAYLIGHT HAD VANISHED BY THE time they arrived at Noyelles-sur-Mer, nearly two hours later than scheduled. Pauline shivered when she stepped onto the platform and quickly tugged on her gloves. Dr. Adams took her over to a group of women.

"This is Frances Newland," Dr. Adams said, speaking French. "Frances, this is Pauline Deng."

Pauline's first thought was that Frances Newland dressed very modestly for a wealthy American. Her clothing was well-tailored, the wide collar of her camel coat was edged with braided trim, but otherwise plain. The four American nurses behind her, busily pointing out their trunks to the porters, were more stylishly dressed. Her smile, however, was very sweet and sincere.

"Mademoiselle Deng, please come with me," Frances said. Her French was perfect. "Have you any luggage?"

"This is everything." Pauline held up Denise's carpetbag. "Thank you, Mademoiselle Newland, thank you so much for your kind offer."

"*À demain,* Pauline," Henri said. "I'll meet you at the hospital tomorrow morning at nine."

"Yes, just come to the hospital tomorrow," Dr. Adams said, "Frances, give my best to your mother."

The two men strode off along the platform and for a moment Pauline wanted to run after them. But she tore her gaze away and followed Frances Newland and the nurses out to the street, where a charabanc drawn by four horses waited. The coachman helped them climb on. Pauline was the last, and he gave her a quizzical but not unfriendly look. There were three rows of seats in the charabanc and he piled their luggage behind the rear seat. The four American nurses gave her curious glances but didn't speak to her. Frances sat with her in the second row.

So this was Noyelles, where Theo had been living most of the time. The train station was at the edge of town and evidently there was no need to go through town to get to the château.

"There it is," Frances said, pointing at a long barrier of posts and barbed wire. "That fence surrounds the Chinese workers' camp."

Inside were rows of Nissen huts and wooden bunkhouses. The fence stretched on for what seemed like half a mile, with an opening at the center where a soldier in British uniform stood guard by the gate. He waved at the nurses from his sentry post, called out something jocular that made the women hoot. Topped with coils of barbed wire, the camp resembled a stockade that kept its occupants inside like prisoners.

"It was disturbing for me, too, the first time I saw it," Frances said, seeing Pauline's expression.

Like the town, the camp was under blackout but a light breeze carried to them the smells and noises of meals being prepared, and with it, the sound of men's voices talking and laughing. Pauline sniffed the evening air and the creases on her forehead smoothed out. Rice. It was suppertime and they were cooking rice. Somehow it comforted her to know that her countrymen, so far from home, had rice to eat.

The vehicle bumped over a hole that had been roughly filled in, and then another one. A scorched crater at the side of the road and a burnt-out farmhouse were evidence of how the holes in the road had been made. Pauline shuddered. She was behind the front lines but still within reach of German aircraft.

"Don't worry," Frances said. "There haven't been aerial attacks all year. The Germans are too busy elsewhere. Anyway, the château has a large red cross painted on the tennis court. They won't bomb us there."

Ten minutes later, the horses clopped through wrought-iron gates and down a broad sweeping driveway, wheels crunching on pea gravel. The château wasn't what Pauline usually pictured when she thought of that word. It was large but not immense or ancient. It was a three-story house of gray stone, topped by a mansard roof with a row of dormer windows. The château's main building was flanked by two wings at right angles, enclosing three sides of a large garden. It was the style of grand house one could see in Paris, discreetly shielded behind hedges of yew and vine-covered walls, only much bigger.

Four steps led to a marble terrace and the front door opened, releasing a sheet of light. Evidently, Mrs. Newland wasn't concerned about the blackout. The charabanc pulled up to the terrace steps and a stout, well-dressed woman came out the door, head turned to speak to the slim younger woman who followed behind, listening intently. Pauline caught a snatch of conversation, instructions about embroidery and mending, the older woman's French fluent if rather oddly accented.

The stout woman called out something in English and Frances replied.

Pauline hung back, standing by the horses. Servants carried the nurses' luggage and boxes into the house. The coachman led the horses and wagon away, leaving Pauline to stand uncertainly at the bottom of the terrace steps, staying close to Frances. Mrs. Newland finished her discussion with the young Frenchwoman, who carried a canvas bag in her arms. A laundress, perhaps.

Frances gestured for Pauline to come up the terrace, into the light.

"Mother, this is Pauline Deng," she said, in French. "I met her on the train. Dr. Adams introduced us. She needs a bed for a few nights."

Pauline thought she heard a gasp from the laundress. Mrs. Newland didn't hold out her hand, just looked down at Pauline and pursed her lips. Unsure of what to do, Pauline settled for a quick curtsy.

"Really, Frances," the woman said. She spoke in French but acted as though Pauline wasn't there. "I'm surprised you'd bring some unknown Chinese person to our home. We're not a charity."

"I do not expect free lodgings, madame," Pauline said, ignoring the insult. "Please let me know what to pay."

"She should stay at a hotel," Mrs. Newland said, still addressing her daughter. "Or at the camp with others of her kind." Mrs. Newland went inside and closed the door, leaving Pauline in darkness and silence, Frances and the young woman with the laundry bag witness to her humiliation.

"Pauline, I'm so sorry," Frances said. "Mother can be such a snob. But what she doesn't know won't upset her. I'll find you a bed in the servants' quarters downstairs for a few nights and you'll be fine. Mother will never know since she never goes belowstairs. If you don't mind, of course."

But Pauline did mind. She didn't want to be in a place where she wasn't welcome. She'd rather pay for a bad hotel room.

"I don't want you disobeying your mother," Pauline said, shaking her head. "It's quite all right, I'll walk back to the train station and see about getting a room at the hotel there."

"If I may interrupt." It was the laundress. The moon came out from the clouds for a moment and lit the Frenchwoman's hair, smoothly pulled back into a tight braided bun. She was thin, with a small, plain face.

"Pauline, this is my friend Camille Roussel," Frances said.

"There are no rooms left at the hotel, and anyway it's not a nice place," Camille said, "but perhaps I can help. There's a hut in our garden, a garden room separate from the main house, it has a daybed. I'd be happy for you to take it. I live but a thirty-minute walk from here."

Pauline hadn't realized there was a knot in her stomach until it loosened. "I would be very grateful to stay with you."

Camille hesitated, looking embarrassed. "Please understand, mademoiselle. I don't want to ask for payment, but my husband will want something."

"Madame Roussel, it's kind of you to even offer." Pauline took out some bills from the purse tucked under her arm. "Will this do? If all goes well, I will only stay until Friday."

"This will more than do for until Friday. This is even enough to pay for meals." Camille smiled. "That is, if you're willing to eat my cooking, mademoiselle."

Pauline changed her mind. When she smiled, Camille Roussel was not plain.

CAMILLE

CAMILLE'S HANDS GRIPPED the handlebar tightly as she wheeled her bicycle out from the alcove at the side of the château. She went through the motions of checking that the trailer was securely attached, then tied a woolen scarf around her head, but her mind was churning.

Pauline Deng. This was Theo's cousin, it had to be.

He had said they looked alike, and she could see his features echoed in Pauline's. The same clean sweep of forehead, the set of her eyes and high cheekbones. Where Theo's jaw was strong and angled, Pauline's softened down to a small chin, making her look far younger than her years.

Theo couldn't have been expecting his cousin or he would've been at the station. And obviously Pauline didn't know Theo was at the Wimereux camp right now. Perhaps she had bad news to tell him and wanted to do it in person. Perhaps something had happened to his father.

Whatever the reason, for Theo's sake she had to look after Pauline, make sure she was safe. Even if she risked Jean-Paul's anger. Camille debated telling Pauline that she knew Theo, but it would lead to further questions even if she said they were just acquaintances. Theo hadn't mentioned her to his family; an affair with a married woman was not something to put in a letter. It was his right to decide when to tell them. If he ever needed to tell them.

She wheeled the bicycle and trailer around to the front of the mansion and put Pauline's carpetbag in the trailer on top of the laundry bag. The Chinese woman looked tired, no doubt drained after a long day of travel. And although she smiled back at Camille, there was something guarded in her expression. Who could blame her, after meeting Mrs. Newland?

"Let's go. It won't take long," she said to Pauline. They made their way down the long driveway toward the road, Camille pushing the bicycle, Pauline walking beside it.

"You're very brave to travel on your own," Camille said.

"I didn't come alone. Our friend Henri came with me," Pauline said. "I'm sorry to slow you down. If you were cycling, you'd get home sooner."

"There's no rush, my husband doesn't get home until much later tonight so I don't need to make supper yet," Camille said.

Above them the full moon gleamed like a silver coin, casting its cold light over the fields, and a veil of mist rose from the ground. It was a perfect night for an air raid, but she didn't say this to Pauline. Camille was accustomed to the road and from time to time murmured a warning to Pauline about a pothole or a crumbling bank.

"Do you work at the château?" Pauline asked.

"No, no. I work at the post office. But I do mending and sewing for the château quite often. Their laundresses are too busy these days to do the sewing."

Since Mme Newland turned her home into a hospital, the château's laundry staff were busy every day washing bed linens and bandages. The stoves continuously boiled vats of water to rid blankets and clothing of lice. They could barely keep up, let alone mend clothes or sew buttons back on.

Noticing again how tired Pauline looked, Camille said, "It's not that far to walk now. See that old barn out there in the field? It's halfway between the château and my home. But what brings you to Noyelles?"

"My cousin," said the girl. "He's with the Chinese Labour Corps. An interpreter."

"You're visiting him, then?" Camille asked.

"He doesn't know I've come. There is a . . . a family situation and I need his help."

"He works here, in Noyelles then?"

Pauline shook her head. "He's at another camp right now. But I'll know tomorrow. I'm meeting someone at the Chinese hospital who will find out for me. Where is the hospital? I didn't see it on the way in."

"It's behind the camp," Camille said. "You wouldn't be able to see it in the dark. If you like, I can take you there in the morning. It's on my way to work."

Another fifteen minutes and then a gentle rise. Camille's pace never slowed as she pushed her bicycle up the incline. At the crest of the hill she pointed out the cottage, its two chimneys and slate roof. Without being asked, Pauline ran ahead as they neared and opened the garden gate for Camille.

Camille leaned her bicycle against the side of the cottage by the kitchen door and took Pauline's carpetbag from the trailer.

"Come," she said. "The garden path is made from crushed white shells so you should be able to see the way. It stands out at night, especially under moonlight."

The year after they moved out of the château, Camille had helped Auguste make the path. She poured and raked crushed oyster shell over the gravel base while her father built the large shed he called his garden room. For the rest of the week she would come out after dark to admire the path, the way the white shell gleamed.

Every now and then the carpetbag brushed against shrubs at the edge of the path. Even in winter the dry leaves held their perfume and released their scent into the night. Camille had planted lavender and rosemary there on purpose. The familiar fragrances calmed her.

"My father called it his garden room," Camille said, opening the door. "It's just a big shed with a window and porch. After my father died, my husband rented it to workers who came for the harvest. But not anymore of course."

"Why not?" Pauline said.

She sighed. "It's the war. Fewer workers are going from farm to farm. The local farmers have been struggling the best they can. All we have are old men and their womenfolk working the fields. The harvest was very bad this year."

Inside, Camille lit an oil lamp and made up a daybed with sheets and quilts from the chest of drawers that also served as a low table. She pointed to the chamber pot under the bed, which she suggested Pauline use for now rather than walking through the dark for the outhouse. Pauline turned down her offer of food, saying all she wanted was to lie down. She had started out from Paris very early in the morning.

With a reminder not to open the window shutters at night due to the blackout, and to come to the house for breakfast, Camille left her guest. She wondered again what family crisis had brought Pauline to Noyelles. Although Pauline spoke politely, there was a tightness in her voice and whenever the forced smile left her face, what remained was anxiety.

On the path back to the cottage, Camille couldn't help leaning down to pull some leaves from a lavender shrub, rub them between her fingers, breathe in the remnants of summer.

Jean-Paul would be home any minute. Fortunately, she didn't have to prepare a meal. She built up the fire inside the stove and heated leftover bean soup, sliced some bread and cheese. In the morning, perhaps the hens would have an egg or two for their breakfast.

Then she settled in the dining room with a bag of mending. Uniform jackets missing their buttons, trousers with small tears and frayed seams. A skirt of fine wool, the embroidered hem torn. The garden gate's creak warned Camille of Jean-Paul's return. She put down the sewing and peeked through the parlor's heavy curtains just to be sure, then hurried to the kitchen and gave the fire in the wood-stove a poke.

When Jean-Paul came in, he said nothing, just dropped his knapsack on the floor and sat in a chair. Camille knelt and unlaced his boots, pulled them off. She put the boots beside the stove to dry and brought over his slippers.

He rolled a cigarette and smoked while she set the kitchen table. She didn't like him smoking indoors but said nothing. When she brought the pot to the table, he threw his cigarette stub into the stove's fire-box. He began ripping off chunks of bread as she ladled the bean soup into a bowl.

"You stopped at the château today, right?" He tore off some more bread from the loaf. "I ran into Lucie on her way home."

"Yes, they had some sewing for me," she said. Then she held out Pauline's money. "Jean-Paul, we have a lodger in the garden room until Friday. A woman from Paris. Room and board."

"From Paris? Ah." He counted the bills. "So you let her think a room here costs the same as a hotel room in Paris? Well done."

He stuffed the money in his wallet and gulped down the soup. When dining with others, he ate carefully, minding his manners, but without an audience he wolfed down his food as though he were still a feral waif.

"She'll join us for breakfast in the morning," Camille said, relieved that the money had put Jean-Paul in a good mood. "Her name is Pauline. Pauline Deng. She is Chinese."

"What is she? A camp follower? Well, as long as she doesn't bring any of those *jaunes* back here." He stood up from the table and wiped his mouth on his sleeve.

"No, she is a very decent young woman. She's here to see her cousin. He's an interpreter."

Almost casually and without warning Jean-Paul slapped Camille across the face, making her stagger against the table. Yet he was smiling. Still in good humor.

"That's for bringing someone to our home without first asking permission. And a Chinoise too." He patted his wallet with a grin. "But I hope she stays longer. A few more days of rent is welcome."

Camille brought the bag of mending into the kitchen where she continued sewing at the large oak table. She knew Jean-Paul liked watching her work in the kitchen, a picture of domestic tranquility. His devoted wife. His obedient wife. He finished his tumbler of cognac, the bottle a gift from Marcel, and made his way up the stairs, his footsteps heavy on the treads. She heard the bedframe creak. She kept on sewing.

CHAPTER 12

Letters from Theo

JUNE 20, 1918

Little cousin,

I'm not sending you this letter, but I had to write something, get my feelings out. There are days when I can no longer keep despair and horror at bay. Perhaps by setting down these memories they will leave my head and stay on the paper, and when I burn these pages their smoke will rise to heaven and the gods will know what has come to pass here.

You must know by now that the Allies are making a big push, hopefully the final one.

All the CLC companies are working day and night to keep the front supplied. Guns, ammunition, fuel, blankets, cans of beef, tins of hard biscuits, sacks of potatoes, even hay for the poor warhorses, all must be loaded onto trucks. It's a never-ending convoy that can't stop or else the soldiers stop advancing. My company, well-accustomed by now to the work of loading and unloading, didn't need me to explain or to communicate the urgency of the situation. They could see the number of troops marching for the front.

Another company lost their interpreter to illness and my
commanding officer loaned me to them just for a few days. It was
a company clearing trenches, preparing for another assault.

It was horrible work even though it was behind the lines in
an area where the fighting was over—for the moment. They
had to work fast in case the battle moved in again. Rather than
stand aboveground the whole time, I climbed into the trenches
to help.

The luckier worked at extending the trenchworks, digging new
ones, laying down duckboards, and shoring up their sides with
lumber. It's work the British Royal Engineers would be doing if
there were enough of them.

The unlucky ones cleared existing trenches. "Clearing
trenches" is a misnomer, Pauline. It is soul-destroying work.

Many sections of the trenches were still waterlogged, and we
waded through large puddles of muddy water surfaced with a slick
film of petrol. At times we worked knee-high in mud and filthy
water that covered the entire length of a trench. I helped pull out
rotten wood and rusty weapons, threw them onto a canvas tarp
that other workers lifted out of the trench. I ignored the bloated
corpses of rats, tried not to think of the lice and fleas that had
already jumped into my clothes. The stench that rose up as the day
wore on was horrible. Spent shells littered the ground and sharp
edges of shrapnel jutted out from trench walls and the ground,
but at least those perils were visible. We were careful where
we stepped, poking in puddles with long sticks before wading
through. We dug drainage ditches to get the water out.

On the second day I removed debris, carried up pails of metal
shards, bundles of shattered timber. This crew was experienced.
If there was a buried piece of metal, they halted work and dug

carefully around the edges until they were certain they hadn't found some unexploded munition.

I used both pickax and crowbar to pry loose the logs and boards shoring up the trench walls. A rat leaped out from between two boards when I struck them with my pickax, and I lost my balance, stumbling back to the opposite wall. I leaned to rest against it, only to startle again at the thing that brushed the back of my head. A decomposed arm stuck out from the trench wall, dangling at the elbow. The man had fallen at the edge of the trench and his corpse had been trampled over and buried under dirt and debris as the months wore on. A dirty uniform cuff showed the soldier had been a corporal, and German. I retched into the foul water, not the first man to have done so that day.

Then I heard cries of protest farther along the trench. I dropped my tools and headed for the uproar, a ganger trying to explain something to his British sergeant while workers behind him shouted and gestured. They paused their shouting to let me speak with the ganger.

"It's considered extremely bad luck to handle corpses unless the proper rituals have been observed," I said to the sergeant. "The men say corpses weren't in their contract."

"Whenever they don't like doing something they say it isn't in the contract," the sergeant snapped. "But the job is to clear out the trenches and if there's bodies in there, you clear them out. If they're British or French, get them on that truck. We'll give them a proper burial. German bodies on another truck." He pulled his pistol from its holster. "Tell them it's in my contract to shoot them if they don't obey."

There was no need to interpret that gesture. The men's faces were grim and sullen.

"The sergeant says that since the dead are foreigners, they will be given proper rituals according to foreign custom," I told the men, "and the officers will also pray to their foreign god to bless you for your kindness."

To show them it was all right, I joined the crew handling corpses. We had gloves and used shovels whenever possible to move bodies onto canvas tarps, rolling up each one and carrying it up the ladder. We laid each bundle on the ground and went back down, going to wherever workers shouted, "Here's another one!"

There were too many bodies, Pauline. Soldiers fallen and left to die by exhausted comrades who never realized they were missing, left behind when the retreat sounded, or when their company advanced over the top. The hard-packed dirt was foul, an odorous reek of excrement, and the ground had absorbed a smell of rotten garlic from mustard gas. My eyes watered. I tied my kerchief tightly around my mouth and nose. It didn't block out the smell, but it made me feel better to have something between my lungs and the foul air.

The crew worked almost without pause until the trenches were clear of dangerous objects. The next day they climbed down with fresh timber to reinforce the walls, dug and filled where needed. Extended the lines farther. Prepared for more death.

I was there for three days. My clothing was soiled with mud, oily water, and worse. I don't see how even ten washings can ever remove the stink, or how my mind will ever erase the horrors. I thought of the patients at the Chinese hospital's mental ward. The one who shrieked at any small noise. The one who was only calm when making willow baskets. The one who gazed with blank eyes at the wall. They could face drought and bad harvests, hunger, and backbreaking work. But they were boys, just peasant boys from rural China. They never imagined living in a guarded camp or getting flogged by commanders who thought they'd disobeyed orders. Or death exploding from the skies.

When the trucks came to take us back to camp that evening, I found myself sitting beside the ganger who'd been arguing with the sergeant.

"Foreign rituals for the dead," the ganger snorted. He took a drink of cold tea from his canteen, accepted the cigarette I offered. "How does that work? No incense, no paper money or paper houses to burn. There will be hungry ghosts haunting this land for centuries."

But do our gods pay attention to what happens outside China, even if it's to our own people? Perhaps they do, but have no jurisdiction, as they say in the military.

Only when I'm with Camille can I forget the horror. I will tell you about her one day. She's my north star, guiding me toward joy. T.

AUGUST 30, 1918

Dear Pauline,

I apologize for not writing more regularly. I've hardly had any days off except for sick leave, nothing to worry about, I was lucky to get over this terrible influenza very quickly. When I do have time off, I visit the hospital at Noyelles where I've been volunteering my services as letter writer.

I got Father's letter that he's on his way to Shanghai for Grandfather Deng's funeral rites. I will find some incense to burn for Grandfather, or at least burn something aromatic. His death will change much back in Shanghai and therefore also in Paris.

The Allies are pushing hard to end this war. Our company is

being moved around a lot, so I'm not in Noyelles anymore. In fact, I am now with a different company, filling in for their interpreter who's in the hospital with influenza.

When I'm settled in the new camp I promise you a long letter, and then you'll have my latest address. Until then, there's no point in you writing.

T.

CHAPTER 13

Noyelles, August 1918

The long summer days were their ally. It was still light when Camille left work in the afternoon and remained so until nine o'clock. It meant no one would wonder if they saw her taking a walk or gathering field greens after suppertime because one made best use of daylight hours. It meant no one would remark on the quilt she hung out to air because every housewife was doing the same. It was just one of the signals she and Theo shared to let each other know when it was safe to meet.

They no longer used the woods. The coppice was common property, anyone could come upon them while cutting wood or foraging. Now they met in the garden room, Theo ducking into the field beside the cottage and pushing his way through the laurel hedge at the back of the garden.

When she thought of Theo, Camille wanted to dance the way she did when she was a little girl, before she'd been fettered by all the rules of etiquette and the prim steps of dancing lessons, when she would spin and spin until she was giddy, arms flying like a pinwheel, face turned up to the sky. She had done this just a day ago while taking laundry off the clothesline. She had looked up at the sky, at the coral-pink streaks of sunset, and begun twirling on the tips of her toes, pirouetting until she stumbled, helpless from vertigo, and fell laughing against the apple tree. Because finally, and for the first time in her life, she knew what she was feeling, she could put a name to the longing and the delight.

But how did Theo feel about her? The giddy sensation faded away.

She wasn't sweet-faced like Jehane at the bakery, eyes like violets and hair a mass of chestnut curls. When unpinned from the chignon, Camille's hair hung straight down her back, fine and wispy, not quite brown, not quite blond. She didn't have a seductive shape like Marianne, the mayor's daughter, whose figure in marble could've graced a Grecian temple. She put her hands to her bosom, breasts that were mere buds, a schoolgirl's breasts. She touched the hollows at her throat, felt the clavicles. Too bony, she was too thin.

Theo didn't seem to mind. He was passionate, there was no doubt about that, yet their intimacies had not yet gone past kisses and caresses. Even timid Édouard Dumont, while courting her, had taken more liberties than Theo.

How did Theo feel about her? Did it matter?

Loving is what makes you happy, not being loved. Those were the last words Grand-mère said to her. Was it true? Édouard Dumont had said he loved Camille, but being loved by Édouard hadn't made her happy. When Jean-Paul said he loved her, she believed he did, in his own way, but his kind of love didn't make her happy. She knew how she felt about Theo, and loving him made her happy. It was all that mattered.

"Hello?"

And suddenly he was there, his arms wrapped around her, his lips brushing the back of her neck. Camille turned around to face him, returned his kisses, until they both laughed simply from the sheer pleasure of being together. If only they could've stood there forever, her head pressed against his shoulder, the warmth of his hands on her back.

"You're early," Camille murmured. "Don't you need to stay in Crécy Forest with your company?"

"I generally stay with the men until early afternoon," Theo said. "Any problems are usually sorted out by then. But they've been doing this work for months so at the start of day, they just need to know how many fascines to make up."

Outside, the sun was slipping down into the fields, glints of gold where it shone through a row of poplars. Farmers and workers had finished for the day and had gone home to their suppers. Inside the garden room, light from its one window laid a long runner of bright-ness on the floor.

"I got up early and baked bread," she said, pulling him down to sit on the threadbare rug. "So for dinner we have fresh bread with last year's plum jam and real butter. Sit here, have some."

She uncovered the basket and handed him a bun wrapped in a linen napkin. He sniffed appreciatively and took a bite.

"It's so good it doesn't need any jam but I'll have some," he said. "Whenever Denise baked bread, Pauline and I found all sorts of ex-cuses for running upstairs to see her."

When they'd finished the meal, he spooned up the last of the jam to clean out the jar and gave her the spoon to lick. Then they lay down together on the narrow daybed. There was a stillness about Theo, a despondency in his silence.

"Did something happen today?" she said.

"Zhao died," he said.

"He was your friend, wasn't he?" she said. "The one whose son fi-nally wrote back?"

The village letter-writer had died, the son explained. They'd had to wait until an itinerant letter-writer passed through before they could read Zhao's latest letter and reply to him.

"Zhao suffered a heart attack," Theo said. "He lied about his age, you know. He told me he's actually fifty-five, not forty."

"The way you described him, I always thought if anyone got through this war unscathed, it would be Zhao," Camille said. "He had already survived so much in China."

"When I first came here, I would fall sleep wondering if the next day might be my last." He pulled her closer. "A railway accident, a stray bomb, infection, I didn't use to worry. But now I'm more cautious. I worry and it's because of you, Camille. I want more time with you."

"And I've become more reckless since meeting you," she said. "Theo, any day could be the last for any of us. Let's appreciate what we have right now, stop worrying about tomorrow."

He didn't reply, just lifted her face to his, his eyes dark and intense, fixed on hers. They undressed each other, haste making them awkward, until they slid under the thin coverlet and soon there was no need for words, only the heat of his body against hers, the shuddering pressure of his weight, the soft breath of his sighs. Only what she had been wanting for such a long time.

Outside, summer's splendor concealed the garden room behind shrubs of yellow rhododendrons and blue hydrangea, fragrant mock orange, and cascades of red, clove-scented climbing roses.

CAMILLE AND THEO HAD BEEN lucky.

No, they had been careful.

But still, they were lucky that Jean-Paul signed up for every extra shift he could get, going away for two or three days at a time, busy working for the Nord and on whatever it was he handled for Marcel. Lucky that it had been a golden, sun-drenched summer and that they had the garden room, a shelter built for warm days.

But at the end of August, Theo had to leave Noyelles.

"It couldn't go on forever," he murmured, stroking Camille's hair. "I'll come back as often as I can."

An interpreter at the Wimereux forestry camp had been hospitalized with influenza. The commanding officer there requested a temporary replacement and Theo was assigned. The train from Noyelles to Wimereux made a long stop at the port of Boulogne so the trip each way took nearly three hours. It would be impossible for Theo to come back regularly without people remarking on it.

"When?" she said, wanting to cry. "When do you think you can get leave?"

"Perhaps in a couple of months? I can write and let you know."

"No. If either of the Dumonts get to the post before I do and find a letter for me, even without a return address, they would ask questions." Camille shook her head.

"What if I find someone discreet to deliver a letter by hand?"

"But who can you trust?" For news of Theo, she was tempted to take a risk, but shook her head again.

"When I come back from Wimereux," he said, "we'll find a way to be together. When the war ends, we'll get away from here, away from your husband."

"Please don't do anything rash," she said. "If Jean-Paul finds out . . . I couldn't bear it if something happened to you."

"What's unbearable," Theo said, "is the thought of leaving Noyelles once the war is over and never seeing you again. I'm more afraid of that than anything else. I'd kill Jean-Paul if I thought I could get away with it."

"Well, one step at a time," she said, giving him her brightest smile. "The easiest thing is to come by the post office when you're back. Buy a stamp or something."

CHAPTER 14

Wednesday, November 6, 1918

PAULINE

PAULINE WOKE UP to frigid air, unfamiliar sounds, and an unfamiliar room. She sat up, then sank back on the bed. In Paris her mornings began with the crooning of pigeons on the window ledge, the soft flutter of wings as they took off. She liked to lie in bed for a moment and listen to the noise of traffic on the Rue de Lisbonne, the cheerful greetings as neighbors opened their doors and swept the sidewalks, the jingle of bicycle bells as errand boys made morning deliveries, the clatter of wagons.

Here, only an occasional birdcall broke the utter silence. She opened the window shutters and startled at the beat of wings followed by loud scolding squawks from high up in the trees. A crow. On the porch she found a jug of water on the wicker chair, the water still warm, and a basin with towels folded inside, a bar of soap on top. Pauline washed her face and straightened her clothes. She had to look decent if she was going to speak with British officers. She had hung her jacket over a chair last night, so even though her blouse was wrinkled, the jacket would hide the worst of it.

She followed the garden path to the kitchen door and knocked. A man's voice called to enter. Inside, welcoming warmth and Camille's slim form by the stove cracking eggs into a bowl. There was a man seated at the table, one hand around a mug of what smelled like coffee, real coffee, the other holding a sheet of paper. He looked at her with blue eyes that were startlingly pale, rimmed with thick dark lashes.

"Jean-Paul, this is Mademoiselle Pauline Deng," Camille said. "Mademoiselle, my husband, Jean-Paul."

"Do you speak French, mademoiselle?" He pronounced each word very slowly and carefully. And loudly.

Pauline smiled politely. "For the past ten years."

"Unbelievable!" He slapped his thigh and laughed. "Why didn't they hire you as an interpreter? Most of the ones I've met are useless." He turned back to study the paper, a hand-drawn map.

"Mademoiselle, please sit down," Camille put cutlery on the table. "Is an omelet all right? With food rationing, so many things are hard to get."

"Eggs are so hard to come by in Paris. An omelet would be wonderful."

The smell of eggs and butter filled the kitchen, and something else, an herb she couldn't identify. Within minutes Camille put a plate in front of her and another for Jean-Paul, then returned to the stove where she took a kettle off the burner and poured some hot water into the large stone sink. She rolled up her sleeves and began washing pans.

"People tell me Camille is a wonderful cook," Jean-Paul said, waving his fork, "but I'm just a country boy, not a gourmet. Food is food, and all I want is enough to fill my belly."

"This omelet is delicious. The bread, too."

"My wife tells me you're here because of your cousin." He smeared fruit preserves on a thick slice of bread.

"Yes, there's a family emergency and I need his help," Pauline said.

"I'm hoping he can take a few days of leave and come back to Paris. But I don't know where Theo's company is right now."

"Theo," he said, musingly. "Can't say I've met anyone by that name, and I do business with a few of them. Clever, some of your people. Unexpectedly so."

"Please, Camille, let me help wash up?" Pauline said, not wanting to sit at the table any longer.

"No, there's no need." Camille reached for a dishcloth and as she stretched out her arm, her sleeve pulled up a little more and Pauline noticed a bruise on her forearm, just below the elbow.

Jean-Paul tore off another large chunk of bread and ate with an intensity that defied interruption. When he was done, he pulled a dark-green coat off a wooden peg by the kitchen door, wrapped a brown woolen scarf around his neck. Then he turned as if he'd just remembered he had a guest, that some extra courtesy was required of him.

"Please excuse me. I must get to work now."

When the door shut behind Jean-Paul, Pauline felt something in the air shift, as though the kitchen had just exhaled or a window had opened to let in the breeze. Even Camille seemed different, brighter and somehow more vivid. Visible.

Camille opened a window and a chill draft of air blew in. "Just for a minute, if you don't mind. My husband's tobacco is particularly pungent. He has a friend who gives it to him. I don't think he actually likes it, but he smokes it to please his friend."

"What is your husband's line of work?" Pauline only asked to be polite. To show some interest.

"He's a railway mechanic with the Chemin de fer du Nord. It keeps him very busy. He also does a bit of trading, bartering used goods." Her smile was rather forced. "We don't need to leave for another twenty minutes. Enough time to enjoy some tea. And there's even a little bit of sugar."

She handed Pauline a teaspoon and a small bowl of sugar. It was glazed in blue and white. Out of habit, Pauline lifted it up to inspect the bottom. "This is Chinese," she said. "Not very old, but a nice piece."

"It's one of the souvenirs my father brought back from his time in China," Camille said. "Here's another; it's very simple, but I like it more than all the others." She reached for a jar sitting on the fireplace mantel and handed it to Pauline.

The jar was rounded, with a wide mouth, glazed in plain white with a design of lotus petals carved into the glaze. The finial on its lid was shaped like a tiny, tightly furled lotus bud. Pauline lifted the lid and peered in.

"I use it for storing chamomile tea," Camille said. "It's a plain thing, but of all the souvenirs my father brought back, this one is my favorite."

"It's lovely," Pauline said and put it back on the mantel. "Take very good care of it."

THEY SET OFF FOR NOYELLES, Camille pushing her bicycle so that she could walk with Pauline. In daylight, Pauline saw the gravel road they had taken the night before, the main road to Noyelles, just wide enough for two vehicles to pass. Tall trees lined both sides of the road, the ground beneath their branches a muddy red brown, a layer of fallen leaves crushed to a wet pulp.

Then she heard singing and a steady, rhythmic sound. Soon they met up with a column of Chinese workers led by a British officer. They marched in twos and many carried axes on their shoulders. When they drew near, the men stared in surprise at Pauline, and a few exclaimed at her in a dialect she didn't understand. Their pace was so quick they soon vanished down the road.

"They must need more workers in the forest," Camille remarked.

"The first squad already marched past our home before sunrise. Perhaps you heard them?"

Pauline shook her head. "I was fast asleep. It does seem like a strange dream, though, so surreal, to be walking along a French country road and seeing a column of Chinese men singing a Chinese folk song."

"Do you know the song? What's it about?"

"It's a children's song about a frog and a rooster, about getting up early to be ready for a new day."

"The melody has become familiar to me," Camille remarked. "The workmen always sing or whistle it on their way to Crécy Forest."

She hummed it, and soon Pauline was humming along, until they broke into laughter together.

When they reached the Chinese camp, Camille took her past the long fence and pointed to the hospital behind it. The Frenchwoman flashed an encouraging smile before climbing on her bicycle.

Pauline took a deep breath and followed the wide path that ran along one side of the camp's perimeter until she reached another fence and the hospital gate. The hospital fence was built using long tree branches as rails, crossed in large diagonals between posts to create a rough pattern. Although the fence was high and a guard stood at the gate, the enclosure was clearly intended to mark boundaries rather than keep people in or out. Through the fence she could see long buildings roofed with wooden slats and then the Chinese pagoda Theo had described in his letter, perhaps fifteen feet high, brightly painted in red, blue, and yellow.

"I'm here to see Dr. Robert Adams, please," she said. "He's expecting me."

The soldier stared at her. British. She sighed. "I suppose you don't speak French."

"I do," he replied in French, "enough anyway. But this is a military hospital and you need a pass."

"It's also the Chinese hospital and I'm Chinese!" she said, refraining from putting her hand on her hips.

"Can't argue with that logic," a cheerful voice said from inside the gate. Henri came striding over quickly to join her. He spoke in English to the guard, who shrugged and gestured for Pauline to come through.

"How was the château?" Henri said.

"I didn't stay there after all. It wasn't . . . there wasn't room. I've taken a room at a cottage not far from here."

Henri frowned. "Is it all right?"

"Yes, it belongs to a woman who works at the post office. Has Dr. Adams got the files for Theo?"

"Pauline, the doctor only just got back last night. Right now, he's doing his rounds and catching up with work."

"Yes, of course," she said, flushing. "I didn't mean to sound so impatient."

"He'll be with us soon," Henri said. "He's going to give me a tour of the hospital later. It was half this size when I first saw it. Have you eaten? Good. Then let's go see an old friend."

They crossed the yard to a building at the northern end of the hospital grounds. A worker sat on a wooden bench, face turned up to the sky. A blanket was tucked around his lower half and a bandage covered the left side of his face, including one eye.

"What happened to him?" she whispered.

"His team was doing salvage work after an attack. One of them found a live grenade and didn't know what it was. He picked it up and the pin dropped out."

Henri called out. "Old Lee, are you still pretending to be an invalid?"

The man opened his eye and waved back. "Are you still pretending to work for a living?" He spoke Mandarin but with an accent. Then he saw Pauline and sat up straight. Old Lee wasn't that old, perhaps in his thirties.

"Lee, this is Miss Deng."

"What's a woman doing here?" he said. "Are you going to marry her?"

Pauline blushed and Henri shook his head. "She's here to visit her cousin, one of the interpreters."

"Ah, do I know him? What's his name?"

"Deng Taoling," she said.

"No. Doesn't sound familiar." Lee squinted with the effort of remembering. "But then I've only been here two weeks."

"How did the two of you meet?" she said, hoping to deter questions.

"Old Lee was one of the first workers I interviewed last year," Henri said, "and he was happy to take a break from digging latrines to talk to me."

"Don't be mentioning shit and mess in front of the young lady," Lee said. "And this journalist, as he calls himself, talked the whole time even though he was supposed to be interviewing me. Did they ever print what you wrote down, Mr. Liu?"

"Some of it, not all of it," Henri said. "Well, I want to interview you again now. How are you feeling? Do they say when you'll get out of here?"

Lee's sun-browned face wrinkled in disgust. "One more week! I say one more day. Two at the most."

"It's dangerous out there, Lee. Why not stay a bit longer at the hospital?"

"I've got a family to support," Lee said. "I lose wages each day I'm not working. The fighting doesn't worry me. I fought in a warlord's army before I came, not like those farm boys, frightened by airplanes and big explosions and dead bodies."

The hospital grounds were busier now with staff and patients. Pauline had become the subject of intense scrutiny from the men, both

Chinese and foreign. Belatedly, she realized she had been extremely lucky. First to have Henri come with her, then meeting Dr. Adams, and then a place to stay at Camille's, away from the town and curious eyes. She had never truly been on her own during this mission. Not yet. She moved a little closer to Henri.

"So your boys didn't get any warnings about unexploded munitions?" he said, opening his notebook.

"No, none at all. Nothing about grenades or shells or anything," Lee said. "They just assume everyone understands. There's so much those boys don't know. Everything looks strange. *I* know what bombs look like. But poor Liao had no idea. His ignorance killed him and injured others."

Henri turned the page on his notepad and scribbled even faster. Then he looked up to see who was calling his name. A tall figure in a white doctor's coat came across the yard, his expression grave.

"Come to my office," the doctor said, "I've been to the Labour Corp's records department. I have your cousin's files, Mademoiselle Deng."

Dr. Adams led them through the center of the hospital, a reception area with offices behind. Unlike the rickety-looking barracks of the CLC camp, the hospital was solidly built, whitewashed and airy. Patients shuffled along the hallways, and Chinese medical aides in neat white jackets carried trays of medication and bandages. They all stared at Pauline openly, some of them gaping with open mouths. She felt certain it was only the foreign doctor's presence that prevented the men from crowding around her, examining her like some strange sea creature.

Dr. Adams's office was just large enough for a desk and a cot along the wall. There were rumpled blankets on the cot and Henri's luggage was stuffed underneath. The doctor offered them mugs of tea from a thermos. Pauline sat by the desk and sniffed at the tea. Chinese tea. She took a sip, the warmth and familiar fragrance calming her impatience as the doctor shuffled through the papers on his desk. She tried not to peer too obviously at the files.

Dr. Adams seemed reluctant to speak. Then he sighed. "There is no easy way to say this. Mademoiselle Deng, I have very sad news. Your cousin was killed two weeks ago."

Pauline's hands gripped the edges of the seat. There was a sharp intake of breath behind her from Henri. Then his hands on her shoulders. But her body refused to do anything but sit upright, her eyes to look anywhere except at Adams. He dropped his gaze to the papers on his desk.

"He died at a forestry camp near Wimereux. He was one of three fatalities at the camp that day, victim of an aerial attack," he said. "Mademoiselle Deng, I apologize that you did not know sooner. The administration here lacks a sense of . . . urgency in these matters since usually the families are in China and letters take a long time anyway."

"Pauline, are you all right?" Henri whispered beside her.

She let out a long, ragged breath. "What more do you know, Dr. Adams?"

"There were no other details. I am so very sorry."

A fist clenched around her heart, clamping down tightly so that grief couldn't seep out to express itself. Her heart hung suspended in her chest, hollow and sullen.

"Is there any chance there was an error, Doctor?" Pauline said. She wouldn't cry. She would not break down.

He shook his head. "I'm sorry. The report about the incident is there. And the paperwork for all three men was signed by their commanding officer in Wimereux."

Pauline pushed herself up from the chair, looking for something else to fix her attention. There were photos pinned to one wall in a sort of impromptu gallery, the pictures neatly arranged. Some were obviously from Robert's time in China, smiling faces of foreign missionaries with their congregations. A lakeside photo of Dr. Adams, surrounded by teenaged boys, one of them holding a YMCA flag. There was a beautifully mounted scroll, a small watercolor of a mountain landscape, the edges of a hermit's dwelling just visible behind groves of bamboo and pine. Several photographs of workers, each seated in front of a painted backdrop of marble columns, obviously all taken at the same photo studio. Photographs given to the doctor as tokens of respect and thanks.

Remember me. Remember my face. Remember.

"I'd like to bring his body and personal belongings home," she said, without turning around. "Can that be arranged, Doctor?"

"I'm not sure," he said. "For that you'd need to see his commanding officer, Captain Maitland. He's still at the CLC camp near Wimereux."

"I have a duty to my cousin and to my uncle, Dr. Adams," she said, still with her back to him. "You know that we Chinese must be buried with our ancestors. I must bring his body to Paris so my uncle can send him home to Shanghai."

"I'll go with her, Robert," Henri said.

"Yes, yes, of course." The doctor looked from Pauline to Henri. "But are you sure? You will have to take the train to Boulogne then go on foot to Wimereux. That's at least an hour's walk."

"It's not a problem," she said. "As long as his commanding officer is still there."

"Maitland wasn't your cousin's regular commanding officer, Mademoiselle Deng," he said. "Your cousin was only on loan to him in Wimereux. I'm saying this so you'll understand if the captain can't tell you much. Maitland wouldn't have gotten to know him very well yet."

THEY LEFT THE HOSPITAL, HENRI hovering beside her. "Would you like a coffee, Pauline? Should I walk you back to the cottage?" He seemed both puzzled and relieved at her cold composure. Only the hard necessity of duty kept her moving forward. She wasn't going to cry, not where strangers could see her. And not in front of Henri.

"Can we go into the town?" she said. "I should send a telegram."

Henri talked nonstop. Noyelles-sur-Mer was a small town surrounded by farmland. But it was also at the juncture of converging railway lines, making it convenient for transporting supplies from the port at Boulogne to the front. He waved at a high brick wall, the manor house inside just visible behind surrounding trees, guards at the front gate.

"That's the mansion the British Army's using as the Chinese Labour Corps headquarters in Noyelles," he said. He kept peering at Pauline anxiously, waiting for some emotion to cross her features.

"Look," he said, when they reached the main street. He pointed at a newspaper pasted on a shop window, headlines in tall, bold lettering. "The German lines are collapsing. The kaiser has lost all support."

Despite the cold weather and threat of rain, doors to cafés and bars were wide open, their clientele spilling out onto sidewalks with drinks in their hands, buoyant with hope. The little bakery had decorated its window with a string of miniature French flags. Soldiers in clean, pressed uniforms queued up outside the photography studio.

"It won't be long now, Pauline. Peace."

A peace that is too late for Theo, she thought. He would never marry and she would never keep house for him and his family. Her uncle would send her to Shanghai.

At the post office Pauline peered in the window. Camille appeared to be there on her own, only one customer inside. "That's Camille Roussel, I'm living at their cottage. Well, a garden room separate from their home, actually."

"Will you send a telegram to your uncle?"

She paused, then shook her head. "I was going to but now I think

I should wait until we're back from Wimereux. Maybe there's been some mistake. And if not, then I'd rather make arrangements to send Theo . . . his coffin to Paris, before letting Uncle know."

And by then, perhaps the numbness that had bound her chest since being told of Theo's death would loosen. She'd be forced to accept he was truly gone.

"Then shall we go to the train station and check tomorrow's time-tables?" he said. Henri's voice was so gentle, his hand on her arm so re-assuring. Pauline wanted to turn to him for comfort but she couldn't afford more heartbreak. It was far better to feel nothing but emptiness.

Why had no one warned her that emptiness could be so heavy?

CAMILLE

MME DUMONT MAY as well have stayed home for all she managed to accomplish. She was out of the post office more often than in, running home to air out bedding and do more laundry, checking on the stew, putting fresh linens in their guest room. Mme Dumont's brother and sister-in-law were coming for a visit.

"Dumont's brother is deputy mayor of Calais and my Dumont only a humble postmaster," she said, "and his wife never actually says it, but in a thousand ways she lets me know how humble."

"Go home," Camille said. "I can handle things today."

Camille dealt with raucous British and Australian soldiers. Mme LeFevre came, as she did every week, begging her to look once more in the back room in case there was a misplaced final letter from her dead son. Camille sorted mail during her lunch break so that the bags would be ready when old Emil and his delivery cart came to the door. Her back ached and so did her feet, but she was glad to be alone.

She had lain awake for hours, arms crossed over her chest in imitation of the stone-carved effigies of saints and queens. It was the only way she could keep still, otherwise she'd toss and turn. But it was no use trying to sleep, so at the first hint of light she slipped downstairs to the kitchen, went outside to feed the hens and check for eggs.

When Camille put the washbasin and jug of hot water outside the door for Pauline, she resisted the urge to wake up her guest in case a conversation led to too many questions about Theo. She wanted to know everything. What he'd been like as a child. What their lives back in Shanghai had been like. What he loved to eat.

Whether he'd ever been in love before.

Would Pauline go to Wimereux when she found out Theo was there? Perhaps she would come back with him. Or at least bring news about him. Had Theo managed to get leave for the weekend?

An hour before the post office closed, an apologetic Mme Dumont came back and took over at the front counter.

"You've done the work of two people all day, Camille," she said. "And I saw Emil's cart go off to make the afternoon deliveries so there's really nothing to keep you here. Why not go home now? You look a little tired."

She hadn't realized just how tired. She had to get off and walk the bicycle. She rounded a curve in the road and saw a couple beside the small roadside shrine, a shrine to the Madonna much beloved by the townsfolk. The two were deep in conversation and when she got closer, Camille recognized Frances Newland and the man in British uniform, the doctor who boarded with the Dumonts.

"Good afternoon, Camille." Frances seemed a little flustered. "This is Doctor Adams. Doctor, do you know Madame Camille Roussel? Pauline Deng is lodging with her."

"Madame, a pleasure." He cleared his throat. "I should get back, Frances."

Frances's eyes followed him up the road. She blushed when she saw

Camille smiling. "Are you on your way home, Camille? I'll walk with you as far as the château."

"Is he the one, then?" Camille said. "Your tall Canadian? Does your mother know?"

"Mother likes him but she doesn't approve," Frances said. "He's a poor missionary. She wants me to marry an American millionaire. Mother says she'll sell the château after the war and take me back to New York."

"Oh, Frances, I'll miss you. And your mother has been most generous to the town and to the war effort."

"Have you heard of a New York socialite named Julia Hunt Taufflieb?" Frances said. "She and my mother have a somewhat . . . competitive relationship. Mrs. Taufflieb turned her château in Longueil d'Annel into a hospital, so of course Mother had to do the same."

There was a long pause. "Well, her motives don't take away from how much good she's done with the hospital," Camille said.

"Oh dear. I've shocked you," Frances said. "But you're right, Mother does mean well. And if not for her hospital, I wouldn't have had the chance to try my hand at nursing."

"And you might not have met Robert," Camille pointed out.

"Yes, and that would've been terrible," Frances agreed as they walked along. "Poor Robert. He's had a terribly upsetting day. He was helping that young Chinese woman find her cousin."

"Pauline told me there's some family crisis. Was Robert able to find out where her cousin's working right now?"

"Oh, Camille, it's terrible," Frances said. "Apparently her cousin was killed two weeks ago near Wimereux during an aerial attack."

Camille stumbled, managing to stay upright only because she was holding on to the handlebars. Her legs kept moving only because she was accustomed to walking this road. She felt encased in a sheath of ice. She would not cry out. She allowed herself only a quick intake of breath, a gasp of surprise and that was all. She called up all the restraint she had honed through her years of marriage to Jean-Paul, giving away nothing through her eyes or voice, the steadiness of her hands.

"Are you all right?" Frances said. "This road has so many potholes. I've turned an ankle just walking. Anyway, poor Robert had to be the one to tell her. He said the girl went absolutely rigid and quiet and it was worse than if she had burst into tears."

How could she not have known? Camille always believed that if something happened to Theo, she would've felt it. An absence of light, a loss of vision. A heaviness in her bones. She would've sensed it in her heart's erratic syncopation, in the laboring of her lungs. She would've felt the way she did right now, every pace forward like stepping off a cliff.

But then again, how could she have known? She and Theo didn't write to each other when he was away, and he had been away for weeks. All she knew was that his company had been sent to Wimereux. Before he left he'd said he would apply for leave, try to come back to Noyelles this weekend.

And now she would not see him. She would never see him again.

She took a deep breath. His death didn't change her plans. She still had to get away from Jean-Paul.

"You've been a good friend, Camille," Frances said, suddenly. "I'll miss you when I leave."

"I'm glad you consider me a friend, Frances," she said. "Because I may need your help."

"Of course. What kind of help?"

Camille shook her head. "I don't know yet. It may involve . . . transportation."

"I see." Frances glanced sideways at her. "Will you be running away from or running to?"

"Is it so obvious?" she said. "Away from. And soon. Perhaps as soon as next week. Please don't ask me more right now, Frances."

They hugged at the tall iron gates at the driveway of the château and Camille continued home. Just the idea of getting through tomorrow exhausted her. She used to think that if Theo died, so would she, if not physically then in spirit, not caring anymore. But now she had something else to live for besides Theo. The instinct to survive surged anew, giving her the determination to carry out her plan. Now, more than ever.

As soon as Camille reached the cottage, she took a lamp down to the cellar, closed the door behind her as she walked down the steps, holding tightly to the handrail. She folded herself into a corner and stuffed her scarf in her mouth. Only then did she give way to tears, her stifled wails those of a wounded animal that refused to give away its hiding place.

Her affair with Theo had put her in danger, and she was still in danger. But she regretted nothing. What mattered most right now was keeping her emotions in check, for her to get through the next few days without Jean-Paul—or anyone else—suspecting.

PAULINE

PAULINE KNOCKED ON the kitchen door. Inside, Camille was by the stove, her back turned.

"I'm not hungry," Pauline said, her voice hoarse from crying for hours, alone in the garden room. "I just came to tell you not to make supper for me, don't waste the food."

"Pauline, you are so pale." Camille pulled out a chair. She looked rather pale herself and her hands were dusty with flour. "Please, at least drink some tea. I have real tea leaves somewhere."

Suddenly, a cup of tea seemed like the most helpful thing in the world to Pauline. While the tea steeped, Camille finished crimping the edges of a pie. She lifted the lid from a cast-iron pot and dipped a wooden spoon into the stew for a quick stir. Then she opened the oven door and dropped a pinch of flour on the bottom of the oven, and waited a moment to see if the flour turned black without catching fire. It was exactly what Denise did to check whether the oven was hot enough.

"I picked those apples at the end of summer," Camille said. "They're a little dried out but perfectly good for baking. I can bring you a supper tray if you're too tired to have dinner here."

Pauline shook her head, attempted a smile. "Yes, please," she said. "I'd like a tray but I can carry it myself."

"Good. You should eat." Camille reached up for a bowl.

Her rolled-up sleeve slid past her elbow and Pauline saw the bruises again. They were too familiar, like the finger marks she used to get as a child when the head housekeeper squeezed her cruelly. The marks on Camille's arm were darker, spaced apart wider, the work of a larger and rougher hand.

Camille put a bowl of stew and another mug of tea on the tray. Pauline took the tray and Camille held open the kitchen door for her.

"If you're still hungry, come back later for apple tart," she said. Pauline noticed for the first time that Camille's eyes were rimmed with red, her nose slightly swollen. Perhaps from leaning over a hot stove.

THE STEW ON THE SMALL table had cooled untouched. Pauline wasn't hungry but she hadn't wanted to hurt Camille's feelings. She lay on the daybed curled up on her side. She had left Paris yesterday, before the morning post. If she had waited until the afternoon, waited another day, would the letter of condolence from Theo's commanding officer have arrived? If there was a letter, it would be addressed to Louis, and Denise wouldn't open it.

But her uncle would be in Paris this Friday. If he came home to news of Theo's death, her disobedience in going to Noyelles would add to his troubles. But if she could give Louis the consolation of knowing he could return Theo's body home to China, it would lessen his sorrow. Perhaps this was what fate had arranged all along, that she should be here at this time, not for her own sake but for Theo's.

Her impending marriage, Shanghai, the fate she wanted to avoid, all of it was irrelevant now. It didn't matter anymore whether she lived in Paris or Shanghai. Theo was dead.

A man's voice called out, a door slammed. Pauline opened the shutter just a sliver and saw Jean-Paul standing by the kitchen door, the small sudden flare of a match casting a brief glow on his face, then the red spark of a cigarette. Then the squeak of the gate and Jean-Paul was gone.

She forced down a few bites of the cold stew, then took the tray back to the kitchen. Camille gave her a tired and rather sad smile.

"Would you like some apple tart?" she said.

Pauline shook her head. She didn't want to say the words. Because those words made Theo's death real, like an incantation that once spoken, couldn't be revoked.

"Camille, I'm going to Wimereux tomorrow with my friend Henri. I don't know when I'll get back, but hopefully I won't need to stay overnight. My cousin was killed and I want to speak with his commanding officer."

Camille clutched the back of a kitchen chair. Tears filled her eyes. "I'm so very sorry, Pauline. How terrible." Her voice was soft, almost a whisper, as if she didn't trust herself to speak any louder.

"I'm probably wrong to hope it's a clerical error, some terrible mistake with the paperwork," Pauline said, staring down at her hands.

"But I must be sure. The doctor at the hospital said Theo's commanding officer would know more. It's our custom to be buried with our ancestors, so I must arrange to bring his . . . his body home."

Abruptly, Camille stood up. "I feel like some chamomile tea. I'll reheat the water. Can you get the chamomile, in that white jar?"

Pauline picked up the white-glazed jar from the fireplace mantel. She turned it over and looked at the bottom, this time more closely.

"This is a very special jar," she said.

"Yes, there's something nice about the way it feels in your hand," Camille said. She sounded preoccupied, distant.

"No, I mean, it's extremely valuable, Camille. I'm prepared to wager this is a piece of Tang dynasty porcelain. A thousand years old."

Camille turned around. "What do you think it's worth?"

"It depends on who's willing to buy it," she said, shrugging. She set the bowl down on the kitchen table. "If I were you, I'd use something else for storing chamomile. Put it somewhere safe in case you need to sell it someday."

"I will," Camille said. "I'll put it away right now. But please, don't mention the jar to my husband. Please."

Pauline nodded, remembering the bruises on the Frenchwoman's arm. "If you ever need money," she said, "I can ask my uncle to buy this jar."

"You're very kind." Camille smiled, and her plain face glowed into beauty.

CHAPTER 15

Thursday, November 7, 1918

PAULINE

THE BAIE DE Somme rail line took them only as far as Boulogne-sur-Mer. From there they'd have to walk. Henri assured Pauline that with so many military vehicles taking men and supplies back and forth, they would be able to beg a ride to Wimereux.

They boarded the first train out of Noyelles and found themselves sharing a carriage with several families of women and small children. At first the adults stared at Pauline and Henri, curious and wary. Perhaps even unfriendly. Pauline didn't care. She closed her eyes, not interested in conversation, while Henri chatted with the women and gave their children candy. She knew when Henri told them about Theo from the change of tone in the Frenchwomen's voices, their words quieter, more respectful. Now she was like them—she had suffered loss.

Eventually the carriage quieted, and the women turned away from Henri and talked among themselves.

PAULINE SAT UP WITH A jerk and realized she had dozed off. She hadn't slept at all last night. Beside her, Henri stopped writing.

"Pauline, can you tell me why you needed to find Theo? I know it's a family matter but perhaps there's something I can do to help."

"Uncle Louis asked his wife to arrange a marriage for me," she said, "but I don't want to marry, I don't want to go back to China. I can't disobey Uncle, but I hoped that Theo could persuade him to stop the arrangements . . . anyway, it doesn't matter now."

What was the point of holding back? Theo was gone, her fate sealed. She told Henri everything.

"And then there was Mah. Theo and I first met him on the way to France ten years ago, he was on the same ship. He turned up at La Pagode after the Mid-Autumn Festival party." She summed up the events surrounding Mah as briefly as she could, the marriage offer, the thefts. Henri's eyes never left her face, his fingers twirling a pencil.

"I think the near miss with Mah made my uncle decide he should do things traditionally," she said, "and have his wife go through a professional matchmaker. Now that Theo's gone, Uncle will probably close La Pagode. The store was meant for Theo. And I'll follow my uncle back to Shanghai."

She sank back against the seat and looked out the window even though there was nothing to see but a steady gray drizzle. Henri took her hand and held it for a long time.

AT THE STATION IN BOULOGNE, they stepped off the train to strong winds and a cold, sleeting rain. Henri tucked his satchel under his arm and opened Pauline's umbrella. "Let's start walking and hope an army vehicle stops to pick us up."

In the end, it was a farmer and his donkey cart who stopped and agreed to take them to the camp for a small fee. Although he was wrapped in oilskins, he was pleased that Pauline held her umbrella over them both. Henri rode in the back of the cart, huddled under a canvas tarp, but even so he kept turning around to ask the farmer questions about how the war had affected him.

"And have you had much to do with the Chinese men in the camp?"

"With your people? They pay good money for fresh food," he said, "apples, pears. That's all the dealings I've had with them. There's a few who take pity on an old man and they give me firewood, leftovers from what they cut."

The farmer drove along Wimereux's main street and pointed out landmarks to help them get their bearings, the church and town hall, a café where they could get lunch at reasonable cost. Another ten minutes' ride past the town and he let them off at an intersection with a signpost marked CLC CAMP WIMEREUX. The gravel road to the camp was rutted from frequent use.

"There it is," he said. "The camp is on the way to the next town, Baston. It's a short walk."

BARBED WIRE FENCING SURROUNDED THE camp, and columns of steam rose from the bunkhouses inside. A few men hurried between buildings, ducking out of the rain. The British soldier at the gate shook his head when Henri spoke to him. He pointed at the huts they had just walked past, a hundred meters away.

"The camp is where workers and translators live," Henri said, returning to Pauline. "The British officers are in those huts outside the barbed wire. Captain Maitland's hut is second from the end."

She stumbled on the path and clutched his arm to steady herself. "Henri," she said. "Thank you for coming with me. It would've been even more awful without you."

"How could I let you do this on your own?"

"I don't blame you anymore, Henri," she said. "I was angry with you at first for not speaking to Theo before you left for England. I was angry at everyone. Even angry with our government for sending men to France at all. But the fact is, Theo had made up his mind to come and there was no changing it."

"I'm glad you're not angry with me," he said and gave her arm a gentle squeeze. "Here we are."

In answer to his knock, a gruff voice called for them to enter.

Compared to the bone-chilling damp, the warmth inside was welcome. After the first few moments, however, it felt stifling. A kerosene heater beside the desk explained the temperature in the room. A chest of drawers against one wall and a cot stacked with blankets made it clear this hut was bedroom as well as office. A man of about sixty with untidy gray hair sat behind a desk, his jacket open, a plaid scarf knotted around his neck. Maitland looked up. His red-rimmed eyes blinked at seeing Pauline.

"Do you speak French, sir?" she said.

"A very little," he said, his words thick and slightly slurred. The end of his nose was red, his cheeks covered in a spiderweb of veins.

"Allow me to explain," Henri said in English, to Maitland's obvious relief.

After listening to Henri, the captain opened a file drawer and rummaged around. He pulled out a folder and perused its contents. Pauline caught a glimpse of a photograph, Theo's face, before the captain turned the page over.

After a brief exchange with the captain, Henri turned to Pauline. "There's no easy way to tell you this, Pauline. The aircraft took a bombing run at the camp and the men who died . . . well, it was a direct hit. There were no remains, nothing to bury, nothing to return to you. But he says that if it's any consolation, Theo would've died instantly."

She bowed her head. So there was nothing. No body to bring back. This had been a futile mission from the start. Tears welled up in Pauline's eyes, rolled down her face. She unbuttoned her coat, felt around the pockets of her skirt for a handkerchief.

"What about personal effects, Pauline?" Henri said. "You can bring his belongings home. Let me ask."

Maitland, looking perturbed by Pauline's tears, nodded at Henri's request. He reached into another drawer and took out a pile of forms. He filled one in and signed it, handed it to Henri. Then he stood up, a little awkwardly, and came around the desk. He limped and only then did Pauline notice the walking cane leaning against the table.

"Mademoiselle, I'm sorry for your loss," he said in heavily accented French. He made a small bow that conveyed both courtesy and dismissal.

Henri tugged at her arm and they left the stiflingly warm hut.

"He gave me a pass to enter the camp," Henri said. "The work squads are out right now. He advises coming back at three o'clock, when they've returned, then I can ask around and find the hut where Theo used to sleep. His belongings may still be there."

"Three o'clock," Pauline repeated. "That's not too long to wait."

"The captain signed a pass for me, not for you," Henri said. "He doesn't want a woman in the camp. Let's walk back into Wimereux, get something to eat at that café the farmer recommended and you can wait there where it's warm."

AT THE CAFÉ, THEY ORDERED soup with bread and cheese. The proprietor looked askance at Pauline.

"We don't see many Chinese women here," he said.

"You mean none whatsoever," Henri said, then laughed, which made the proprietor laugh also.

It didn't take long before the café and its few customers knew

Pauline's reason for coming. There were curious looks but also sympathetic nods. Eventually the café emptied.

Pauline found herself looking at the clock on the café's wall every few minutes.

"The work teams should be back soon," Henri said. "I'll head for the camp. Wait here."

But Pauline wasn't listening. She sat frozen, eyes on the door. Or rather, on the man who had just entered, a man whose uniform and greatcoat identified him as being with the Chinese Labour Corps. Not one of the workers, an interpreter.

So this was where he had ended up.

She would've recognized that wolfish smile anywhere, ingratiating and insolent at the same time. She couldn't think of anyone whose face could've been less welcome, no matter where or in any situation. And in this small café there was no way to avoid him.

"Mademoiselle Deng," Mah said. His voice was friendly. "This is the last place I expected to run into you."

"Mah," she said, with a nod. She didn't introduce him to Henri, who looked at her, a question in his eyes.

Mah turned away from her and put his hand out to Henri. "Mah Fuliang. Interpreter. My company just arrived in Wimereux. I used to work at La Pagode in Paris. It's how I know Pauline, her uncle and cousin Theo."

Henri shook his hand. "Henri Liu. Journalist."

"May I ask why you're here, Baoling?" Mah sat in the chair beside her without asking. His coat reeked of damp wool cloth and stale cigarette smoke. It reminded her of the tobacco Jean-Paul used, pungent and strong.

What did she have to lose? If the camp here was anything like the one in Noyelles, her presence and the reason for it would be known to all very soon anyway.

"Theo joined the CLC last year as an interpreter. He was killed. I'm here to bring his . . . personal belongings home."

"I'm so very sorry." The regret in Mah's voice sounded genuine, but his eyes lacked compassion. "I'm new to this camp but is there something I can do to help? I could try and get you a pass to enter the camp."

"I have a pass from Captain Maitland, and that's what I was going to do this very minute," Henri said, standing up and pulling on his coat. "I need to find someone who can show me to Theo's quarters."

"Then we'll go together," Mah offered. "I'm not busy at the moment. I'll just get a small coffee first."

He went to the bar. Pauline stood up and helped Henri button his coat. She leaned in closer as she did the top button for him.

"Is that——" he began. She put a finger to her lips and nodded.

"Be careful what you say," she whispered. "I'm going for a walk to sit in the church. Come find me there, but don't let him come with you."

At the bar, Mah gulped down his coffee and came back to the table. Pauline was still sitting, her coat on the seat beside her. "You're not coming, Baoling?" he said.

"No. Just Henri." She saw a brief scowl that quickly turned into a smile.

"Well then, perhaps later," he said.

Pauline watched the two men head out, chatting amiably. She noticed that one of Mah's shoulders stood higher than the other. From an injury perhaps. She put on her coat and left the café, then turned in the direction of the church. Outside, the wind was even colder but at least the rain had slowed to a misty drizzle. It seemed to her that the dark skies were not the consequence of a winter storm but Mah's presence.

THE CHURCH WITH ITS TALL single tower loomed out of the fog as she got closer. All she had to do was keep it in sight as she walked.

Despite the foul weather, the streets of Wimereux were crowded. British, Australians, New Zealanders, Canadians. Wimereux was a hospital town, its population swelled by the presence of several Allied hospitals and Red Cross centers.

Pauline pulled down the veil on her hat and kept her umbrella low, moving briskly, purposefully. Young women attracted attention from soldiers, but even during her short time in Noyelles-sur-Mer, she'd learned that her Chinese face drew comments. Some of it good-natured, but she didn't need to put up with any teasing today.

The town hall was a tidy and handsome building with a clock above the main door. Pauline crossed the square in front to L'Église de l'Immaculée-Conception. She had no real interest in the church itself. It was just a place for some quiet and solitude, to get out of the wind while waiting for Henri. She hadn't wanted to sit in the café alone.

She barely glanced at the architecture and artwork inside the church. It smelled musty. Decades of incense smoke had settled into altar cloths and the grain of wooden pews and choir stalls. She sat in a pew near the door of the south transept to gather her emotions, her head bowed as though in prayer. An old man with a broom was sweeping in the north transept and didn't pay her any attention as he moved between the aisles, bent over his work.

Seeing Mah had unnerved her. Pauline hadn't thought about Mah in months and when she did, it was with relief that he was gone. They had been told he'd been put on a ship back to China, yet here he was. But he couldn't harm her, not with Henri by her side. And he certainly couldn't harm Theo.

The custodian and his broom were moving closer, so Pauline left the church. The rain had ceased for the moment and she spent a few minutes on the bridge looking down at the river Wimereux. Its waters flowed cold and gray, a dull pewter indistinguishable from the sky above. Shallow steps beside the bridge took her down to a path along the riverbank lined with poplars and willows, their bare branches holding on stubbornly to a few shriveled leaves. The wind was even colder by the water, the path empty of other foot travelers except for a man walking ahead of her. He wore a dark blue knitted cap, and his shoulders were hunched against the cold, his hands buried in the pockets of a military-issue greatcoat. Then he tugged the cap farther down over his right ear.

Pauline ran.

She had never run so fast in her life. She pulled up the veil on her hat as she ran, waved her umbrella, not caring that her boots splashed through puddles and squelched through mud.

"Stop, stop," she called. "Theo! Theo!"

The man stopped in his tracks and turned around. She threw her arms around him.

"Pauline?" An incredulous voice.

"It was a mistake, oh, it was a mistake!" she cried. "You're not dead. They made a mistake, it was someone else, not you. Oh, Theo, you're alive!"

She stepped back, puzzled by his stillness. He patted her on the cheek, the way he used to whenever she got upset, then held her by the shoulders and looked at her. Then he smiled and took her hands in his.

"Pauline, what are you doing here?"

"I came to bring your body home," she said, clutching his hand. "I mean, that wasn't the original reason but when I got to Noyelles they told me you'd been killed."

He shook his head. "I don't know what to say, Pauline."

"You didn't know there had been a mistake? I can't believe that Captain Maitland thought you'd been killed." She babbled on. "Oh, won't you come back to Paris, even if it's just for a few days' leave? Denise will be so happy to see you and so will your father."

"Tell me everything, Pauline. But let's go someplace quiet and dry, where we can talk without anyone overhearing."

THE OLD MAN WITH THE broom was gone and the lights inside the church were turned on, a string of bare bulbs that hung between the stone pillars of the nave, their feeble glow not much better than candles. They sat down in the pew near the south transept. Pauline hadn't let go of Theo's gloved hand, squeezing it every now and then to reassure herself that he really was here, beside her. Alive.

She started to cry. All the pain she had pushed deep into the corners of her heart, all the sorrow she had buried so that she could carry on with her mission, the grief she wouldn't show, all of it now welled up and she wept on his shoulder, smelled the familiar scent of his soap mingled with the fusty odor of damp wool. She wiped her eyes with the handkerchief he offered, a plain white square with his initials in one corner, her own inept embroidery work. Finally, sniffling and red-nosed, she sighed and leaned back against the hard wood of the pew.

"I can't believe you came alone," Theo said. "What were you thinking?"

"I'm not alone," she said. "I mean, I was ready to come on my own if need be, but Henri was back in Paris so I asked him to come with me since he's been to Noyelles before. That's where we're staying, at Noyelles-sur-Mer. He's at the Wimereux camp right now, trying to find your hut in case your personal effects are still there."

"Henri is here too?" Theo said. He didn't sound pleased.

"And something else. Remember that horrible Mah? He's here too. We ran into him in town. His company only just came to Wimereux today. He went with Henri to the camp. But I warned Henri not to say much."

"Mah?" Theo frowned, but Pauline didn't notice. She was still giddy with joy, with relief. He really was alive. The past twenty-four hours had been a nightmare, but now she knew she'd been right. Someone had mixed up the paperwork.

"We arrived in Noyelles yesterday. Henri's staying with a doctor who works at the Chinese hospital and I've taken a room at a cottage outside Noyelles, it's about a forty-minute walk to town."

"Outside of town? Is it a decent place for a woman on her own?"

"Very decent, it's actually a little garden room separate from the cottage itself. The couple is very nice, at least the wife is, her name is Camille."

There was a long silence and Theo put his hands on the pew in front, leaned his head on his hands for a minute. He sat up. "Pauline, when does Henri come back from the camp?"

"He's meeting me here, so let's just wait," she said. "Oh, Theo, if only another of your letters had come, then I would've known right away that Dr. Adams was mistaken when he said you'd been killed two weeks ago. Maybe your letters were lost in the mail. Of course you probably had no idea of this error. Or have you been too busy?"

Then she saw the look on his face.

"You wanted us to believe you were dead," she burst out. Pauline jumped to her feet. "How could you? Theo, how could you? What have you done? Why?"

He stood up slowly to face her. She flailed at him, pounding against his chest when he crossed his forearms in front of his face.

"Pauline, please," he said, "let me explain."

"Why? Why?" Her cry echoed through the stone pillars. Her cousin, who she trusted and loved. Who she thought cared about her. "Why would you hurt us like this?"

Theo took a deep breath and lowered his arms. "Because the family is better off without me."

"How can you even think that? You're going to run La Pagode.

Grandfather picked you; he picked *you* to come with your father, not one of your brothers, not one of your cousins."

"Pauline, listen to me. Grandfather sent me to France with Father because I'll never be of any use to the business in China," he said. "I'm an embarrassment to them. And you know why."

"But to pretend you were dead!"

Theo sighed. "I'll explain everything to you when Henri gets here. But, Pauline, please go to the door and make sure he's alone. If Mah is with him, I'm going to hide until you get rid of that odious man. Do not let Mah know I'm here."

HENRI ARRIVED ALONE. HE HELD a folded newspaper over his head to keep away the light drizzle of rain. He waved when he saw her at the entrance and hurried over.

"I found Theo's hut, it looks like another translator lives there now," he said. "There was a book with 'Deng Taoling' written on the flyleaf so I took it and a few other things. Mah looked around, too, but he had to go settle some brawl out in the yard and I left before he came back."

"Come with me," she said, pulling him along the rows of pews.

A woman with a kerchief tied around her head was setting fresh candles on the altar, getting the church ready for vespers.

"Theo's bunkmate is probably back at the hut now," he said, still talking, "I would've waited longer but I didn't want you to worry. But I'll go back and . . ."

Theo's tall figure rose from the pew. Henri whistled.

The woman at the altar cleared her throat and glared at them. "No whistling in church. Heathens."

"A thousand pardons, madame," Theo said, bowing slightly. She glared again and began arranging a bunch of wax flowers beside the altar.

Theo greeted Henri with a wry expression and a handshake. They sat in silence for a few moments, Pauline and Henri on either side of Theo. Finally, Henri gave Theo a punch on the shoulder.

"Explain. According to Maitland's paperwork, you are definitely deceased."

"It wasn't a clerical error," Theo said. "I did that paperwork."

MAITLAND HAD BEEN UNLUCKY WITH his interpreters, the first dying from a small wound that turned septic, the second sent to the Noyelles hospital with a suspected case of influenza only a few weeks after arriving at the Wimereux camp. The CLC workers in Wimereux were on loan to a Canadian Forestry Corps battalion with a portable sawmill that cut logs into railway ties. The work at the mill was varied, from hand sawing lumber and feeding wood chips into the steam engine, to looking after the horses that hauled logs to the mill. Some squads felled trees, some made bundles of brushwood into fascines, and others loaded railway ties onto trucks. They couldn't do without an interpreter.

Theo had never been so busy, up at the break of dawn with the men, circling constantly from one work site to another with the young lieutenant in charge of their group. They couldn't afford any misunderstandings that might slow down work now that the Allies were succeeding in their big push.

Theo shared his hut with a senior ganger who went to the main bunkhouse after supper, more interested in gambling than conversation, so at least Theo was able to rest and read quietly after hours.

He returned from the forest one day to find the little woodstove in the hut already burning, the kettle about to boil, and his predecessor back from Noyelles.

"I'm Chao Te-Yin," the other interpreter said.

"You're over the influenza then?" Theo said, shaking his hand.

"It was bad but I pulled through," Chao replied. "I tried reporting in to Maitland earlier, but he wasn't answering his door, so I came here to wait a bit. I'm sure you've noticed by now that Maitland is rarely sober."

Chao had draped his damp uniform jacket over the back of the chair near the stove, and steam rose from the jacket's shoulders. His greatcoat was on a wall peg, and Theo hung up his own coat beside it. They talked while Chao made tea.

The other interpreter was an orphan, raised by missionaries. He had been teaching school in Weihaiwei when the British set up a recruiting center there. Wanting a chance to see more of the world, he signed up in November of 1916, one of their first recruits. Fluent in English, he was put to work immediately giving workers basic English lessons while they awaited transport.

"They kept me teaching for so long I didn't board a ship for months," he said. "Once the war is over, I really hope to go home by train when it's safe to take the Trans-Siberian again."

"Seasickness?" Theo said sympathetically. "Same with my father."

"How's it been here?" Chao said. "I heard the British aerodrome in Marquise was bombed a couple of weeks ago."

"We've had some air-raid alerts but no actual bombs during my time here. The men are all ragged from lack of sleep, though," Theo said, standing by the stove. He handed a mug of tea to Chao. "The Germans are always on the way to some other target, but we all run for shelter when the siren sounds just in case."

After a second mug of tea, Chao helped Theo put up blackout curtains over the door and windows.

"I suppose you'll be heading back to your own company tomorrow," Chao said. "Let's get our coats on and head for the mess hall. I missed lunch today."

The gravel walkways in the camp were edged with white stones to make the paths more visible in the dark. The moon slid out from a bank of clouds, casting a shadow beside the long building that served as the mess hall. At the far end of the camp, a bunkhouse door opened and light slanted out, then the door closed. A pair of red sparks glowed in the dark; two workers had come out to smoke.

"You'd think by now they'd know about smoking outside at night." Chao gave an exasperated sigh. "I know who those two are. I'm going to remind them again about blackout rules. Meet you at the mess hall."

He hurried toward the pair of thoughtless workers, shouting as he approached. Theo continued on toward the long building at the center of the camp. His hand dug into the pocket of his greatcoat, touched the letter from his father. It was brief, informing him of his grandfather's death, then a tersely worded reminder that as soon his contract expired or perhaps sooner if the war ended, Theo was to go home and get married.

Theo knew that his father had managed so far to frame his defiance in favorable terms to the family, first praising Theo's desire for education when he enrolled at the Sorbonne, then Theo's patriotism when he joined the Chinese Labour Corps, making it seem as though he was in accord with his son. The words of an indulgent father. In the rigid hierarchy of the Deng family, these were Louis's decisions to make.

But if Theo disobeyed his father now, refused the arranged marriage, refused to go back to Shanghai, Louis would lose face for raising an unfilial son. Beyond that, it would bring shame to the Dengs as well as the bride's family, expose rifts in the family to outside gossip. It would be unforgivable. The family would convey their displeasure, perhaps relegate Louis to some inconsequential part of the business.

But Theo didn't want to marry a stranger. He didn't want to go back to China, even for a month. He wanted a life with Camille.

The growl of engines overhead drove all thoughts away. The sound grew louder with every second, approaching with frightening speed. Fear and instinct kept his legs moving and when he realized he couldn't get to the shelter in time, he threw himself behind a stack of empty barrels and put his hands over his ears.

A single explosion and then the roar of fire. The smell of charred wood, a taste of metal in his mouth, acrid air stinging his eyes. A piece of corrugated iron landed six feet away from him, clattered and then lay still. Then the stench of burning meat. He retched, knowing what it meant.

Just as quickly as it came, the drone of aircraft engines faded away. Theo sat up, dazed. Why just the one bomb? Around the camp, shouting and bustle, officers setting men to work slinging buckets of water over the burning bunkhouse. The bunkhouse where Chao had gone to give two careless men a dressing-down.

Flakes of ash floated in the air, settled on Theo as he returned to the hut and reached for the matches beside the door. He lit the oil lamp and sat down on his cot. Across from him was the chair with Chao's uniform jacket draped over its back.

The badge pinned to the front of the jacket winked in the lamplight, the dull metal stamped with Chao's CLC identity number. Theo looked in the breast pocket and found Chao's identity booklet with his number, his name written out in Chinese and English. Chao Te-Yin, then a birth date and height. They were almost the same height. If Chao had been wearing his jacket, all of this would've burned. But he'd left it in the hut, and Theo had all the information he needed to fill out paperwork for Chao's death.

Next morning came the news that German planes had bombed the nearby aerodrome in Marquise again. The one that attacked the camp had probably just been lightening his load, dropping one more bomb before heading back over the border.

The work crew's mood was somber, and the ganger took his instructions for the day's work from Theo in silence. After the men set off into the forest, Theo spoke to his officer.

"Lieutenant, I need to get paperwork done for the men killed last night," he said. "Permission to leave now and come back after lunch?"

The lieutenant sighed. "Those poor buggers. Go ahead. It's all pretty straightforward work today."

THEO KNOCKED ON THE DOOR of Captain Maitland's hut. This was the second time he had tried the door. The first time he'd knocked he heard what sounded like an answering grunt, but when he pushed open the door, Maitland was snoring on his cot. Even from across the room, Theo could smell the reek of alcohol. Maitland had been wounded while serving in India, and at the start of this war had been assigned to the CLC. Theo suspected the captain's drinking was a long-established habit, and that constant pain from his injuries gave him excuses to indulge even more.

This time, Maitland was up and sitting at his desk. He had washed his face and shaved. Theo felt sorry for him, an elderly officer who had given his best years to the military, hoping to work long enough for a decent pension.

Many members of the regular officer corps looked down on CLC commanders, regarding them as babysitters, unfit for real military duty. Theo had met some who justified this opinion, men who resented the posting and treated Chinese workers abominably. There were others, far fewer, who took a genuine interest in their workers' welfare and knew every interpreter, every worker and camp cook under their command by name.

Maitland was one of those who didn't pay attention, who couldn't remember names. He claimed all Chinese looked alike, ignoring the differences in height and facial features between the men in his company. Yet he wasn't cruel, Theo had decided. Just indifferent. Lost in his own sad world.

"I'm here to do the paperwork for the men killed last night, sir," he said. "I need some forms."

"Ah yes. Terrible, just terrible," Maitland said. "The files are in those drawers. And Tang, remember to write condolence letters to those poor chaps' families on my behalf when you've finished the paperwork."

Maitland, as always, got Theo's name wrong. Theo had never bothered correcting him, since this was a temporary assignment.

"Of course, sir," Theo said, "and may I borrow the typewriter? Then I can work in my hut without disturbing you." Actually, he wanted to work in his hut because Maitland's office was overheated and smelled.

"Excellent suggestion, Tang, excellent."

Theo searched through the folders, the records filed by identity number, and found the two workers' documents. He couldn't find Chao's, then guessed that Maitland hadn't bothered to keep up with filing since his first interpreter died. Theo found his own file stuffed at the front of the drawer and behind it, Chao's.

He hesitated for a moment, then took both files.

Back at his hut he sat at the table, laid out his papers beside Chao's, studied the photographs in their identity booklets. His had been taken last year, upon his arrival at Noyelles. He looked confident, eager. Had he really been that young? Chao's face swam in his memory, looking nothing like the solemn visage in the photo. Carefully he slipped a razor under the dead man's photograph and removed it, then did the same with his own. He glued his picture into Chao's identity booklet. Removing Chao's badge from his jacket, he pinned it on his own. After only a moment's hesitation, he pushed his own identity booklet and Chao's photo into the woodstove.

On the three files from Maitland's office Theo printed the words

Deceased Wimereux, October 21, 1918. He filled out three forms to report the three deaths.

And finally, he addressed three envelopes and wrote three letters of condolence. One to his own father.

Theo walked back to Maitland's hut. "Here they are, sir," he said. "The reports and letters of condolence for your signature."

He breathed a silent sigh of relief as Maitland dashed his signature across the bottom of each form and signed the letters, not bothering to check names or identity numbers. All of that was the interpreter-clerk's responsibility. Theo's responsibility.

Theo took the papers and slipped them in a mail pouch to send on to headquarters in Noyelles. Maitland looked up. "Ah, no need for you to take them to the mail room, Tang. I have some other things to go out, I'll do it myself later."

And just like that, Theo was no more. Deng Taoling was officially dead.

He was now Chao Te-Yin, assigned to Wimereux for the duration. From now on, he would use Chao's identity number and collect Chao's wages, and only someone who knew both his face and his Chinese name, someone who bothered looking up the records, would realize the discrepancy.

To his family, he would be dead. There would be no marriage, no shame on his father or the family.

"MAITLAND PROBABLY DIDN'T TAKE THE pouch to the mail room for days," Theo said. "Since your doctor found the death report at Noyelles headquarters, it means the paperwork finally did arrive. It also means the letter of condolence is on its way to Paris, if not there already."

Pauline shook her head. "We took the early train on Tuesday, before the first mail delivery. If I had left home even just a few hours later . . ."

"It was hard writing that letter," Theo said. "There's a standard form letter, so I only had to copy the words and fill in the name. But it was hard, thinking of you and Father reading those words, Pauline."

"How hard do you think it was for me, believing you'd been killed?" Pauline cried. "Why are you doing this to us?"

"I couldn't see any other way, Pauline," Theo said, reaching for her hand. "My death gives Father less trouble and shame than if I refused that marriage."

"But you've known for a long time about your marriage," Pauline said. "You've known it since you were fourteen."

"And I accepted it, reluctantly. But here, away from Father, away from family, I've realized I can't be the dutiful son."

"But La Pagode will be yours. That's been the plan all along," she said. "You, running the European side of the Deng family enterprise when Uncle retires."

"La Pagode," he said with a wry shrug. "I don't want it. Neither does Father, not really. He was being dutiful to Grandfather and to the family business. He doesn't ever complain but he's only in France because Grandfather sent him."

Pauline thought of her uncle leaning back in his armchair, eyes closed, a Chinese opera record on the phonograph, his fingers tapping unconsciously to the beat of the drum, his hand chopping the air at the clash of cymbals. She thought of their apartment, filled with Chinese furniture. The magazines and newspapers from Shanghai.

"What you're saying doesn't add up, Theo," Henri said, frowning. "You've committed a serious fraud and cut yourself off from your family. What's really going on?"

A long silence as Theo pulled at the fingers of his gloves. He cleared his throat. "I've met someone. The woman I mean to marry is French.

But it will take time so I need to stay until . . . conditions are right. No one can know, not yet. It's a bit complicated."

"Because you're Chinese and she's French?" Pauline said.

Theo looked away.

"Because she's married," Henri said, sitting back and crossing his arms. "Whenever men say a love affair is complicated, it means the woman's married."

Pauline turned to Theo. There was a crooked smile on his face.

"Yes. She's married. But I love her. We'll find a way to be free of her husband and then we'll get married."

"Oh, Theo," she said in despair.

"I have to get back to camp now. But I'll be in Noyelles on Saturday," he said. "Can you stay in Noyelles a bit longer and wait for me there? I've really missed you, Pauline. Let's talk some more. Please don't do anything, don't send Father a telegram, not yet. Promise me."

She sighed. "Yes. All right. But I'm only staying so I can talk you out of this madness."

"You should go now," Theo said. "I'll find a truck driver who can take you to Boulogne so you don't need to walk all the way there. Otherwise you'll miss the last train back to Noyelles."

"But how will I meet you in Noyelles?" she said.

"Wait outside the church at noon on Saturday," he said, standing up. "Now let's go to the British hospital down the street. It's almost time for the supply trucks to head back."

The wind had picked up and the drizzle of rain was now a torrent. Theo put up her umbrella and they walked together, Pauline holding his arm tightly. Henri followed behind holding a newspaper over his head in a futile effort to stay dry.

The top floor of the building that housed the British hospital boasted a sign on its ornate façade that proclaimed its previous function, CASINO HOTEL SPLENDIDE, but placards on the iron palings that enclosed the grounds read NO. 14 BRITISH GENERAL HOSPITAL. Several trucks waited on the street and a driver with a Red Cross armband returned Theo's wave. He jumped off the back of his truck. Theo gave the driver a package of cigarettes and the two shook hands.

"What will you tell that Mah if he sees you here, Theo?" Henri said, climbing into the back of the truck beside Pauline. "He came to your hut with me. If he goes again, he'll find you there."

"I'll tell him there was a clerical error and hope Mah believes it. And it's what you should say, too, if anyone asks."

"But you haven't deserted or anything," Pauline said. "Is it so bad?"

Theo banged on the side of the truck and the driver pulled away. Theo stood in the rain, framed by the opening of the canvas, one gloved hand raised in response to her farewell.

"This whole thing's a mess." Henri shook his head. "Theo wasn't thinking. Too many people in Noyelles know him. What happens if Chao Te-Yin's services are required there? The questions when Theo arrives instead?"

"Henri"—Pauline held up her hand, a plea for silence—"don't say anything. Please don't say anything for a while."

MIRACULOUSLY, HENRI REMAINED QUIET FOR the rest of the ride to Boulogne. But on the train from Boulogne to Noyelles, Pauline knew he wouldn't be able to hold back his curiosity much longer. He squinted and scribbled, throwing glances in her direction.

Pauline slumped against the seat, eyes closed, exhausted by the revelations of the day. She tried to imagine the desperation that had driven Theo to such a rash decision. Tried to imagine herself wanting something so badly that she was willing to cut ties with her family. Even with her eyes closed she could tell Henri, seated across from her, was restless.

"That Mah, I've been thinking," Henri said. "Imagine his life. He started out working for a merchant, joined the Chinese consulate, quite a step up, something his family would brag about. But then he was caught stealing. He didn't want to go back to China in disgrace."

"He should've been on a ship back to China," she said. "We thought he was gone. The consulate sent someone to escort him onto the ship in Marseilles."

"But ships make stops along the way. He could've gotten off at the next port and made his way back to France. Or if his escort left before the ship pulled away from the dock in Marseilles, he could've walked down the gangplank without anyone knowing."

"But why join the CLC?" Pauline said.

"Maybe he didn't have a choice. Any Chinese employer in France would soon learn about him if they didn't already know. But the British need interpreter-clerks very badly, and Mah is more than qualified."

Pauline closed her eyes again. "Well. Anyway, you understand why I worry. Mah has reason to hate us. To harm Theo if he could."

For a while the only sound was the steady, rhythmic metallic rumble of the train.

"Pauline," Henri said, "what about your reason for coming to Noyelles in the first place? All swept to the background when we thought Theo had been killed. What will you do now?"

"What's the point?" she said. "How can I convince Theo to speak to his father on my behalf if he prefers to be dead?"

The lantern inside the carriage cast a weak light, just enough that she could see her face reflected in the glass pane of the compartment door. Then her features faded, replaced by Theo's face and the crooked smile on his face when he said, "But I love her."

CHAPTER 16

Thursday, November 7, 1918

CAMILLE

CAMILLE WAS STILL a bit dizzy, but if she pushed against the wall she could stand up. The toilet at the back of the post office was inside the storage room, which was furnished with an old dresser whose drawers held cleaning supplies. There were plenty of rags for cleaning up the sink. She washed the dirtied rags and hung them to dry on the wooden pegs beside the dresser, splashed her face with cold water to clear her head, and gargled. She took a few anise seeds from the pillbox in her pocket and chewed on them to get the taste of bile out of her mouth. Another mouthful of water, another rinse, and she felt ready to face Mme Dumont.

"All those boys in uniform," Mme Dumont said, looking out the window, "getting their photographs taken before the war is over. The lucky ones, that is, still alive and able to walk into a photo studio."

Camille returned Mme Dumont's smile, trying not to think about Wimereux. Or Pauline. Or Theo. Fortunately Emil had come from the train station in the morning with a sack of mail, so there was plenty to keep her busy in the back room. She put another stack of letters into the mail bag for Emil's delivery route.

"Don't tire yourself out, chérie," Mme Dumont said. Her smile was knowing and questioning at the same time.

"My breakfast didn't agree with me," Camille said, retreating to the back. "I think the egg wasn't fresh but I didn't want to waste it." She couldn't have anyone suspect, couldn't start any gossip that might reach Jean-Paul's ears. After she was gone, it wouldn't matter. But not just yet.

WHEN CAMILLE RETURNED HOME, PAULINE had not yet come back.

She paced through the house, peered out at the deepening darkness, moved from kitchen to front door. She felt the now-familiar pangs of hunger, cravings for cheese and fresh fruit, so she opened a jar of preserved plums. Restless, she threw on a coat and went to the garden room, lit the kerosene heater to warm the space, and checked that the shutters were firmly closed. But what if Pauline was staying the night in Wimereux?

Finally, she went upstairs to undress for bed, but not before lifting up a corner of the blackout drapes. She sighed with relief when she looked out the window. Two people were on the road from Noyelles. She could see only their silhouettes but one was unmistakably Pauline. The other was a man, short and square. Perhaps it was Henri, the friend who had come with Pauline. The two figures paused for a moment at the top of the rise and Pauline continued toward the house. She reached the garden gate and turned back to wave. Only then did the man walk away, his shadow sinking behind the crest of the hill.

Camille hurried downstairs and heated up the pot of soup. She ladled it into a bowl and carried the tray to the garden room, her shoes crunching on the shell path. The shutters of the little room were closed, and she could hear furniture being moved around. She called out quietly and Pauline opened the door.

"It's only soup and bread," Camille said, putting the tray down on the chest of drawers. "If you were coming back tonight at all, I guessed you would be on the last train from Boulogne, without any dinner."

"Thank you," Pauline said. "I'm quite hungry, but I didn't want to disturb you this late. And thank you for warming the room." She had already spread out her coat on the coverlet to dry and moved the heater a bit closer to the bed.

"It's no trouble. Jean-Paul isn't home until tomorrow so this is just reheated leftover soup." Camille perched at the end of the bed so that Pauline could sit on the little wicker chair beside the tray. The Chinese woman smiled her thanks and began eating. The soup was thick with lentils and vegetables, something she often made for Jean-Paul, who only cared that his meal should be filling.

"Were the authorities in Wimereux helpful?" she asked, leaning forward slightly in the chair. She could tell Pauline was tired, perhaps didn't want to talk, but she had to know what happened.

There was a moment of hesitation. "Yes. It turns out the whole thing was . . . an administrative error," Pauline said. "My cousin is alive."

Camille had compelled herself to move carefully through each hour since hearing about Theo's death, holding her emotions in a vise, telling herself she would not give in to grief. Now the knot in her heart loosened so suddenly she couldn't hold back the gasp, couldn't stop her face from crumpling.

"Theo's alive? Oh thank God!" She began to sob, shoulders sagging, both hands covering her face.

Camille heard the clatter of a spoon falling on the brick floor.

She stooped automatically to pick it up, wiped it on her apron. She handed it back to Pauline, who silently finished the soup, scraping the bowl clean. Then the two women regarded each other.

"You've known all along who I am," Pauline said. She glared at Camille. "You never told me you knew Theo. That you're his lover."

"I knew who you were when you first arrived at the château"—Camille wiped her eyes with a sleeve—"but I had promised Theo not to say anything. He wanted to tell you himself when the time was right. Then you heard he'd been killed, so what was the point of saying anything? But now we know he's alive, it was all a mistake. Let's be happy about that."

"Let me tell you about that mistake, Camille." Pauline's voice was flint. "He did it on purpose. He stole another man's identity so he could pretend he'd been killed."

Camille could only stare. "But . . . I don't understand. Why would he do such a thing, why cause your family so much sorrow?"

"He wants to be free of our family so he can be with you!" Pauline said, throwing down her napkin. "Abandon us because of you, Camille."

"He shouldn't do that," Camille murmured. "What sort of person would hurt the ones who love him like that?"

Hesitantly, Camille reached out to Pauline, to touch her on the shoulder or hold her hand, but the younger woman jerked back. Camille looked at her, at all that anger and hurt looking for someone to blame, someone other than the cherished cousin who had betrayed her.

"Please, please, Pauline," she said, "you must tell me. When does he come back to Noyelles?"

"Saturday." Reluctantly.

Thank goodness, Camille would get to see him one last time. "I know you're angry and confused, I don't blame you. But don't be angry with Theo. He's your family. He loves you like a sister."

"I feel as though the world has gone mad!" The words burst out of Pauline. "You, a Frenchwoman, married, in love with a Chinese man.

Theo, fabricating his death so he can escape his arranged marriage, the future his parents set out for him."

"But that's where you're wrong." Camille's voice was soft, sad. "It wasn't sudden. Don't you see he's been trying to escape for years?"

"He's been given everything!" Pauline cried. "My uncle came to Paris and opened La Pagode, a business for him to run, for his future."

"First the Sorbonne, then the CLC. Sometimes, Pauline, I wonder if I'm another excuse for another escape, a final attempt."

"So now you think he doesn't really love you? That you're just an excuse?"

"Whether or not he truly loves me, does it matter?" Camille said. "Loving him is what's made me happy. Loving him has given me the strength to live for myself."

"I can make him give you up," Pauline said. "Tell me, Camille, what would your husband do if he knew you were having an affair with my cousin?"

"He would kill me. I mean that literally. And then he'd kill Theo."

"Get away from me. Just get out!" Pauline burst into tears, shoulders shaking with sobs.

CHAPTER 17

Friday, November 8, 1918

PAULINE

PAULINE STRUGGLED TO sit up, sensing the lateness of the morning, but every movement seemed to require conscious effort. How could she be so tired?

Then she remembered. Theo.

The plunging sorrow of his death, the strain of holding her grief in check. Then to see him alive, only to realize she didn't understand him at all. She had set out for Wimereux anchored by the conviction she was doing what was necessary. And that conviction had sunk like debris tossed in a river.

Had she ever truly known Theo? Or understood how deeply he felt the stigma of his condition, his inability to work with numbers? Pauline swung her legs over the bed and sighed. A childhood memory came back to her, the two of them perched on a garden wall in Shanghai, sharing a paper cone of sugared walnuts. When Theo climbed off the wall and walked away, he avoided the other children in the courtyard. In his own way, like her, a lesser member of the family.

She could barely pull her own thoughts together, let alone summon up arguments to make Theo understand the futility of his romance.

But Henri would help her talk sense into Theo. Persuade him to give up Camille, come back to Paris, and speak to her uncle. What would it take?

On the chair outside there was a pitcher of water, no longer warm, with a clean towel folded over it. There was a note pinned to the towel: Camille had left for work but breakfast was on the kitchen table.

Pauline washed her face. Her boots seemed reasonably dry after a night beside the kerosene heater. The mud on the hem of her skirt had dried and she did her best to brush it off with a corner of the towel. Then she finished dressing and, taking a deep breath, went to the house for breakfast. She was ravenous.

A covered plate on the kitchen table contained bread, a hard-boiled egg, a small pat of butter. The water in the kettle was still warm and she added some coal to the stove's firebox and reheated the water. Someone, no doubt Jean-Paul, had stubbed out a cigarette on the edge of the stove and she threw it in the firebox, then regretted it as the strong, rank tobacco scent rose up with the heat.

She buttered the bread and thought of Theo's sisters. Or rather, their wedding photographs, posed solemnly for the occasion, their faces radiantly lovely. Then there was Undersecretary Chang's wife, her fine eyebrows and bold red lips, the way she strolled up the driveway with the assurance of someone accustomed to wealth and beauty. She thought of the minister's daughter with her sweet oval face, eyes brown and docile like those of a fawn.

Then there was Camille, her plain little face and that quiet voice. So nondescript she could be wallpaper. Pauline sighed. She knew she was being unfair. She needed to know more about this woman, needed to understand why Theo loved her.

She prowled through the lower floor of the cottage, not certain what she was searching for. She examined the framed photographs, ran her finger lightly over the piano. There wasn't a speck of dust anywhere, not a single cobweb clinging to ceiling beams. Pauline stood at the bottom of the staircase, her hand on the newel post, and paused a moment before climbing up.

She opened one bedroom door and then the other, looking briefly inside each one before entering the largest. The window overlooking the back garden was almost obscured by the leafless stems of a climbing rose. The double bed and pair of mismatched armoires told her this was Camille and Jean-Paul's room. A large oil painting dominated the wall across the bed, a rather pudgy man holding the reins of a chestnut horse. Opening one armoire, she saw it was Camille's. The Frenchwoman owned surprisingly few clothes, most in soft faded tints of green and brown, all much washed, carefully mended in places. There was one hanger with a sheet pinned over the dress, the fabric a rich green brocade. Camille's one special dress.

The room across the hall contained a desk as well as a bed, a collection of leather-bound volumes in a low walnut bookcase, most of them on military history. There were framed maps on the wall, a bust of Napoleon.

The third room was the smallest, with a narrow bed. It was neatly made up, a calico spread covering the blanket. A long, fine hair on the pillow. Camille's hair. It appeared she slept in this room sometimes. A pencil sketch of a cat dozing on a chair and a watercolor of sweet peas were pinned above the bed. A framed watercolor portrait of a man hung on the wall, his long nose and narrow face an older, masculine version of Camille's. A small silver frame stood on the chest of drawers, a tinted photograph of a woman with gray hair styled in a pompadour, deep-set eyes that looked out with disconcerting directness. The chest of drawers contained clothes that Camille had outgrown, of finer quality than the ones in the other room, soft wool skirts and linen blouses, ruffled and beribboned, a fall of lace around a neckline. A pair of blue leather shoes wrapped in muslin.

The bottom drawer held sheets of drawing paper, some blank, some used. Sketches of the man with the narrow face, obviously studies made in preparation for the watercolor. Pencil drawings of the countryside, workers bringing in the harvest, picking fruit. Watercolors of mushrooms and ferns, as detailed as botanical drawings. Then a series of small studies in blue ink. Pauline immediately recognized the intricate scenes. Lady Ch'ang O escaping to the moon. The Eight Immortals. Chuang-tzu Dreams He Is a Butterfly. All copied from the blue-and-white porcelains in the cabinet. She arranged everything back in the drawer, feeling grudging admiration for Camille's talent.

She looked under the bed and pulled out a leather suitcase. There were paintbrushes, clean and carefully wrapped inside a paper bag. Boxes with tubes of paint, almost used up but neatly arranged. Two small blank canvases, each wrapped in brown paper. Three oil paintings that resembled the ones she and Theo had seen at the Louvre, the ones that entranced him so much. Impressionist, he called them. Wheat fields heavy with golden grain beneath cerulean skies. A pond reflecting clouds, sunbeams on its surface. A farmhouse, its thatched roof capturing the rosy glow of a setting sun.

Even if Theo had never seen these paintings, this was Camille. This was the light in her soul. This was why Theo loved her.

She wasn't angry with Camille. She was afraid. Because she couldn't see a way out. If Theo refused to give up Camille, it wouldn't matter if he went back to Paris and pleaded with Louis on her behalf. Disgraced, his words would count for nothing. And if she let him go on pretending to be dead, he wouldn't be able to plead for her at all.

PAULINE HAD PROMISED HENRI SHE would meet him in town so she trudged to Noyelles with her umbrella pulled tightly over her head, wrestling every step of the way with a wind that tried relentlessly to pull it from her hands. Few people were out in this weather and she returned a mumbled "bonjour" to anyone who bothered greeting her.

M. Antoine's photography studio was just a few doors down from Noyelles's main intersection. As Henri said, there was only one photography studio in town, she couldn't miss it. The studio had been extremely busy and Henri had been helping M. Antoine develop prints in exchange for use of the darkroom.

Pauline shook the rain from her umbrella and rang the bell. She heard voices behind the door and peered through the window. A great flapping of canvas and two men emerged from behind a backdrop mounted on the wall, one of them Henri, the other an older gentleman in spectacles, stylish and trim in a paisley waistcoat.

"Pauline, come in, come in," Henri said, opening the door. "This is Monsieur Antoine. And this is Monsieur Antoine's newest backdrop." He waved at the canvas, a mansion in the background that vaguely resembled the Château Beaumarchais, dappled light in the foreground shining through a canopy of leaves. When posed, the client would appear as though standing under the trees.

"Now I can open, Henri, thank you for your help," said M. Antoine. "I have several appointments this morning and must prepare the cameras. My darkroom is yours." He bowed to Pauline.

The darkroom was lit by an oil lamp with a red glass chimney mounted on the wall. Henri pulled a heavy black curtain across the door. Pauline wrinkled her nose at the sour smell, the odor of stop bath solution, familiar from all the times she had been in the Girards' darkroom watching Theo and Armand work. There were two stools and she took the one at the end of the worktable.

Henri said, "Monsieur Antoine has been very busy. If the war ends in the next few days, those soldiers will be demobilizing, heading home, and want to take their photos with them."

"Will it really end so soon?" she said.

"Germany's allies are surrendering," he said. "Austria-Hungary signed an armistice a few days ago. And now the Imperial German Navy has mutinied against the kaiser. Apparently, the Allies have given Germany seventy-two hours to agree to terms."

Seventy-two hours. The war could be over in seventy-two hours and Theo could come home. If she could persuade him.

"But the Chinese laborers will stay on, you know," Henri said. "They signed three-year contracts and the British will hold them to it. They'll be doing the cleanup, terrible work. Theo knows what that's like, but I'm betting he will stay anyway to be near his lover."

"Camille. Her name is Camille Roussel."

"You don't mean the same Camille . . ." he began.

"Yes, Camille my hostess. Camille with the barbaric husband. Who will kill Theo if he ever finds out about them and that's not a figure of speech," she said. "How can I convince Theo to change his mind? I'm so angry at Theo, but at the same time, I know Theo doesn't . . . he isn't . . ." Pauline faltered.

"Theo isn't always practical," he finished for her.

"But he listens to you, Henri," she said. "Talk to him. This is madness."

"I can't promise I'll succeed. But I promise to try. Good enough?"

Pauline sighed. "I can't ask for more. He's made up his mind, just as he made up his mind to attend university and enlist with the CLC, so all anyone can do is try."

"Let me finish these photos and I'll take you to lunch." Henri clipped another photograph to the wire strung above the sink, paused to examine it, and shook his head.

"Are those photographs for your newspaper?" she said.

Henri looked up from the tray he was bent over, a pair of long-handled forceps in his hand. "No. My editor doesn't want these kinds of photographs. They're not the sort readers want to see. But without them, my record of what happened here would be incomplete."

Pauline stood up to take a look. From a few feet away, it looked like a horse. When she looked more closely she realized the horse was dead, lying on the ground with its front legs lifted, lips drawn back over its teeth in a final shriek of terror. The lower half of the horse was partly covered by the body of a soldier. Another picture, of Chinese men with grim faces standing beside a bomb crater. Another picture, workers moving between barbed wire, cutting it, taking it down.

"Did you go into the trenches to take these, Henri? Into No Man's Land beyond the barbed wire? How did you ever get permission?"

"I found a ganger willing to let me rent his spare uniform for a day," he said. "His company was fortifying the trenchworks behind Arras. No one pays attention to yet another Chinaman. Not all the photos are horrible. I have a nice one of workers weeding their vegetable garden, and another of a worker whistling to his tame sparrow."

His voice grew despondent. "I tried writing an article about what I saw. But I couldn't. Still can't. No matter how many different ways I approach the story. I've tried while drunk and while sober. It was a nightmare I couldn't bear to relive. I just can't write about it."

He sat on the stool and looked up at the photographs again. Pauline could see his hands shaking even though he rested them on the table.

"Henri," she said and put both her hands over his. "You don't need to write that article right away. Not right now. There's so much else you could write about."

"I can't write about it, and no one else is bothering to write about the men," he said. "That's why I must get this film developed. I'm sending the film and prints to my father, so he can look at them and understand what it's like here. He'll keep them safe for me, for the future. For whenever I can face those scenes again. But if not, those photos are the only way of telling the world what it's been like here for our countrymen. If the world even bothers to listen."

His eyes shone in the red light, dark and haunted. They sat together for a long time, saying nothing. His hands never let go of hers, even after their trembling ceased. Then Henri let go of Pauline's hands and pulled her into his arms.

CAMILLE

SHE HAD PUT Pauline's breakfast on the kitchen table and left a note, judging it best to keep her distance. There was no point. At the end of the day, Camille's own plans had not changed. She would go see Frances on the weekend and, finally, she would confide in someone, ask Frances for help. All the way home after work, she tucked her hands under her arms to keep them warm and pulled her scarf up to cover her cheeks and nose. At least the rain had given way to clear skies.

When she got home, Jean-Paul was sitting at the kitchen table, the floor around him littered with rags and tins of shoe polish. He was slowly and deliberately buffing his boots. Then she saw it on the kitchen table.

A blue metal canister painted with a garland of roses.

She turned quickly to hang her coat on the wall peg by the door, forcing down nausea and fear. She coughed a few times to steady her voice.

"You don't have to polish your boots, Jean-Paul," she said, "I can do that for you after dinner."

"I've almost finished," he said, not looking up. He continued plying the brush over the side of his boots. "Is our Chinese girl eating with us?"

"She didn't say," Camille replied. "She wasn't up when I left the house this morning."

She built up the coals in the firebox, added a little water to the left-over stew, and put it on the stove to heat. She set the kitchen table, all the while waiting for the blow to fall.

"Come here," Jean-Paul said, patting the chair beside him. "Sit."

He picked up the blue biscuit tin and slammed it down in front of her. Camille's heart stopped for a moment and when it started again, the sound of blood pounding in her ears was deafening.

"I found this when I was in the cellar, looking for rags," he said, twisting open the lid. He poured out its contents. Her money. Every-thing that had been left to her and all that she had saved was spread on the tablecloth in front of her, banknotes and gold Napoleons, the jewelry, her own miserable contributions of small coins. When did Jean-Paul ever pick up a rag, ever clean his own boots? Why now?

Camille debated what to say, wondered if she should admit to knowing about the tin. She touched an earring, "This was my grand-mother's."

The tin was clean. She thought of the dusty corner where she had hidden it. Had she absentmindedly wiped it with her apron the last time she put money in? He could tell it hadn't been hidden away and forgotten.

"How did you get this money? And why hide it from me, Camille?" Jean-Paul's tone was deliberately casual, but she could see his hand closing into a fist.

"I think it must've been Grand-mère. Near the end, her memory wandered and she hid things in strange places. When I found it the other day, I just left it there. In case we had need one day." She hoped this would mollify him. She couldn't let him suspect she had been adding to this little hoard.

He pulled her up from the chair and grabbed her shoulders, pushed her backward until she was pressed against the wall. "Never, ever keep secrets from me," he snarled. "What other secrets do you have, Camille? Better confess now."

She shook her head. "Nothing, Jean-Paul. There's nothing to confess."

A slap. Not the worst she'd ever received.

"And you think I would ever let us be in need?" he said. "Why do you think I take all those extra shifts? Why do you think I work at repair yards up and down the line, far away from home? Why do you think I'm in business with Marcel?"

She told herself afterward it wasn't that bad. She'd expected much worse.

It was a silent meal, the contents of the blue tin spread out on the table like an accusation. Jean-Paul swabbed the last chunk of bread around the bottom of his bowl. She took his bowl to the stove, gave the stew a stirring it didn't need, and ladled out another serving for Jean-Paul.

She felt dizzy and a sharp needling pain jabbed inside her head. How would she ever get enough money in time? Even before she met Theo, she had begun saving so that she could leave one day. She hoped Jean-Paul didn't suspect the money was for running away.

"Was the stew all right?" she asked, after he had gulped down the second bowl. "Would you like more?"

He waved a hand dismissively, he'd had enough. If there was one thing Jean-Paul never complained about, it was food. The cure for a hard, stale loaf was to dip it in soup or coffee. Bread had to bloom with mold before he threw it out and even then, sometimes he'd cut off the spoiled surface and toast the rest to make it edible. He never wasted food.

He scooped up the money, left the jewelry.

"We won't sell your grandmother's jewelry," he said, standing up. "You'll need it one day. Marcel and I have a big deal set up for this weekend. Our supplier arrives tomorrow. This money is very useful."

Just like that, he was in a good mood again. Not for the first time Camille wondered if her husband might be insane rather than merely cruel.

Jean-Paul laced up his boots and took his coat and hat from the wooden peg by the door. The heavy green coat and hat once belonged to Auguste, clothing Jean-Paul decided he'd keep for himself. She hated seeing her father's clothes on Jean-Paul.

"I'm meeting with Marcel," he said, wrapping a scarf around his neck. A brown one she had knit for her father. He whistled on his way out.

She slumped over the sink. How would she ever get enough money again? She was running out of time. She didn't know how long she stood there before hearing the garden gate creak.

Pauline had returned. But she didn't come to the kitchen.

CAMILLE KEPT AN EYE ON the clock above the kitchen mantel while she washed up and waited another half hour. Pauline still didn't come in and Camille couldn't wait anymore. She threw a shawl over her head and went outside into the rain-drenched garden, making her way along the familiar path. The night was cold, the rain already turning to sleet. She knocked and without waiting for a reply, opened the door of the garden room.

"I don't want anything from Theo," Camille said, as soon as she stepped inside, before Pauline could say anything. "I want you to know that. But if you want me out of his life, you need to help me."

The younger woman looked startled. Then doubtful. "What kind of help?"

"Money. To leave Noyelles. By myself. Then I'd be out of his life."

"Money. If you care so little for Theo and would leave him for money," Pauline said, "why not just tell him so? Tell him it's over between you two?"

"He'd never believe me," she said. "He knows how much I love him. But it's because I love him that I must be the one to leave. This is a small town. Sooner or later, Jean-Paul will find out."

And Theo would be in danger.

"But how do I know you won't persuade him to leave with you? That you won't disappear together?"

"Because the pair of us would be too noticeable. A white woman and a Chinese man? That would make us so much easier to track down. Jean-Paul mustn't find me. Not ever."

"I'll give you all the money I have right now but it isn't much," Pauline said. "And when I'm back in Paris, I can get you more. If you mean what you say."

"I won't need your money if you can help me with something." Camille took a dishcloth-wrapped bundle from her apron pocket and put it on the bed. The white porcelain jar. "You told me it's worth a lot. Would your uncle buy it?"

Pauline sat on the bed, all of a sudden very businesslike. She examined the jar more closely. "It depends on whether he thinks he can sell it. He has some very discerning clients. But that was before the war. Now, who knows?"

"Please, Pauline, how much? Just a guess."

"If this is really Tang dynasty, then I recall my uncle selling a similar piece a few years ago for fifteen hundred francs."

Camille gasped. More than a year's wages for a female postal clerk.

"I'm not as expert as my uncle," Pauline said, "so I could be wrong. But there are reasons why I think it's that old and valuable."

She ran a finger across the glaze. "The color isn't pure white, there's a grayish tone to it that's typical of the seventh century. A hundred years later, white glazes became more creamy." She turned over the jar and showed Camille the unglazed bottom. "No reign marks pressed into the bottom. Reign marks have only been used since the fourteenth century on ceramics made in the Imperial kilns. My uncle would know what else to look for."

"Will you take it back with you to Paris? Sell it for me?"

"And you trust me with this?"

Camille leaned forward, took the jar from Pauline. "I trust that you want me out of Theo's life." She wrapped it up again in the dishcloth and handed it back to Pauline.

"I'm meeting Theo tomorrow," Pauline said. "He doesn't know I've figured out you're his lover. The woman he was willing to die for. Or at least, pretend to die for."

"I never wanted him to hurt you like that," Camille said. "You're his family."

"What will you do when you see Theo? How can you face him without giving yourself away?"

"I can hide my feelings. I've had a lot of practice since being married to Jean-Paul," Camille said with a wry smile. "When you see Theo tomorrow, tell him not to come here. I don't know what Jean-Paul is doing. It's too risky."

Only the small catch in her throat as she spoke those words betrayed Camille's desperation. Yet her back was straight, her gaze direct and determined. This, more than anything else she had said, convinced Pauline that the Frenchwoman was prepared to leave Noyelles. To leave Theo.

CHAPTER 18

Saturday, November 9, 1918

If there was one good thing about the icy rain, Pauline reflected, it was that it made her as anonymous as the next person. Everyone was hurrying to get under cover, huddled under umbrellas, shoulders hunched against the icy wind. It wasn't just any Saturday. The armistice would be signed in two days. News reports said the German delegation had already crossed over to France under a flag of truce. Stores and cafés on the town's one main street were busy, everyone euphoric at the prospect of peace, every window brightly lit. The bakery and grocery store had stocked up in anticipation of festivities. She bought a dry sausage, some cheese and bread, a pound of dried apricots. The storekeepers were both amused and astonished at hearing perfect French spoken by a Chinese woman.

Soldiers and civilians alike were already celebrating, even though many couldn't bring themselves to hope, not quite yet. They'd suffered years of grinding hardship, had lost husbands and fathers, sons and cousins. Only when guns fell silent and bells rang out would they believe the war was over.

When Pauline reached the small church, it was just past noon, and the drizzle had turned to a fine, cold mist. She stood in the churchyard, keeping close to the oak trees even though it meant standing under their dripping leaves. She wore a hooded oilskin cape she'd found hanging on the door of the garden room, old but still far more practical than her little veiled hat. A contingent of the faithful left the church, umbrellas mushrooming as they dispersed from the steps. Gusts of wind carried a drift of voices, farewells and snatches of conversation, none of it clearly audible.

A familiar figure approached from the street, turned onto the path toward the church. She couldn't decide whether she was furious with Theo or relieved he was alive. But since Wimereux, since her talk with Camille, mostly she felt sad for him.

"It's going to rain harder soon," Theo said, not slowing his stride. "Let's go to a café."

"Henri is working at the photographer's so let's go there to talk," she said, "in a nice, warm darkroom. Then the three of us will walk to Camille's and have supper in the garden room. I believe you know the way."

He stumbled. "So . . . you know it's Camille."

"Yes, and she says not to visit her right now. She doesn't know whether Jean-Paul is in town or going away. But you can come to the garden room. I'm family, you're there to see me. Just don't go near the house."

A jangle of bells announced them when Pauline pushed open the door of the photo studio. She greeted M. Antoine, who was posing an Australian soldier in front of the new backdrop. He waved her in the direction of the darkroom and when she knocked, the door opened to Henri's smile.

"Is it all right that you're here in town?" he said to Theo. "Has anyone seen you?"

"No, I don't think so, but it doesn't matter. They'd only wonder if they'd seen my death report," Theo said. "Anyway, everyone knows that paperwork is a shambles. Duplicate names, identity numbers copied down wrong, death and injury reports lost."

Henri put another print into the tray and Theo moved around the table to watch the photograph develop. A Chinese worker slowly emerged on the paper, solemnly looking into the camera. Henri looked at his watch and gave Theo the thumbs-up, and Theo transferred the print to the next tray, the stop bath. When the print was clipped to the wire, they began talking about cameras.

Pauline coughed and glared at Henri. He cleared his throat.

"Theo, what are you thinking, getting involved with a married woman?" he said. "And Pauline tells me the husband is a brute. He'll kill you if he ever finds out."

"I'm aware what sort of man he is, believe me. All the more reason to stay here so that Camille and I can make plans together for us to run away together," he said.

"Have you saved any money to do that, Theo?" Pauline said.

"Some, but not much," he admitted. "But we have time. At least another year. Henri, time to take that one out."

Pauline sat in the corner of the darkroom, listened to the two men talk. Could Theo even calculate how much money he needed to run away? He'd always had a roof over his head, food in his belly, and clothes on his back. First his father had provided and now the British Army. If he disobeyed his father, who would look after him when the war was over?

"All done!" Theo said. His voice jolted her awake.

She had dozed off in the warm room. She hadn't even heard whether Henri had tried again to talk sense into Theo. But there was still tonight.

"Good to have a well-trained assistant," Henri said, clapping Theo on the back. "If I ever open a photography studio, you've got a job."

"Henri, come eat with us tonight," Pauline said as she slid off the stool. "In the little garden room where I sleep. Nothing fancy, just a few things from the bakery and grocer. Theo and I are going back there now, so whenever you've finished helping Monsieur Antoine, just come over."

THE RAIN HAD STOPPED, AT least for the moment. Theo led Pauline to a lane behind the church. He helped her jump across a ditch then pulled her up onto a path.

"We're actually walking on top of a berm marking the boundary between two fields," he said. "It's a handy shortcut to the road leading out of Noyelles."

The long ridge was wide enough that people had been using it as a path, walking single file. One side had been planted with a sheltering windbreak of poplar trees, the other was a tangle of wild shrubs that snagged at Pauline's coat. Damp leaves covered the path but it wasn't muddy, its sloping height quickly shed water. Although the rain had stopped, the trees still dripped and Pauline kept the hood of her borrowed oilskin up.

After a few minutes, Theo spoke. "You and Henri. Is there something between you?"

"I think we're just friends," she said, "but closer friends since coming to Noyelles. Since he agreed to help me."

"I think you mean more than that to him," he said. "While you were asleep in the corner he told me . . ."

"It isn't anything serious, Theo," she said firmly. "I don't want to talk about it."

Pauline had been telling herself this since Henri kissed her yesterday. That it was only because he'd needed comfort after remembering the horrors he had seen. They were just friends. That's all she could ever be to him. She was not part of his future.

"Then let's talk about something else," he said. "You haven't told me yet why you came to Noyelles in the first place. I asked Henri and he said I should ask you myself because it's a family matter."

Now at last, the conversation she imagined having with Theo when she first made up her mind to come find him.

"Uncle is sending me back to Shanghai," she said. "Your mother is arranging a marriage for me. Theo, you must come back to Paris and ask Uncle to stop the matchmaking. Have him send a telegram to your mother. Before it's too late."

"I don't follow. You don't want to be married?"

"Not an arranged marriage to a stranger. Not one that takes me away from France. You of all people should understand. But you can't help me if you're dead."

"Maybe there's another way. I'll ask Henri to propose to you."

Pauline turned to face him. "Theo, this is not funny. This is my life, my future."

"I'm sorry. I do understand. Look, there it is." Theo gestured ahead of them to a gap between trees and shrubs. "Voilà! The main road out of Noyelles."

Pauline realized she must've walked right by the path several times on her way to and from the cottage. Its opening was almost completely screened from the road by brambles. A gust of wind made her clutch at Theo, pulling him back, suddenly uneasy. Uneasy about something carried on the air. Not a sound, but a scent. A rank, pungent tobacco smell that was horribly familiar.

"Theo, be quiet," she whispered. "Someone's out there on the road."

He frowned, but the distress on her face made him obey. They edged closer to the gap. She couldn't see them, but she could hear two men talking. It sounded as though they were on the road just beyond the shortcut. The voices were loud and agitated.

"I told you to bring two proper knapsacks," said the first man. He spoke French with a Chinese accent and was clearly annoyed. "Two, not one knapsack and a paper bag."

"That's Mah," Theo said quietly. "What's he doing in Noyelles? His company only just arrived in Wimereux the other day."

"Piss off, you stinking chintok," said a second voice, equally annoyed. "It's your fault for bringing too much at one time."

"That's Jean-Paul," Pauline whispered.

"This little business might be all over once the armistice is signed," Mah said, "and then you'll complain I should've brought more today. Put what you can in your pockets and get to the train station. I'll hold on to the rest. Tomorrow at the usual time and place."

A figure passed the gap in the shrubs, his hurried steps taking him in the direction of Noyelles. Then the second man walked by, moving more slowly, but also in the same direction. Pauline let out her breath, waited another few minutes. They were gone. The two men she least wanted to see.

"What do you suppose that was all about?" Theo said in a low voice. "What sort of business could a CLC interpreter possibly have with a French railway mechanic?"

"Who cares? As long as neither of them saw you." Pauline ducked under an arching stem of blackberry and came out onto the road only to see Mah crouched on the ground beside a brown paper bag. It was torn and Mah was gathering up small white boxes that had fallen out, stuffing them in his knapsack. He looked up, as startled as she was, and the smile that came over his face widened when he saw Theo behind her.

"Ah, Baoling," he said. "And young Master Deng. How fortunate. I was going to look for you here in Noyelles, young master. Now could you hand me that box over there beside your foot, I missed it."

Pauline picked up the small white cardboard box. It was spattered with mud but the labels were still legible, as were the hospital markings.

"Morphine tablets," Theo said, taking it from her hand. "Supplies from the hospital. You're stealing from the hospital."

"I steal, my partners sell," Mah said amiably. "We all make money. We have contacts for buying and selling all kinds of goods in every town along the front. But you won't say a word. Not a word."

"You're stealing from our own countrymen, Mah. I'm not keeping quiet."

"But you will keep quiet." The older man grinned. "Unless you want me to show your commanding officers proof that you stole another man's identity. I'd say that would mean arrest followed by a military tribunal."

Suddenly Pauline couldn't breathe.

"I don't know what you're talking about," Theo said, rather stiffly.

"I asked around before I left Wimereux last night," Mah said, "and according to workers who knew him, the interpreter who died was called Chao. They were sure it wasn't you, no, not the handsome one, not you. I went to CLC headquarters this morning and said I wanted Chao's file to get his next of kin's address, to write a letter of condolence. Well, I'm sure you can guess what the nice British army clerk handed me."

Both Theo and Pauline were silent.

"There you were, filed under the dead." Mah wagged a finger. "You've been clever, very clever."

"An error," Theo said.

"A deliberate act, young Master Deng," Mah said with a sneer. "Your drunken Captain Maitland didn't do the paperwork. You did. You were the only interpreter-clerk he had. It was no error. But now I wonder why you'd do such a thing."

"All right," Theo said, cutting him off. "I won't tell anyone you stole drugs from the hospital."

"You'll do more than that," Mah said with a satisfied nod. "You owe me, Deng. You're the one who had your father call the consulate and the gendarmes. I plan on taking a large supply of drugs out of the hospital tomorrow night and you're going to help me."

Theo's shoulders sagged. Mah's smug smile told Pauline they both knew Theo had no choice. "Are you expecting Theo to break in?" Pauline said.

"Not at all. Not when you have these," Mah said. He grinned and pulled a chain from his pocket, dangled it so that the small collection of keys tinkled. "Camps can be so careless with their keys. Meet me in the mess hall on Sunday night, Deng, just before lights out. Bring a large bag with you. Not too large or obvious."

Mah turned toward Noyelles, then stopped.

"Young Master Deng," Mah called. "One more thing. I haven't figured out yet why you'd want to change places with another man. But I will. Before we're through with each other, I will."

They said nothing until Mah vanished around the bend.

"What did he mean, a military tribunal?" Pauline said.

"Court-martial and imprisonment." Theo looked down at the ground. "Everyone in the CLC is subject to British military law even though we're civilians."

"So fix it, Theo," she cried. "Go and correct the paperwork before anyone else notices. Steal them, so there's no evidence at all."

"I wouldn't know how." He shook his head. "The CLC bureaucracy may be inefficient and chaotic, and I took advantage of that. But stealing documents is another matter. I can't get inside that building."

"But a court-martial," she said. "I can't lose you again, Theo. There must be something we can do."

"Hush, don't worry," he said. "Mah is the only one who's put the pieces together and he needs my help."

Words failed her. Why couldn't Theo see that if he helped Mah steal drugs, that was one more crime Mah could use to blackmail him? Pauline put up her umbrella and pulled him under it.

"Let's go," she said, looking up at the gray sky.

She had to get Louis to buy Camille's jar, get the money to Camille as quickly as possible, even if she had to take the train from Paris to Noyelles and deliver it personally. Then Camille could disappear from Theo's life. Then Theo might reconsider his feigned death, at least explain to his father it had just been a paperwork error. Then he could appeal to Louis on Pauline's behalf. Would any of this happen in time, before First Wife settled her marriage contract?

None of it mattered. Pauline almost stopped in her tracks.

Cold as the November wind, stark reality blew through her mind, clearing her thoughts of all but the most immediate danger. What mattered most urgently was for her and Camille to prevent the calamity that was sure to come: Jean-Paul learning about the affair. Jean-Paul going after Theo. Camille had to disappear without a trace. And soon.

INSIDE THE GARDEN ROOM PAULINE closed the shutters. She spread a dishcloth on the daybed and laid out her groceries. Theo flopped down on the daybed beside the food.

"This is horrible," he groaned. "Camille is right there, and I haven't seen her in weeks."

"She said you weren't to go near her," Pauline said. "It's too risky. We don't know when Jean-Paul's coming back. Maybe tonight. Maybe in time to meet Mah at their usual spot tomorrow, whenever that may be."

"He's not in Noyelles," Theo said. "He ran to the train station. He's gone."

"Or perhaps he just had to give those drugs to someone getting on a train and he's still here." All the possibilities and risks had been clicking through her head, the way they never seemed to for Theo. She sighed.

"We need some utensils and cups. I'll get them from the kitchen."

Pauline didn't have to knock on the kitchen door. Camille was already there and pulled her inside.

"What are you doing?" she gasped. "Why did you bring Theo here? What if Jean-Paul finds out? What if a neighbor should see and tell Jean-Paul?"

"You can explain he's here to be with me, his cousin," Pauline said. "No one will see, it's getting darker as we speak. We're having supper together, and Henri is coming later. Can I borrow a knife and three forks, three cups?"

Silently Camille set the items on a small tray, added three napkins, and handed them to her.

"Camille, I didn't bring Theo here just to have supper," she said. "I wanted him to take a look at the jar. He knows more about Tang porcelain than I do, almost as much as my uncle. If I'm wrong and the jar is worthless, I will get some money to you, I promise. Even if I have to steal from my uncle, I will get money to you."

"No, I don't want you to do that," Camille said.

"Unless you can afford to run away, I don't know of another way to separate you from Theo." She picked up the tray. "I'll make sure Theo doesn't come to the cottage."

When Pauline returned to the garden room, Theo was peering out from the shutters. It was obvious he'd been hoping for a glimpse of Camille. He opened the door and closed it behind Pauline.

"This romance of yours is madness," she said, putting the tray on the chest of drawers.

"Madness? She is the only thing that makes sense in a world gone mad." Theo's expression was soft. "My life would be as desolate as No Man's Land without Camille."

"There's something I want you to look at." Pauline pulled her carpetbag out from the corner, lifted out the dishcloth-wrapped bundle. "Be careful, it's porcelain."

Theo knelt by the low table and brought the jar closer to the lamp. He removed the lid and examined it, set it down carefully. He turned over the jar to look at the underside.

"No reign marks, but you can see that. Not a pure white glaze, more of a grayish white, a good sign. Some tiny brown spots and fine crackling, a good sign. Give me some water."

Theo took the basin Pauline held out, dipped his finger in it, and dripped some water on the bottom of the jar. They watched the water vanish, absorbing quickly into the unglazed surface, leaving behind a dark stain. "Another good sign. Sniff where the water dripped. Does it smell slightly musty, like old earth?"

She nodded. "So it's real? Not a copy?"

"It's rare to see one with the original lid intact. Where did you get this?"

"It's Camille's. Something her father brought back from China. She had it on a kitchen shelf. I was curious and she let me take it for a closer look."

"She should put it somewhere safe, not the kitchen," he said, shaking his head. "It isn't the most expensive piece I've seen but quite valuable. If this were at La Pagode, we would probably sell it for fifteen hundred francs, maybe eighteen. The lid makes a huge difference."

Fifteen hundred francs. Pauline had been right. And it would be enough for Camille.

AFTER PAULINE TOOK AWAY THE tray of utensils, Camille moved through the cottage, pulling all the drapes shut. Was there even any need to follow blackout rules, with peace only days away?

A knock on the front door, and she peered through the parlor window. Darkness hid the man's face, but she knew from his height and bulk that it wasn't Theo.

A wide smile had greeted her. "Madame, I am Henri Liu. I'm a friend of Pauline's."

"Yes, she's in the garden room, over there." Camille pointed it out.

Henri peered into the night. Beyond the sliver of light from the open door behind Camille, the darkness was impenetrable. She imagined him crashing into the birdbath, tripping into her flower beds.

"Just a moment, please; I will show you the way."

Camille lit an oil lantern and pulled on her coat. Henri kept pace beside her, stumbling only a little when the curved path took them under the apple tree and bare branches grazed their heads. She didn't have to take him all the way. The door of the garden room opened and Theo stood there in a wedge of light, Pauline beside him.

"Camille, please," he called. "Come join us."

Pauline's voice, softer. "Leave her be, Theo. Henri, come in out of the cold."

Camille turned away and didn't look back.

Then she had undressed in the cottage and wrapped herself in a blanket, sat by the window with the bedroom in perfect darkness. How many hours did she sit there until she saw the two men leave? She drew back a bit, in case Theo looked up and saw her pale face behind the glass. She watched them walk over the rise in the road and then they were gone. She let out a long breath.

CHAPTER 19

Sunday, November 10, 1918

I t was freezing outside; no, colder than freezing. Shivering, Camille went downstairs to stoke the woodstove, then bundled up to go feed the hens. She put a dried corncob inside the coop as a treat and laid down another layer of bedding straw. Back in the kitchen she sat on a low stool by the stove to keep warm, head buried in her arms. The events of the previous night ran through her mind over and over. She had done the right thing last night by refusing to join the little party.

If Jean-Paul's plans had changed, if he had come home unexpectedly, it wouldn't matter to him that Theo was supposedly just visiting his own sister. Not because Jean-Paul suspected anything, not yet. Just because one could never be sure what set off his rage.

Camille made porridge, something she only cooked when Jean-Paul wasn't there. He hated porridge. It was the only food he refused to eat, even when she flavored it with cinnamon and slivers of dried apple. Suddenly the sight of the mushy porridge made her sick. She retched into the stone sink, her legs too unsteady to support her without her holding on to the sink. When she'd stopped panting for breath, she splashed cold water on her face, drank from the tap to rinse her mouth. With a deep sigh, she stood upright.

Cold air blew around her legs. She turned around to see Pauline at the kitchen door. There was a shock of comprehension on the younger woman's face.

It was the way Camille straightened up, one hand pressed to her back. A memory surfaced in Pauline's mind of Lise. After her friend moved to Sèvres with her new husband, they only saw each other when Lise came to Paris to visit her parents. In the middle of one such visit, Lise abruptly scrambled up from her chair and ran to the kitchen sink. Mme Girard murmured soothing words, holding back Lise's long hair while she retched violently. Once it was over, Lise pressed a hand against her back as she stood up. Lise's mother didn't seem concerned and Lise smiled before rinsing her mouth with a cup of cold tea. Mme Girard patted Lise's stomach and they both laughed.

"The baby, is it Theo's?" Pauline said. She didn't know if it was fear or excitement that made her tremble.

"The odds are good," Camille said.

"But you can't be sure?"

"No, but I am sure of one thing. If the baby is Jean-Paul's, what sort of father would he be?" Camille said. "I'd fear for my child's safety every day. And if the baby turns out to be Theo's, well . . ."

Pauline didn't want to imagine what Jean-Paul would do.

"So now you know all of it," Camille said, stirring the oatmeal. "Jean-Paul doesn't know I'm pregnant, but soon I won't be able to hide it from him. Or from Theo."

Theo, who was bound to do something foolishly valiant.

"I understand." Pauline sighed. "You have to get out of Noyelles. Sooner rather than later. But I have good news."

"The jar. Does Theo think it's valuable?"

"Extremely valuable. Theo thinks his father would pay fifteen hundred francs."

Camille stopped stirring the oatmeal. "Can you take it to Paris for me? Will your uncle really buy it?"

"I'll make sure he does." A baby. Theo's child.

Pauline would be like an aunt to the baby, if she could help raise the child. "Camille, when you run away, come to Paris. You could leave with me tomorrow, next week, I've got enough money for train fare. Theo will follow, I'm sure he'll find a way to leave the CLC once he knows about the baby."

"Absolutely not." Camille shook her head. "You will not tell Theo anything. I don't want him to feel obliged."

"He won't feel obliged. We're talking about his baby!"

"But what if it's Jean-Paul's baby?" she countered. "What then? And even if the baby is Theo's, what would I be to your family or to Theo? A mistress like Denise? I must make my own way, Pauline. All the decisions I've made have been for the baby's welfare. The most helpful thing you can do for me is sell that jar."

Pauline hardly noticed the porridge as she ate, her thoughts muddled by excitement and worry. "Yes, all right. How should I send the banknotes? To you at the post office?"

"No. Nothing addressed to me," Camille paused. "Send it to Frances Newland, Château Beaumarchais, with a note to contact me. She's the only one I trust."

"I'll go home tomorrow then," Pauline said. "My uncle will be home by now, and I should be there. Even if I don't know yet what to say about Theo."

Then she remembered. "Camille, I have something to tell you about your husband and a man named Mah. And Theo."

It felt like another blow to Camille. Theo's reckless decision to forge his own death had led to this. Now he was vulnerable to extortion, forced to help this man Mah steal drugs from the hospital. And if that wasn't bad enough, Mah was one of Jean-Paul's partners in their black-market trade. Mah must've been the "little Chinaman" Marcel mentioned.

"Theo didn't seem to take us seriously last night," Pauline said. Her voice revealed the depth of her exasperation. "Henri and I kept pointing out that if he helped Mah steal from the hospital pharmacy, he would be giving the man even more to hold over him. He seems to think that since Mah can't give him away without giving himself away, it will be fine."

"Unless he's caught," Camille said, "or unless that Mah makes him do more dangerous things."

Pauline shook her head. "If only Mah hadn't seen me in Wimereux. Then if he ran into Theo it would've been awkward but he wouldn't have had reason to look deeper."

So many "if onlys." If only Pauline hadn't come to Noyelles. If only Theo hadn't exchanged identities with Chao. If only Camille and Theo hadn't fallen in love.

"You'd better go to the railway station today, Pauline," Camille said, "make sure of tomorrow's schedule, and buy your ticket. Take my bicycle, it'll be faster."

"Yes. And I'll find Theo and Henri, let them know I'm leaving in the morning."

VOICES OUTSIDE BROUGHT CAMILLE TO the kitchen window. Jean-Paul stood on the road beside Old Fournier's wagon, the two of them evidently finishing a conversation. They laughed and Fournier's donkey cart rolled away.

"Your bicycle isn't outside," Jean-Paul said. "I thought you'd gone out." He dropped his knapsack on the kitchen floor and sat on the bench by the door, feet thrust out slightly so that Camille could pull his boots off.

"Pauline borrowed it. She's gone to buy a train ticket. She's leaving tomorrow. Will you be taking a nap before supper, Jean-Paul? You've worked at least two shifts." She placed his boots by the stove to dry.

"I ran into Madame Dumont," he said. "She asked after your health, because you didn't go to Mass this morning."

"I decided not to attend Mass. I had to finish all that sewing for the château." Camille gestured to the dining room, where piles of fabric rosettes sat on the table. "And it's done now. I'll deliver them when Pauline brings back the bicycle."

"The good Madame Dumont gave me a rather stern look," Jean-Paul continued, as if she hadn't spoken. "She told me I should be more careful looking after you this time. This time, Camille? What are you not telling me?" He pulled her around and tapped a finger on her stomach.

Camille took a deep breath before speaking. "I wasn't sure, Jean-Paul. I didn't want to tell you until I was sure. Madame Dumont shouldn't have said anything. It's still too soon."

"Not so soon that an experienced grandmother like Madame Dumont wouldn't notice."

Something was wrong. He had been so happy the first time he learned she was pregnant. But Camille had to pretend everything was normal. "I'll be careful, Jean-Paul. Don't worry."

It had taken years for her to train body and face and voice to be her accomplices so that she could lie to Jean-Paul and present a blank expression. For her eyes and ears to observe his every twitch and change of tone. Even her heartbeat and breathing collaborated to dampen spikes of panic.

"Let me tell you what worries me," he said. "I got a ride home today from Old Fournier. He strolled past our home last night. You had company, he said. A party going on in the garden room."

She put a bottle of beer in front of him as gently as she could, willing her hand to stay still. "Pauline's cousin was here. They had dinner by themselves in the garden room."

"I thought her cousin was dead," he said. "Theo, didn't she say that was his name?"

"It turned out to be a paperwork error. A good reason for them to celebrate, don't you think?" Camille spoke the words lightly, prayed that was the end of the matter, but Jean-Paul remained ominously still.

"Fournier saw you heading for the garden room, walking beside a chintok. No mistake, you were holding a lamp."

The old farmer, walking home in the dark. She cursed her luck. First Mme Dumont and now Fournier. Desperately she tried to remember her actions from the night before.

"One of them called you by name, Camille. 'Camille, come join us' was what Fournier heard one of them shout to you." A blow across her face sent her sprawling to the floor. "Just how friendly are you with them that they knew to call you by name?"

"Jean-Paul, please. It was just Pauline's cousin and his friend. They were visiting Pauline." She looked up from the floor and knew what came next would be bad.

"First, only Pauline's dead but now not-dead cousin was here. And now the cousin's friend."

Camille did her best to hold her arms over her belly while his blows fell on her. She couldn't lose this child. "Please, Jean-Paul, the baby. Your baby." He might be kinder if he thought the baby was his. She just needed a little bit longer.

"But is it mine, dear wife?" He crouched beside her. "You've been running a whorehouse for Chinamen? The money I found in the biscuit tin. Did you earn that opening your legs for foreign scum?"

More shouting. More pain. Jean-Paul shaking her. "And the other man, who was the other man with that Theo person?"

"Jean-Paul, I wasn't doing anything improper," she sobbed.

"You've humiliated me in front of Fournier! Ruined my reputation. Who was the other chintok?"

"I don't remember." She couldn't think. She couldn't remember. A name pushed itself onto her tongue. "Mah. They said his name was Mah."

He cursed loudly, kicked her again. "You're lucky I have a meeting now," he said. "But it won't take long. And before I come home tonight both your Chinese boyfriends will be dead."

But the irony of it all, she thought, just before the world turned black, was that even though he didn't know she loved Theo, Jean-Paul was going to kill him anyway.

SWIRLS OF FROST ETCHED THE glass on shop fronts with fronds of ghostly ferns. Every window on Noyelles's main street was festooned with tricolor bunting, strings of small flags. The war was nearly over. There was no doubt anymore that the armistice would be signed tomorrow. Despite the cold, doors to cafés and bars stood open, celebrations already starting.

After Pauline bought her ticket at the railway station she had gone to the photography studio. Henri was still working in the darkroom, now with Theo helping. They had spent the night at the studio, on a pair of settees M. Antoine used for posing large families.

"The less time I spend at the camp, the better," Theo said. "And helping Henri develop prints gives me something to do."

"Good to have you here, Theo. Together we should be able to finish all these prints in a couple of hours."

Pauline patted her bag. "I'm taking the train home to Paris tomorrow morning."

"What will you tell my father?" Theo said.

"I'm not sure yet," she said. "But whatever I say, I won't mention Camille for now."

"Thank you, cousin," he said.

"If Pauline is leaving Noyelles in the morning, then I'll go with her," Henri said.

Theo rummaged in his shirt pocket. "Can you take this note to Camille for me? I simply must see her before I head back to Wimereux tomorrow. It might be weeks before I can take leave again."

"It's up to her, not you," Pauline said, "and shouldn't you worry more about tonight? When you become a criminal? What if you and Mah get caught?"

"If it's any consolation," Henri said, "I think Mah knows what he's doing and won't get caught. It sounds as though he's made a career of it."

"It's just this once." Theo sounded glum, not at all as though he believed it. Pauline suspected Henri had made him understand the hold Mah would have over him.

Pauline rode back to the Roussels', grass and dried leaves stiff with frost crunching beneath the bicycle's tires. She crossed over icy puddles with leaves trapped inside, each pool an album of frozen specimens. A strong gust of cold wind made the bicycle wobble. She had put on her heavier wool skirt and wrapped her head and shoulders in a shawl Camille insisted on lending her; now she wished she'd put on an extra pair of stockings. But at least cycling was keeping her warmer than walking.

The Chinese camp was lively when Pauline passed it. There didn't seem to be anyone in the yard who wasn't busy. The workers were organizing their own Armistice Day celebrations. Some men were applying paint to a wooden arch and others were building an outdoor stage. Men in bright costumes practiced walking on stilts while others turned cartwheels in a display of acrobatics. Strains of broken melodies from an unseen orchestra assaulted her ears, the crash of cymbals and high-pitched whistling of pipes as the musicians rehearsed.

The château was equally busy, with gardeners raking the gravel driveway and delivery wagons pulling up to the side entrance. A small donkey cart turned onto the road from the château, and a blast of wind sent debris flurrying from the planks of its load bed, bits of greenery and a few pale petals. Even in winter, Mme Newland had somehow managed to get fresh flowers.

The wind picked up even more as Pauline reached the fork in the road that turned toward the hamlet of Sailly-Bray. This section of the road was lined with plane trees, branches now bereft of leaves, no longer useful as shelter for birds. She cycled a little faster, encouraged to see she was already at the ruined barn. It stood at the boundary of two fields, the weathered planks of its broken door barely hanging onto a single hinge. The field was scarred with craters, evidence of a bombing from the early years of the war.

Pauline tugged the shawl over her head more securely and thought longingly of Camille's warm kitchen. Even if Jean-Paul was at the cottage, it was worth going in just to stand by the stove for a few minutes.

Then the sound of a gunshot, quickly followed by a second shot. She scrambled to crouch behind a tree, bicycle flung to the ground.

When no other gunfire followed, she stood up and slowly, cautiously, peered around the trunk. A man hurried out of the barn, a knapsack over one shoulder. She froze against the tree, then let out her breath as she realized he was running away from her, moving across the fields toward Noyelles. He wore a greatcoat like Theo's, a CLC winter coat. One shoulder hunched higher than the other.

It looked like Mah but she couldn't be sure.

The man paused and looked around, his movements furtive. When he turned in her direction, Pauline saw it was indeed Mah. He stiffened when he saw her. But had he recognized her, all bundled up like a farm wife? He quickened his pace almost to a run and didn't look back.

Pauline rescued the bicycle from the side of the road and pedaled as fast as she could. Had Mah fired the gun or had someone else? What happened inside that barn? She'd ask Camille what to do.

Ten minutes later, she leaned the bicycle against the house and knocked on the kitchen door. There was no reply, but the door wasn't locked so she pushed it open, called out a greeting as she entered.

The first thing Pauline noticed was that one of the chairs at the kitchen table had been knocked over. Then the two bowls on the table, both scraped clean of soup, the cutting board with a heel of bread and crumbs of cheese. An empty beer bottle, knocked over. An empty flask of cognac.

And through the table legs she saw Camille's inert body curled on the floor.

CAMILLE FELT A DAMP CLOTH pressed against her face, heard a woman's voice call her name. There was a salty, coppery taste in her mouth. The pain in her ribs as she turned over made her cry out, but she opened her eyes.

Pauline. Thank goodness, it was Pauline.

"Theo," she managed to gasp. "You must go warn Theo. A neighbor saw us last night and told Jean-Paul there were Chinese men here."

"How would Jean-Paul know it was Theo?" Pauline slipped a hand under her back.

Camille wanted to cry, but just drawing breath hurt. "I told him Theo was visiting you, that it was nothing to do with me. But it didn't matter. Old Fournier saw me and heard Theo call my name."

Pauline sat back on her heels. "Oh, Camille. It's my fault for asking Theo and Henri to come here for supper. I didn't think there'd be any danger . . ."

"It doesn't matter now." Camille sat up, one hand on her side. "He knows Theo was here. He accused me of entertaining men while he's away. He's gone into town. Pauline, he will kill Theo if he finds him."

"Theo's probably still at the photo studio with Henri," Pauline said, helping Camille onto a chair. "But you need a doctor."

"No, you ride into town. Warn Theo. I'll be all right here." But Camille's breathing was ragged and she couldn't help gasping. Her ribs. Instinctively, she put an arm against her stomach, feeling for damage.

Pauline saw the motion and knelt beside her. "The baby? Is it all right?"

She managed a weak smile. "Go. Go warn Theo."

Pauline stood up. "Camille, what about that little trailer-wagon? Can you sit or lie in it? I'll take you to the château, to the nurses and doctors there. Then I'll go into town and warn Theo."

"No. I'm not moving. I can't. I can't risk it." She moaned and drooped to the floor again. "I can't lose the baby."

"You risk more by not getting immediate medical attention," Pauline said. "I'm not leaving you here."

Pauline attached the trailer to the bicycle and lined its bottom with a quilt. Camille tried not to cry out as Pauline helped her outside and had her lie down in the trailer, head and neck propped on a cushion. She curled up as best she could, but her ankles and feet still dangled over the end of the trailer bed. Pauline pushed the bicycle onto the road and began pedaling.

Camille could tell Pauline was trying to avoid potholes, but her bruised body felt every small bump. They reached the rise in the road and Pauline climbed off the bicycle to push.

"We only need to get as far as the château," she panted, "and then you'll be in good hands. If a wagon or automobile comes by, we'll stop them to give you a ride to the château."

It was easier as they neared the main road to Noyelles where the terrain leveled out. With Pauline pushing, it would take at least another twenty minutes to reach the château. Camille turned her head to look up at the uncertain light. Broken through the trees, the winter sun was just starting to make its descent. She'd always loved cycling beneath the trees on this stretch of road in the summer. She tried to think about the summer, about the way sunlight winked and fluttered through the leaves above. Tried not to think about the agony in her ribs each time the trailer rattled over uneven ground.

"I'm stopping," Pauline said, her voice strained. Somehow Camille could tell it wasn't from the struggle of pushing the bicycle. "There's something in the ditch."

She stopped at the side of the road, close to the trees. Camille sat up slowly, using the sides of the trailer to pull herself upright. She could barely breathe without pain flaring in her ribs. They were by the d'Amervals' old barn.

Cautiously, Pauline moved to the edge of the embankment and looked over the side. She turned and put a finger to her lips before Camille could call out to ask what she'd seen. Then she clambered down the bank, vanishing from sight for some minutes. She appeared again, scrabbling on hands and knees to get over the top of the bank, eyes wide, her face pale despite the exertion.

Without saying anything, she helped Camille out of the wagon and half carried her to the side of the road where she could lean against a tree. Pauline pointed down.

A man lay crumpled at the bottom of the embankment, facedown in the wide irrigation ditch that ran along the foot of the berm. If not for the wind lifting his hair, he would've been utterly still.

A familiar hunter-green coat, a brown woolen scarf. Black hair.

From the trail of blood and broken grass stalks, the women could tell that Jean-Paul had crawled some distance before losing consciousness, too weak to climb up the embankment's steep sides. The ground beneath his body was dark with blood.

"He's unconscious, still alive," Pauline said, her voice low. "I think he was shot, Camille. On my way to the house I heard two gunshots and saw a man running away from the barn. It was that horrible Mah."

"Mah? You think it was Mah who shot Jean-Paul?" Camille pressed one hand against a tree, head spinning from vertigo. She wanted to vomit. They both whispered, as though the unconscious man could hear them.

"I was frightened and just wanted to get back to your cottage," Pauline said. "I didn't know your husband was in the barn. But why would Mah shoot him? They were in business together."

"What should we do, Pauline?"

In reply, the Chinese woman looked at her. Camille understood. Jean-Paul was her husband. Her decision.

"Can we put him in the wagon, too? Take him to the château?" Camille spoke the words, but her tongue felt wooden.

"Camille, I don't know if I could even drag him up to the road," Pauline replied. She took Camille's hand in hers and clasped it tightly.

The fear in Camille's chest that fluttered like a trapped bird was all for her unborn child and for Theo, not for herself. She could barely walk, and pain bloomed in every part of her body, but the sight of Jean-Paul's inert form sent a rush of relief through her.

"He'll freeze to death if he lies out in the open much longer," Pauline said. "We should tell them, when we get to the château."

They looked at each other. Camille, with one eye swollen shut, blood still trickling from her nose and a cut lip. Pauline, her expression carefully neutral, only the dark light of her eyes betraying her thoughts.

"Whatever you decide, Camille, it's between the two of us. No one else will ever know."

After a long silence, Camille looked down the bank one more time and squared her shoulders. "Then let's go." Her voice was like the dry snap of twigs.

Pauline helped Camille back into the trailer. They continued along the road toward the château, the last of the afternoon sun shining through bare branches.

AS SOON AS FRANCES CAME to the front door, she took charge. She had Camille carried on a stretcher to a room in the private wing of the château. A doctor arrived minutes later; he spoke French heavily laced with an American accent.

He leaned down to look more closely at Camille's bruised and swollen face, shook his head. "Who did this to you, Madame?"

Camille realized she'd never be able to explain away her injuries. The marks couldn't have come from anything but a brutal beating. She didn't have to say anything however, because Pauline answered for her.

"Her husband. And it's not the first time."

There was a shocked intake of breath from Frances, but the doctor just nodded and continued his examination.

Camille felt strangely relieved now that Pauline had blurted out the information. She didn't need to make the effort of hiding behind the façade of a decent marriage anymore. She knew of other marriages, other husbands who abused their wives. It was frowned upon, but no one interfered. These were matters between husband and wife.

"Bruises on face and limbs," he finally said, "nasty, but ice packs will help. The worst thing you have are two cracked ribs, but without an X-ray machine I can't be certain."

"The Chinese hospital has an X-ray machine," Frances said. "We could take Camille there."

"I don't think that's necessary, Frances," he replied. "Whether her ribs are broken or bruised the treatment is the same. Bed rest and try not to jolt your ribs, madame. Press a pillow against the chest to reduce movement if you must cough. Ice packs to bring down the swelling. Stand up and walk a little now and then to keep your lungs clear. A turn or two around the room is sufficient. If you develop a fever, have the nurses call me."

"Doctor?" Camille's voice was weak. "There is one other concern."

Pauline held Camille's hand while the doctor conducted another examination. Frances hovered for a few minutes then left the room.

The doctor straightened up. "Your baby is fine. Same instructions as before. Bed rest, ice pack, and so on."

He left and the nurse followed. For the moment the two women were alone.

"Don't tell Theo anything, not yet," Camille said. "Not until I've decided what to do."

"There's nothing for you to do except get better," Pauline said. "We wait for someone else to find Jean-Paul. How can we decide anything until we know?"

Until they knew whether Jean-Paul was dead or alive.

THERE WAS NO URGENCY ANYMORE for Pauline to find Theo. It was more important for her to stay with Camille. To be with her when someone came to tell her they'd found Jean-Paul. For the questions that were bound to come once that happened. For the decisions they would have to make.

"Hush, someone's outside the door," Camille murmured. "No more talk."

It was Frances, with water and sedatives. "You need to sleep, Camille. Stop worrying. You're safe here. No one comes in that you don't want to see. No one." The determination on her sweet, plain face was evident.

Obediently, Camille swallowed the pills and sank back onto the pillow. Her eyelids fluttered, then stilled.

"We have so many wounded," Frances whispered to Pauline, "and I don't want to ask the nurses to look after Camille. But I'll check in on her as often as I can, and we can always call for the doctor if she's in distress."

"There's no need for you to inconvenience yourself," Pauline said. "I can stay in that chair, stay with her all night if need be."

"I think we can do better than the armchair," Frances said and vanished out the door again. A half hour later, two maids came into the room with a cot and bed linens, which they set up in the corner.

Pauline had just finished making up the cot when a loud female voice in the hallway outside reverberated through the door. An imperious woman bustled in, followed by a nurse. Given how many townspeople worked at the château it wasn't a surprise that Mme Dumont knew about Camille. She'd come to size up the situation for herself. But Camille could barely keep her eyes open, let alone greet her visitor.

Camille dozed off again. She knew she was dreaming but couldn't control the panic rising in her throat. There was snow falling on her shoulders and she was clutching Pauline's cold hand in hers. Jean-Paul lay motionless below them, facedown in a trench that was slowly filling with snow. Blood spread out from his body in scarlet veins that stretched out like a giant cobweb. Then she was alone in a church, kneeling in the darkness of a confessional stall, her lips almost touching the wooden screen as she whispered her sins to the hazy shape of an unfamiliar priest.

Was letting a man die the same as actually killing him? What if he was going to kill you and your child, kill the man you loved? He would've killed them all in his rage. Camille knew this as surely as she knew the names of all the plants in her garden. Jean-Paul showed no mercy when his pride was hurt, she explained to the priest. But the priest said nothing, offered no comfort or condemnation, prescribed no prayers. When she peered through the carved quatrefoils of the screen, the other side of the stall was empty.

I don't care. If I'm damned then so be it was her last thought before falling into a deeper, dreamless sleep.

CHAPTER 20

Monday, November 11, 1918

Pauline had been standing at the window since before sunrise. It wasn't as though she'd been able to sleep. The bedroom was at the end of the château's north wing and Pauline couldn't see the garden or driveway, but she could see out to the road, which was busy with vehicles and carts delivering supplies.

The night before, Mrs. Newland hadn't been pleased to learn of the two women under her roof, one a convalescent, the other one Chinese. Fortunately, an imposing automobile arrived, more houseguests. That, and arrangements for the party, prevented Mrs. Newland from turning her full attention to her less-welcome guests. Pauline and Camille had been glad to take Mme Dumont's offer: that Camille recover in the Dumont home.

With all that had happened, Pauline nearly forgot the date. November 11. In a few hours, at eleven o'clock, the war would be over. Artillery barrages would cease, airplanes would return to airfields, and refugees begin their journeys home to a life that was still uncertain. But the world would stop killing.

And in the smaller drama of her own life, she and Camille waited for someone to find Jean-Paul.

A small parade of townsfolk were making their way to the château, extra workers hired to help with the party. But none of them seemed to be in a hurry, none of them were rushing to deliver urgent news. Frost dusted bare tree branches and frozen puddles gleamed like pools of dull glass. Pauline tried not to think of what happened to a person lying out in the open. She pulled the drapes shut.

A soft knock on the door and Frances came in with a tray. "Breakfast," she said, "and I have arranged for one of the ambulances to take Camille to the Dumonts."

They woke Camille, who opened her eyes, startled. "Is it Jean-Paul?" she whispered.

"No," Pauline said, glancing at Frances. "No sign of him. No word although apparently most of the town know you're here. Have some breakfast and then I'll help you dress. We're going to the Dumonts'."

Frances cleared her throat. "Dr. Adams has offered to take over your care, Camille, since he is living at the Dumonts' anyway. I'll come see you every day, in case you need anything from the château."

"That's very kind of him," Camille said, with a slow smile.

IT WAS JUST AFTER NINE o'clock when they arrived at the Dumont home. Camille insisted she didn't need them to carry her on the stretcher again, that she could manage the few steps from street to door. Inside, old Mme Dumont's bedroom had been prepared for an invalid: fresh sheets, washbasin, towels, and a wooden chair by the bed. A folded nightgown on the pillow.

Frances put a packet of tablets in Pauline's hand. "These are for the pain and also to help her sleep. I must go now." She made a face. "Mother's big party."

The bedroom window faced the front yard. People were leaving their homes, heading for the main street where the parade would start at the stroke of eleven.

A low rumble alerted Pauline to the military vehicle making its way along the street, not an unusual sight in Noyelles. It stopped in front of the Dumont house and the driver stepped out. He wore a British military doctor's uniform. Pauline ran to the bedroom door and looked down the corridor toward the front door.

M. Dumont opened it, and Mme Dumont joined her husband at the threshold. The sounds of low, hushed conversation. A gasp from Mme Dumont, then she put her hands over her mouth.

Pauline returned quickly to Camille's bedside and shook her gently. "Wake up, Camille," she said. "Get ready for the news. I think our wait is over."

Camille put her hands over her cheeks for a moment, fingers covering her eyes. She nodded at Pauline, who helped her sit up and propped a pillow behind her back. The Dumonts entered, then the doctor.

"Oh my dear Camille!" Mme Dumont said. She sat on the chair and held Camille's thin hand in hers. "You know Dr. Adams from the Chinese hospital."

"The doctor brings very distressing news," M. Dumont said. "It's your husband, Camille. Some Chinese workers found Jean-Paul in a field early this morning. They carried him to their hospital. Dr. Adams was on duty."

Camille closed her eyes and exhaled, a long slow sigh. "How is Jean-Paul doing?"

There was a silence, then Dr. Adams spoke. "I'm very sorry to tell you that your husband is dead, Madame."

"How?" Camille's voice was soft and drowsy. "How did he die?"

"He had been shot, Madame."

"Who would want to do that? Why?"

"We'll find out, Camille," M. Dumont said. "The doctor has already alerted the military police at the camp. You have my word and that of our mayor. We'll not rest until Jean-Paul's murderer is brought to justice."

"You said a field? Which field?"

"At the edge of the d'Amervals' barley field," Dumont said, "the one where their old barn stands."

"He was out in the open all night," Dr. Adams said, "and I would say he froze to death while unconscious, Madame Roussel. He would've died painlessly."

Camille closed her eyes. "Please, I'd like to be alone now."

"Of course," the doctor said. "But would you permit me to examine you? Then I'll leave you alone for the rest of the day."

"And after you examine Camille," Mme Dumont said, "you'll have some coffee with us, Dr. Adams. It's already made. Just a quick cup. Dumont has official duties at the celebrations and we must leave soon."

In the kitchen, the Dumonts asked all the questions. Pauline only had to listen.

The workers at the Noyelles camp had invited men from other camps to their armistice celebrations. A group of workers on their way to Noyelles saw Jean-Paul from the road and brought him to the Chinese hospital.

"But why call the military police?" M. Dumont asked. "How is the British Army involved?"

Adams looked down. "Something I didn't tell Camille. We found drugs in his coat pockets. Medicines from the hospital. Stolen. Most likely to sell or trade on the black market. We have to investigate it as a crime against the military."

Two military police had gone to search for clues at the spot where they'd found Jean-Paul. There was a trail of blood all the way from the bottom of the embankment to the barn. The evidence pointed to Jean-Paul having been shot inside the barn; then he had staggered part of the way before crawling the final few yards and collapsing, too weak to climb up to the road.

"The old barn," Pauline said. "Is it the one close to where the road forks at the Noyelles main road? The one where the door is barely hanging on to its hinges?"

"Yes, yes. That's the one," M. Dumont said, "it belongs to the d'Amervals."

"I saw something while cycling back to the Roussels' cottage yesterday," she said. "Well, actually I heard what sounded like two gunshots. Then I saw a man leaving the barn. A Chinese man wearing a CLC greatcoat. Walking very fast through the fields toward town."

Dumont and the doctor looked at each other.

"Jean-Paul was shot twice," Dr. Adams said. "I don't suppose you would recognize the man if you saw him again?"

"Yes. In fact, I know him. His name is Mah, an interpreter. He used to work for our family in Paris before the war. I'm sure it was Mah because Henri and I ran into him when we were in Wimereux."

"Mah. I think I know the man you mean." Dr. Adams looked thoughtful. "He's always hanging around the hospital when he's in town."

"We should go now," M. Dumont said. "The celebrations. My speech."

The Dumonts hurried out the door, Mme Dumont still straightening her best hat, her husband glancing down occasionally at the paper in his hand as he muttered the words of his speech.

Pauline poured a fresh cup of coffee and took it to the bedroom. Camille was groggy but sat up to sip from the cup Pauline held to her lips.

"I told them about hearing two gunshots, then seeing Mah leave the barn. The doctor says Mah must've killed Jean-Paul because he'd been shot twice," Pauline said. "If they find Mah, he'll be arrested for murder. But why would Mah kill Jean-Paul if they were in business together?"

Camille was silent. "I think it was Jean-Paul who wanted to kill Mah, not the other way around," she said, "and Mah shot him in self-defense."

"Why would Jean-Paul want to kill the person supplying him with stolen goods?"

"Because when Jean-Paul asked me about the second man at the cottage, I said his name was Mah." Camille's eyes closed. "It wasn't even on purpose. My mind went blank and I couldn't remember Henri's name at all. 'Mah' was the only Chinese name that came to me."

Pauline went back to the window. Everyone had made an attempt to affix tricolor ribbons to hats or a lapel. Many carried small flags. One young boy ran up the street, hitching up the pants of his band uniform with one hand and clutching a trumpet with the other. She smiled.

Two men caught her attention. They were hurrying toward the house, in the opposite direction everyone else was walking.

Theo. And Henri.

Pauline flew out the room and opened the door. Theo was the first to rush in. "Pauline, are you all right? Where's Camille?"

She pointed at the bedroom door.

"Are you all right, Pauline?" Henri said, echoing Theo's words as he stepped over the threshold. "You're not hurt, are you?"

She shook her head, then let him gather her into his arms. More than the luxury of the château, more than the Dumonts' kindness, Henri made her feel safe. She wanted to lean against him for hours, feel his cheek beside her hair, smell the clean disinfectant scent of soap on his skin.

Finally, Pauline moved back but left her hands on Henri's shoulders. "So, you know about Jean-Paul?" she said.

"That he's dead? Yes, Robert told me. Then he told me what that man did to Camille."

They paused at the open door of the bedroom. Theo was kneeling by the bed, his face buried in the quilt. Camille was stroking his hair as though he was the invalid who needed care and not her. She looked up at them, her face bruised, her smile radiant.

First faintly, and then louder, as though growing in confidence, the sound of church bells came through the window. Cheers echoed from the street. Henri pulled Pauline to the front door and flung it open. He gazed out as though he could see two streets away to the parade. The brass band struck up "La Marseillaise."

The war was over.

A war in a foreign land, a war that wasn't supposed to kill any Chinese, Pauline thought, bitterness rippling through giddy relief. Now the workers could go home.

Then Henri pulled her into a long kiss, and all she could feel were his arms encircling her, his lips on hers. And for a moment she stopped thinking about all the men who could go home, stopped worrying about Theo and Camille.

THE FOUR OF THEM HUDDLED in old Mme Dumont's bedroom while the rest of the town celebrated, the music and cheering from outside a backdrop to their conversation. Jean-Paul's death changed everything. Camille no longer needed to fear he would come after her or Theo.

When Camille confessed her pregnancy, Theo had been stunned, then ecstatic. He wanted to marry her right away. He didn't care whether the baby was his or Jean-Paul's, as long as they could be together.

"No, Theo," she said. "First I must bury my husband. Then I will go away somewhere to have the baby."

"Where will you go? I'll come with you," he said.

"I don't know yet. I need to think it over." She smiled at the anxiety in his eyes. "We can make that decision together. But not right away. Pauline needs to sell the jar first, we need the money."

"I'll change my ticket and go back to Paris tomorrow," Pauline said. "The letter of condolence must've arrived by now. Your father and Denise will be in mourning. Theo, I have to tell your father you're actually alive."

Theo protested. His death gave Louis an honorable reason for ending the marriage contract, maintaining the family's reputation for always meeting their commitments.

"Perhaps your father would prefer damage to family reputation than to have you dead," Henri said.

"When I refuse the arranged marriage, he'll disown me." Theo pushed nervous fingers through his hair. "He has to. It will shame him."

"Oh, Theo," Pauline said. "You were willing to be dead, so why do you care about being disowned? It won't be easy, but pretending to be dead is so . . . . so dishonorable."

"And cowardly," Henri added. Theo looked abashed.

"Theo, I want your father to know about me," Camille said. "If he disapproves, then at least it's based on the truth."

But Theo had to remain in the CLC pretending to be Chao or risk arrest. Between Maitland's alcoholic stupor and the chaos of the Allies going home, Theo would be able to stay out of the limelight, avoid doing anything that attracted attention. In the end, Theo agreed to write a letter for Pauline to take home. He would give it to her at the train station the next morning.

"Then I'll return to Wimereux tomorrow." Theo lifted Camille's hand to his lips. "Please rest and be careful."

"There's a doctor living here," she reminded him. "And Madame Dumont is a wonderful nurse."

"I'm glad you'll be traveling with Pauline," Theo said to Henri, "and thank you for coming to Noyelles with her. You're a good friend."

Pauline smiled at Henri. "And this good friend will go with me to the cottage so I can get my belongings."

THE WALK THROUGH TOWN WAS slow, their path blocked by rev-elers. Henri and Pauline pushed their way through, returned cheers of "Vive la France!," and smilingly refused bottles of wine offered to them. The entire street was a tidal wave of jubilation.

Columns of steam rose into the cold air from the barracks of the Chinese camp. The noise of clanging gongs and shouts of encourage-ment told them that acrobats had taken the stage. The drummers began a lively beat and musicians struck up a tune.

"Ah. 'Dance of the Golden Snake,'" Henri said. "A festival favorite."

Farther along, the wrought-iron arch above the château's gates was draped in red, white, and blue fabric. Even the huge chestnut trees that guarded the gates were decorated, tricolor ribbons tied to bare branches waving in the breeze.

When they neared the old barn, Pauline averted her gaze, looked ahead along the road at the skeletal branches of poplar and elm that lined each side. But she couldn't stop the memories.

Mah, turning to look in her direction.

Jean-Paul, facedown at the bottom of the embankment, wind flick-ing his dark hair.

Camille's voice, bleak and brittle, saying *Then let's go.*

At the cottage, Henri helped Pauline tidy up the kitchen. They swept broken glass and crockery into the trash bin, mopped the floor, and washed the dishes. Henri stacked kindling beside the stove. Then in the garden room, she packed her clothing into the carpetbag and checked that the white jar was still there. She hoped her uncle would pay a good price for it. She had to coax as much as she could from Louis for Camille. And the baby.

"Is that the famous Tang jar?" Henri said.

She held it up for him. "I won't tell my uncle it belongs to Camille," she said, "in case he's angry with Theo and refuses to buy it."

"Does your uncle know you don't want an arranged marriage or to move to Shanghai?"

She sighed. "It doesn't matter what I want. He's asked First Wife to bring in a matchmaker. She hates me, so who knows what kind of bargain she will make."

Henri looked thoughtful. "You could marry me."

CHAPTER 21

Tuesday, November 12, 1918

They parted in Paris at the Gare du Nord.

"I'll send my father a telegram," Henri said, "and tell him I want to marry you. And that he should send a matchmaker to your uncle's home, and do everything according to tradition."

"How can you be so sure he'll approve?" Pauline said. They'd talked of little else on the journey down to Paris, Pauline not daring to believe that Henri would be allowed to marry her, Henri confident and reassuring.

"My father is not like the rest of the family," he said. "They consider him eccentric and just shrug."

"But Henri," she began.

"Pauline, I can marry you without my father's permission," he said. "He's not the sort to dictate my life. I'm only asking his permission to make your uncle happy, to give your family an honorable reason to cancel all other matchmaking. Now, I'd better get to the post office and send this telegram. I'll come by La Pagode as soon as I have my father's reply."

Henri was so optimistic, Pauline thought, but the reply telegram might deny his request. It was best not to hope.

At the corner of Rue de Lisbonne, Pauline glanced up at the windows of the apartment. There was a movement at the drapes and when she reached Number 53, the door flew open and Denise rushed out to greet her.

"You're home! You're safe, thank the blessed saints! Pauline, there was a letter from Theo's commanding officer. Did you know . . ."

"No, no, it's all right. He's alive, it was a paperwork error, Theo is alive," she said, hugging Denise. "I saw him. He gave me a letter for Uncle. Where is he?"

She followed Denise upstairs, where Louis sat in the parlor staring at a record on the gramophone. It spun soundlessly, the needle still up.

Why, he's old! That was Pauline's first thought. It had only been a few months since she last saw him on the platform waiting to board the train to Marseilles, but her uncle seemed suddenly smaller, his shoulders more stooped. A funeral for his father, then coming home to the news of a son's death. Thank the gods Theo had seen sense. That Camille had been firm with him.

"Uncle." She bowed her head. "I've caused you worry and for that I am sorry. I hope you forgive me after reading this."

He looked at the envelope, at Theo's handwriting, and tore it open. He read slowly and when he looked up at her, he shook his head.

"What I feared most was losing him to the war," he said. "Instead, it's a woman. A Frenchwoman." He read the letter again and put it down.

"I went without permission, Uncle," Pauline said, "so please don't blame Denise. But because I went, you know that Theo isn't dead. Perhaps the gods had a hand in this outcome."

"This letter," Louis said, tapping the paper with one finger. "Theo says he expects me to disown him for refusing his arranged marriage. And that if you hadn't found him, he would've let us go on believing he'd been killed. This foreign woman means more to him than his duty to our family."

"Theo isn't dead," Denise said. "And Pauline is safely home. The armistice has been signed and the war is over. Be happy, Louis." She patted his shoulder and he reached up to touch her hand.

At dinner, Louis spoke very little, letting Denise ask all the questions. Not for the first time it occurred to Pauline that her uncle relied on his mistress to express his concerns and probe for information. Pauline recounted the events in Noyelles. She noticed that from time to time he touched the pocket of his vest as if to assure himself that Theo's letter was still there. That Theo really was alive.

Denise wanted to know about Camille, of course. A widow from a good family, Pauline told them. A good influence on Theo. She tried to describe Camille, her sweet and stalwart nature, but couldn't give Denise a consoling answer when Denise worried how Theo would be treated by the citizens of Noyelles for marrying a Frenchwoman. She could only say that Theo and Camille planned on moving away from Noyelles.

"But they should come to Paris," Denise exclaimed. "Here, where the neighbors know your family. And of course, Theo will work at La Pagode again. All will be as it was before the war."

Louis stood and went to the sideboard, came back with three small glasses of cognac. It was the first time he'd offered liquor to Pauline since the day they toasted the new Republic of China. It was raining again and cobblestones glistened under the streetlamps. The cold drizzle sent pedestrians hurrying along, the sound of their footsteps dampened by the rain's drumbeat. He peered through the rain-streaked panes and downed his glass.

"With Grandfather Deng gone, my eldest brother is in charge," he said. "He discussed some changes now that he's running the family business."

"What sort of changes, Uncle?" Pauline said.

"Changes that would've affected all of us, but mostly Theo. Since he's decided he's no longer a member of the family, it hardly matters now."

"Louis! Don't punish Theo for refusing an arranged marriage."

"It's not punishment, Denise." He turned away from the glass. "Theo knows our family. He knows the consequences of his decision."

"He doesn't expect any help from the family, Uncle," Pauline said.

"My elder brother feels it's time for this European experiment to end." Louis cleared his throat. "Our family is selling La Pagode. So you and I are returning to Shanghai, Baoling. Theo, too, if he changes his mind."

"Sell the store!" Pauline exclaimed.

"Louis," Denise said very quietly. "This is unexpected."

"I've thought things over and made plans," he said. He folded his napkin and placed it on the table. "We'll talk about it tomorrow."

Wednesday, November 13, 1918

The next morning, Pauline joined her uncle in the storeroom. He had the inventory ledgers out and a trunk was on the floor, lid opened. Louis held up a stone disc.

"A fine collection," he said. "Han dynasty jades. A dozen discs and ten belt hooks. Five archer thumb rings. This one is nephrite, olive green with brown streaks, rice grain pattern."

Pauline sat down and took the pen and ledger from him. "Measurements?"

There was an easy and familiar rhythm to the work, and it didn't take long before each piece was noted in the ledger and labeled with a price. Louis leaned back in his chair.

"I've written to an antiques dealer I know in London, a merchant from Ningbo. He wants a store in Paris now that the war is over. He's interested in La Pagode, all the inventory, even the lease on the building."

In Shanghai, Louis's older brother had made it very clear that La Pagode, even with the luxury import business, had not been successful. Only Grandfather Deng's determination to give Theo a future had kept the Paris store in play. Now Louis was to sell up and return home to run another part of the family business.

"I never admitted to myself how very much I've missed Shanghai," he continued, "not just our family and friends but the city itself. I didn't want to come back to Paris. This city has worn me out, the effort to make myself understood every day in a language that's not my own."

"What about Denise?" she said.

"Don't worry about Denise," Louis said. "I'll make sure she's looked after."

"Uncle, I have a favor to ask. Can you take a look at this jar?" Pauline held out the bundle she had brought with her.

Louis held it to the light, examined the lid and then the bottom of the jar. He dipped a finger in his water glass and drew some water across the unglazed bottom. He looked up at her.

"Where did you get this?"

"The . . . family in Noyelles I was staying with. I told them you owned an antiques store and they asked whether you might buy it. They need the money. It's Tang dynasty, isn't it?"

"I'm sure of it. You've always had a good eye." Her uncle nodded, still turning the piece over in his hands, as gently as though he were holding a baby bird. "It's worth quite a bit. Do they know that?"

"I've only said I thought it was valuable. They were very kind to me. And also to Theo, so please buy it at a good price."

"Now that I'm giving up the business it doesn't seem so important anymore to grind out every possible penny of profit." He smiled. "We can afford to be generous."

"Uncle, you know how grateful I am that you've taken care of me all these years," Pauline began.

"Baoling, your father was my youngest and dearest brother. Even if he hadn't asked me on his deathbed I would've taken you in." There were tears in his eyes. "When I thought Theo had died, when I didn't know where you might be . . ." He grasped her hands. Louis had never touched Pauline before, either in anger or affection. "When we are back home in Shanghai, I will adopt you formally. You've been by my side for ten years, you've been like my daughter."

"I am honored, Uncle," she mumbled, too astonished to say anything else.

But where was Henri? He'd sworn that an exchange of telegrams wouldn't take more than a day or two.

Thursday, November 14, 1918

Louis had asked them to make the store look its best for the buyer. Two elmwood chairs with curved armrests posed on a fine silk carpet, a tea set positioned on the elegant side table between them, and an inlaid lacquer screen provided a background for the little scene. Near the front door, Denise had created a display of yellow porcelain bowls and jars, with a few blue-and-white pieces for accent. An arrangement of silk magnolias bloomed in the vase on the counter.

Louis was in the storage room with M. Lin, taking him through an inventory of the contents stored there. It was really happening;

M. Lin was going to buy La Pagode. He had come to the store at noon, an affable and handsome gentleman who had given the store a thorough inspection.

"Your uncle knew Theo didn't want to go back to China," Denise said to Pauline, who was on a ladder cleaning a lamp, laboriously polishing the beveled glass while Denise held the ladder steady. "But he did hope. He hoped Theo would marry, immigrate to France, bring his wife over, raise a family. Then Louis could go home to Shanghai."

Immigrate. A permanent move for Theo, the troubled and troublesome son. Pauline climbed down the ladder and they moved it under the next lamp.

"Denise, I wish you would let Uncle take you to Shanghai. He's truly fond of you. He'd set you up in your own household."

"And I am fond of your uncle, but China is not for me," Denise said. "I've seen what it's like for Louis to live here as a foreigner. I would not do well in Shanghai. M. Lin will be taking me on as a sales clerk."

More than that, Louis had struck a deal with Lin, who was taking over the building lease. Denise would continue living in her apartment as Lin's tenant. Louis was giving her enough money to help with the rent for several more years. Since the apartment had more rooms than Denise needed, she would take in boarders for extra income.

"I won't be rich, but I won't starve, either" was how she put it. Denise seemed to have made her plans. She wouldn't have to be anyone's mistress.

The back door opened and Louis came in, followed by M. Lin, who set down a large cardboard box on the glass top of a display case.

"Gentlemen, please," Denise said. "We only just polished that case. Put it down on the floor."

Startled, M. Lin looked at her then chuckled sheepishly and moved the box. No, Denise wasn't going to be anyone's mistress. The men returned to the storage room, still talking.

There was an excited rapping on the door. Denise opened it and Pauline almost fell off the ladder with relief. It was Henri.

"Hello, hello." His cheerful greeting lifted her heart. He wouldn't sound so pleased if something had gone wrong. "Good day, Denise. I'm here to see Pauline."

Denise pointed to the top of the ladder and held it as Pauline climbed down.

"May I speak with you a moment, in private?" he beckoned her outside.

"What's happened?" she asked. "Tell me quickly, it's cold out here."

"I hope you still love me," he said, kissing her hands.

"I do, of course. Why are you saying this?"

"Because we're getting married."

Suddenly, Pauline felt shy. "But are you still sure you want to marry me?"

"Why do you even need to ask?" he said.

"Because it might cause problems between you and your father. I'm not the usual sort to marry into a family like yours."

He chuckled. "My father isn't the usual sort either. He adopted a street urchin, remember."

"YOUNG MAN," LOUIS SAID, "DOES your father know? We are humble merchants, not at all in the same class as your family."

"I have his telegram right here," Henri said. "He's quite happy someone is actually willing to marry me. He's sent our family's matchmaker to your home in Shanghai to discuss the matter. I hope your family hasn't come to any final decisions yet about Pauline's marriage."

Pauline could see it in her uncle's eyes. Shipping companies, banks, and railways. Cabinet ministers and judges. Newspapers and hotels. The Liu clan included some of China's wealthiest and most influential men. Even if First Wife had settled her marriage contract, there would be no shame in breaking it, not for connections such as these.

"It would be an honor for our family to be allied with yours," Louis said, "but a suitable dowry . . ."

"No dowry necessary. I want Pauline for herself."

"Well, then, you should know that I am planning to adopt Pauline officially," Louis said, "so that she's a legitimate daughter of the family."

She knew what the Dengs would think. That Louis was adopting her so that Henri's family wouldn't be insulted by her illegitimate status. So that with Pauline as a legal daughter of the family, the Dengs would have a stronger claim on her and therefore on her exalted in-laws.

But she knew better. Louis was adopting her because he loved her.

CHAPTER 22

Thursday, November 21, 1918

The cottage felt different. Camille felt like a stranger walking into someone else's home. She took a deep breath when she entered. There wasn't the faintest reek of cigarettes, nor the smell of woodsmoke. It might've been her imagination, but the lurking sense of menace was gone. Emil brought in the small valise and got back on the donkey cart to continue his route. He returned her wave with a toothless smile and clucked at the donkey.

The kitchen was tidy. All the broken crockery was gone and the kitchen floor swept, no sign of empty liquor bottles. There was kindling and coal beside the stove. Camille hung up her coat and put the paper bag of bread and cheese on a shelf. The house was cold and she began laying a fire, wincing a little bit as she bent to open the grate.

She and Theo still had so much to overcome. He had gone back to Wimereux the day after the armistice, but a few days later, while his unit was being transferred to the port of Le Havre, he had hitched a ride into Noyelles to see her.

When Mme Dumont opened the door to him, her smile was friendly but her body positioned itself firmly across the threshold. Camille hobbled to the door using old Mme Dumont's cane and stood behind her.

"You can't come to the Dumonts' now that Pauline has gone," Camille said. "She was your only excuse. Please think of my reputation if nothing else. I still need to live here in Noyelles for a while longer."

"You mustn't come in, Monsieur Deng," Mme Dumont said. "Please leave. No one can know about you and Camille. It could harm your safety as well as Camille's reputation."

"I don't see how," he said, his brow furrowing.

"Madame Dumont and I have discussed the risks," Camille said. "You and Pauline are outsiders and also Chinese. The authorities only have Pauline's word that it was Mah who ran away from the barn, that Mah is the likely murderer."

"If anyone learns about you and Camille," Mme Dumont said, "they might think up another scenario: that you killed Jean-Paul in a fit of passion and that Pauline lied to protect you. We are very fond of the *crime passionnel*."

"That's ridiculous." But Theo's shoulders slumped, and he looked cautiously up and down the street, the truth of their words sinking in.

As the war dragged on and the number of foreign workers increased, so had antagonism toward them. There were workers in France from faraway Indochina and China, and from closer to home, Spain and North Africa. Now, with the coming of peace, people felt it was time for foreign workers to go home—and in Noyelles, that meant the Chinese Labour Corps. It wouldn't take much for Jean-Paul's murder to be blamed on a Chinese.

Theo nodded, then pulled a small drawstring bag from his coat. He held it out, but Camille stayed in the shadows behind Mme Dumont, who took the bag from him.

"It's a seal," he said. "Everyone in our family is given a seal when we come of age, it's how we sign documents in China. It's yours, Camille. My pledge that I will never go back to China. I never need to use it again. I will find a way to stay with you in France."

"Now go, young man," Mme Dumont said, still blocking the door. Then she shut it.

Camille opened the bag and took out a slim ivory cylinder. One end was rounded, the other end flat, stained with red ink, carved with Chinese characters. Theo's Chinese name. Deng Taoling. His name, his identity, in the palm of her hand.

CAMILLE FILLED THE KETTLE, SET it on the stove. The sun was setting and she lit a lamp, went to close the drapes out of habit and remembered there was no need anymore. Nor was there any reason to worry about the Dumonts seeing the letters Theo sent, now that they knew. She and Theo discussed their plans in writing; in fact, they wrote to each other almost daily.

The sound of an automobile engine brought her to the kitchen window. Frances climbed out of the car and almost skipped up the path. When Camille opened the front door, her friend's face was pink with excitement, her eyes sparkled.

"I wanted to tell you sooner, but I had to be sure," she said. "But now everything is settled."

Robert had proposed to her on Armistice Day.

"I went to see him at the hospital the next day," Frances said, "just in case he'd only asked because, well, you know, everyone was just so ecstatic that day, carried away with joy. But he said he meant it."

"Such wonderful news, Frances," Camille said, hugging her. "I hope your mother was carried away with joy as well."

"Mother has threatened to disown me," Frances said, "but the advantage of being twenty-five and an old maid is that I'm long past legal age. Mother can't interfere, all the arrangements are in place."

"Why, Frances," Camille said, "are you actually giggling?"

Her friend twirled around the kitchen. "Robert's going home to

Canada, and then back to his mission hospital in China. I'm leaving with him. We'll get married on the ship, I'll meet his family in Vancouver, and after a short visit, on to China."

"I'm leaving, too, Frances," she said. "I can't stay in Noyelles anymore."

"So a new chapter for both of us," Frances said. "No, no tea for me. I must go. But I'm dying for a longer chat. I'll come back tomorrow."

After Frances left, Camille returned to her meal of bread and cheese, and to her thoughts.

The war was over, but depending on when they joined up, Chinese workers were still on contract for another year, some as long as another eighteen months. The sooner Theo could leave the CLC, the sooner they could start their life together. There was a benefit to Theo keeping Chao Te-Yin's identity. Chao had signed his three-year contract a good eight months before Theo, so by pretending to be Chao, Theo would finish sooner.

The workers had shifted to salvage and cleanup. Even before the armistice, they had been clearing battlefields so the ground could be returned to pastures and farmland. They rolled up miles of barbed wire, dug shrapnel out of trenches, removed spent artillery shell casings from battlefields. Moved corpses of men and animals. They cleared away the rubble of shattered buildings in towns so their citizens could start rebuilding.

Camille was thankful Theo's unit was not one of those clearing No Man's Land. She recalled how he'd come back after one such assignment shaken, silent and haunted. Theo's unit was at the port of Le Havre, sorting through wreckage brought in by the salvage crews. The mountains of shell casings alone were worth a fortune in scrap metal, a fortune being shipped back to England.

They needed money. Theo's small translator's income was not

enough. Henri had come to Noyelles the day before and delivered the money from selling the white jar. It was a good amount, but it wouldn't last very long. Not if she was to rent a home that was clean and airy, suitable for raising a child. Not for all the things a baby would need. So the day after Jean-Paul's funeral, Camille asked M. Dumont to sell the cottage for her. Whether the cottage sold or not, she would move from Noyelles after a decent period of time to Le Havre. Or wherever Theo went next.

A loud rapping on the kitchen door interrupted her thoughts. Mme Dumont had promised to check in on her, even though Camille protested there was no need. But it wasn't the kindly postmistress. It was Marcel.

She took a step back.

His face and clothing were dirty, his blond curls disheveled, the hems of his trousers edged with mud. He looked at her closely, and she knew what he was seeing—the yellowing bruises on her face, the cut on her lip, the black eye.

"*Merde*," he said, "what else did he do to you?" He didn't sound angry or threatening. Just mildly curious. She took another step back from the door but he didn't come in.

"He cracked two of these." Camille touched her ribs. "Why have you come, Marcel?"

"To offer my condolences," he said. "Jean-Paul was my oldest friend. And my business partner."

"I appreciate your condolences. But you didn't need to come. You were at the funeral yesterday."

Despite the cold, all of Noyelles seemed to have turned up. It wasn't every day they got to bury a man who'd been murdered. It was a brief graveside ceremony and then Camille stood on the path as mourners filed past, Mme Dumont holding an umbrella over her. The townsfolk murmured words of sympathy and she could tell they were trying to peer through her black veil to see for themselves what Jean-Paul had done to her. She had caught a glimpse of Marcel standing on his own away from the main group, lingering by the low stone wall just past the entrance to the cemetery. He was bareheaded, rain dripping down his face. The sight of him had made her pull her coat more closely to her body.

"There were too many people at the funeral. I came to give you this." He held out a drawstring bag, brown leather, stained at the edges.

She looked at him, puzzled.

"It's Jean-Paul's share of the business," Marcel said. "I know you don't like me, Camille. You don't like that I got Jean-Paul into the black market. But I don't steal from my friends. Or from their widows."

He pressed the bag into her hands and stepped back. "One more thing, Camille. Is it true what they say, that it was a chintok named Mah who killed Jean-Paul?"

"Yes. There's no doubt at all."

Marcel swung a leg over his bicycle and pedaled away. He rang the bell four times and lifted a hand in farewell without looking back.

Only after he crested the hill did Camille realize she had been clenching her hands tightly around the bag. She opened it at the kitchen table and pulled out a roll of banknotes. And there were gold coins. Her grandmother's gold Napoleons. She sat at the kitchen table and quickly counted the money. Money that Jean-Paul often boasted would set them on the road to prosperity, wealth enough to make him a respected citizen. He had not been exaggerating.

Camille dreamed of Jean-Paul almost every night, a motionless figure lying in the ditch. Sometimes she and Pauline hovered above him, angels of death at the cusp of a decision. Sometimes it was Theo and not Pauline who held her hand. Most of the time she was alone, her heart the weight of an anvil. The first night she'd had such a dream was when she and Pauline had been in the château. Pauline, in a cot by the bed, immediately sat up and came to her side, listened to her account of the dream.

Listened to all her agonized what-ifs.

Pauline reminded Camille over and over that Jean-Paul had been half frozen; by the time they reached the château, he might've been dead already, or at least beyond saving. Most of all, that Jean-Paul had been on his way to kill Theo.

"If you had begged me to take Jean-Paul instead, I would've tied you to the trailer and pedaled away," Pauline said. "I have no regrets. No regrets for not telling anyone when we got to the château."

When she woke from such a dream, Camille fought with her conscience. She took a mental inventory of every scar on her body, every cigarette burn on her arm, the kinked little finger that had been broken, and the baby she'd lost. Most of all that first baby, all testimony to the precariousness of life with Jean-Paul.

Then guilt would give way to relief, so much relief that he was out of her life, that her unborn baby was safe, that Theo was safe.

But it wasn't the same as having no regrets.

CHAPTER 23

April 30, 1937

At the Gare de Calais-Ville, the couple on the platform drew some curious stares, but most travelers were more preoccupied greeting relatives and gathering up their luggage to give them more than a passing glance. The man was tall and Chinese, middle-aged and strikingly handsome in a tan trench coat, his fedora flecked with rain. The woman who held his arm pushed wisps of light brown hair back under her hat. Her complexion was rosy with excitement, the lines on her face faint as fine pencil strokes, her expression one of joyful anticipation.

"Hello, hello!" Henri shouted from a carriage window. "Hold on, we'll be right there." Behind him, Pauline gave a quick wave and proceeded to jam a hat on her head while pulling a bag off the overhead rack. But Camille didn't wait. Before they'd even managed to set down their luggage, she had enveloped Pauline in a bruising hug. The men shook hands in a dignified manner before breaking into grins and slapping each other on the back.

To Camille's eyes, neither of them had changed much. Henri was still vigorous and animated, Pauline's dark eyes alert, missing nothing. They gave the impression of having dressed carelessly even though Henri's jacket was beautifully tailored and Pauline's simple cashmere coat more expensive than anything in Camille's own closet. On a previous visit Pauline had explained rather apologetically that whenever they went to Shanghai, Henri's aunts and cousins took her to their dressmaker, not trusting her frugal nature to uphold Liu family standards.

AS SOON AS CAMILLE KNEW Henri and Pauline were coming, she had declared a vacation, adamant that while their guests were in Calais, she wasn't going to work. She gave her staff two days' holiday, closed the Café Barbier, and over Theo's weak protests, flipped the sign on the door of his photography studio to Closed. The day before Pauline and Henri's visit, Camille did nothing but cook.

And now they sat around the large kitchen table, so replete with food that they refused Camille's desserts. Until later.

This was the first time Henri and Pauline had missed seeing young Auguste, who was away at his first year of university in Lille.

"It's his birthday today," Henri said, "so we brought him a gift. But when does he come home next?"

"Not until his exams are over, middle of May," Theo said. "He'll be sorry to have missed his Oncle Henri and Tante Pauline."

"What about your daughters?" Camille said. "Do they like boarding school? The Nanking Girls Middle School, isn't it?"

"The novelty of living with a hundred girls their own age has not yet worn off," Henri said, "and they're happy in Nanking, yes. In Shanghai there are too many aunts and uncles scrutinizing their behavior. We don't do well under surveillance."

As Camille and Pauline cleared the table, the men's conversation grew more heated. A year ago, Germany had ignored the Treaty of Versailles and put troops along their border with France. Both France and Britain were unsure of what to do. In China, the Japanese were aggressively pushing south from Manchuria, both sides already taking part in conflicts their governments had so far politely declined to call a war.

The women sat by the kitchen window, talking about their children. Pauline had brought photographs of her two daughters in their school uniforms. Camille, who had suffered complications when young Auguste was born, could have no more children and gazed wistfully at the pictures. Their conversation was interrupted by good-natured shouting from the street below.

Camille opened the window and leaned out, then laughed. "I'm on holiday, Monsieur Joubert. We open again on Tuesday. Come back then and I will make your favorite tart."

WHEN THEO FINISHED HIS CONTRACT with the CLC, he and Camille had settled in Calais. At first, their neighbors looked askance at the young couple who opened a café and then a photo studio. Although mixed-race marriages were not forbidden, newspapers warned Frenchwomen against marrying foreigners, and these articles cast doubts on the character of women willing to do so. But Camille's quiet, well-bred manner and Theo's flawless educated French confounded the neighborhood's expectations, especially when the deputy mayor of Calais dined frequently at the Café Barbier and appeared to be on more than friendly terms with the couple. Then there was little Auguste, with a smile so endearing that women crossed the road to fuss over the little half-Chinese baby.

Pauline had traveled with Henri on his assignments whenever possible, until the birth of their first child. Now she traveled only when their daughters were at boarding school, but even so, she had seen much of Asia and Europe. She was most comfortable as a tourist, with no need or expectation of acceptance. She thought of Shanghai as her home now, but never managed to feel at home there even though it was the most cosmopolitan city in China, as many Westerners strolling its streets as Chinese. The Dengs and, to a lesser degree, Pauline's in-laws, considered her too foreign. Even the way she walked, one of Henri's aunts remarked, was foreign, her body loose, her strides too long. And much though she loved Paris, she knew she couldn't live in France like Theo and pretend she belonged. She was too foreign there also.

The two women kept current with each other's lives, corresponding regularly. A year after Pauline and Henri were married and living in Shanghai, Camille mailed Pauline two newspaper clippings. The first contained a brief paragraph about the murder of a Chinese man in Paris, near the Gare de Lyon. Police were looking for a suspect, a man of slim build with curly blond hair. The second clipping, dated a week later, stated that with help from the Chinese community, the police had identified the dead man as Mah Fuliang; there was nothing more about the suspect. *Is this the same Mah? Could the suspect be Marcel?* Camille had written.

Their letters frequently enclosed photographs. Pauline's favorite was one of Camille seated on a garden chair with baby Auguste on her lap, Theo standing behind them. Camille's face was rounder, her smile beaming out with so much joy it made Pauline happy every time she looked at the photo.

Camille had sent two copies, one for Pauline to give Louis. He'd led a life of leisure upon returning to Shanghai, mostly because his role in the family business was a token one, his responsibilities vague. Yet he seemed quite content to step back. The rest of the Deng family never mentioned Theo, and they turned a blind eye to the fact that Louis stayed in touch with his disgraced son. Louis died during a cholera epidemic only five years after selling La Pagode, followed by First Wife, who had exhausted herself nursing him.

"Are you still in touch with Madame Dumont?" Pauline said, after Camille closed the window. "How is she doing since her husband died?"

"I last saw her in Noyelles at the funeral. I've invited her to stay with us later this summer."

M. Dumont had acted as Camille's agent, selling the cottage for her after she left Noyelles. Then he wrote a letter of reference vouching for Chao Te-Yin's character, stating that he should be allowed to obtain French citizenship. This recommendation from the postmaster did much to smooth the way for Theo and Camille. They wed quietly in Calais just before Auguste was born. Calais, because M. Dumont's brother was deputy mayor there and issued them a marriage license without any fuss.

"Do you think the formidable Madame Dumont coerced her husband and his brother into helping you?" Pauline said. They both laughed, and then Camille looked thoughtful.

"I think, actually, that it was Jean-Paul's doing. I mean, what Jean-Paul did to me was so terrible that it swayed Madame Dumont to help, even though she disapproved of my affair with Theo."

Pauline wiped her hands on a dishcloth. "Camille, come with me. I have a gift for you."

In the guest room, she took a small wooden box out of her suitcase and handed it to Camille. They sat on the bed together and Camille unlatched the lid. The box's interior was padded on all sides, lined in dark blue satin.

Nestled in the satin was a white porcelain jar.

Camille exclaimed when she took it out. "Is it the same jar?" she said, looking at Pauline, whose smile answered her question. "But how did you get it?"

"Entirely by chance, while we were visiting Denise," Pauline said.

"I went downstairs to La Pagode just as a crateload of porcelain came in. The man who bought the jar all those years ago had died and the estate was selling off his collection. I bought it from Monsieur Lin."

"Oh, it's too valuable, I can't take it," Camille said. But her fingers stroked the jar's glazed sides, lifted and replaced the lid gently.

"I promise you it was quite affordable." Pauline looked stern. "Remember that Henri's father is worth a fortune, so stop worrying. I know that of all the things your father brought from China, you loved this jar the most. Take it, and remember him."

Camille held the jar, felt the familiar rounded sides that fit so comfortably in the curve of her hands, remembered the first time she had dreamed of Theo holding her face in the curve of his hands. Remembered how this piece of white porcelain once contained all her hopes for a new life.

"All right." She put an arm around Pauline. "Thank you. I'll keep it, but also to remember you by. You're the one who first recognized its value."

"Good, no more arguing," Pauline said. "Let's get those boys out of the kitchen and go for a walk on the beach."

CAMILLE AND PAULINE STROLLED ARM in arm, their husbands walking ahead, still talking about China. The skies had cleared and the tide was going out. Out in the channel, the water threw off glints of light, and a ferry bound for Dover cut through the waves. Gulls wheeled over the beach, diving down to fight for scraps.

The women paused for a moment to watch the froth of waves crashing on sand. Pauline breathed in the fresh tang of salt air. "I always love being in Paris, but it's so nice by the sea. I'm glad you moved here."

"I love being by the sea. It's why we bought our house here, facing the water," Camille said. "And being near the beach is good for business. Can you see Dover across the channel now that the clouds have lifted?"

"Do you ever think of Noyelles?" Pauline said, suddenly.

Camille knelt down to pick up a shell from the sand, shook her head. "Sometimes, yes, when I think of my childhood, my grandmother, my father, the château. But most of the time, I try not to. And this life keeps me busy and happy." She stood up and smiled.

Pauline pressed Camille's hand tightly in hers. It was hard to believe there had been a time when they didn't trust each other. Now, even without the secret they shared, they were close as sisters, willing to place their lives in each other's hands.

"Look at them, so far ahead," Pauline said, gazing up the beach. "They're walking so fast, we'll have to run to catch up."

"It's like they're doing a quick march," Camille said. She began humming under her breath. Pauline knew the tune.

And as she and Camille began running along the beach, laughing like children, another time and place filled her mind. Pauline remembered when they'd first walked together in sunshine, on a road lined with poplars and plane trees, daylight filtering through bare branches. And passing them on the road, a troop of Chinese workers singing the same tune, a children's song, as they marched to Crécy Forest.

AUTHOR'S NOTE

THE CHINESE IN FRANCE

UNTIL THE ARRIVAL of Chinese workers during the First World War, most French had never encountered any Chinese. A 1911 census shows only 238 Chinese living in France, consisting of consulate staff, artisans, businessmen, and students.

The 40,000 men who signed the French employment contract had the option to apply for residency after the war. It is estimated that between 2,000 and 3,000 workers stayed on under this provision. Zhu Guisheng (French name: Jean Tchou) was one such worker. He married a Frenchwoman, raised three children, and fought for the French army in World War II. He died in 2002, aged 102. There are other instances of Chinese workers who married Frenchwomen, even though mixed-race marriages were strongly discouraged (but not illegal). Most workers who remained in France settled in Paris near the Gare de Lyon, which became the city's Chinatown.

The 98,000 men who signed with the British Chinese Labour Corps (CLC), however, did not have the option to apply for UK residency. Nor did the UK offer CLC translators scholarships to enroll at British universities after the war, despite the Chinese consulate's efforts.

Thus, one of my research questions was: Since Theo signed the British contract and not the French, would it have been possible for him to remain in France and marry Camille?

The answer is a plausible yes. France did not have an official immigration policy back then. Employers could hire foreign workers and the approvals for their contracts, medical examinations, residency status, and naturalization were carried out by a mix of departments and public authorities. It wasn't until the 1930s that all these functions merged into a single department under the Ministry of Labour. For someone like Theo, well-spoken and educated, fluent in French, and who had respectable citizens such as the Dumonts to vouch for him, the odds were good that he would've been allowed to become a French national after marrying Camille.

LA PAGODE

LA PAGODE IS a magnificent building on the Rue de Courcelles near the Parc Monceau. I made La Pagode of the novel a far more modest establishment on the Rue de Lisbonne, just around the corner from the real one. La Pagode was built in 1927 by C. T. Loo, an antiques dealer whose life is worthy of its own novel. It's because of C. T. Loo that I made Louis Deng an antiques dealer.

Loo went to Paris in 1902 as part of the Chinese embassy's entourage, but soon left to follow a more entrepreneurial path. He worked at a store owned by one of the embassy's staff and also had an affair with the staff member's wife. In 1908 he opened his own antiques store and used his network of connections to import Chinese antiquities, many significant enough to be purchased by museums around the world. Loo is credited with bringing ancient Chinese artifacts to the attention of the West at a time when collectors were only interested in porcelains. He is also condemned for pillaging and selling off some of China's most valuable treasures.

Loo's true love and longtime mistress, Olga Libmond, refused to marry him for fear of losing financial support from her other lover, so Loo married her daughter Marie-Rose instead. He raised four daughters with Marie-Rose, all the while still carrying on a relationship with Olga. After Loo's death in 1957 La Pagode fell into disrepair. It has now been refurbished and is used for events.

DYSCALCULIA

THEO HAS DYSCALCULIA, a learning disability that makes math hard for him. People with dyscalculia may have problems counting, doing basic math, or estimating; sometimes they also have dyslexia or ADHD. According to the UK Dyslexia Association, 3 to 5 percent of the population has dyscalculia in varying degrees of severity.

NOYELLES-SUR-MER

THE BRITISH CHOSE the small farming town of Noyelles-sur-Mer as the site for the general headquarters of the Chinese Labour Corps. It had the advantage of being on the Boulogne–Amiens line, a convenient railhead where other transportation routes converged. It's close to the seaport of Saint-Valery-sur-Somme as well as Crécy Forest, important as a source of timber.

The Château Beaumarchais of the novel does not exist, at least not in the Somme region. Its description and use as a hospital are based on the Château Longueil d'Annel, owned by American socialite Julia Hunt DePew Taufflieb, who was honored with the Legion d'Honneur and Croix de Guerre after the war. Her daughter Frances married the hospital's head surgeon. The Château Franssu, which the CLC administration used as their headquarters, does exist and now operates as a hotel.

There's nothing left in Noyelles-sur-Mer of the CLC camp or the hospital. The farmland where they stood had been requisitioned for military use, so the land was returned to its owners as soon as possible once the war ended.

There is a Chinese cemetery of 841 graves and a memorial in nearby Nolette. It is one of dozens of cemeteries in France and Belgium that contain the graves of Chinese workers, around 1,900 in total. Some of these cemeteries are maintained by the Commonwealth War Graves Commission. There are ongoing arguments over the actual number of Chinese workers who died, ranging from 2,000 to 20,000.

THE FORGOTTEN WORKERS OF THE GREAT WAR

I FEEL THE Chinese workers—why they went to Europe and what happened afterward—deserve a section here of their own.

It was in 2017 that I first came across a British news article about a monument in East London being raised to honor the Chinese Labor Corps of the First World War. A hundred and forty thousand Chinese workers went to France and England during the First World War. The first group arrived in France at the end of 1916, and the last contingent went home in 1920.[1]

Some 90,000 men made up the Chinese Labor Corps companies, which were part of the British Expeditionary Forces. The rest, who signed up with the French, worked for private French companies in war-related industries and in agriculture. After the United States

---

1   For the sake of keeping the plot moving, this novel only touches on other aspects of the workers' experiences, such as life in the recruitment camps in Weihaiwei while waiting for transportation to Europe, or journeys across the Pacific to William Head Quarantine Station on Vancouver Island, Canada, followed by a cross-Canada train ride, and then from the Atlantic coast of Canada to France or England.

entered the war, the French loaned around 10,000 laborers to the Americans.

The Chinese were the largest and longest-serving contingent of non-European labor, manpower that kept the machinery of war running. Afterward they cleaned up battlefields and cleared the rubble from devastated towns. Yet they seemingly vanished for decades from the historical record.

The big question everyone asks is: Why?

One reason is (not surprisingly) that Western historians of the time tended to gloss over the contribution of nonwhites in the Great War. This despite the fact that France and England drew troops and laborers from colonized territories such as the West Indies, India, North Africa, and Indochina.

There is also a dearth of firsthand accounts from Chinese workers. This is not surprising when you consider that the vast majority were peasants, of whom perhaps only 20 percent were literate. Only two CLC memoirs have come to light so far: those of interpreter-clerk Gu Xingqing and of Sun Gan, a schoolteacher who decided to volunteer as a worker. The epigraph to this novel about flares lighting up the night sky is from the latter's memoir.

On the European side, it's clear that scholars had to comb laboriously through journals and memoirs to glean even brief mentions of the Chinese presence. I've come across only two memoirs with extensive accounts of the CLC, by officers Jim Maultsaid and Daryl Klein, whose diaries indicate they recognized how unusual and unique an experience they had being part of the CLC. There are reports and anecdotes from YMCA members who staffed recreation huts at some of the CLC camps. Decades later, local historians collected personal reminiscences from civilians who observed and interacted with the workers. European accounts of the Chinese express a range of sentiments from admiration to hostility, with the majority at the negative end of the spectrum.

But as Dominiek Dendooven, curator and researcher at In Flanders Fields Museum, remarks, "There is a general lack of sources on the Chinese Labour Corps and the little that is available is quite fragmented. . . . One telling example: for only one of the companies of the Chinese Labour Corps, the 4th, has a war diary been preserved, be it only for the month of May 1917. As the war diaries are the day-by-day reports of a unit, the consequence is that it is nigh impossible to establish where a particular company has been working, at what time, what the nature of the work was, nor any other events related to that group's service."[2]

The workers were promised civilian duties safely behind the front lines of the war, but the reality is that front lines shift. The first 279 deaths came when the SS *Athos* was torpedoed by U-boats in the Atlantic; its passengers included Chinese workers on their way to France. While in France, workers died from aerial attacks, artillery fire, unexploded munitions, and industrial accidents. They died from the Spanish flu, tuberculosis, and other illnesses.

The Chinese men were mostly farmers, peasants hired as unskilled labor. Some were tradesmen and mechanics. There is ample documentation that by the end of the war, Chinese workers and mechanics were responsible for maintenance, repair, and sometimes total rebuilds of tanks at the Central Workshops of the Royal Tank Regiment.[3]

Often lacking timely access to translators and unfamiliar with Western culture, institutions, and labor practices, they couldn't argue

2   Dominiek Dendooven, "Asia in Flanders Fields. A Transnational History of Indians and Chinese on the Western Front, 1914–1920" (PhD diss., University of Kent, 2018).

3   Gregory James, *The Chinese Labour Corps (1916–1920)* (Hong Kong: Bayview Educational, 2013).

their grievances effectively. Language and cultural differences led to frustration on all sides and at times ended in violence. Despite being hired as civilians, Chinese workers for the British were subject to military discipline, something the worst officers took advantage of to dole out beatings and other harsh punishments. There were occasions when workers went on strike to protest their working conditions.

Some CLC companies were lucky enough to have sympathetic commanding officers who made the effort to understand their concerns; the result was mutual respect and a highly productive work environment. It must be said however that a job with the CLC was scorned by "regular army" because it was considered no better than babysitting, a job for either injured officers unable to serve in the field or, worse, officers of low caliber that no one else wanted.

The Chinese government was also at fault, doing little to advocate for laborers' rights and working conditions. The consulate representative appointed to look after Chinese working for the French was proactive and mediated with reasonable success on issues such as proper food and winter clothing. The representative assigned to help Chinese workers on the British side, however, proved nearly invisible.

There was more to come after the war. Workers were sent to battlefields and bombed-out towns to clean up the devastation so that French and Belgian refugees could return to their farmlands and homes. The Chinese took away barbed wire and dug up mountains of spent ammunition shells. Some were killed when their tools struck unexploded munitions. They cleaned out and filled in trenches and bomb craters so that battlefields could return to their former use as pastures and farmland. They carried away decomposing corpses of men and animals, loaded barges with abandoned equipment, clothing, and blankets.

"When you picture most of this stuff covered with hard blood, mud and filth, not to mention the fleas and bugs in their billions, you get some idea of what our Chinese boys had to handle day and daily."[4]

At the same time, with the war's end, the CLC was demobilising their personnel, leaving companies of workers with fewer experienced officers, less direction, and less stability. The military was skilled at preparing for war but not so good at winding down for peace. CLC workers had to leave established camps for lodgings closer to their new work locations. These might be temporary compounds of canvas tents, former POW camps, or sometimes shelter they had to find on their own. These makeshift camps lacked decent facilities for cooking, washing, and hygiene. The military was shutting down its supply lines and the CLC fell through the cracks. Some companies stopped getting their food. Morale dropped when the Chinese saw their officers go home while they were required to stay behind, carrying out some of the most soul-destroying work after the war. Deprived of the safety net of a fully functional CLC, hungry and cold, sometimes without officers who were willing or able to advocate for them, the workers felt betrayed. Some men resorted to stealing while others refused to work.

When French and Belgian refugees returned to their ravaged homes, they were shocked to see thousands of foreigners in their streets and farms, some clearing rubble, some wandering aimlessly. There's no doubt that Chinese workers were to blame for some of the reported crimes; there's also no doubt that Chinese were often the scapegoats in too many cases. French and Belgian accounts of Chinese workers, relatively positive during the war years, became very negative during this postwar period.[5]

---

4   Jim Maultsaid, *Dawn of Victory, Thank You China!: Star Shell Reflections 1918–1919* (South Yorkshire, UK: Pen & Sword Military, 2017).
5   Dominiek Dendooven, "Asia in Flanders Fields. A Transnational History of Indians and Chinese on the Western Front, 1914–1920" (PhD diss., University of Kent, 2018).

Between racism, politics, and historians' penchant for documenting battles rather than drudgery, the contributions of Chinese laborers, along with those of other men of color and women, were painted
out of history. In one case, the workers were quite literally painted
out. The United States entered the war just as artists in France were
finishing work on a huge mural known as the Panthéon de la Guerre, a
painting that featured groups of figures representing the twenty-three
nations on the Allied side. In order to fit in the latecomers, its artists
painted over the Chinese.

But why didn't Chinese historians of the time write about the
workers and their experiences?

At the risk of oversimplifying, the workers were pushed aside by
other events unfolding in China. The Republic of China was barely
a nation in 1912 when the last Qing emperor abdicated. At the time
of the Great War, the country had devolved into a loose affiliation of
territories ruled by warlords, each with their own armies, some more
modern and better-equipped than the government's. The Nationalist
government faced one crisis after another until the warlords finally
agreed in 1928 to unite under the Nationalist government—which
then promptly went to war against the Communist party of China.

Conflicts between the Nationalists and Communists abated some-
what in 1937 during the second Sino-Japanese war, which flowed into
the Second World War, followed immediately by the Chinese Civil
War, which saw the Nationalists retreat to Taiwan. Chinese under
Communist rule lived through the Great Leap Forward, the Great
Chinese Famine, and the Cultural Revolution.

These were tumultuous chapters that affected all Chinese, whereas
the workers' sacrifices affected only their families and barely merited
a footnote in the nation's history.

Sometimes I wonder if Chinese historians of the time preferred to
forget about the workers after the embarrassment of the Paris Peace

Conference in 1919. The Imperial government of China had leased part of the Shandong Peninsula in 1898 to Germany for 99 years. The new Republic of China hoped that by providing Chinese manpower to the Great War, they would have a seat at the bargaining table during peace negotiations and regain the Shandong Peninsula.

But Chinese delegates at the Paris 1919 peace talks were bitterly humiliated by an utter lack of acknowledgement for the workers' contributions, and worse, betrayed by their own government, which had already signed secret agreements to lease the Shandong territory to Japan without informing the delegates.[6] For decades, Chinese narratives about the peace talks focused on political betrayal by Western powers and skimmed past the fact that the workers' sacrifices had ended up counting for nothing during negotiations.

As a personal comment, it's also possible that the Chinese elite of the time (scholars and political leaders) were still hampered by a feudal mindset and did not consider the lives of mere peasants worth documenting.

Both Chinese and Western scholars are now taking an interest in the workers: in their personal experiences and perceptions, the impression they made on the foreigners they encountered, and their impact on the war's outcome. Hopefully this interest will lead to uncovering additional documentation that provides a more comprehensive picture of the workers' lives.

To learn from the mistakes of the past, we need accurate accounts. This chapter in world history, along with its long-term, global consequences, remains incomplete without the stories of women and nonwhite combatants and workers.

---

6 Roger Chapman, "Elleman, Wilson and China: A Revised History of the Shandong Question, 2002" review of *Wilson and China: A Revised History of the Shandong Question* by Bruce A. Elleman, H-Net Reviews, June 2003, https://china.usc.edu /elleman-wilson-and-china-revised-history-shandong-question-2002.

REFERENCE BOOKS

James, Gregory. *The Chinese Labour Corps (1916–1920)*. Hong Kong: Bayview Educational, 2013. Of the 1,285 pages, 770 are text and the rest are appendices and meticulous references to source materials that are just as interesting to read as the text. Available through:

Peter Morris, Ltd.
1 Station Concourse
Bromley North Railway Station, Kent
020 8313 3410
info@petermorris.co.uk

Klein, Daryl. *With the Chinks*. Wentworth Press, 1916. The title gives you some idea of prevailing attitudes. Klein considered himself a good and sympathetic officer to the Chinese "boys."

Maultsaid, Jim. *Dawn of Victory, Thank You China!: Star Shell Reflections 1918–1919*. South Yorkshire, UK: Pen and Sword Military, 2017. This is a unique memoir. Maultsaid kept an illustrated diary of his time with the CLC and this book reads like a graphic novel. Maultsaid's granddaughter has published two other memoirs. This one focuses on his experiences with the CLC.

Xu, Guoqi. *Strangers on the Western Front: Chinese Workers in the Great War*. Cambridge: Harvard University Press, 2011.

ONLINE SOURCES

Boehler, Patrick. "The Forgotten Army of the First World War: How Chinese Labourers Helped Shape Europe." *South China Morning Post*. https://multimedia.scmp.com/ww1-china/.

Boissoneault, Lorraine. "The Surprisingly Important Role China Played in WWI." *Smithsonian Magazine*, August 17, 2017. https://www.smithsonianmag.com/history/surprisingly-important-role-china-played-world-war-i-180964532/.

Dendooven, Dominiek. "Clearing the Battlefields. The Chinese Labour Corps in 1919." *Stand To!* no. 116 (2019): 64–68. https://www.academia.edu/40837867/Clearing_the_Battlefields_The_Chinese_Labour_Corps_in_1919.

Kennedy, Maev. "First World War's Forgotten Chinese Labour Corps to Get Recognition at Last." *The Guardian*, August 14, 2014. https://www .theguardian.com/world/2014/aug/14/first-world-war-forgotten -chinese-labour-corps-memorial.

Report Giving the History of the Chinese Labour Corps Used Behind the Lines in France 1917–19. March 24, 1920. British Library. https://www.bl.uk /collection-items/report-giving-the-history-of-the-chinese-labour-corps -used-behind-the-lines-in-france-1917-19.

Sultan, Mena. "Forgotten Heroes of the First World War." *The Guardian*, November 8, 2018. https://www.theguardian.com/gnmeducationcentre /2018/nov/08/forgotten-heroes-of-the-first-world-war. Includes information about other non-European participants.

ACKNOWLEDGMENTS

A very wise author once said to me, "It's hard being friends with an author because even when we're there, we're not there." I began writing this book in 2020, at the start of the pandemic. So the first person I want to thank is my husband, who survived lockdown with me and The Damn Novel, which meant he survived a lot of it by himself since I was there but not really there.

I am grateful to Gregory James for his masterful work *The Chinese Labour Corps (1916–1920)*, and for answering my many (too many!) questions. Sincere thanks to Dr. Dominiek Dendooven, curator and researcher at In Flanders Fields Museum, for generously sharing his research with me, as well as for his many published articles and papers. Most of all, thank you for caring enough to research the Chinese workers and their role in the Great War.

If I were allowed to thank only one person, it would be the late Captain James Maultsaid for treating the Chinese workers in his company with respect and humanity. He was in the minority. His illustrated diaries, *Star Shell Reflections*, offer a unique and fascinating firsthand account of the Great War and his time as an officer with the Chinese Labour Corps. Many thanks to his granddaughter, Barbara McClune, for editing Maultsaid's diaries and getting them published. They are a treasure and I'm grateful she has shared them with the world.

Writing is a solitary profession and even more so during a pandemic. Big hugs to each and every one of the Lyonesses, my agency sisters and fellow historical novelists. It makes such a difference to know we have each other to lean on in this challenging industry and through these crazy times. Kate Quinn and Jennifer Robson—one day the Hysterical Fiction Tour will ride again!

Thank you to my agent, Kevan Lyon. I'm lucky to have your guidance and support.

During the editing stage of this novel, it dawned on me that finally I felt like a career author instead of an imposter and it's because of the team at William Morrow and HarperCollins Canada that's now seen me through four books. Thank you, Jennifer Brehl and Iris Tupholme, for trusting that the story outlines I submitted would return to you as full-length novels. Nate Lanman, thank you for project managing this novel. It isn't easy dealing with authors on deadline and I fully and humbly acknowledge this. Janice Zawerbny, I agonized much while writing *The Porcelain Moon* but not at all while you were editing, thanks to your endless patience and brilliant instinct for story. Laurie McGee, Shelby Peak, Christine Vahaly—I am so grateful for your careful copy editing. Where would authors be without your eagle eyes? To Camille Collins, Amelia Wood, Elsie Lyons, Alice Tibbetts, Cory Beatty, Neil Wadhwa, and everyone else at William Morrow and HarperCollins Canada: thank you again and always.

ABOUT THE AUTHOR

Born in Taiwan, JANIE CHANG has lived in the Philippines, Iran, Thailand, New Zealand, and Canada. She writes historical fiction, often drawing from family history and ancestral stories. She has a degree in computer science and is also a graduate of the Writer's Studio program at Simon Fraser University in Canada. She is the author of *Three Souls*, *Dragon Springs Road*, and *The Library of Legends*.